NO LON ☙ S0-CBE-029

SEATTLE PUBLIC LIBRARY

# PRAISE FOR JASMINE SILVERA

The TOOTH & SPELL series is so fresh and broadly appealing, that even romance readers who don't normally read paranormal will be hooked. A perfect balance of wry humor and angst; sweetness and heat.

— JEN COMFORT, AUTHOR OF *THE ASTRONAUT AND THE STAR*

DEATH'S DANCER weaves suspense and romance into a story as smart as it is sensual... Silvera deftly choreographs the action using lush depictions of Prague's storied scenery and deliciously dark humor. A thrilling debut.

— CAMILLE GRIEP, AUTHOR OF *LETTERS TO ZELL AND NEW CHARITY BLUES*

Silvera's worldbuilding is exquisite... a rollicking, romantic, riveting ride.

— THE PINK HEART SOCIETY (*THE TALON & THE BLADE*)

A spellbinding urban fantasy.

— BOOK BUB (*THE TALON & THE BLADE*)

# ALSO BY JASMINE SILVERA

## GRACE BLOODS

Death's Dancer

Dancer's Flame

The Talon & the Blade

## TOOTH & SPELL

Binding Shadows

# CONJURING MOONLIGHT

## TOOTH & SPELL BOOK TWO

### JASMINE SILVERA

This is a work of fiction. Names, characters, organizations, events, places and incidents are the product of the author's imagination or used fictitiously.

Copyright © 2022 No Inside Voice, LLC

All rights reserved.

No part of this publication may be reproduced, distributed, or transmitted in any form or by any means, including photocopying, recording, or other electronic or mechanical methods, without the prior written permission of the publisher, except in the case of brief quotations embodied in critical reviews and certain other noncommercial uses permitted by copyright law. Violators subject to punishment by necromancers.

First publication date March 2022

Published by No Inside Voice Books, Seattle, WA

ISBN: 978-0-9976582-9-3

Cover design by The Book Brander

Book Design by No Inside Voice

*In memorium...*
*The howl rises and falls, leaving silence behind.*

# RIVERSIDE, CALIFORNIA, 1990

THE ENVELOPE ARRIVED ON A TUESDAY. It was such an ordinary thing—off-white and business-sized, printed with the return address of the NorAm Territory Citizenship and Immigration Services—to mark a day Markus Vogel would never forget.

Mama juggled the mail and her keys around his baby sister. She swore under her breath, tossing her head to clear a stray lock from her eye as Isela fussed.

His younger brother whined about a kid at school who had stolen his book during recess and called him a nerd.

Mama listened with half an ear, sighing softly. "You've got to learn to ignore people like that, Tobias."

Mark made a mental note to find that kid tomorrow and have a word with him.

"Go put that on Papa's desk." She handed Mark the mail when the door swung open. "I need to put your sister down for her nap. Can you take your brother out into the courtyard to play for a little while before you start homework? Papa or I will help you finish after supper."

"Yeah, Ma."

He didn't bother telling her that six-year-old Tobias would have been happy curled up with his books for the rest of the afternoon. She had a strict rule on outdoor playtime every day, even on rare rainy days.

Mark'd rather be outside no matter the weather. Herding Toby back out into the courtyard on a mild spring afternoon took the kind of effort that involved his favorite action figures out in the dirt. He had to let Toby play Lady Samurai even though she was Mark's favorite.

They played Nightfeather's Agents, pursuing the dreaded *Others* that threatened humanity. He was Mad Irish, cornered by an evil snake monster and fighting his way free until Lady Samurai and the Strongmen arrived.

Mark forgot all about that envelope until after dinner. He finished his homework as Papa swept the table clear of crumbs and looked over his shoulder occasionally to correct an answer.

Papa paused at the envelope tucked beneath his laptop. He pushed his glasses up his nose and studied the return address. "Was ist das?"

"Keine Ahnung." Mama shrugged and traded the baby for the wet dishrag. She turned to the boys. "All right, wild ones, head to the bathroom and brush teeth. Papa will come read you a story in just a minute."

As Mark turned to go down the hall, he caught a glimpse of his father's bushy eyebrows lowering, and the single page unfolded in his hand. The baby grabbed for it. He tucked her under his chin, out of the way, to finish reading. His frown deepened.

"What's wrong, Lukas?" Mama asked quietly.

He didn't answer.

She glared down the hall, spotting Mark in the shadows. "Hop along. Make sure your brother gets his back teeth."

Papa read a short story at bedtime. His mind was somewhere else: he kept forgetting to switch voices for the characters like he usually did.

The scent of fear woke Mark in the dark hours before dawn.

Fear had a peculiar tang, metallic and dull. His parents often worried about money and work and something they were careful not to talk about when he or Toby was nearby. This was different.

"I don't know how they can do this after all these years." His father's voice, anger tightly leashed.

Mark slipped out of bed, crept down the carpeted hall. He must be extra quiet. His mother's sense of her children was the only thing sharper than his own nose. She just seemed to *know* when they were close by, awake, or upset.

Mark leaned against the doorway until he could just see his parents in the little breakfast nook at the end of the narrow kitchen. Even sitting across from one another—tension drawing the air tight between them—their fingers were intertwined on the peeling table.

Papa looked up finally. "This is your home. Take the savings, stay with your cousins. I can send money, and when the kids are older—"

Mama fixed him with one of her long stares—the same one that made Tobias admit who broke what and Mark confess when he provoked the fight. "We stay together."

Papa released a long sigh and bowed his head. Pale brown hair flopped over his forehead in an unruly wave. His voice thickened. "I couldn't ask, but the thought of leaving you all—"

"It might be safer if... Better now than later. Later might be too late. They say Azrael is more lenient. As long as we follow the codes. And there's so much wilderness there, not like this city. So the boys will have a chance to just be."

He exhaled. "Better now than later."

"We stay together no matter what," Mama said.

Mark tried not to groan when they kissed. They were always doing that. *Gross.*

Mark headed back to bed.

The next few weeks were lost in the sea of arrangements to be made.

Papa sat Mark and Toby down and told them he'd gotten a new job offer overseas, near where he was born, and he and Mama had decided to take it. There was no word about the letter.

Mark searched, but it was gone.

They were allowed one suitcase apiece with necessities and one small personal bag for the plane. Suddenly the pocket-sized two-bedroom apartment seemed full of indispensable treasures.

On the last day, Mark came into the room he shared with Toby to find his little brother trying to close the zipper of his small backpack, which was stuffed with books. Toby's glasses were fogged from crying.

"Pop says we have to be ready to go to the airport in an hour," Mark said.

Toby sniffled.

"Mr. Henderson will look after things. He's going to find a nice family that needs all our stuff and send us the money so Mom and Dad can buy you new books."

"I want *my* books." Tobias sobbed.

Mark hurried to his side. The baby was sleeping, and Mama was trying to nap too. Before leaving, Papa warned him not to disturb them.

Their baby sister had been named after their grandmother: Isela Rose. Mark had only the haziest memories of the old woman. By the time Mark was born, Gramma Rosemarie could barely rise from her rocking chair, but her smile was bright for her first grandson. His only firm memory was of her skin, wrinkled as an old walnut, the same deep shade of brown as his own.

Mama had kept her picture with the other ancestors on the fake mantel. Now they were all packed carefully in her suitcase. She often spoke of the courage of the woman who had survived the war between the gods that nearly destroyed the world. She must have been strong. If an old woman could be that tough, so could he.

Confronted with a hysterical younger brother, Mark did the first thing that came to mind. He grabbed the backpack from his own bed and undid the zipper. He dumped the contents and shoved the mess of it under his blanket, then dropped to Toby's side.

"*Genug*, Toby." He grunted the command, reaching for the books spilling out of the smaller pack. Speaking German like Papa did always soothed Tobias. "Hush. Pick the ones you can fit in here too."

Toby gave a few lingering snuffles, and together they packed both bags full of books. At the sound of Mama's footsteps in the hall, Mark froze with a finger over his lips. He zipped up the bag and tossed it on his bed. Then he grabbed his action figures and set them up between himself and Toby.

The door creaked as he'd settled. Mama yawned, poking her head in. "I thought I heard crying?"

Mark pushed Mad Irish into Toby's hand. "No, Ma, just trying to get Toby to play with me."

She sighed, squatting beside them on the carpet. "Tobias, honey, everything's going to be okay."

She repeated herself in German. That seemed to do the trick.

Toby sniffed obediently as their mother's fingers traced the wavy hair away from his face. He even looked more like Papa.

She touched Mark's cheek and shared a rare smile with him. "Thanks for trying."

"Sorry to wake you, Ma," Mark murmured as she stifled another yawn.

"Wasn't really sleeping," she admitted. "What's Mad Irish doing out... *and* Lady Samurai? These are your favorites. Papa told you not to take anything out of your bag."

He nodded. "I just wanted to play for a bit."

She sighed heavily. "But when we gotta go, we gotta go, Markus. No time to go looking for lost toys. And you don't want to leave them behind, right?"

He shook his head, unable to speak.

The front door opened, and their father called for them to leave.

Mama levered herself off the floor. "Hurry up—get these guys packed. Come on, Tobias, grab your bag and let your brother have a minute."

Tobias tugged his small pack over one bony shoulder as Mama clasped his hand. She took the bag from him. "Good gracious, Tobias Henry Vogel. How many bricks are you bringing?"

Tobias grinned up at her, his round baby face shining. "No bricks, Mama. Books!"

"Of course!" She beamed back at him, adjusted his glasses, and steered him toward the door. She cast a look at Mark over her shoulder, and her smile faded a little. "Don't take too long, okay?"

When they were gone, he scooped up his action figures. He carried them to the bed, fingers tracing the familiar edges fondly. He pantomimed the sweep of the Strongmen's powerful arms flexing, Mad Irish's dancing feet, a few strokes of Lady Samurai's blades. He tried to think of some other kid playing with them and swallowed the hot lump rising against the back of his throat. Then he stuffed them under his pillow and grabbed his backpack.

"Markus," his father called. "Komm her mein Junge, wir gehen jetzt."

The time had come. Mark hurried to the door at his father's call to leave. Halfway there, he turned back. Maybe just one. He grabbed Lady Samurai and tucked her into a small corner near the zipper, tugging it closed as best he could.

His parents waited in the doorway of the tiny apartment, framed by the light of the glaring afternoon sun.

Papa pushed the door open and extended a hand to Mark. "Komm, schatz," he urged. "Wir haben ein Flugzeug zu fangen."

He imagined the plane rolling down the tarmac and them chasing after.

At the airport, armed guards patrolled from the curbs to the checkpoint. Some had dogs, but the ones without made him shiver. Their strangely colored eyes seemed to be gazing beyond anything an average human could see. The departure hall bustled with people, and security lines wound through the endless mess of it all.

Mama kept Toby close, squeezing Mark's hand. Every time eyes skimmed her or the boys, she tensed. A whisper seemed to be constantly on her lips, though he picked up no sound.

Papa returned from dropping off their luggage, tickets clutched in one hand. "Just a flight delay. It's normal. Nothing to worry about."

Flights in and out of the country were still hard to come by, made trickier by the *real* borders crossed depending on the destination.

The night before, Papa had sat him down at the dining room table, unrolled a map, and pointed out hand-drawn lines over the printed ones, each highlighted in bright yellow. Some encompassed whole countries by the handful. Others covered enormous territories of land or sea. Eight in all. He tapped the West Coast. "Wir sind hier."

"The Nightfeather!" Mark exclaimed. He'd seen images of the Allegiance of Necromancers in school. Eight all-powerful sorcerers who commanded death itself. They'd emerged from the shadows after the godswar to rule, keeping humanity, which was bent on self-destruction, safe from powers they didn't understand. Mark liked the long dark hair and piercing gaze of their necromancer.

Papa nodded, but his expression didn't lighten. "Und wir gehen hier."

His finger slid across the ocean to Europe, stopping on a tiny landlocked country in the center of a highlighted area. This territory ran to the Mediterranean in the south, north over the islands and peninsulas, and east to the Caspian Sea.

"The Angel of Death," Mark whispered. "And the Red Death above."

The necromancer Azrael's territory was bordered by a female necromancer known for her vicious nature. Rumor was that Azrael and Vanka were fighting over disputed territory on the Black Sea.

Mark looked at his father's finger, well within the boundaries of Azrael's territory. As safe as anywhere could be.

"But Papa," he whispered. "We can't cross borders."

"It is difficult to impossible usually," his father agreed. "But with the East Coast unlivable, Raymond Nightfeather's territory is too crowded, so he and the Angel of De—Azrael—have worked out an arrangement. A kind of repatriation. I have skills that can be useful there, and I have been invited to return."

"But not to Germany?"

Papa shook his head and tapped the map with one blunt finger. "The city of Prague is a new technological center. I should be able to get a good job. I will need your help to take care of this family on the long trip. You can do that, yes?"

"I promise."

At the airport, Mark remembered his promise and stayed close to Mama and Toby while Papa checked the monitors for updates. He tugged the straps of the backpack on his shoulders. Books were much heavier than action figures, CDs, and his favorite Mariners T-shirt.

"Come now," Papa murmured. "Let's get through security early. We can get something to eat on the other side."

The slow-moving line made Toby wiggly and restless. The hot air smelled of too many humans in a small space. Mark breathed shallowly. Sweat trickled down his back.

"Take your brother's hand," Mama said as they shifted their backpacks off their shoulders.

Obediently, Mark grabbed for Toby. Toby tried to slip loose, but Mark was faster. When Mark looked back, Mama and Papa had stepped ahead in line, murmuring to one another.

He gave Toby a tug.

They turned and came face-to-face with an enormous Belgian Malinois on a short leash, held by an airport guard. The young, light-skinned man wore a black utility jumper emblazoned with the distinctive form-line raven, wings spread. The Nightfeather's symbol.

The dog fixed Mark with a deep stare, chest expanding like a bellows as its nostrils flared, scenting him.

An answering snarl rose in Mark's throat, and he strangled it back. *Where had that come from?*

He edged Tobias behind him, unable to tear his gaze away from the dog's shiny black nostrils framed in dark fur. The dog growled.

The muscles above Mark's lip twitched in response.

Papa shouted, scooping him off his feet and away from the dog. Mama pulled Toby behind her.

"What is the meaning of this?" Papa snapped.

The guard's eyes never left Mark. Instead, he touched the radio on his shoulder, muttered a number code, and then his gaze flicked to Papa. "Please come with me, sir."

Mama gasped as the dog tugged at the leash, closing the distance.

Papa snapped, "Restrain your animal. They are children."

The passengers around them edged away as more black-clad enforcers materialized in the crowd. No one would meet their eyes. Pity at best, suspicion at worst hovered in their faces. But no one spoke in their defense. No one dared.

Mama's voice lowered. "Lukas."

"Please come with us," the handler ordered. "All of you."

The air-conditioning that had been absent in the main hall turned the waiting room off the security checkpoint into a refrigerator. Below the unit, a slow drip formed an uneven blotch of water stain on the wall.

Their carry-ons were piled on the stainless-steel table on one side of the room near the scanners.

Mama sat in the only chair, tugging Mark close. She swept her fingers over his cheek, down his ear to his collar. Her mouth moved the whole time, silent lips forming words as she stroked his shoulder and his arm to his fingers. She moved to the other arm. Her occasional shudder had become a steady shiver.

Papa shrugged off his sweater and made her put it on. Tobias snuggled into her chest around Isela, whimpering softly.

Mark clenched his teeth to keep them from clacking. His hoodie irritated the goose bumps springing up on his arms and neck.

Papa paced. He'd surrendered their papers. He met Mama's eyes, saw something that made the color drain from his face. But he nodded without speaking and resumed pacing.

There were no clocks. Mama touched the crown of Mark's head. She looked faded, her skin dimmed somehow. "Will have to do."

Finally the door opened. Three guards entered—an Asian man with a ponytail, the dog handler, and a dark-haired, pale woman in plainclothes with an official-looking lanyard around her neck. She smiled tightly, gesturing for the one with the dog to wait by the door.

This time Mark kept his eyes on the tile, ignoring the clack of the dog's nails on the floor.

"What is the meaning of this delay?" Papa asked, but indignance bowed to the strain of worry in his voice. "You want us gone. We're leaving."

"Everything is in order, Mr. Vogel," the woman said with the weighted air of one overworked and out of patience. "We'll just do a quick check of your bags and you'll be on your way."

Mark snuck a glance at the guards as papers shuffled. The guy with the ponytail scanned the bags with a wand before unzipping each and poking through the contents.

"Sir?" The dog handler spoke. He sounded younger in this small room, less authoritative than he had in the main hall. The dog was attentive but not focused on anything.

The woman's brow rose. "Yes, Private?"

The handler reddened, acne scars visible under his flush. He didn't look much older than the high school boys who played pickup games in the park in the afternoons. "The boy."

Mama's grip on Mark's shoulder tightened.

"My son." Papa's voice held a note of iron Mark had never heard before. "A child that you menace with an animal."

Mark almost broke his stare to look into his father's face as heat and tightness wedged themselves into the back of his throat.

"I apologize, Mr. and Mrs. Vogel." The woman sighed before turning to the young guard. "It must have been a false positive."

"But, sir," the handler said.

"Enough, Iglesias," she said. "They don't show so young—you know that. Your dog needs a break."

"Ma'am," the handler mumbled, and the dog heeled to his side.

Mark's gaze darted up once more. The dog huffed once, then followed the handler obediently from the room.

Mama exhaled a deeply pent breath beside him. Mark felt like his knees might melt and soak into the legs of his jeans.

Papa knelt in front of him as the first tear slipped free.

Mark wrapped his arms around his father's neck, and when the man stood, Mark's feet left the floor. His father hadn't carried him in years.

Papa's free arm lowered, and Mark didn't need to look to know he and Mama had clasped hands. Tobias kept his face nestled in Mama's collar. Isela began to protest the pressure.

The second uniform finished the inspection. The woman in charge returned their papers. Papa shifted Mark to handle both documents and their carry-ons but didn't put him down.

The woman opened the door leading to the departure hall. Mama was outside, and Papa was halfway through when the uniform called, "Hey! Just a minute."

Mark tensed. Papa's expression was calm and mildly irritated, but Mark could feel his heartbeat against his chest, fast and hard.

The guy with the ponytail held out a small plastic figure with a hesitant smile. "This must have fallen out. Is it yours?"

Mark saw the familiar figurine, and his stomach heaved.

Papa rocked him gently. "*Mein schatz?*"

"Lady Samurai," the uniform said, offering it up. "She's my fave. Yours too?"

Mark shook his head and buried his face in his father's neck, breathing deep. Papa smelled like aftershave and hazelnuts, and that pervasive tang Mark now knew too well: fear.

Papa shrugged at the man. "Guess not?"

The overhead paged their flight number, and the officer nodded. "Have a good flight."

Mark's last glimpse of the worn figurine was the uniform tucking it into his breast pocket as the door closed behind them. He pressed his cheek against his father's collar and wept.

# CHAPTER ONE

PRAGUE, 2014

Mark cranked down the tired window as his wolf rose to scent the humid breeze. The wolf's nose picked up forest loam and slow-moving water. They were close.

"Careful, boss." Sam laughed from the passenger seat. "Any farther and you're going to be leaning your head out the window like a dog."

Mark pressed his shoulder blades back into the thin, worn seat.

He put some weight on his right foot and willed a bit more speed out of the reluctant van, briefly regretting not taking the newer, more efficient vehicle he'd been offered a year ago. This had been his first company rig and ran fine most days despite all its familiar imperfections. Maybe it was time to stop being sentimental—showing up late to the jobsite on the first day of demo because the van hadn't charged fully wasn't going to earn him any points.

"You sure we got the right directions?" Sam muttered, squinting between hastily scrawled Czech on the paper in his hand and the thin trunks of the beech trees pressing against the road from either side.

The oldest member of Mark's crew, Pavel, leaned into the gap between driver and passenger, pointing at the road ahead. The skin at the corner of his eyes settled into crinkling lines to match the deep furrows bracketing his mouth.

"Jevany pops up out of nowhere." After decades of cigarettes, his voice had a permanent rasp. "You can tell because the pavement is fresh at the municipal line. Fancy cars hate potholes, you know. Markus, watch the limit."

Mark slowed to the residential speed limit. Last thing he needed was a ticket on a company rig. Glimpses of water that had been appearing between the trees became a lake as the road entered the village.

"Left." Pavel twitched a finger in the general direction.

Mark took the turn a bit too fast. Pavel grunted and gripped the seat back to keep from sliding.

"This is not the Formula One." Sam hung on to the handle above the door.

The narrow, tree-lined main street ran perpendicular to the lake into the sloping hills. Since the Middle Ages, the ten man-made cascade ponds in the natural stream basin around the village had been used for farming fresh-water fish. Across the pond, the national reserve stretched, dense and dark as any good storybook forest, crossed only by deer and hiking trails. Though it felt a thousand miles away from anything, two other small villages were a twenty-minute ride away by narrow, winding roads.

The village consisted of a restaurant, small municipal and primary school buildings, and a grocery, all comfortably settled in the landscape. No more than a few hundred people occupied Jevany year-round. The number swelled in the summer as city dwellers sought refuge from the heat in the surrounding countryside. If not for the perfect pavement of the road climbing the gentle slope away from the water, it could have been any outlying village.

Jevany had a reputation for attracting the famous and the notorious. The estates they passed as they left the village behind were obscured by fences both ornate and plain, all designed to preserve privacy. More than a few gates had secured entry, and some even had guardhouses. Each expansive property was cushioned from the others with trees and overgrowth.

Pavel pointed out one owned by an opera singer, a former politician, and a movie star. He sucked his teeth as they passed immaculate walls made to look like real stone. "Look at those shitty modular block columns."

"Stone is pricy and heavy as hell," Mark said. "And modular looks just as good as the real thing."

"Nice inset lighting." Sam leaned forward to get a better view out the window. "And the manned guardhouse."

"That is Little Saint Peter," Pavel announced.

"Peter—"

"As in Petersburg," Pavel said. "Russian. Originally a diplomat. But the only Russian diplomats in town these days are the Crimson Saints."

"The mob?" Sam's eyes widened.

"Even necromancers can be bought." Mark exhaled sharply, unable to keep the bite out of his tone. "Figures."

He ignored the sensation that Pavel was staring at him. One didn't talk shit about necromancers in public. Especially when they had as much to hide —to lose—as he did. He'd worked with Pavel since he started demo. He trusted the old man and Sam. Still, he'd do better to keep his opinions to himself.

Mark whistled. "Who did the reno?"

"Anton, of course," Pavel said. "Before your time; last one he ran himself."

They left behind the prime real estate to the less grand—and less protected—villas, many of which had begun to show their age. These were more his style. They wore their experience like veterans of time. A bit of patina here, a crumbling wall there, a half-replaced roof, or a boarded-up cottage beside the main house. All he saw was beauty in those old spaces.

"Hey, pull over here," Pavel called as they passed one weather-beaten wood-and-metal fence.

Mark pulled the van off the road.

"We're already late," Sam grumbled.

"Time is a construct." Pavel levered himself out of the back, landing on the pavement with a little grunt.

Mark climbed out. "I'll square it with Anton."

It had rained before dawn and the air was still damp and relatively cool. The warm pavement hissed steam whenever a tenacious raindrop clinging to the branches above surrendered to gravity.

Otherwise, a pervasive stillness filled this stretch of road.

Mark caught a glimpse of something between the broken boards. He glanced back at Pavel.

"Heard about it on a blog, wanted to see it for myself." The older man's eyes followed Mark, and he tilted his head in the direction of the property beyond the fence. "Have a look."

Mark hopped up onto the stone base of the nearest fence post, craning his neck for a view. Behind him, Sam's door opened and shut, accompanied by the man's sigh.

In the distance, down a long-degraded driveway and partially obscured by trees on either side, was a magnificent old villa in the uniquely Czech take on art deco style. The crumbled facade revealed brick beneath in places, and the roof had aged to a lovely green patina. Moss crept through cracks and the edges of the broken window frames. It would need to be completely gutted.

Beside him on the post, Sam whistled. "Wonder why nobody's fixed this old bird up? Or torn it down, though that would be a shame."

The bones were beautiful. A reconstruction filled Mark's vision, replacing fallen structures and excavating the years and the decay until he could see it as it had been.

The crown of an enormous tree rose just over the far side of the roofline.

A chill settled over him. He passed his fingertips over the invisible charm at his throat, expecting to feel something: heat, tingle.

Nothing. The chill remained.

"It was a family home until the Second World War," Pavel said quietly. "Made their money in manufacturing."

Pavel prided himself on being an amateur history buff and knowing stories even most locals didn't, particularly gruesome or strange. The fact that he was interested also meant there was something supernatural involved. Unlike most humans, Pavel didn't pretend the world wasn't full of unexplainable things. Mark braced himself for a horror story.

"The Nazi commander hung the entire lot, even down to the swaddled one, from that tree." Pavel lowered his voice. "And then lived in the house until he was run out. It's traded hands a few times. But... nothing sticks."

Mark's nostrils flared. "It's been empty since?"

"More or less."

That the villa had stayed empty for so long was likely a sign of restless dead on the property. Releasing them was a job for a necromancer. Trouble was, no one knew precisely how many necromancers existed beyond the eight that formed the Allegiance. Not enough if, even this long after two world wars and a godswar, many places were still haunted.

Mark made a mental note to talk to his mother about it. Perhaps there was something she could do to soothe the ghosts until one of the necromantic overlords got around to doing their damn jobs.

When his attention returned to the present, Pavel's eyes remained on him. It wasn't the first time Pavel had shown him a place like this. Mark nodded once.

Pavel's thin smile seemed relieved.

"Back in the car," Mark said. "Now we're late."

The eerie stillness dissipated as soon as they continued up the long road. A few minutes later, Mark took the turn Sam pointed out, following the driveway to a modest estate nicely situated on a big plot overlooking the farmlands beyond the village. He parked by the Land Rover and newer company van.

Anton was already there with the architect, the construction foreman, and a kid Mark didn't know but who looked vaguely familiar.

Mark liked the architect well enough. His designs were clean, modern but often uninspired, and safe. However, he had much stronger feelings for the foreman.

The man returned his expression as he spat into the dirt. "We can start. Finally."

"What have we got, boss?" Mark aimed the question pointedly at Anton.

The project, a fancy new country home, was one of the nicest residential bids the company had won. Mark went over the plans and the sketches, the image of the completed home forming in three dimensions in his mind. He mentally tweaked a few details, corrected a few cosmetic issues.

If he could see it, he could build it. Too bad he wouldn't be building it.

He wondered when he was going to stop hoping the next project would be his chance. He just needed one. One Anton wouldn't seem to give him for reasons Mark couldn't figure.

He shunted that thought aside. There was a job in front of him, and Anton had called him in on this for a reason. "Samuel, you're up."

Sam put on his hard hat and headed into the structure.

Pavel remained at Mark's shoulder, listening to the architect as his eyes scanned the plans.

When Sam reemerged, rubbing his chin, Mark knew he was about to get bad news. They'd worked together long enough for Mark to read his expression.

"How long've we got?" Mark asked Anton but kept his attention focused on Sam's face.

Anton spoke. "Four weeks."

Sam coughed hard, covering it with a few empty huffs as he pantomimed brushing dust away from his face.

It was a bigger job than it looked.

Great. Mark rubbed his palm over the tight coils of his dark hair. He'd been growing it out to let his younger brother practice fades for barber training but working demo on a tight deadline in summer heat made a quick buzz sound better and better.

"Why the rush?" Pavel fisted his hands on his hips and toed a clod of dirt at his feet.

"What rush, old man?" The foreman snorted. "Other crews get a job like this done in two."

Pavel spit, aiming it too close to the younger man's feet to be an accident.

"Not with the amount of preservation we want," Mark countered, pointing out the notes the architect had made. "We're retaining a lot of the old facade. And this interior stonework is a nice touch, but that means we have to be extra careful about how we pull out the wiring. Plus gods only know what condition those pipes are in, but I assume you want to keep as much as you can. Save on costs."

The architect grunted approval.

"I have more good news." Anton beckoned to the kid lingering outside the circle of men. The boy came, dragging his feet. Anton clapped a hand on the kid's shoulder. "This is my wife's nephew. He'll be doing summer work for us. Getting his start in demo, just like all my crew does."

*Only some of us never get to leave.*

The kid was tall with good shoulders. His hands were soft though. And looked like he still hadn't grown into his oversize feet.

Mark sighed. "How old are you?"

"Seventeen," the kid said, eyes darting between his uncle, Pavel, and the architect. Anywhere but Mark. Anton's big hand squeezed, and the boy coughed out, "Sir."

"Just Mark," Mark said. "Or Markus if you need to feel formal."

Mark met Anton's gaze, unflinching.

Anton looked away first. "He's a strong kid. Just needs some focus. I know you'll have him in shape quick."

Anton gave him the fresh meat because he was good at his job—and everyone else's too. Sticking the kid out here for the summer was likely just a way to keep him out of trouble.

"I got this."

Anton beamed. He shoved the kid aside and took Mark's shoulders in his hands. The wolf bristled at the contact, but Anton, oblivious as always, gripped him hard and pressed kisses to both cheeks.

"Good man, Markus," he crowed, drawing Mark to his side as if presenting him to the others for the first time. "You see? The finest demolition lead in all of our great city and now beyond!"

The foreman's face flushed angrily. Even the kid looked wildly uncomfortable.

Mark locked his teeth together and forced a smile. One thing was for sure, Mark wasn't spending the rest of his life running demos for Anton. Sooner or later, he'd take his shot.

When Necromancer Azrael had chosen Prague as his seat, the money followed. Politicians, business, industry leaders, the mob—all wanted to be close enough to have his ear. Construction had tripled over the past twenty years. As companies like Anton's grew, they created an opening for smaller ones to fill in the space left behind.

Companies like his, Mark hoped.

"Walk with me," Anton said, slapping his shoulder.

In their wake, Pavel stepped up to the newest member of their crew. Mark knew the talking-to the boy was about to get very well. *No favorites here. Hard work, no mouthing off. Boss is a god, and you're an ant climbing out of a hill,* that kind of thing.

"My boy," Anton said when they were out of earshot of the others. "I am grateful for you. Every day."

*Funny way of showing it.* Mark kept his mouth shut.

"This job doesn't seem important," Anton said apologetically. "Out here, in the center of godsforsaken nowhere."

"Jevany isn't nowhere," Mark said. "Lots of rich people out here that do business in the city. We show them what we can do. Might lead to more jobs. Bigger ones."

Anton pounded Mark's shoulder. "Smart man. Going to make a good construction boss someday."

"Someday, eh?" Mark tried to keep his voice even, but he heard that note of hope creep in.

Anton faced him, his back to the jobsite. "A lot more riding on this job than you'd think. Do good work. It will come back to you."

Mark must have let his skepticism show.

Anton splayed his palm over his chest. "On my father's grave."

"Jesus, Tony." Mark rubbed his forehead but couldn't help laughing. "Don't get dramatic."

Anton bellowed a laugh, and Mark feared the older man was going to hug him. But Anton just shook his hand again with a toothy grin. "Pull this off, and your next job is a build. My word, Markus."

Anton clambered into his Land Rover, leaving the architect and the foreman the work van. He was on a call before he'd started the engine.

The abandoned nephew-in-law stood in the dust as the two vehicles disappeared down the road, looking a bit like a dog preparing to be kicked.

Mark rubbed his hand together, palms scraping as he surveyed his team. "Sam, you've had a look. What's the job?"

Sam dragged the hard hat off and patted his wild bristles of dirty-blond hair as though it would have any effect. "If we don't stop to sleep or eat or shit, we'll be done in *five* weeks."

"A normal job," Mark said.

Sam grimaced. "Exactly."

"Good," Mark said. "Keep us in shape and plenty of beer money in our pockets. That's the way we like it, right?"

"Right, boss." Sam laughed.

Mark started for the van. "Let's hit it then. Fresh meat, you're with Pavel."

"My name… it's Ondrej," the boy called after him.

The kid wasn't entirely a wet rag. Good. Maybe they'd get some work out of him after all.

Mark spun on one heel midstride, walking backward, and showed teeth.

"If you make it till the end of the job, we'll call you whatever you want. Put on your gloves and get to work."

Sam joined him watching the two men, young and old, head inside. "We grind him?"

"What else do you do with fresh meat?" Mark nodded. "Anton's counting on it. Wonder what his fuckup is. Drinking?"

"Girls." Sam reached for the door handle as Mark unlocked van's rear doors. "Clubs. Stays out too late partying and doing the drugs."

"Isn't that *your* life story?"

Sam snorted a laugh. He stood as Mark went about unloading. "You know Anton's full of it, yes? Putting the heat on to make himself look good."

"Something's stressing him out. Something big." Mark shook his head.

Sam's shrugs were a language all their own. This one said *who cares.* "I know a guy with a little company might need a few hands. You know this guy? Name's Vogel?"

He'd been running small side jobs for years, but launching his own business would be tricky—it took more than paperwork and equipment. He needed references, word of mouth, a reputation. He'd been in the trade long enough to know that many deals were still done by handshake and business conducted by relationship. Going off on his own without Anton's blessing might make it impossible to get the bigger gigs.

"Why're you going to wait on that old man to decide you're ready?" Sam asked, too perceptive as always.

"*I'm* not ready," Mark said. "I do this wrong and I lose my job and my chance. I can't afford to blow this. My parents. I can't be a drain on them. They're counting on me."

He liked working for Anton, not having to handle his own payroll and taxes and deal with the endless paperwork that was Czech bureaucracy. Staying on Anton's rolls was safe.

Anton's promise dangled before him like ripe fruit. If he could just get this job done right and on time, the next job was his.

Sam pursed his lips to speak but only blew out air and shrugged again with recognizable resolve. *Your decision, boss.*

"I'll see if Chris can come up for a couple of days of work." Mark changed the subject.

"Get us through the worst of it." Sam brightened.

The youngest Vogel sibling, Chris, got on famously with Mark's crew but had so far resisted Anton's offer for permanent work. Mark gave his little brother's determination to become a barber another month or two before Chris decided he wanted to lead walking tours or some shit. In the meantime, he could damn well earn some money and help Mark out.

Mark glared at the house after Sam lumbered off with the first load of tools.

The breeze blew a gust of something strange from the forest. Mark sneezed. The wolf rose in his chest, curious. *Focus on the job, Big Guy.*

Pollen, dust, old buildings. Whatever else was out there was not his problem. This was his shot. Finally. He wasn't going to blow it.

# CHAPTER TWO

A MURDERESS AND A WITCH, Evie expected to feel much less conflicted about drugging a man for a bit of peace and quiet. She liked to think she wouldn't have even considered it if she hadn't been put into such a ridiculous position.

A week ago, she arrived at the club to find one of the many well-dressed goons that were now a fixture in her life waiting at her desk to deliver her to someplace known as the Summer House. *Valentin's orders.*

The Summer House turned out to be a sleek modern villa in the Czech countryside that looked like something out of an architectural magazine, from the manicured lawns and meticulously kept garden to the two original cottages near the back of the property renovated as guesthouses. She expected Valentin to be waiting for her, or at least his second-in-command, Nikolai, with an explanation. Instead, she'd been installed in the smaller of the two cottages by the housekeeper.

The refrigerator was stocked with essentials, and the furniture was prepared. On the table was a bouquet from one of the most expensive florists in the city. She ordered flowers for Valentin's anniversary and his wife's birthday every year. This time it was her name on the envelope. She broke the seal, making no effort to hide from the housekeeper's attempt to catch a glimpse.

*Be patient, my darling. Enjoy some relaxation time—you have earned it. I will join you shortly.*

*—V*

The blocky script was Nikolai's.

The housekeeper tutted like an angry hen, looking her up and down before leaving her alone. *"Harlot,"* Evie had thought she heard the woman mutter. Or maybe it was just her imagination.

The following morning Evie had walked to the front gate. It was impossible not to admire the estate—peaceful in the day's early light. The grounds were bordered on all sides by mature stands of beech and pine, and her cottage was perfectly positioned to benefit from afternoon shade.

It would have been a lovely retreat from the sunbaked stone buildings lining the narrow streets of the city if not for the walls. A cage was a cage no matter how picturesque.

Taller than most men by half, the stone walls were unbroken except for the front gate where the driveway connected with the main road. A guardhouse occupied twenty-four seven by a rotating shift of security monitored the gate with firm instructions that she was to stay on the grounds.

It had taken all her practiced calm to smile and wander back down the long driveway to her cottage.

What would Tal have said? *There's always a way out. The trick is to be patient and wait for it and stay calm enough to take advantage when it arrives.*

She did what she always did when she was stressed: calculations. Under the guise of exploration, she counted the steps from the gate to her door. She measured the distance from wall to wall in meandering strides, calculating the time to get there at a walk, a jog, a flat-out run. She studied the angles of the windows from the main house where she had seen the housekeeper come and go with her meal tray and the small, black-eyed cameras pointed at the driveway and main entrance.

Her lucky break had been finding the metal gate behind her cottage where the old walls met the new, covered in brambles and rusted shut, out of view of the main house.

Now she had options.

But the next day a sturdy man, stooped and entirely gray, had presented himself at her door as her companion. He was something of a rarity—life as a henchman didn't lend itself to age. He provided her a single, supervised outing to the village for supplies, then proceeded to make himself at home during the days on her patio, next to the picture window overlooking the garden.

The heat of summer crept earlier into the morning with each passing day. Sweat dotted the space at her collarbones and slid between her breasts. It would be a record-setting year if this kept up. Without air-conditioning, she kept the windows of her cottage open for whatever cross breeze might be had.

Her keeper seemed to take that as an invitation for a one-sided conversation.

Desperate, she retreated to her sketchbook. If she drew as he talked, the deep, effortless focus allowed her to tune out most of his words. But after a week, even that was failing.

Meanwhile, her keeper droned on. The novel he'd brought lay unopened on the table. Instead, he'd spent much of the morning describing the first necromancer who had claimed Europe—the so-called Queen of Diamonds.

At fourteen, Evie had lost everything she loved to lingering hostilities between two of the most powerful necromancers in the world. In the twelve years since, humanity's overlords had done nothing to soften her opinion of their rule.

She didn't need history lessons. She needed to know why the hell she'd been dragged to the middle of nowhere and apparently forgotten.

The pencil snapped in her hand.

*Damn it.* That was her last one.

She swiped damp hair from the back of her neck before cleaning up the pieces.

This was her own damn fault. Her plan had been to leave Prague before summer. But instead, she'd let doubt create excuses to delay her. Another month or two to save. A few more weeks studying the transit timetables to figure out how far and fast she could get out of the country. And now she was stuck in the countryside, an hour away from her go bag and caches with no idea how long it would take Valentin to remember he'd stashed her here.

She had nothing but the clothes on her back and the sketchbook she carried everywhere. A housekeeper and gardener lived year-round on the other side of the property in addition to the rotating guards. Even if she could run, near constant supervision meant she wouldn't even have a twelve-hour head start before someone noticed she was missing.

She had to see this through. Whatever it was.

If only she could get a little peace and fucking quiet.

Drugging him was extreme, but desperate times…

She also knew there were ways to make a man sleep with the right words or a combination of herbs. But that took training or knowledge of plants. All she had was an affinity for metal, her glamour, and an education of trial and error on the road from the refugee camp near the Black Sea to the center of the European necromancer's territory.

One lesson was that near-hysterical women complaining of insomnia were always likely to get more sleeping powder than they needed. On her trip to the village, she'd visited the pharmacy first.

Now she calculated his dosage by height and weight. She had enough mint to disguise the flavor, and honey would help. She knew he took his tea sweet.

She just wanted a few hours alone in the woods to walk, to think, to plan. She longed for a swim in the lake. She would be careful not be seen, and she would be back before anyone knew she was gone. The decision made itself.

She slammed shut the battered leather portfolio over her sketchbook.

"How about some tea?" She interrupted him midsentence, phrasing her Russian carefully to hide her abysmal accent.

"Tea?" Her guard blinked up at her as though he didn't recognize her.

She must have let her glamour slip. Damn. Another reason for solitude. Maintaining the illusion that covered her scars was tedious.

Her second mistake—looking at his face. The vision of his death wavered like sun-dappled water over his living features. Sepia-toned and deeply wrinkled, it was far from the worst she'd seen. Faded color meant it was still a ways off. The more violent ones had taken her years to register without reaction. It was easier to avoid eye contact altogether.

Distraction was making her sloppy.

She needed to regain her calm.

"I would make a pot of tea," she clarified, subtly drawing the illusions back into place. "I thought your throat might be dry. After all your... storytelling."

"Stories?" He leaned back in his chair. "Saw much of it with my own eyes. I was a boy, yes, but old enough—"

His pocket chimed, surprising her with the cacophony of a pop song. A hurried, anxious pat-down followed, as though he were on fire and trying to put himself out rather than searching for his phone.

He squinted at the screen, then tucked it away.

"Pardon, my dear." He rose with a grunt. "Another time for tea. I must go into town on an errand."

Evie ignored her curiosity and suspicion. She wanted to demand the phone and the reason for dumping her without a word. Second best, she held up the broken pieces of her pencil. "May I go with you? I could use more pencils and maybe another sketchpad."

"Not today." He shook his head, sliding his book onto the windowsill. "Perhaps you would like to read?"

She eyed the title. Russian. Of course. She'd grown up with Bulgarian, Hebrew, Turkish, and bits of Arabic at home. She'd picked up English from the aid workers and enough Czech not to get taken advantage of in the market. For a short time, she'd studied Russian in primary school, and the rest she'd learned from the club. She was in no way ready to tackle the literature.

She pasted a bored smile on her face and fanned her cheeks. "I'd rather nap in this heat."

"I'll see that you are not disturbed." He turned, his next words just loud enough for her to hear. "These days. Young people have no respect for classics."

"You are too kind to me," she called after him as if she hadn't heard, relieved she wouldn't have to resort to drugging the man after all.

When he was gone, she closed the windows and drew the drapes. Immediately the room became a dim, stuffy box.

She twisted her hair into a knot at the back of her head and put on the shapeless old sundress she'd found in the charity shop in the village. The back door opened into the garden.

On her way past the potting table, she took the small handled basket and clippers for whatever forage she might chance on—or protection if she encountered trouble. Whoever had managed the renovation of the estate had cut corners. At the back of the property, where it was unlikely to spoil the view from the house, the original stone walls remained. They were chipped by time and weather and covered in climbing brambles that had come inside from gaps in an ancient iron gate that had probably rusted shut. Not that that would stop her.

When she was fourteen, months before she'd lost everything she loved, she discovered she could make a pile of metal buttons dance just by waving her palm over them. That night her mother had taken her into the workroom of their tailor shop below the family apartment. The pattern her father had been cutting on the worktable before he'd answered the call to prayer rustled faintly as Evie approached. Each of the pins trembled. She could feel them vibrating toward her, an almost audible sound. She hummed in response, a summons.

Her mother had placed a hand over hers, and the pins quieted. *Your notion is strong, but your father worked hard on this all day. You mustn't play with his effort.*

Evie had not understood the hot squeeze in her chest at the way her mother's face seemed to glow with more than candlelight. *Is this magic?*

*We call them notions*—she gestured around them to the bolts of fabric, strips of ribbon, snaps, elastics, and colorful threads—*as a way to disguise them in plain sight in this world of necromancers. Your notion is an affinity to metal, it seems.*

Evie had stared at her fingers. *My notion?*

*Our family has carried these talents for generations. With proper focus and training, your notions will be more than simple tricks.*

Perhaps she should have been afraid. The charge of witchcraft had been dangerous long before necromancers came to power. Instead, pride had warmed her.

The first lesson had come with warnings: a notion that revealed itself came without much effort, almost for free, but when used with intention, it came with a cost—strength, energy—and if too much was asked, it could drain the user dry. The line between them blurred, and her first duty was to learn where that line fell. For her own safety.

*Be glad you found your notion early and safe ways to exercise it,* meleğim. Her father's voice, soothing the frustration of her initial attempts to control it going awry and sending an entire box of pins scattering across the fitting room floor. *There is no mercy from necromancers for those who do—or can—not.*

*Your father too has his gifts,* her mother had said wryly. *It is his charm and good looks. How he is always fresh as a new day even after a full book of fittings.*

*Silence, woman.* He'd grinned, dancing her across the storeroom on his way up the stairs. *We were once great sorcerers. The power of spoken word. We were scholars and poets. Masters of illusion.*

Evie wished she could have asked if her ability to glamour came from him. But like the sight of death masks, illusion had come much later. Too late to save them.

She had given up pride in the magic that was her heritage, used it grudgingly only when necessary, and never trusted it to do anything more than get her into trouble.

Standing before the gate with a deep breath in her lungs, she decided this was a risk she would have to take. She'd stolen oil from the gardening shed for the hinges earlier in the week. She hummed a lullaby, and the metal sang in response beneath her palm before quieting again. Rust flaked away, the tumblers ground in the lock, and the gate swung open the slightest bit. Convincing the brambles and ivy to let her pass took more work, and she paid her due in itchy welts as she emerged on the other side.

Still, it went off better than she'd expected. Without any formal training, most of what she could do had come by way of experiment. The belief that she could do a thing seemed to go a long way even if the result wasn't always predictable.

Securing the latch behind her, she set off into the forest as the brambles resumed their tangle.

One of the smaller ponds was her best bet for solitude.

She let the glamour fall away and flexed her fingers on the basket handle. The knobby balls of her joints, skin thickened by scar tissue, protruded without the illusory smoothness. She'd always had strong hands, capable. But they had not been nearly strong enough, not when it counted.

She turned over one palm, where the scars ran deepest. A jagged white line bisected her palm all the way to the base of her thumb.

*Any deeper and you'd have severed the tendons, lost the use of it.* The bleary-eyed doctor had examined her hands in the field hospital. *They found you digging through the rubble without gloves.*

Evie's throat closed on the words. How could she explain what she had seen in the minutes before stones that glittered like stars and fell like bombs destroyed everyone she loved? How she'd tried to sing to the metal in the ruins but that had only made it worse, compacting the layers of brick and concrete and sending up clouds of dust.

When she had blinked away tears, the image of the faded old man the doctor would become, peaceful in death, overlay the purple half-moons of exhaustion beneath his living hollowed eyes. She panicked, thinking more bombs were coming. It took two nurses to hold her down for the doctor to administer a sedative.

The next hours passed in a blurry collection of images. Her own mangled hands. The distant pain of needle and suture. The flickering generator-powered lights. The doctor's voice, coming from a watery distance at her side. *I am a surgeon. I came here to do some good, but this was a massacre… You are lucky to have survived.*

She had spent three days in the field hospital, sealing her eyes shut whenever anyone approached to avoid seeing their death masks. She should have died that night. But she'd run, and she'd lived. And death would never allow her peace.

Cold, sinking muck splashed around her ankles to her calves. Evie swiped at her damp cheeks, swearing softly. She'd stumbled into the marshy ground surrounding a modest, shady pond. The forest around was still, quiet.

She headed for the little stand of pale birch trees and the broken log bench near the high bank. Halfway there, a splash caught her ear, this one from the center of the pond. She froze.

The pond was not empty. Water rippled away from the curved brown arc of shoulders and a spine, the taut bulge of a flank as a swimmer dove again. A moment later, a little flurry and a pair of pale soles flicked the surface a few times before disappearing.

The surface calmed to a few quieting puckers.

When the swimmer didn't reappear, she stared outright.

Hurrying the rest of the way to the trees with her gaze on the lake, she stumbled over a root and caught on the nearest trunk, scraping her palm on the rough mound of a knot beneath paper-thin peels of bark. She brushed the bits of bark and dust free, checking for injury. She had little sensation on the skin of her hands anymore, and it wouldn't do to get blood on her only dress.

When the swimmer broke the surface with the explosive release of held breath, she jumped. He shook the water from his short hair before flipping onto his back.

Evie slid close to the trunk and huddled behind a leafy branch. The swimmer was sleek and brown as a river otter; naked as one too.

*Oh.* She blinked hard. *What did you expect, you ninny?*

For a moment she envied his boldness. He might not have anything to fear from onlookers, but she did.

Jevany's fame as a summer retreat for the wealthy and infamous exceeded its size twofold. Locals loved to track the comings and goings of the summer people and gossip at the beach or the bar.

The moment the furniture covers were drawn in the little cottage and the groundskeeper hired extra hands to clear the garden, the word had probably gone out that Valentin Dimitrov was bringing his mistress to town for the summer. The housekeeper, who brought her breakfast and dinner, seemed to enjoy taking her measure every day, like a gardener deciding to see what came of an exotic plant that had appeared among the roses.

A tasty bit of gossip in the village, Evie presumed. Or perhaps she, too, was keeping tabs on Evie for Valentin. Hard to say.

The glamour only hid Evie's flaws. The staff knew her face well enough. All she needed was for one of them to overhear mention of seeing a strange woman in the woods and connect it to her.

It would be wise to leave before he saw her.

With a low sigh, he sank into the water again and swam directly toward her. With the sun at his back, she couldn't register his expression, only the brief tension in his shoulders when he spotted her. He paused at waist level. The barrel of his chest expanded and contracted again with a big breath.

It wasn't too late to run. He would need time to find his clothes. He wouldn't follow her. She could be well away before he got a good look at her face.

"*Dobrý den.*" His voice, low and steady, filled the space between them, and something in the tone of it made her skin prickle with warmth.

"Good day." Her English was rusty but passable.

He resumed his approach.

Desperate to avoid his face, she followed the beads of water pearling on his shoulders and pooling in his collarbones before sliding down his chest. His was an even shade of brown all over, as though he spent much of his time without his clothes. A public service, or at least a kindness to humanity that might look on him and marvel at the strength of his legs, the graceful wedge of abdominal muscle above the dark hair nesting the thick line of his manhood.

"Eyes are up here, buttercup," he said in English, a few feet away now.

Embarrassed, she made the mistake of meeting his eyes. His were pale, almost copper, circled by an earthier shade of brown. Her vision shifted, doubled, and her belly clenched hard in anticipation of the worst. But it was not his death mask she saw.

Instead, he became a window into an endless night sky full of unknown constellations. The brightness of a crescent moon hung where his brow should have been. Each movement caused the view to shift, but not the stars themselves. As though where he stood, the world peeled away to reveal a starlit sky, an unknown galaxy.

Her gaze darted about, counting the stars until she ran out of numbers, "You're infinite."

He cocked his head in amusement and confusion. "That's a new one—"

And then he sneezed.

The look on his face was priceless. He barely caught the next sneeze in the crook of his elbow. Even then, the strength of it made him shudder. "Sorry. Allergies."

She blinked hard, but instead of melting away, the vision of stars softened into his skin, giving him a faint glow. *What* was he?

Never mind that. She had enough mysteries to solve. She should take this opportunity to make her apologies and be gone.

She didn't move.

In one more step, he was close enough for her to feel the cool clinging to his skin. Pond water on human flesh shouldn't smell so good, or was that sunbaked earth and fresh pine scent just him?

She remembered the first time she'd seen these northern forests—the damp hollows and air redolent with the smell of green things. Growth and rain and wooded places she couldn't see but felt in her bones. The sense that if she lay down in the grass and the damp, she could be swallowed whole without a trace left behind.

She wondered if being in his arms would feel like that.

His ears came to slight points at either side of his head, a perfect conclusion to the stark angles of his jaw and chin and a contrast to a decadent mouth.

Arousal streaked through her, a flush of heat and possibilities.

She'd drawn the woven basket to her chest like a shield. Self-consciously, she curled her hands so that only the backs showed.

He stopped when she didn't move away. His chin lifted. "My clothes."

Reluctantly, she dragged her eyes from the slab of pectoral under his collarbone. Hanging from the low branch of the tree behind her was the kind of scrunchable athletic bag she saw kids on the tram carrying, often stuffed with tennis shoes. Draped on the branch beside it were a T-shirt and jeans.

His clothes.

He wasn't coming on to her.

Without her glamour, she was little more than a scarred woman with hair just a shade darker than the bags under her eyes. Nothing a man like this would find the least bit interesting. She tripped over a root in her hurry to get out of his way. "Pardon."

With his back to her, he shook out his pants and briefs and stepped into them. He didn't seem to possess an ounce of modesty. He did have a lovely ass.

"Take a picture. It'll last longer."

She cleared her throat and looked up at the pond. "What are you doing here?"

When he looked up, he winked at her, dragging on what turned out to be a faded T-shirt with a logo for something called a Kid Cudi. "This is your spot?"

"I don't own it." Evie straightened her spine.

His smile bucked loose again, almost against his will. His gaze swept *through* her. He might have been most recently naked, but she was the one exposed. She shouldn't like that feeling as much as she did.

"I just started on a job not far from here," he said. "My crew is out of the city. Work gets hot there, but we don't have this."

He splayed an appreciative hand at the pond and the forest, and somehow it seemed to encompass her as well. Perhaps she wasn't so uninteresting after all. Heat flooded the tips of her ears and the skin under her jaw. She resisted the schoolgirl's urge to fidget with the mess of her hair.

"Anyway, it seemed like a nice way to cool off." He cleared his throat. "If I'd known, I would have brought a suit."

"That would be a shame." The words escaped before she could catch them, dancing ahead like disobedient children.

His lips curled in amusement. "You live around here?"

"Something like that."

He stuck out a hand, fingers gracefully splayed from a broad palm. "I'm—"

"No." She jerked backward. Touching her could be dangerous, and like her death masks, it was a part of her notion she could not control. "Please. Don't."

Something passed over his face, a dimming of that brilliant moonlight. "Okay. That's cool. Well."

He shouldered his pack.

"Yes, very well." She floundered.

"Nice not meeting you?"

He would leave her here. Walk away and take a whole galaxy with him. She didn't want it to end. "Your crew. Do you stay in the village?"

"Nope, drive the whole way out and back, every day. Cheaper that way."

He wouldn't be trading stories of scarred women in the woods over a beer with the locals. What harm would it be to have this... flirtation?

She tried out a smile that didn't belong to one of her roles. It hitched and stumbled like an engine that had sat too long in the cold. "It's just best we don't do... names."

That got his attention. "You going to have to kill me?"

"You don't think I could?" This time the smile came easier.

"I should warn you, I'm pretty tough to kill." He lowered his voice. "But I like a dangerous woman."

The confidential tone buzzed up her spine. "It's more interesting that way. Don't you think?"

He hesitated, seemed to consider, but his eyes never left her. "No names. Deal."

Her stomach squeezed under her rib cage. It hurt distantly, a low ache.

"You're hungry." He narrowed his eyes as if he could hear the inaudible gurgle. She started to refuse, but this time her stomach growled in threat. He laughed. Again, she glimpsed a star field in a mysterious night sky.

She should walk away.

This man, with starlight beneath his skin and his big easy laugh, reminded her she was more than her notions and what others would use them for. She wanted to be seen.

Instead, she admitted the truth. "I am."

# CHAPTER THREE

HE'D BEEN aware of the woman as soon as she stepped out of the trees. A villager on a walk, he assumed. From scent alone, he could tell her approximate age (late twenties), where she was in her cycle (ovulating in a day or two), and what she'd had for breakfast (tea and bread).

But it wasn't until he got close that he caught something more remarkable.

The scent of magic was all over her, clinging to her hair and skin, carried on her light exhales. The wolf's awareness rose. *Witch*.

He hadn't met many witches aside from the one who raised him, but he knew the old stories of the war between witches and wolves. Even at the height of the conflict between them, most wouldn't recognize each other by sight alone. Both had to be trained to detect their enemy.

His mother's charm protected him and his brothers against all but the most powerful eyes. But she must have some awareness that he was not what he seemed. It was in her expression and that penetrating gaze.

Mark was used to being looked at. His dark skin earned him everything from interrogative stares on the tram to covetous ones in nightclubs. Being seen was new. Her gaze kept sweeping him with a wary curiosity that matched her foxlike face, as if searching for something.

And she'd called him *infinite*.

A long scar bisected the edge of her eyebrow before continuing down her cheek to her jawline. It puckered against the smooth motion of her cheek when she spoke or smiled. It was old but would never fade entirely. From the way her pulse beat beneath her jaw and her pupils widened, she was startled but not afraid.

Gorgeous in a harried, witchy sort of way wasn't usually his type. But then, usually his type didn't come wandering out of the woods, eying him like a snack.

The sudden heat uncoiling in his core caught him by surprise. He clamped the lid down on that. It wouldn't do for the stories to get around town that there was some strange man seducing village women in the woods.

The rumble of her stomach came again.

"I brought a lunch," he said, lifting the bag between them. "We could share it."

She eyed him, her hands still clutched awkwardly around her basket handle. "You would feed a stranger?"

"My mom always says be generous to strangers in need." He shrugged. "You never know when they're a powerful being in disguise, testing you for great reward."

"Wise." Amusement softened her mouth, but her eyes darkened.

"You have a spot you like?"

When she shook her head, loose hairs from the hasty knot at the back of her head stuck to her temple, jaw. Shades of carob, amber, and marigold coiled free, and sweat-darkened waves frizzed at the base of her neck. "These woods are new to me."

"I know a nice place. Not far."

She stared into him for a beat too long to be comfortable. He didn't look away.

"Lead on."

He paused when they emerged from the wild forest at the edge of a lane of overgrown grass, waiting for her to catch up.

She stepped around him, her voice hushed. "What is this place?"

On the other side of a wire fence, orderly rows of trees forming an abandoned orchard extended away from them. Overgrown, heavier branches split and arced to the ground. A few had gnarled and broken from lack of tending, but most were still green and crowned with fruit.

"Lot of these farms got abandoned after the war," he said. "State owns it now. Eventually it will get sold and plowed under for development. Prime real estate bordering the forest, a stone's throw from the lake."

He thought he'd kept the skepticism out of his voice, but when her dark eyes turned to him, they danced with a smirk.

"Not a fan of the bourgeois?"

"I just like open spaces."

She dropped to her haunches and spread her palm over the dirt. Her ass curved over her dusty heels, plump when outlined against the shapeless, faded dress. Nice.

Mark tore his gaze away just in time to see her fingers before they disappeared into the grass.

When she'd curled them against her chest at the pond, he'd assumed she was hiding a wedding ring. But her fingers were bare except for scars that crisscrossed each digit, turning her knuckles into knotty lumps not unlike those of the old trees before them. Her fingernails were short, warped by old damage, and on her pinky missing altogether. Whatever monster she had battled that left her with such scars she'd survived. She was strong.

"Shall we?" He lifted the top wire.

After she stepped through, he vaulted over the nearest post. Among the trees, the scent of young apples filled his nose.

He led her to a spot where three trees formed a loose triangle: one down, one still standing with massive boughs full of apples, and one that bore the blackened streaks of lightning where its trunk had been sheared almost in half. Ground ivy and periwinkle grew dense as a carpet amid wild grasses in the sheltered space between them. Where dappled shade cast darker coverage, a patch of wild ginger had taken root.

At their approach, a couple of butterflies rose sunward on lazy wings. Sparse birdsong filtered from the forest they'd left behind, but a bee sang through blossoms here and there. He spread his hands with a flourish. "Ta-da."

The witch made a soft sound that might have been pleasure and dropped her slippers at the edge as though she were entering a house, not a thimble-sized glade. She wiggled her toes in the grass. Then, in a graceful move, she folded neatly to a seat, her legs tucked beneath her. She set down her basket and dragged her dress into her lap, tucking her hands into the folds of fabric.

He flopped down a short distance away, ignoring the bits of dirt and detritus. He'd be covered in worse by the end of the day. He began unpacking his lunch, offering her the packet of almonds. "Go ahead."

She demurred.

Mark set them down and went on unpacking.

Out of the corner of his eye, he glimpsed her hand darting out. She slipped a few almonds into her palm and drew it back into the safety of those faded folds. He wondered if they hurt. He pulled apart the wrappers of two crescent-roll sandwiches the tiniest bit so they would be easy for her to open, just in case, and set the chocolate bar beside them. Then he took a sandwich and angled his body slightly away from her.

As soon as his gaze followed his body, he heard the crinkling of foil. "Sweet tooth?"

"Life is short, so eat dessert first," she said around a piece of chocolate. The hum that followed teased him, sending the hair standing on the back of his neck. "This is delicious."

"The best," he admitted. He wanted to see more of the boldness, the flirt, the hint of that dazzling smile that brightened her liquid brown eyes.

"Something is funny?" A smile lit her voice as the foil crinkled open.

"I also have a sweet tooth, Evergreen."

"Evergreen?"

"Gotta call you something."

A tiny wrinkle creased her brow. "Why that?"

"Because you are an evergreen in a sea of deciduous trees."

*No names.* This witch was running from something. And cagey as all get-out. She was a red flag in a faded housedress.

Too bad he'd always liked a good mystery. "Where are you from?"

"What makes you think I'm not from here?"

"A hunch."

She snorted. "And you?"

"Not from around here."

He flopped onto his back, so close to her carefully tucked knees he could almost brush them with his elbow when he pillowed his head on his hands. "Tell me a story."

She laughed. "You *are* a strange man."

"Seems like a fair trade." He caught another wave of surprise. "For lunch."

He enjoyed her surprise more than the glimpses of hunger and hints of flirtation.

"Fine. Anything particular?"

"Make something up."

She chewed for a bit, thinking. The fabric of her dress rustled. She cleared her throat.

"Once upon a time," she said. "That is how they begin, right?"

"It's a bit of a cliché."

She snorted. "Do you want the story or not?"

"Sorry, go on." He wanted the story, but more than that, he wanted the sound of her voice husky with laughter.

"Once upon a time," she said, "there were two merchant families who would not have given each other the weather and a good day under normal circumstances."

"Why?"

"Every reason you can imagine." She shifted in her seat. "Different faith, different custom, different class. Then the godswar came, and they were thrown together in the same low place, and they found they had much in common after all. They saved each other: shared bread and protection and stories until the worst passed and each was on their feet again. By then they had become close. And so it should have been no surprise when the youngest daughter of one and the middle son of the other fell in love."

"Is this going to be like Romeo and Juliet?" he asked. "Everybody always thinks it's so romantic... but it's a tragedy."

"More like Yusuf and Miriam, and it's not... Just listen." She sighed, exasperated. "The families did not object. Why should they? The children were well suited, both clever with a head for business. Both families had demonstrated themselves as honorable and observant, if not the most traditional perhaps, but in their own way. And the godswar changed many things regarding faith."

He snuck a glance at her face. She looked so severe he couldn't help himself. "Are there going to be dragons?"

"No dragons." She huffed.

"It's just that once-upon-a-time stories usually involve things like dragons and princesses." He was pushing it. "These sound like very normal, unroyal people."

"And I suppose you are the expert." There it was, the laugh quivering at the edge of her voice.

"Just establishing expectations."

"Should I continue?"

"Please," he said. "Yusuf and Miriam fell in love."

She took a breath, laughing under it. "Their names don't matter. But it turned out they both were suited for other reasons. He was a very bright boy, charming and good with cloth and people. She was a clever girl, excellent with numbers. They opened a tailor shop and took every job that came. She even learned a bit of stitching, though she preferred handling the accounts. The first years were hard. But they worked even harder. And eventually people would come from all over the countryside to patronize their shop. They had three children: a girl, followed by twins, a boy and a girl, one charming and clever, one industrious and wise beyond his years."

"And the firstborn," he said, liking this glimpse of her, "what was she like?"

"She had her mother's gift for numbers and her father's passion for cloth and thread," she murmured.

The silence stretched. He hovered at the edge of sleep, lulled by the heat and post-swim lethargy. At the shift of her body, he lifted his forearm and opened one eye.

She stood, staring up at the trees, and dusted her hands off on her dress.

Before Mark could call out, she began to climb the standing apple tree. He watched, speechless.

Of all the things he imagined, seeing her scale a tree sent a burst of pleasure through him. He grinned and slipped a quick glance at his watch. He was due back at the jobsite soon. But if he was a bit late, Pavel would get everyone started and he'd drive up early the next morning and get a head start to make up for it.

"Where are you going?"

"I bet some of these are ripe," she called down, reaching for the next branch. "I want to try them."

He rose to his feet. The tree wasn't incredibly tall, but it was old. Its branches had spread, not as thick as he'd like, but enough to bear her. He stepped back to avoid an unintentional glimpse up her skirt and shaded his eyes against the sun with one hand.

She plucked an apple from a cradle of leaves, inspecting it briefly before bringing it to her lips. The skin broke with a juicy crunch.

The crisp, sweet scent tickled his oversensitive nose. "Any good?"

"Tart." She tucked the bitten apple into her teeth and reached out again. "Catch!"

Mark caught a half dozen apples before he called up, "Are you gonna pick the entire tree?"

She chewed another bite before answering. "Better to leave them to the birds?"

"Bombs away." He made a small pile near her basket.

As she descended, some of her sureness left her. She stopped just higher than a comfortable drop to the ground.

"Need a hand?" He gripped a low branch, testing it.

"I don't think it will bear the weight of us both," she said, leaning back. "Maybe if I just let go."

"It's too far." He stepped closer. "Wait. I'll catch you."

She scoffed.

"I'll break your fall."

This time she laughed.

"I've got you." He moved right underneath her, careful to keep his eyes on her face, and waited. He wouldn't rush her. "I promise."

She considered the distance. Then those dark eyes turned on Mark, really taking him in. More than likely, she was just trying to figure out if he was full of shit. He held her gaze when she met his and hoped the steadiness would reassure her.

"How hard are you to kill exactly?"

He thought of a four-hundred-year-old witch and smiled. "Tougher than I look."

Tension softened with her laugh. "All right."

He smiled and angled his body into a better position. "Your count. On three."

She faced the trunk, gripping it with both hands. Her shoulders rose and fell with a deep breath. At last they softened away from her ears, and her voice came, clear and steady. "One, two, three."

She let go gently, as if she could somehow slow the fall. He'd calculated well: with only a little fumble, he caught her in both arms.

The bare skin on the back of her calf pressed against his biceps, and a low, snapping tingle arced between them. Without thinking, he bounced her, taking her weight more securely behind her knees.

At the unexpected movement, her arms tightened around his shoulders. Faces a breath from one another, his smile met her wide eyes. "You feel that?"

❧

EVIE LAUGHED A LITTLE, hearing the edge of nerves. "Static electricity."

She'd forgotten the danger to him. He seemed so solid standing beneath her, confident he could catch her. All she had to do was fall.

In midair she realized the mistake, but it was too late. To catch her, he would have to touch her, and between her dress and the T-shirt there was no way she could avoid skin-to-skin contact. She flinched instinctively when his arms closed around her.

The jolt of contact—a buzz less sharp than static but with a similar crackle about the edges—was a surprise.

A slow smile tugged the corner of his mouth up, revealing brilliant white teeth in a grin that was both sly and pleased. "Nah. That's something else."

He released her knees, and she slid down his chest, toes settling against his in the grass, but didn't let go of his shoulders as the steady buzz echoed between them. Their height difference was so slight that she could almost look directly into his brown-flecked copper eyes. Surprise and delight brightened them.

He was warm, more real than anything she'd held in a long time.

His newly freed palm joined the other at her back, fingers splayed wide. How long had it been since she'd held anyone or been held? He must feel her heart pounding against his palm through the muscle and bone of her shoulder.

His hands tightened reflexively on her back. She should let him go.

Instead, her fingertips settled where his neck met his T-shirt. A tremor went through him when her mangled pinky scraped the skin at his collar.

He liked it. When her fingers traced the back of his neck, his pupils grew, deep starlit wells banded by thin strips of gold. His gaze searched her. She'd been silent too long.

She rose on her toes, and her eyes closed. One kiss wouldn't hurt.

She wasn't prepared for the way he surged back, bringing one hand to the base of her neck between her shoulder blades to hold her against him. That sensation intensified, deepened beneath the skin, and arrowed to her spine.

She gave him her weight, breasts pressed flat between them, the long line of her stomach against his own, the mound of her outlined in the faded dress centered against the junction of his thighs. His erection stirred against her, sending new waves of that prickly warmth from her legs to her toes.

She answered his need with her own, hands sliding down to grab his waistband and drag him closer. A low growl vibrated in his chest. The kiss deepened, a breath too long to sustain.

Somehow he managed to avoid the spent picnic and the pile of apples, navigating backward until she was pressed against the tree trunk she had just been climbing.

Restless and urgent, she bucked her hips against his hard-on with a demanding noise of her own. She hiked a thigh up his hip, making more space for him in the junction of her thighs.

"Hey." He threaded his fingers through the damp curls at the base of her neck and squeezed his palm, parting them.

"You're thinking," she murmured, breathless and idle at once, "I am a stranger you met in the woods. You don't even know my name."

"When you put it like that," he drawled, bracing his palms against the branch behind them.

He was entirely too far away. Evie wanted the sensation of being enclosed again.

"I am an adult." Her hips ground into his again, demanding. "And I know what I want. And you are also an adult. What do you want?"

He met her eyes. The control was there, ragged around the edges from an onslaught of desire but still in place. She wanted to see what might happen when he let go.

"This doesn't have to be more than a fuck beneath an apple tree in the woods." Her split brow bounced. "We can agree to that, can't we?"

She watched the stark words rocket through him, distantly aware that her lopsided smile puckered the scar on her cheek. He didn't seem to notice it or care. There was freedom in that.

"Is that what you want?" Tension graveled his voice.

She nipped his lips, ran her fingertips over the skin of his collarbone, rewarded by his deep shudder. "That is all this needs to be. Deal?"

"Okay," he panted. "Deal."

❧

THIS WAS MOVING FASTER than he expected. But if there were no expectations, who was he to argue?

He did a mental check that he had a condom somewhere on his person and slipped a hand up her rib cage. A shiver coursed through her when the pad of his thumb found her nipple, passing lazily back and forth over it until it hardened.

Her fingers scrabbled for him, yanking impatiently at his thick leather belt, the heavy buckle.

He hiked her hips onto the low branch behind them. A tiny shriek of delight escaped her at the motion as she wrapped her legs around him.

So she liked his strength then. Most women did. He traced his fingertips over the curve of her ass where skin met cotton until he confirmed she was already wet. He stroked, lightly, until her breath juddered unsteadily against his neck. Her scent bloomed, deepened.

Need pressed through him when she curled her hips, the heat of her though fabric tempting him to push the cloth aside and slide inside her. Instead of giving in, he teased its edges until it became nearly unbearable and she made a frustrated noise.

How he managed to get to the condom in his back pocket and keep hold of her at the same time was something of a miracle. Especially when she kept wiggling on the branch. What was she doing exactly?

Then a pair of plain, lace-trimmed cotton panties landed in the grass at his feet.

*Oh.*

"I like to be helpful." She winked, dragging her skirt up along a mile of soft, full thighs.

He met her eyes, laughing, as he lined himself up at her entrance, the heat there almost more than he could bear. "Come to your senses?"

Her brow ticked up. "Have you?"

They shared a collective noise of satisfaction when he slid inside her.

Maybe it had been longer than he'd thought since he'd gotten laid. Because this was like walking into a room he'd visited a hundred times and finding it brand-new. He lingered, rocking his hips until her breath hitched, and she clenched him as hard inside as out.

He fisted a hand in her hair, dragged her mouth to his, and matched the rhythm of their kiss with his body.

The pressure tightening low in the base of his spine built too quickly. It didn't help that her body was a vise and a furnace. When her hand slipped between them, he obliged with a bit of a gap, giving her the room she needed. The quick twitch of clever fingers resulted in her keening cry of pleasure.

The sensation of her breaking around him destroyed his control. He locked her to him, thigh and shoulder and mouth and hips, and instinct took him, bringing release on its heels.

In the aftermath, his forest witch hummed softly, draped against him. It left him free to lay a line of kisses from her ear down her neck to the edge of the dress. Tilting her head back, she opened herself to him.

She broke the contact first. "Your legs."

His thighs shook. Somewhere in the middle of it, he'd taken most of her weight on his hips. The rest of him was the same: spent. He braced a hand on the branch and eased her down.

She gently extracted herself, shaking out the crumpled mess of her skirt with a secret little smile that drew her farther away from him.

Mark shoved off the branch, giving her what he hoped was a careless grin. "I'll go take care of this."

*Get a grip, man. It's just sex.*

Hard to focus with a wolf howling in his chest.

When he returned to the picnic, she'd begun cleaning up. Her dress was wrinkled over her thighs to her waist.

He regretted not stripping it off her completely, the missed chance to admire the body he'd only felt hints of in the warm daylight. "Leaving so soon?"

She jumped. Her surprise was different this time. It didn't ease when her glance skated over him. A new tension tightened her jaw and the skin around her temples. "I have to go."

He didn't ask. Instead, he began to help her pack.

He gathered the apples she'd picked in the grocery sack. Some of the tension left her features when she looked at him, the sly playfulness returning to her eyes.

He took a breath. Better to clear things up now. He didn't want any confusion about this, and if he'd made a mistake, he was going to try to make it right. "Things went a little… fast. Maybe too—"

"It was… perfect." She shook her head doggedly, and the scar puckered with the hint of her smile. She leaned forward and kissed him lightly on the mouth. "Thank you."

Perfect.

Knowing he wasn't the source of her anxiety didn't take the edge off the uneasiness. It only meant there was something else giving her scent a familiar acid tang. He didn't like the idea of her being frightened.

She rose to her feet, dusting off her knees and shins. She didn't seem to notice she was no longer hiding her scarred hands. Mark rose with her, packing his own bag.

"I'm sorry to leave so abruptly." The smile she gave him was forced. "But I should get back."

"It's good, my lunch break ended, oh... let's not talk about it."

Guilt swamped him. He was in town to do a job, a job that might make his career, and while his crew was hard at work, he was getting laid in the woods. "I'll walk you back."

When they reached the fence, he lifted the wire. She slid between the strands. By the time he found his way over the top, she was already moving back the way they had come.

At the pond, they both studied the water.

"Meet you here tomorrow?" he said, smiling.

"I'm not as free as you seem to be." The skin between her brows puckered, her frown tugging at her scar.

"When are you free?" What was wrong with him? It was a brush-off if he'd ever heard one.

"And how does your boss feel about you sneaking away to seduce strange women on your lunch break?" She pursed her lips, trying to hide a smile.

"I am the boss," he said with a shrug. He probably sounded cocky as fuck. He didn't care. "I wouldn't call you strange. A little unusual perhaps. I like unusual."

Her face collapsed, expression at once sad and tight with worry. "I'm only here for a short—"

"Look, I've got another three weeks on this job." He wished he knew her better so that he could understand the look on her face. If he had to guess, he would say maybe longing or astonishment, but it might have also been the kind of disbelief that came when somebody just couldn't take a hint. "If this weather keeps up, a daily swim doesn't sound like a terrible idea. When you decide you have the time to go wandering, you know where to find me, Evergreen."

A smile transformed her face the way moonlight moving through broken clouds suddenly lit the sky. He could almost feel the shafts of that light against his skin. A shiver of pure pleasure raced through him. The air lodged against his throat, and the blood in his chest surged with some unspoken need.

*More.*

She closed the distance between them and reached up to cradle his cheek. Rising onto her toes, she brought her mouth to his before slipping away again. "It's Evelia, but I go by Evie."

"Evie." Mark shoved his hands into his back pockets to keep from reaching out to her.

She turned her back to him, striding away. After a pace or two, she spun on one heel, walking backward. "Aren't you going to tell me yours?"

He smirked. "Gonna have to come back for that."

# CHAPTER FOUR

EVIE WAS out of breath by the time she reached the brambles at the rusted gate. The metal sparked at her touch, tongue sliding free of the groove before she asked. She slipped inside and eased it shut behind her, feeling as though she were waking up from a dream.

In the little rose garden behind the cottage, she held her breath, listening.

She shouldn't have left. It had been dangerous, foolish, reckless. If she were to get caught—

The villa was as it had been every hot afternoon since she arrived, idle and quiet. There were no searching guards or staff, no cries of her name.

She hadn't been caught. Giddiness filled her. It hadn't been a dream. Her skin was sticky with sweat and exertion, bearing the faintest scent of him.

She would run a bath and celebrate her little victory, savoring the memory of the way the man in the woods shivered under her touch. How he set her skin alight with his mouth and his hands.

On the other side of the villa, the gate slid open on metal tracks. The main house was between her cottage and the front gate, obscuring her view. Her breath caught at the barely audible whine of an electric motor growing louder as it passed the horseshoe driveway at the front of the house. She pressed her back to the wall of the cottage and willed herself calm. The weekly grocery delivery perhaps. Gardening supplies.

Unlike the delivery trucks, it didn't pull around to the back entrance.

The engine cut off before it reached the garage. If Evie had to guess, right before her cottage door.

She had a visitor.

She stashed the basket of apples under the hydrangea bush and smoothed the disarray of her hair. She could do nothing for the sheen of sweat, the sticky afterglow of sex. Full glamour would take more time than she had, so she did her best, applying it too fast judging by the way her pulse began to beat against her temple—she'd pay for that later.

On her way to the front of the cottage, she grabbed the abandoned novel from the patio table and stuck her finger inside.

A familiar pearl-white BMW parked between her cottage and the garage. Valentin's second-in-command, Nikolai.

Anticipation knotted under her rib cage. The driver's door opened, revealing the oil-slick hair, blunt pale features, and bearded jaw. He rolled his head on his neck like a boxer entering the ring as he stepped out of the car. Cradled in one arm like a forgotten toddler, a bouquet of hothouse roses was so vivid she knew they were dying.

In the main house, the kitchen curtains twitched. The gardener appeared from nowhere beside the garage in his waxed apron, dabbing at the immaculate lawn with a rake. She wondered where her keeper was.

She bit back impatience. They had an audience. Her role: Valentin's mistress.

"My warden returns," she said with her most winsome smile.

As always, his death mask remained hidden from her. She told herself it meant nothing; there seemed to be no rhyme or reason as to why she saw some deaths and not others. Still, she wondered if seeing it would have made him any less unnerving. The knowing that he *could* die might have settled her in some immeasurable way. Instead, she lived with the irony of having one of the few people whose death she did not see be a face she would do almost anything to avoid.

Nikolai surveyed her. It took all her strength not to flinch away from that look. The back of her neck prickled with a sudden chill.

She focused on the paper-wrapped bouquet in his arms and clapped her hands to her mouth with a squeal. "Are those for me?"

"Valentin sends his regrets that he was not able to join you this weekend," he said perfunctorily. "Business keeps him in town."

She turned her lips down and sucked her teeth lightly. "Again? I'd so hoped. Ah well. At least *you* haven't forgotten me out here."

When she took the flowers, she ghosted kisses in the general vicinity of his cheeks, holding her breath to avoid the pervasive scent of his cologne.

Her keeper shuffled down the drive from the main house, sweating in the sun. "Hello, sir, Nikolai, sir. As you can see, she is fine. Behaving herself."

She'd wondered what excuse he'd been given about why she needed a keeper. *Misbehaving, was it?* He had no idea. She snugged her teeth together but kept the smile. "Sergei has been *such* good company."

Nikolai narrowed his eyes. "You have been getting sun."

"Sergei was kind enough to loan me his novel." She closed the book and offered it to her keeper. "I was reading in the garden. I lost track of time. And now you're here!"

"Valentin sent you a few things to make you more comfortable," Nikolai said.

She turned her back to him though it made the tiny hairs on her arms rise and opened the door.

"Come inside, Kolya," she called over her shoulder, using the affectionate nickname. "These need water before they wilt. I want to hear *all* about the club."

He touched the fob in his pocket, and the trunk eased open. "Sergei, bring the packages in from the car."

Inside, the cottage was blessedly dim. Evie left the lights off, opening the drapes and the windows before puttering about, locating scissors and a vase as though she hadn't explored and categorized every square inch and object in the cottage on arrival.

Tal's first rule: always know your surroundings better than anyone in the room.

She hummed as she returned to the sink. "I've finally figured out the fancy espresso machine. Would you like one?"

"No." Nikolai took a seat in the small sitting area by the window, ankle over knee. The casual posture did nothing to dull the bladed energy that filled the small space.

Couldn't he even pretend at small talk? She fought the urge to throw a glare at him. Wasted effort. His had been the sole voice of dissension when she and Valentin had agreed to play this game.

The night Nikolai had dragged her before Valentin for murdering a man in his club, she recognized the moment Valentin decided putting her to work for him would more than cover the cost of cleaning up the mess she'd made.

With a few quick calculations, the numbers screaming through her head as her heartbeat drowned out her own breaths, she'd revealed a scheme to skim off his liquor earnings and gone from the certainty that she would never see another dawn to kindling hope.

Valentin had laughed and lifted her chin, unbothered by the sticky residue of another man's blood. *I could use someone with your particular talents. Consider it a promotion. You will make sure all my money makes its way to me unimpeded and is handled with care. You will find it lucrative. Do we have an agreement?*

Valentin liked to think of himself as a businessman. As though he didn't owe everything he was to the Crimson Saints. It took a lot of creative accounting to keep the appearance of being aboveboard. Bookkeepers were notoriously valuable targets for rivals and law enforcement—knowledge of the operational details made them a high prize.

But if Valentin locked her away under guard to keep his empire's secrets, escape would be nearly impossible. The seed of a plan had formed—if she played this right, no one would know what she really was to him. *I could work in the office as a secretary. Wealthy businessmen screw their secretaries all the time. Who would believe otherwise?*

Then Nikolai had leveled her with that steady, cutting stare. She knew better than to look away. In a way, it was easier than watching the death mask image of three bullet holes appearing on Valentin's forehead.

*Come, Kolya,* Valentin had insisted. *She's right. A young, attractive woman capable of keeping the books for the most powerful businessman in Prague? Unbelievable. But my new girl… Well, the story tells itself. She'll pass. It keeps her close. We'll give her an allowance.* He'd stared at her critically. *A sizable one. You must dress yourself up. Play the part.*

Evie had nodded so hard her teeth rattled. *Hide me in plain sight.*

Let the whole world believe she was the latest entry on the list of Valentin's dalliances. Evie simply leaned into the assumption people made when he brought her up from serving drinks on the club floor to the desk beside his door. Valentin controlled the liquor and clubs, and over time her role grew from checking the numbers to calculating them in such a way that kept him aboveboard.

Day to day, she spent her time thumbing through magazines and taking far too long to answer calls. She could still socialize with the girls at the club and maintain her chosen apartment in the city. At first working upstairs hadn't seemed so bad. He'd fixed her immigration situation, showered her with cash and clothes and jewelry as befitting a new mistress, all without the expectation of physical contact behind closed doors.

Several times a month, she stayed late to do the actual work: making the bulk of Valentin's money appear legitimate and the rest disappear into the coffers of the Crimson Saints. But she hadn't been lulled into complacency for a second. It only took one such night's work to understand how illegal his operations were and how thoroughly tied to the Saints he was.

She began to plan her escape. It came with rules. She would not steal, only save. She would not make friends, would not care about anyone she would have to leave behind.

For two years, she'd checked the numbers daily in her own head. How much it would take to find another city to disappear into, set up with the money she had earned keeping Valentin rich, and live a quiet life alone with her ghosts. She could already imagine herself seeing winter in London or Rome.

She'd spent almost half her life moving from place to place. It was the only thing she was any good at. When she finally disappeared, she'd leave no trace that she had ever been in Prague.

Like a nesting doll, she built a shell within a shell, her true self tucked away so completely she'd begun to wonder who or what remained.

Perhaps the man beside the lake had glimpsed it. He'd seen the scars that lay at the heart of it all. He hadn't asked, hadn't reacted to the touch of her ruined hands with anything other than pleasure. He'd wanted more of her.

It would be wise not to let herself be distracted. Or to consider him at all. People she cared about had a way of getting hurt. It was for his own good.

As she trimmed and prepared the roses for their slow funeral in a vase and collected her thoughts, Sergei made trips from the car with an absurd assortment of shopping bags and brightly wrapped packages. This display was over the top. The flowers would probably have sufficed, but she knew Valentin well enough. He enjoyed both the favor and largesse of his proximity to the head of the Crimson Saints, and he liked people to know it.

The final load was plain cardboard boxes. Document boxes. Whatever they contained was the real reason she'd been brought here.

The final load deposited, Sergei excused himself with a stiff bow and closed the door silently behind him.

As Evie filled the vase from the tap, she watched her keeper on the doorstep. He wiped desperately at the sweat pouring from his brow. By the time he shuffled up the rise toward the main house, she had decided on her approach: confusion, mild aggravation, humor.

"Is all this really necessary?" She turned to Nikolai, smiling. "Poor Sergei."

Nikolai looked up from flipping through her sketchbook. She tamped down her anxiety.

He'd stopped at the half-finished sketch of a gown. "Sergei is being paid handsomely—"

"To watch a woman surrounded by walls." She retrieved the pitcher of water from the refrigerator. She poured two slim glasses. "Lemon?"

"Two slices," Nikolai ordered. "He is *guarding*."

Her brows lifted as she set the glass on the table beside him. "Rapunzel is safe in her tower."

She turned to leave, but his hand snaked out, circling her forearm. She kept her expression even, though her stomach rolled against her rib cage.

Unlike their boss, Nikolai had done his share of physical labor. The pads of his fingers were tougher than she expected. Now they closed on her wrist, squeezing to roll her palm up. "You've damaged yourself."

Drops of blood wet her palm and fingers, drying in tacky smears. The brambles from the garden gate had taken their due. She hadn't even felt them. Scar tissue dulled sensations.

Evie focused on the glamour that overlay her hands, admiring what they would have looked like if she hadn't broken them in grief. She knew her glamour would bear up under standard human inspection, but she'd always been afraid that someone like her would recognize it for what it was. An illusion.

Still holding her, Nikolai fished a handkerchief from his pocket, dabbed it in the glass, and wiped at the spots of blood. He ignored her protest.

"Have you eaten since you've arrived?" He stared up at her critically. "Slept?"

"You abandoned me here without so much as a change of clothes." She put frustration and a touch of annoyance in her voice as she tugged her wrist. "Did you think about what that might do to my mental state? It's a wonder I can sleep at all."

He released her, and she closed the portfolio on her sketches.

"What is this old thing you keep?" He kept it pinned beneath his fingers when she would have removed it.

"It has sentimental value." To distract herself, she stalked to the table, brushing aside bags from cosmetics stores and lingerie and an expensive boutique she hadn't even dreamed of walking into. "What is all this?"

"Gifts," he repeated. "From Valentin. Who regrets the lack of preparation for your departure and wanted to send you tokens of his appreciation."

Valentin did not care for her convenience beyond how it suited him. But the gifts provided a cover for the actual delivery.

She drummed her fingers on the first of three plain document boxes. "No. This."

Nikolai rose, surveying the garden through the window and the drive toward the house. The quiet property had gone even more still since he arrived. Satisfied, he turned back to her, folding his arms over his chest.

"The boxes contain the accounts," he said quietly. "The most recent ones at least. Valentin suspects someone is stealing from him."

"He wants me to investigate?"

"Who better to find it than one who has already proven herself so capable of identifying such schemes?" Nikolai smiled.

Evie shivered at the reminder of the ties that bound her to Valentin. The blood on her hands.

At her hesitation, Nikolai's voice turned soft, almost gentle. Dangerous. "You can do this, can't you?"

"It will take time." Evie forced steel into her voice.

"Which is why we have removed you to the countryside," he said, a little laugh in his voice. "Fewer distractions."

"If I find—"

"*When* you find," Nikolai said gently. He slid a paper onto the table toward her, a number she did not recognize, written in his blocky script. "You will call me. You will give me the account, the amount, and any personal names you encounter. Only me."

"What will you do?"

"As I always do. Deal with it." Nikolai rose and gestured at the door. "I'll bring the rest over the next few weeks. We must be careful not to alert whoever it is that we are coming."

"Then I can come home?" Hope and relief tangled in her throat, and she was finally able to admit the thing she had been afraid of all week—that they had brought her here because they knew she planned to run. That the only way she would leave this place was in pieces.

"When the work is done."

Once she was back in the city, she would clean out her stashes and run. First she had to get word to Tal that she was all right.

Evie retrieved an envelope from the counter. "I hate to ask, but I left some clothes with my tailor."

She'd written a note out of hope. Tal did most of the tailoring for the dancers at the club. Hers would be just another bill to be settled. They had been at this too long to be reckless. The note would keep him from worrying, for a while at least.

Nikolai's lips curved into a sardonic smile. He slipped the envelope from her fingers, removing the single sheet folded around a few crowns. She'd expected he would read it and had chosen her words carefully. *My mother is ill. I will remain in the countryside until she is well or worse. Here is something toward my bill.*

Nikolai now removed the money and set it on the table. He held up a hand to silence her protest and slid the note into his jacket. "It will be taken care of. Consider the rest a bonus for the additional work."

"Please send him my gratitude."

"It is the least he can do." Nikolai inclined his head regally. "Walk me out."

She trailed him to the door. "Kolya, favor?"

He paused, eyes narrowing.

"A television."

"A television?" Nikolai glared at her.

"Every day, Sergei sits outside my window, babbling about the godswar," she said, genuine exasperation easy to come by. "Assign him regular check-ins and give him a television for his off-duty time. It would keep me from having to make up stories about what I'm doing with ledgers and sums instead of painting my nails and tanning."

It would also keep her from having to drug him to slip out of the villa. Not that she would. She'd done some foolish things in her life, but fucking strangers in the woods was a madness she had no intention of repeating.

*Oh, but the feel of him inside her. She wouldn't regret that. Nor the way his hands moved, callused and warm, against her skin.*

"I'll see what can be done."

"Thank you."

From the shadow of the doorway, she watched the white BMW disappear around the drive.

Inside, she paced a circle around the table. She wanted to stuff all the packages in the closet, unopened. But she was sick of the two dresses she'd found at the charity shop, and the pharmacy toiletries were nearly expended.

Out of defiance, she saved the top box for last. The rest was standard. Lingerie, a silk robe, makeup, and skincare products that smelled like candy and floral bouquets. Too expensive and impractical for a country vacation. Valentin was hopeless.

At last she slid the gold ribbons aside and lifted the lid reluctantly. Cradled in tissue was a summer dress. It was a simple wrap made of silk so gauzy and lightweight it felt like feathers on her fingertips. She recognized the quality of the workmanship immediately, the hand-overcast seams and matched lines of the small white dots in navy fabric. This wasn't Valentin's taste.

The silk weighed nothing in her hands, the sensuality a sensation she wasn't accustomed to giving herself.

Beneath the dress was an envelope, wadded full of Czech crowns.

Evie thumbed through the stack of new bills, calculating by the thickness. Twice her regular income for the month. Valentin was not usually so generous. He must be seriously concerned.

She folded the dress carefully and replaced it. She would have to decide where to hide the money. Somewhere she could get to it in a hurry—outside the walls preferably.

But that could wait. For now she had a way to get back on track to leave this city for good. For the moment that would have to be enough.

"NICE OF YOU TO turn up, boss," Sam called as Mark hurried back onto the site.

"Went for a little walk—got lost on my way back," Mark muttered.

Sam grumbled under his breath, but considering he intended for Mark not to hear it, Mark did him the courtesy of ignoring it.

Pavel called out a *dobre vecher*, acknowledging the lateness of the hour.

*Geez, a guy slips one time and nobody lets them off the hook.*

Annoyance was immediately replaced by shame. He had no business sneaking off into the woods and hooking up with a stranger in the middle of the day. They were up against an impossible deadline, and they depended on him.

Anton's promise waved like a beacon. The next job. He needed this chance.

He threw himself into work the rest of the afternoon. This was his favorite type of demo. The bones of the villa were good, and he took pleasure revealing them beneath a few decades of neglect, hastily made repairs, and amateur improvements. He felt as though he were uncovering the truth of something rather than hastening its destruction.

Sure, sometimes buildings needed to come down, to be replaced by bigger, better, safer structures. But one thing he saw over and over was how often humans, through impatience or greed or a lack of resources, had simply neglected the treasure beneath.

His mind kept returning to the pond and the mysterious witch. Was she visiting for the summer? Maybe she was someone important seeking privacy. Witchness protection? He snorted.

"Hey, look what the kid found," Sam called.

Mark jogged over to where Pavel had the kid clearing out the old fireplace. It was dirty work. Perfect for breaking in fresh meat. Mark clapped a hand on the older man's back as he passed, grinning.

The kid was crouched in the ashes, hands and clothes blackened from soot. He'd made good progress.

He was probably a nice kid. Mark resigned himself to having to learn his name. Eventually.

The kid dragged down the cloth he'd tied over his nose and mouth to reveal a huge toothy grin and said in English, "Look, boss!"

Mark exchanged an annoyed look with Pavel. The older man spread his palms. "He says he wants to practice."

Mark sighed and sank to his haunches to get a closer look at the boy's outstretched palm.

"I found—" The boy paused as his English abruptly ran out and he switched to a rapid stream of Czech. "These stones, precious stones, you know. In the ash."

"Who owns the house?" Mark asked.

"Anton's doing it on speculation for a real estate guy?" Pavel said. "Owner abandoned."

"Legitimate salvage," Sam muttered.

Mark raised his eyebrows. Born in this landlocked country, Sam didn't have a maritime bone in his body. Must have been something he'd gotten out of one of the battered science-fiction paperbacks tucked into his toolbox for his lunchtime reading.

The boy twitched his hand, and the six chunks of black tektite-like substance winked prettily in the fading afternoon light, drawing Mark's eye. Gods only knew how they'd wound up among the greasy ash. Each threw iridescent rainbows when struck by light, their heavily pocked surface flecked with glittering bits that shone gold and then silver and then gold again. The material was like nothing of earth, but everyone knew divine-stone when they saw it.

It was hard to believe something this beautiful was a remnant of the cataclysmic war that brought humanity to its knees. The power of gods, weaponized by governments, ideological parties, and religious factions, had produced results often strange and illogical. After all, they were not arms created by science to maximize destruction but magic harnessed by human imagination and bent to slaughter. They could be terrible and beautiful.

Prague suffered less during the godswar than many cities, so there were far fewer artifacts of the war recovered here. Whether they had been consigned to the fire intentionally or not, these had been forgotten long ago.

"They're valuable, right?" the boy asked.

Human collectors weren't the only ones willing to pay a high price for such remnants of gods. The name, divinestone, wasn't entirely a misnomer. They might not possess a power of their own, but they did have the ability to be charged to amplify power or protect against it. The crew looked up at Mark expectantly.

"Yeah, maybe." Mark straightened up. "You found them. You get first pick."

"Boss?" Sam frowned.

The kid's grin grew even wider. He plucked not the biggest one but the shiniest from the pile. Smart kid.

"Gimme your handkerchief," Mark ordered.

The boy obediently undid the scrap of fabric and handed it over.

"We sell the rest and split it even," Mark swept the rest into the cloth. "Pavel, you still know that guy?"

Pavel nodded.

"We agree?" Mark surveyed them.

The men nodded. The boy contemplated his and then added it to the pile. That would cover all their rent for a month with a bit of beer money left over.

Mark paused, thinking of his forest witch. Evelia. *Evie.*

Something about her expression had made him think just maybe she'd be back.

Anton's words—his promise—needled at him. He had to bring this job in on time. His chance to work on a build crew was riding on it.

But if he kept sneaking away at lunch, he was going to have to call Chris in to make up time. Keeping Evie secret from prying coworkers *and* a sharp-nosed younger brother would be tricky.

If she came back.

She wasn't coming back.

But maybe she would.

He hated being an optimist. It was only going to lead to disappointment.

He plucked the smallest stone. "You can split my share if I can keep this one."

Sam shrugged. *Your loss.* Pavel nodded. Fresh Meat—Ondrej—agreed.

"You have a need for such a thing?" Pavel asked as he started back for the brick walls. The older man's eyes were too sly, too knowing.

Mark shrugged. "Probably not. But doesn't hurt to hang on to it just in case."

# CHAPTER FIVE

THE FIRST BOX INCLUDED LEDGERS. The second, blank notepads and sharpened pencils, her preferences. After a bath and dinner, Evie started on the accounts.

For the first time since she'd come to Jevany, her mind grew still and focused. Instead of counting dust motes and paint chips or her own breath, she lost herself in columns of numbers.

Numbers obeyed rules and logic and came to provable, reliable conclusions.

That her skill with numbers was anything more than a nervous habit was Tal's fault. After they'd been reunited in the camp, he'd traded tailoring for some old algebra and accounting textbooks from a college professor who'd gotten work tutoring outside camp.

The first pass was for obvious signs of fraud. Looking at each account over history, she followed the pattern of first digits. The appearance of each number should follow a predictable curve. When it didn't, she highlighted those accounts for deeper analysis. It wasn't proof, but humans attempting to randomize numbers often introduced inconsistencies and patterns that would not follow the way numbers appeared naturally.

It wasn't magic, but she supposed someone watching her might assume it was if only because of the speed with which she did it. The night she'd used her skill with numbers to save her own life, she'd had to walk Valentin through her accounting more than once.

After that night, she'd been careful to set a pace for herself that seemed impressive but wouldn't raise suspicion that she was anything more than quick with numbers. Without an audience, she moved quickly, pausing to shake out her fingers or massage her wrist as her body labored to keep up with her mind.

Within a few hours she'd made it through half the ledgers and set the work aside. It wouldn't be good to finish the whole batch in a single night when she had all week. Three of the accounts bore more scrutiny. Evie made a note to do a complete examination.

Just as hunger had startled her earlier, surprise followed her yawn, accompanied by the sensation of heavy eyelids.

In the bedroom, she dragged herself out of her clothes and onto the sheet. It was too hot for blankets. She shut off the light and sank into the pillows, prepared to stare up into the darkness of the ceiling, listening to the frogs calling to each other and the distant cry of an owl before drifting to an uneasy sleep. She hadn't lied to Nikolai. Sleep had been hard to come by and interrupted by nightmares.

But when she woke, the birds had long given up their morning songs. No dreams. Nothing at all. Just blissful oblivion.

The housekeeper had come and gone, a tray with a covered breakfast plate in the shade on the porch. She eyed the sausages in congealing grease and the waxy store-bought fruit. She'd known what it was like to feel hunger for days on end. She never took food for granted. But she'd never learned to endure pork. She took the bread, butter, and jam instead. Accompanied by one of the orchard apples and strong tea, it made a reasonable breakfast.

When she set the tray back on the porch, her keeper was there. She braced for another day of stories. He took the tray silently and mumbled a thank-you.

"For what?" she asked, fixing her gaze on his sternum.

"I'll be back with your lunch," he said. "Nikolai says you sleep poorly. You are to nap in the afternoon. I will make sure you are not disturbed."

Evie wouldn't let herself smile. "How thoughtful."

She spent the morning on the patio, dutifully painting her nails. In the afternoon, she closed the cottage. She lay in the dimness and sweltering heat, listening for any sounds of people snooping around the cottage. If she was being tested, she wouldn't disappoint.

The frenetic racket of a Russian game show drifted down the hill from the open kitchen window of the main house. She recognized Sergei's guffawing laughter and the housekeeper's hen-like chuckle. The television noise turned into the drone of a soccer announcer. She rolled onto her side and tried not to think of her lover cutting long strokes across the pond.

She worked from dinner until midnight, and this time she dreamed of him—unfamiliar constellations moving through the trees. She ran after him, but he was too fast.

She kept the routine for the rest of the week. She even managed to sleep a little after the second day. That was mostly a result of boredom, and she woke up sweaty and irritable.

She had to deal with the money stash, sooner rather than later.

She dug the box containing the silk dress out of her closet and put it on. It felt like a crime to wear it for manual labor, but it was the most practical of her new wardrobe. She wrapped the money in plastic and slid it into the bottom of her basket by the back door.

She fidgeted until the lunch tray was delivered and nearly snatched it from poor, gaping Sergei. "I'll bring it up to the house before dinner."

"There is no need," Sergei said grudgingly as he tried not to stare. "I can retrieve—"

"It's no trouble at all." She beamed at him, the full effect of her smile making his jaw slacken. "I'm happy to pull my weight. And I'm sure you have a show to enjoy after lunch?"

He grunted and took his leave.

*I'll take that as a compliment.* As soon as he was gone, she eyed the stewed pork shoulder and shuddered. She managed a few quick bites of the creamed potatoes and asparagus that had been steamed well into its afterlife, but her stomach wasn't in it. Perhaps she could talk the grateful Sergei into another trip to the village for her own groceries. Later.

For now, she slipped the remainder of the apple tart she'd baked from the orchard fruit into the basket with a bottle of wine. She could have a picnic when the work was done.

She slipped out the back door, grabbing a trowel from the gardening table behind the cottage. She hoped it wasn't just decorative. The metal gate responded to her touch easier than the first time. She'd debated where to go. In the end she decided on the pond. If she had to run, the pond would be on the way to the village.

She played with the edge of her glamour as she walked. It was like pulling a loose thread from a piece of cloth—she could feel the unraveling against her skin until there was nothing between her and the air.

Digging was harder than she expected and took longer. She was sweaty, and dirt had crusted under her nails by the time she arranged the soil and rocks. She repacked her basket, too hot to think about baked goods no matter how delicious her tart was.

She stripped off her dress and slid into the water. It was every bit as cool and refreshing as she'd hoped. More even, because of the work before. She was not an elegant swimmer, but she could get herself across the length of the pond a few times before she had to pause for breath. She treaded water. No sign of her mystery lover.

He'd probably given up after she hadn't shown.

She quit kicking and allowed herself to sink below the surface. Eyes open, she watched the shafts of sunlight pierce the murky gloom, a few disturbed fish streaking by. She counted, letting the ache in her lungs build. A distant splash startled her. She looked up.

A pair of familiar legs kicked at the water hard, pausing above her and spinning. Her lover. The muted noise of her name reached her. He dove, searching the gloom. She waved, grinning. Shock kicked the air out of his lungs in huge bubbles, and she pushed off the pond floor, shooting to the surface just as he emerged.

"I saw you go down, and then you didn't come back up and I thought— Gods," he said around coughs.

"Boo?" She grinned softly, giving way to concern as he struggled clear his airway.

"You were under for…" He stared at her.

"I can hold my breath a long time."

"You trying to kill me?" He splashed a handful of water in her face.

She shrieked, laughing, and splashed back. "You said you were tough to kill."

He ducked and dragged her under with him. When they surfaced, he was grinning again, starlight in his eyes. "Didn't seem like you were coming back."

"I wasn't," she said honestly.

"Glad you changed your mind." He dragged her close.

Kissing him unmoored her from her worries about Valentin and Prague.

When he parted them, his breathing was ragged and they smashed knees as they tried to stay afloat and locked together. Even in the cool of the pond, he was warm, a solid presence against her.

His eyes fixed on her in earnest question. "Are you hungry?"

Hunger had been her companion. The kind not even a freshly baked tart or a portion of lovely penne pasta with garden herbs and a delicate, almost floral olive oil could cure. Wine did no good. Even her favorite pieces of chocolate did nothing to satisfy her. Nor her hand between her own thighs late at night while the other stroked her breasts and throat, imagining his mouth there.

She'd tasted pleasure with him—sweet tart, buttery warm. Nothing else satisfied.

A slow smile curled his lips. He cupped the back of her neck in one broad palm. "Nah, you're *hungry.*"

"Hallo!" a voice called.

"Dobry den," her lover called cheerfully over her shoulder. He kept one hand splayed where her neck met her shoulders, the light pressure holding her in place.

Just a hiker, looking for directions to the village. She tried to help keep them afloat with a few little flutter kicks, but their legs mostly tangled. He dragged her thighs around him. He didn't seem to tire as he carried on a pleasant conversation. The entire time, his hand at the back of her neck stroked lazy circles that managed to turn anxiety into arousal.

Strength *and* stamina.

The hiker went on her way.

"The coast is clear. You can come out now." Evie's lover brushed her ear with his lips.

Evie laughed despite herself.

His eyes were grave. "Don't want to be seen with me?"

"Don't want to be seen at all. It's… complicated."

*No complications, Evie girl.* Tal's voice, wise as ever, served as her conscience and her reason.

It didn't have to be, not if they kept it simple. She met her lover's eyes, brushed the curve of one sharp ear with her fingertips. "I can't explain. Or make any promises. But if this could be enough—"

"Evergreen, I'm not a promises kind of guy." He grinned. "And *this* is more than enough."

He stroked her mouth with his lips, teasing her tongue in a slow, decadent dance. She shifted her hips, fitting them together, but he gripped her thigh to stop the natural conclusion.

When their eyes met, his were bright with desire, tense with restraint. "Maybe someplace a little more private?"

She grinned, letting him go and splashing toward shore. A much better swimmer, he passed her in a few easy strokes, and when she emerged from the water, he was waiting, hand extended to help her onto the muddy rocks.

Naked, he was just as beautiful as she remembered. Self-consciousness tightened her belly. Without her glamour, she was—

"Gorgeous," he said, the long look heating the air between them. He released her hand. "But I want you all to myself, so put on that potato sack and let's get out of here."

"Potato sack?"

He tossed her dress to her but grabbed her underwear before she could and balled it in his fist with a wink. "You don't need these."

Wriggling into fabric while wet was a challenge. He had a lot more practice. By the time she smoothed the dress down over her thighs, he was already buckling his belt. Today he wore another T-shirt that was worse for wear, covered in smudges that looked permanent, but this time for a British band named for a French prison she recognized. He stayed barefoot, boots thrown over his shoulder with his lunch sack.

His gaze skated over her, warming everywhere it lingered. "I stand corrected. *That* is a dress."

"It was a gift," she admitted. When she looked up, he was watching her, copper eyes inscrutable.

He started into the trees. "Come on."

"I don't even know your name," she said stubbornly, peeved at the way her heart still hammered long after the alarm had faded.

"Whose fault is that?" He turned to her with a wry smile. "You coming or what?"

He stood perfectly still as she approached. His nostrils flared as she drew close, and his chest rose beneath the thin, faded shirt like he was pulling her in or restraining himself.

"Where are we going?"

"Another perfect spot for a picnic." He offered a hand. "Ready?"

She gathered her basket and slid her fingers between his. This time she felt it: that strange electricity that seemed to draw them together rather than push apart. The fear that she might hurt him fled. Touch had never felt like this before. She missed it, and she was eager for more. "Yes."

Hand in hand, they moved deeper into the woods.

He certainly had a knack for finding secret places. The clearing appeared after a brief—slightly harrowing—passage through overgrown brambles and undergrowth, invisible to all but the most determined. It was a shady glen amid a stand of slender beech, the ground covered in a thick blanket of moss.

She wandered around the perimeter, but her eyes kept returning to him—to starlight and the hungry look on his face. He was waiting for her to decide on the first move. She had no doubt that if she sat down to eat, he would sit with her without complaint.

She untied the belt of her dress instead.

"Stop that."

Her fingers froze at his words.

"Come here."

He laid her out on the moss, cushioning her head on a pile of discarded clothing, and then took his time exploring her. When they finally came together, she wondered if she had a bone left in her body, spent as she was and driven to her peak by his mouth and hands. She floated above herself somewhere in the thin summer clouds overhead, like a kite on a string until her final release brought her cascading into her own body.

Afterward, she cushioned her head on the thunder of his heartbeat. She allowed herself to drift again under the sensation of his palm sweeping her side, shoulders, arms.

He'd circled her hand with his before she could draw it away. He pulled her fingers to his mouth, kissing the tip of each—even the horrible pinkie finger.

It still surprised her to find what sensations registered through scars. The pain of rose thorns hadn't reached her notice until Nikolai called them out. But the pleasure of these slow, delicate kisses rang through her like the peal of silver bells.

He just looked at them when he was finished, studying the scars and ridges of healed flesh. Evie's fingers curled reflexively, but his gentle grip held her firm.

"We don't have to talk about them if you don't want to," he murmured. "But you don't have to hide them from me either. Scars are just... a history we can't cover up. You're gorgeous."

Heat swelled into her throat, making it hard to breathe. She'd gotten so used to her masks that she'd begun to judge what lay beneath against them. Acceptance felt new, frightening. She pulled her hand away.

He let go, only to run his fingertip along the line of her jaw and up her cheek. The sensation of his finger on the scar was a phantom. "I like this one. Makes you look dangerous. Like a pirate queen."

Laughter bubbled through the complex tangle of emotions in her throat. "A *pirate* queen?"

"Aye, matey," he growled, tilting her chin up.

This kiss shattered something deep in her she hadn't known was held in such fragile trust.

When he pulled back, tiny creases formed in the corners of his eyes and the left side of his lips in the otherwise flawless brown skin. She saw him in five years, in ten, and twenty-five. Eventually the threads of silver would trace through the tight black curls. The lines would deepen around his eyes and mouth, a lifetime of smiles she hoped someone who loved him would see.

For a single foolish moment, she envied the woman who would claim a place at this man's side.

This was not the beginning of a forever. She would never endanger him that way. But she would enjoy what time they had. And she would set him free to give that kind of acceptance—and pleasure—to someone who truly deserved him.

Her chest ached, but her stomach demanded her attention.

"Have you eaten?"

"No," she admitted. "But I brought dessert."

"Dessert?" He kissed the swell of her breast. "I thought we already did that."

"Suit yourself. More for me."

＊

WHEN EVIE DIDN'T COME BACK the first day, Mark should have felt relief.

This job was the one he had been waiting for, the gateway to his future. A skittish forest witch—no matter how sexy and uninhibited—was a distraction he didn't need.

*Keep your head down, do good work, and reap the damn reward for once.*

Which didn't mean he couldn't swim at lunch. And her pond *was* the closest.

She wasn't coming back anyway. She'd all but run from him. That single wild-eyed look was probably *I'm trying to give you the brush-off, dummy.*

But she'd also given him her name. Evelia. Luminous.

Once, he'd seen a photo of moonlight on a desert landscape. It hadn't looked cool silver at all but gilded and warm, stretching over everything it touched like liquid gold. She was that kind of moonlight.

When he'd scented her again, he'd wanted to tackle her in the grass and kiss her senseless for making him wait to see her.

Mark took her to the glade. He wanted to feel that achy sparking that eased when their fingers slid against each other. He'd felt it all right. He might have gone a little overboard with the feeling of it. But it ended with her limp and drowsy, draped on his chest, and he had no regrets at all.

He liked women, their softness and strength, their scent and the timbre of their laughter, the way both changed with desire. The value of a woman's satisfaction was not lost on him. Satisfied women were much more fun. And he liked having fun—and keeping it that way.

Except sooner or later, things got serious. Or people expected them to get serious. He had enough on his plate—keeping his siblings in line, taking care of their parents, plans to get his own company off the ground. He'd inevitably let someone down.

Wanting more than casual encounters felt wrong when he didn't have more to give.

And he didn't need the trouble another witch would bring. They had gotten lucky once in avoiding bringing the necromancer down on their heads. Two things that never struck twice were luck and lightning. And since Beryl Gilman-Vogel wouldn't have the sense enough not to try to help this witch, it was up to him to create some boundaries. The last time she'd gotten involved, they'd had to put down a four-hundred-year-old witch and he'd gotten a sister-in-law.

Mark and Evie were consenting adults having a lunchtime fling. That was all this would be. And speaking of lunch, based on the sound her stomach was making, he wasn't the only one who had worked up an appetite. He withdrew a series of wax-paper-wrapped baguettes—sandwiches stuffed with cucumber, tomato, and cheeses.

"The mushroom-eggplant spread they use is incredible." He pushed one at her. "And it's kosher."

Her head tilted, eyes bright and curious. She looked good after sex. Better than good. Tousled hair and flushed chest and that sheen that made her full-moon glow warmer and softer. "How did you know?"

How could he not? He'd heard the grief in her voice when she told him of the tailor and his wife. Her parents. Her family.

"You didn't eat the ham in your sandwich the other day," he said instead, remembering another detail of the family. Miriam and Yusuf. "Or halal? Or you're a vegetarian, and I went way too far jumping to conclusions over some truly second-rate deli meat—"

"You didn't," she admitted, her voice soft and rasping over emotion she tried to hide by digging through her basket. "I was raised... Well, I'm not particularly observant, of anything, anymore..."

He withdrew a pair of containers with a flourish. "Hazelnuts. Dates. These are my sister's favorite. She says they're the best in the city. I was supposed to see her yesterday, but she was busy, so now they're ours."

"You have a sister?"

Did casual lunchtime flings talk about their super-annoying families? He shrugged a shoulder. They'd make the rules up as they went. "One. And two brothers. What's for dessert?"

She'd baked a tart from the apples in the orchard. That was the enticing smell coming from the basket. The dates were soft in the heat. Almost too sweet, though he enjoyed sucking the stickiness from her fingertips.

He'd promised not to ask her about her scars, so what came out was, "Are you going to tell me the end of the story?"

"What story?"

*The one that ended with you alone in Prague instead of surrounded by the family who loved you.*

"The one about the princess and the dragon," he said instead.

She laughed, taking an impressive bite of her sandwich and tucking a stray slice of pickled cabbage between her lips. She covered her mouth with the back of her hand and shook her head. "I think it's your turn."

He rolled onto his back with a handful of hazelnuts, popping one into his mouth. "Okay. I'll give you a story. Once upon a time, there was a young man—"

"A prince?" she chirped.

"Not a prince." Mark shook his head. "What is it with princes anyway? Stuck up, inbred... He's a kid, okay? Just a regular kid."

"Establishing expectations," she sang.

"Funny," he drawled, but he could feel the laughter rising effervescent in his chest.

"Go on."

"His mother was beautiful and powerful like a queen. Happy?" he conceded. "His father was good with his hands and making languages his own. Anyway, when the regular not-a-prince kid was small, they were forced to flee their home."

"Exciting."

"Hush, I'm not even getting started," he said. "But the boy was unhappy because he was far from home. Then one day, he discovered he had something inside him."

Her eyes widened theatrically. "What kind of something?"

"Are you going to keep asking questions?"

Her smile flashed. "Please go on."

"Thank you." He topped off her glass. "The something inside him had always been there. Perhaps he had never known it. But gradually he had no choice but to answer it. And when he did, he discovered it had secrets revealed only to him. And he found for the first time in his life, he understood who he was and the world he belonged to. He allowed its voice to be his guide and his companion where he once had none."

Mark was quiet, self-conscious. That's not where he'd intended the story to go. Only now it seemed obvious, and he wondered if he had given himself away. But she only looked at him, perturbed.

"That was your story?" she asked, so offended he knew it was an act.

He narrowed his eyes. "The story thing was your idea. I was just trying to enjoy my lunch."

"I didn't think anyone could be quite as bad at it as you are." She smirked. "It was vague, and the ending made no sense at all."

He clutched his chest as if the words had done damage before grinning up at her. "I do have a knack for finding wonderful picnic spots. You have to admit that."

"The best."

"I need to get back," he admitted reluctantly.

When they reached the pond, he reached for her hand to find her fingers curling around his. Her smile matched his own.

"This is fun, yes?" she said, squeezing his fingers even as her slow steps put distance between them.

"It is," he admitted warily. Still not letting her go. Or was that her holding him.

Was this where she asked if they could do, be more?

"Maybe we can keep seeing each other while we're both in town," she said. "When it's done, it's done, and we're okay with that? No plans, no promises."

"No plans, no promises?"

"Keep it easy. And fun." She nodded as if it were the most reasonable request in the world. "Whenever it works for both of us. But no expectations."

"I can do that." He exhaled he released her. It was exactly what he wanted. Why wasn't he relieved?

She paused mid-turn into the forest and glared back at him. "Will you at least tell me your name?"

"Thought you'd forgotten." He winked. "It's Markus. Mark."

"Mark." She smiled as if he'd given her something much more valuable. "Will I see you tomorrow?"

His chest was light as a balloon, and he couldn't keep the grin off his face. He took a few backward steps, drawing a big breath as if he were considering. "Boss is working me *way* hard on this job."

She narrowed her eyes at him, a smile twitching in answer at the corner of her mouth. "Aren't you the boss?"

He grinned. "See you tomorrow."

She walked into the trees. Mark made sure to be gone before she looked over her shoulder to find him. He was definitely going to have to call in his little brother to finish this job on time.

# CHAPTER SIX

THEIR DAYS WENT in the hazy way of summer—endless until it was suddenly gone. Looking back, perhaps she could have anticipated the end. But for the first time in years, Evie allowed herself to settle into a routine.

As in the city, she preferred to do her work in the cool, silent night hours. She found two cases of minor skimming—a few thousand crowns here or there, "misplaced" by someone whose bookkeeping was less creative than they imagined it to be.

She spent the hottest part of the afternoon with Mark, swimming in the pond before or after sex.

When they were together, she became someone new, untouched by grief and unhindered by scars. Someone closer to who she was beneath the masks she wore. She'd grown accustomed to the unfamiliar constellations beneath his deep brown skin. As if he wore stars instead of freckles. They were gone as quick as they came, especially when he met her eyes and his lips quirked in a smile. She'd counted them repeatedly and always came up with a different number. She'd never seen anything like him.

Maybe, with time, they would have trusted each other with their secrets.

She refused to acknowledge the melancholy that sometimes slowed her pencil late at night. It came with the knowing that his touch, his taste, would someday fade from memory. She would no longer be able to smell him, remember what he sounded like when he laughed. Just as every day when she left him at the tree line, she'd turn back to look and, like Eurydice, he was gone.

She had no choice. Valentin thought he owned her. He'd gotten—or likely forged—the documents that made her legal. The only power she had was to disappear.

And even if she could stay, what kind of life could she make for herself? She was an orphan, a refugee. She had no skills other than her wits and a bit of notion. No reputable accounting firm would hire her without a degree or certifications, no matter how good she was with numbers. And her work as a mobster's bookkeeper was worse than worthless as a reference.

Pleased with her progress on the first set of books, Nikolai doubled the next batch. He also brought her a present—a small, colorful bird in a gold cage. "I thought you might like some company. Something as exquisite as you are."

She couldn't read him well enough to know if he intended the irony, the cruelty. Perhaps it was a reminder.

She took the cage and peered at the little bird to keep the disgust off her face.

"I'll call him Kolya," she said sweetly.

Evie endured the songbird for a single afternoon before she set it loose. She would cage nothing.

The current set of books lay on the table where she'd abandoned them for a cup of tea. She lit a few candles, placing one in the empty birdcage near the stove. She put on the kettle, plucked fresh mint from the pot she'd transplanted to the windowsill.

The outside air moved, damp and heavy against the curtains. Rain was coming. Still a ways off, but the prospect of it made the humid air even thicker and the breeze less of a relief than usual.

Waiting for the water, she leaned against the counter and eyed the books. Something was off, something different about these. Columns of numbers itched at her brain, biting like flies. A new entry had begun appearing in the past six months or so. Eyebrow-raising amounts, irregular but increasing with some numbers repeated, as though it was a standard size or item quantity. It wasn't what Valentin had asked her to look for, but now that she'd found it, she couldn't look away. She was missing something.

No. *Something* was missing.

She flung herself off the counter, returning to the books. Most of the descriptions were kept in code, but she'd seen them long enough to recognize liquor, tobacco, protection fees. But there was no code leading into the amount on the new income, only three letters behind each.

The whistling kettle startled Evie out of her thoughts. She made tea, bringing the cup, saucer, and a small crock of honey to the table. She lit a few more candles and went back to work.

She turned the letters beside each entry over in her mind, searching for some sort of connection. She listed all the clubs and operations she knew of under Saints control, including their locations. Her eyes snapped back. These were cities. Two cities.

Moscow. Saint Petersburg.

Some borders were more permeable these days than they had been after the war. But the European territory's relationship with its eastern neighbor was tenuous at best. Contested borders resulted in gray areas claimed by both, though there had been no recognizable conflict between them for a decade. Fourteen years exactly since the last one.

Rumor had it the head of the Prague arm of the Crimson Saints, Yan Petrov, had brokered a gentleman's agreement with the necromancer Azrael to operate in the city. The deal was viewed as a minor miracle—based in Saint Petersburg, the Saints had deep ties to the necromancer known as the Red Death, Azrael's rival.

Nevertheless, the Saints were allowed to operate in the city if they kept his codes and didn't stir up trouble fighting over turf.

Evie suspected Azrael was keeping his enemies closer than his friends, but she saw no need to point it out.

Flights back and forth to Moscow were not available commercially. Saint Petersburg—impossible. But for the Saints, perhaps it was part of the exception Azrael had made or been paid to look away from.

When the faint whine of the electric motor reached her, muted gray light filtered through the windows and all the candles but one had guttered out in their own melted wax. She was still in her robe, her hair a nest on top of her head. She contemplated whether she should try to make herself presentable. In the end, she compromised. She flung glamour about her, ignoring the sway of nausea and the throbbing at her temples. Too fast.

She started for the door but went back to her work instead. She was close to something. What would Valentin be selling to Moscow and Saint Petersburg that would command the fee of a luxury car? Where was he keeping this new product, and how had she not noticed a new operation?

Information was currency all its own. Protecting it was priceless. A seed of hope sprouted under her rib cage. If she could figure out what he was hiding, she might have something that could be used as insurance to guarantee her freedom.

She missed the first knock. Perhaps the second.

"Come in," she said, unable to keep the impatience out of her voice.

The door opened slowly, Nikolai's measured steps on the parquet. "What has happened to your bird?"

Evie spoke before thinking. "The cat got it."

His steps halted.

She looked up to see him standing in the entryway with an expression on his face she so rarely saw it almost made it worth the slip. "The. Cat?"

He looked as if he had come from a long night at the club. His eyes were bloodshot, and he reeked of smoke and perfume. His collar was open, a winking cross flashing at her in the low light.

It would not serve to irritate him now. She wasn't going to be able to figure out what Valentin was up to from a tiny cottage in Jevany. She needed to get back into the city. And she needed to stay in Nikolai's good graces.

"Forgive me," she said in a perfect simulacrum of a penitent woman. "I slept poorly, and I have been struggling with this last set."

Nikolai took another step, scanning the gutted candles, the mess of mint leaves, the potting soil on the counter. She must have looked like a storybook witch midspell. The image almost made her smile. If only.

Maybe she didn't need Prague to solve this mystery. How much did Nikolai know about this new business, and what would he reveal? She gnawed her lip for a split second, then made a decision. It wouldn't hurt to ask. Probably.

"It appears the information is incomplete." Evie tried to modulate her tone, aiming for concern, not suspicion.

"What is the trouble?" Nikolai perked up.

"This account, it's new," she said. "And this income. I don't understand the code like the others—"

He closed the distance, one hand spinning the open ledger to look down at it. Then he settled back on his heels and his face closed, becoming impenetrable. Whatever it was, he knew about it.

"It would serve you not to be distracted from the task you were given." A warning.

She drew a measured inhale through her nose, releasing it slowly with a laugh she hoped betrayed exhaustion and apology. "Where are my manners? Would you like some tea?"

"No, thank you." He stared at the counter and her full, now cold, cup.

"I just want to do a thorough job for Valentin," she said, rising to collect her work into neat piles. "I wouldn't want to make a mistake, you understand, so I consider everything. Do you have the rest for me?"

"Not today," he said slowly. "This is just a check-in. You still have difficulty sleeping?"

She paused, keeping her hands steady. "I'm fine, working. As you instructed."

"And the bird?"

The fucking bird again.

She dropped her gaze, wringing her hands at her chest, and knit her brows together in regret. "It escaped as I was cleaning the cage. I am terribly sorry. Was it expensive?"

Nikolai's lips sealed in a thin line briefly before his expression cleared. "It was nothing. I only thought having something to take care of would be good for you. Give you some purpose."

Purpose. Like Evie needed some helpless, captive creature to give her day meaning.

She fought the urge to spread her hands to take in the table full of ledgers and paper. Instead, she pasted on the smile of a sleepy coquette. "Well, if you're here for a visit, I'll take a coffee."

He hooked her elbow in one hand, restraining her.

"You have always been something of a mystery to me, Evelia," he said softly. "But now I think I understand you."

"Where is the fun in that?" She forced a bright smile, tugging lightly.

His grip was firm.

Adrenaline coursed through her, and it was all she could do to keep the sleepy, lax expression on her face. He'd had enough time to comb through her apartment. She'd hidden her caches well, but maybe not well enough for intense scrutiny.

"You are very independent," he said, head tilting as if trying to solve a puzzle, a line etching between his thick brows. "You make your own way in the world."

"It's what I know."

Her heart hammered against her rib cage. If this was it and Nikolai was about to close the noose, she vowed not to go down without a fight. The knife on the counter, forgotten from slicing lemons. The letter opener beside the door. The sharpened pencils on the table. All too far away.

*Let your opponent reveal his cards first.* The memory of Tal's words steadied her.

"Valentin needs me to keep his books in order," she said, reminding them both that she had a purpose to the one they both answered to.

"He underestimates your worth," he said. "One as precious as you should be protected."

It took an effort to keep her voice light, and she couldn't stop the way it trembled. "Which Valentin provides, in exchange for my... work."

"Perhaps that is enough for now." Nikolai spread his palms as if accepting her answer. Evie started for the coffee machine, but his following words froze her in place. "But know that when the time comes, you have options. Shelter."

"*If* the time comes, you mean?" Evie inclined her head.

She always thought him too smart to risk his comfortable place operating in Valentin's shadow and the freedom it gave him. Was he planning to make a move against Valentin? She wondered who his allies were and how he planned to dethrone Valentin if that's what this would be.

"Perhaps I didn't recognize you at first because you and I are so alike," he said, his voice low.

She fought to keep her surprise off her face as she waited for him to elaborate.

"We are survivors," he explained. "And survivors know the only thing we can depend on is change. Our dear Valyusha imagines himself capable of control. But you and I know better. Don't we?"

"We do?" she whispered.

Her mind scrambled briefly around the possibilities. Valentin liked the spotlight and the notoriety that had come with rising in the Saints. And he'd reached the top. He was in Yan Petrov's inner circle. Only Petrov outranked him.

If Valentin was preparing to make a move up the chain and was found out, or tried and failed, Petrov would kill him and anyone who helped him, if only to send a message to the rest of his vassals. Petrov was Crimson Saints by birth—his family had *built* the Saints. She doubted they would look kindly on his usurper even if Valentin succeeded.

Maybe it was Valentin—not Nikolai—who was about to overreach his grasp.

The very thought of how unstable the Saints operation would be in a power shift made her sick to her stomach. But the chaos might provide the perfect cover for her escape. Calculations of the unknown raced through her.

She needed to know who was planning a move and when. It all came back to the money.

"And what would you ask in exchange?" She kept measured consideration in her voice. Perhaps Nikolai saw the coming storm and wanted to protect her. Maybe he anticipated filling Valentin's shoes and keeping her in place.

"I would ask no more of you unless you wished it." Nikolai cocked his head, and the smile indulged the assumed naivete of her silence. "Change is inevitable. Fortunes rise and fall with it. We survivors, we know the only thing to do is position ourselves properly and prepare to ride out whatever comes."

She moved to the kitchen window. Outside, clouds darkened the sky. "I appreciate your consideration, but you worry too much, Kolya."

She followed Nikolai dutifully to the car and filled her lungs with the ozone and damp earth scent of coming rain.

"The final set will come in the next few days," he said as he climbed into the sleek white BMW in the driveway. "Remember my words, Evelia. Shelter."

"I will."

Inside the cottage, she slumped against the table as the front gate closed behind the BMW. The ache that came with applying her glamour too quickly pressed the base of her skull. She couldn't remember when she'd last eaten. She needed to be outside the walls, surrounded by trees, feeling the rain on her skin. She checked the clock. It was well past noon. Mark had probably left the lake. She had to try. She slipped on the silk dress and tugged her hair into a ponytail.

Their time was running out.

# CHAPTER SEVEN

MARK HAD GOTTEN USED to the sight of her appearing in the trees, her wariness resolving to a smile when she saw him. But as he squatted on his haunches under the trio of birch trees where they had first met, the spot remained empty well past their usual meeting time.

Maybe she wouldn't show up.

He hated the sinking in his chest that came with the thought. Uneasiness settled in his belly.

So far, he'd resisted the urge to follow her after they parted. It seemed like crossing a line somehow. No plans, no promises.

But if she was going to leave, she would say goodbye. Wouldn't she? At least an awkward breakup scene was in order.

Something was wrong.

He stripped off out of his shirt and kicked out of his boots.

The wolf rose as the last of his clothes settled at his feet, giving him barely enough time to stash the pile under a bush before taking over.

And then he was jogging through the trees on four feet instead of two, scenting. Mark thought of it less as changing shape than sharing a body. Unlike his middle brother, Mark never leashed the beast inside. The wolf's consciousness was his own—closer than blood—and understood in this time and place they were better served by the man's ability to move through the world.

In exchange, Mark respected his wolf and gave him the freedom to run as often as he could.

Now he relied on the wolf's superior nose to pick up Evie's scent trail, well established after weeks in the woods, consolidating on the same route to the lake. *Witch.*

*That's our girl.* A hitch in the man's brain made the wolf stumble. *Sorry, Big Guy.*

Our girl. Where the fuck had that come from? They weren't anything to each other but a good time. After all, he had no idea how long she was in Jevany, and maybe she hadn't felt the need to say goodbye.

The wolf pressed on.

He slowed when the trees thinned, turning his full attention on his surroundings. Daylight made getting around as an oversized adult male wolf tough, but the storm was close, casting deep shadows in which to shelter.

He left the trail briefly, staying deep in the brush as he made a wide half circle around the walls of the villa nicknamed Saint Petersburg.

When the gate began to open, the wolf shrank backward, belly down beneath the low brush. A pearl-white BMW coupe slid out, pausing briefly at the guardhouse before pulling onto the road. He couldn't make out much through the deeply tinted glass. He drew in a breath for the scent but got mostly petrol and the sharp ozone smell of a coming storm.

While the gate was open, Mark scoped out the inside of the villa: manicured lawns, modern buildings alongside the traditional structures. Cameras where the gate and the walls met watched the road or the guardhouse. Aside from the bored guy at the gate, it was empty from what he could see—no other cars in the circular driveway.

When the BMW was gone, Mark picked Evie's trail up again. It led from the dense forest to the oldest part of the villa where overgrown brambles formed as much of a barrier as the crumbling walls. Her scent was strongest here, a touch of blood in the brambles carrying magic in its metallic tang.

As he watched, the leaves began to tremble. They peeled back as elegantly as pages of an old book, withdrawing to reveal an old metal gate. The lock twisted on his side, and then the gate swung open.

Evie emerged, wearing the silk dress that spilled over her like a caress. The gift from someone who knew her body well. With a glance at the darkening sky, she tugged on a yellow rain slicker and stepped into the wood.

The gate slipped shut behind her, and his sharp ears picked up the squeak and rasp of rusted metal, though she hadn't touched it. The brambles closed on her heels as she slipped into the woods, passing just a few feet away.

Mark watched her move down the trail she'd walked for weeks, headed to the pond. When she was gone, he rose, shaking off the stillness, and surveyed the bramble-covered gate one more time.

Beneath the overhang of a gutter spout, in a place as unfriendly to electronics as could be imagined, sunlight reflected off round glass. A lens.

Mark had missed it the first time.

Maybe it wasn't wide enough to catch the gate or the brambles. But it certainly caught her figure disappearing into the trees. He kept to the brush and the growing shadows, hoping to avoid the camera's range. And then he broke into a run.

He barely beat her back to the pond. In the end, he had no time for clothes, so he dove into the water to make it look like he'd been swimming all along.

"Are you out of your mind?" Evie called as he met her at the shore. "I've been hearing thunder all morning."

"I was hot." It was true. The wolf didn't blow his coat with summer as he would in nature. Shifting in summer left Mark drenched in sweat.

"Get out of the water before you get struck by lightning," she ordered, laughing. Gone was the drawn, worried witch who had magicked her way out of a rusted-shut gate. Not the flirtatious mystery woman either. This, the lover he'd come to know in her freely given smiles, was even better.

Whoever she was, whatever her circumstances, she was happy here with him. He liked it. He shook off the lingering thought. No plans, no promises.

He came out of the water slowly, the way he knew she liked, and enjoyed the way her eyes devoured him.

"Eyes are up here, Evergreen," he murmured as he passed, stepping into his clothes.

"I'm not interested in your eyes," she snapped smartly, trailing a hand down his back.

The wolf arched his spine, craving the brush of her scar-roughened fingertips. *Down, buddy.*

Mark caught her wrist, his thumb sweeping passes over the heel of her hand. He lowered his voice, sliding his mouth close to the spot where her scent was strong between her jaw and her ear. "What are you interested in, huh?"

She purred.

And then the wolf caught a whiff of another male on her skin, and his teeth closed hard on each other.

"What's wrong?" She went perfectly still, prey to predator.

When he let go, the worry returned to her brow.

"Wasn't sure if you were coming." He tried to shake off the scent, but it clung to his nostrils. Cologne. He'd never smelled the man on her before, but an uncomfortable doubt filled him. It wouldn't have been the first time a woman who had given her promises to someone else had slipped past his guard. He'd tried never to be that guy. "It's going to rain."

"I hadn't noticed." She smirked, giving her jacket a little tug. "I am prepared."

But the half smile didn't clear the concern between her brows. The smudges of weariness below her eyes were back.

"I've got a place to get out of the worst of it," he said. "It's a bit of a walk though."

"Okay." She stepped close again. The heat of her body carried her scent and the man's. The wolf bristled.

Mark thought about how frank she'd been in asking for what she wanted. He might not know much about her life, but he'd never picked up the acid sourness of deception in her scent. Even when they'd been telling each other stories, she hadn't been able to stop from interjecting hers with the truth. The certainty that she'd never lied to him should have been enough.

*Let it go, Big Guy.* The man could have been anyone: brother, friend, even a bodyguard. She hadn't earned his possessiveness. It wasn't his business. No plans, no promises.

He didn't realize he was walking ahead until her hand gripped his.

Her fingers tightened. "What's special about this place?"

"Can it be a surprise?" He slowed his pace, taking her basket.

"Will there be dragons?"

The innocent joke calling back to the day they'd met shattered him, spilling warmth and a kind of tenderness he didn't need to be feeling. She never questioned where he led. Her trust seemed absolute.

The rain began to slap against the tree canopy overhead, a few scattered drops leaving cool streaks down his skin. Then it was as if every cloud opened at once.

"How far are we?" She tugged the hood over her head.

"Not far." He squinted as the air thickened with rain.

A few days ago, he'd left a sweet juju pouch his mother had made at the abandoned estate of the murdered family. It would not send away the ghosts, she warned, but it might ease their turmoil. Eventually they would rest and perhaps find release on their own. On his way back to the jobsite, he'd glimpsed a wall of weathered glass panes and a patinated metal frame through the trees. He'd circled the property. No ghosts.

"Wanna make a run for it?"

They ran. She slipped on a wet root, and he caught her, bringing her back to her feet. Her eyes met his, full of surprise and delight. "Good catch."

The memory of the camera's steady, unblinking eye on the crumbling villa walls tugged at him. Little Saint Pete belonged to the Crimson Saints.

She *was* connected to the Saints. It was a matter of time before someone picked up on her sneaking out—if they hadn't already.

It felt good to have her trust. But it came with the responsibility to keep her safe.

He needed to warn her. But how could he without revealing the wolf? Everything sounded lame in his head—there were dozens of villas around here. There was no way he could have just happened to stumble onto the right one, happened to see her sneaking out, and somehow beat her back to the pond. Just admitting that he'd followed her felt like a breach of some unspoken promise.

Would she be sneaking out so much if it wasn't for him?

He focused on the path ahead, jogging through the little clearing between the trees. He could just make out the glass when lighting reflected off the panes. At the back of the house was an old-fashioned conservatory. Vagrants or kids had broken in at some point and someone had boarded up most of the lower windows. But he knew his way around an abandoned site.

"No one comes up here." He reassured Evie when she hesitated.

"No one but you, it seems." She laughed, wiping wet hair from her face. She stamped a little from one foot to the other, then tugged the door handle, her arms covered in goose bumps. "It's locked."

They both knew this had to end. He just hadn't expected this would be the why.

*Not yet.* Without a thought to moderating his strength before her, he ripped the lower board away from the door with his bare hands.

Evie stood back, eyes wide and fixed on him. Her smile trembled.

"Loose nails," he claimed lamely.

The broken glass formed a guillotine's edge. Mark slipped his arm nimbly through the opening and around, popping the handle on the door. "Open, sesame."

He let the door swing open, pretending to inspect his arm for cuts to allow her to pass.

The room had once been filled with plants, circling an enormous fountain tiled in patterns that evoked Al-Andalus. But only echoes of life remained inside, moss clinging tenaciously to the cracks in the tile, dried leaves and organic detritus collected in corners.

She dropped her yellow jacket on the edge of the fountain and circled the room. That slip of watered-down silk, obviously expensive and damp around her thighs, highlighted her body and made him feel like he was seeing her for the first time. Not a forest witch or a village girl out for a good time.

There was so much they hadn't done together—sneaking around in the woods hadn't led to the most leisurely encounters. It had been a lot of rushing and avoiding splinters and finding bug bites later in awkward places. He'd been so excited to bring her here, somewhere dry and relatively clean. It wasn't sheets and a bed, but he'd stashed a blanket in the dry fountain. Finally they could take their time. Now?

Lightning flashed, a crack of thunder on its heels, and rain sheeted onto the glass around them. She didn't even flinch. Her smile returned in force.

She shouted over the roar. "This is... incredible."

She closed the distance between them and cupped his cheeks. It lit a fire in him, the way she wanted him so plainly, enjoyed him so freely.

He lifted one shoulder, suddenly seeing himself as she must have all these weeks—in faded old work pants and boots and a stained T-shirt. Gods, she was really slumming it here with him.

He had a stupid desire not to kiss her until he figured out what to do about that camera. In the end, he wasn't strong enough to resist.

Evie tasted like lemon, mint, and honey. She fit him perfectly. Her body lined up—all his favorite parts of her against the parts of him that needed them the most. She was all surrender and sweetness.

The confession escaped before he could catch it. "You're everything."

Her brows drew together, and her eyes shone with a watery glow. Then she blinked hard, smiling seductively at him, her hands tangled in his belt buckle. "Eat first or...?"

He drew the firm length of himself lightly against her, conscious of the roughness of his jeans and the softness of her everything. A full-body shiver wracked her.

"I want you too." He drew his knuckles rhythmically back and forth over damp cotton, letting his words in her ear punctuate each slow, dragging stroke. He replaced his hard-on with the knuckle of his index finger. He brushed the fabric, and he didn't know why the idea of those plain cotton panties soothed something in him. "What's the hurry?"

"Don't you have to return to your work?"

"If it rains like this all afternoon, the guys will spend it lying around and smoking or napping in the back of the truck," he murmured, thumb brushing the center of her pleasure as he drew cotton aside. "Nobody will miss me."

"The boss." She shifted to give him better access.

"Exactly." He paused, waiting.

"Yes." A low, shuddering moan escaped her when he slid a finger slowly inside her grasping heat. "More."

His thumb traced lazy circles through cloth, slipping the occasional brush directly over her in the way that made her clench and tug at him. A second finger joined the first, and she gasped, tightening around him with a quiver he recognized too well. Her first orgasm always came fast, a release of tension he hadn't understood until now.

He circled her wrists gently when she reached for his belt buckle. She made a noise of protest, but he was firm, drawing her hands away. They'd always had this. He wanted more.

Her smile puckered the scar on her cheek, falling a little at his ongoing silence. Tension curled her arms. Instead of releasing her as he always did, he closed his eyes and brought her hands to his mouth. One after the other, he pressed kisses to her palms. He closed them between his own, curling his fingers around hers and drawing them against his chest.

"Tell me"—he kissed the words into her temple—"about your scars?"

Her hips stilled. Her whisper was so soft even the wolf strained to hear it. "Why now?"

"I need…" He pulled back to meet her eyes. He expected wariness, even anger. But there was only resignation, pain.

She didn't push him away. Instead, rough fingertips cupped his jaw. "What do you need? If I can give it to you, it's yours."

He closed his eyes. *If.* If what—if they had made plans, if they had made promises, maybe he had a right to know, to ask. If they were anything other to each other than— "Nothing."

"It doesn't sound like nothing."

*Enough of this.* He could feel the time slipping away from them with every breath. It ended today, and if this was all they had left, he'd make the best of it for them both.

⬥

EVIE WOULD NEVER FORGET the cool glass against the sweat-damp silk on her back, the vibration of raindrops on the other side, and Mark, supporting her weight, so warm and solid inside her the world could have washed away outside and she would not have noticed.

Afterward, they sat on the cool tiled edge of the fountain and watched the lightning while they ate.

After weeks of knowing him, she could make a list of the things she found remarkable, and the constellations embedded in his skin had become the least of them. It still amazed her that her scars didn't repel him. He even seemed to enjoy the touch of her ruined hands. Why did he ask about them now? Something had changed.

She cleared her throat. "How is your work?"

"My brother came up for a bit," he said. "That helped us get back on schedule. I'd say we have another week."

"I imagine you'll be pleased to be done," she said, too cheerfully.

"What about you?"

"I don't know." She hated that she could not make the truth sound less like a lie. "Soon perhaps."

A shadow flitted over his face, darkening the brightness of the starry night. He didn't make a sound. Wet heat scored the inside of her rib cage, hitched her breath. Perhaps they'd been lying to each other. No plans, no promises might have worked if this had been once or twice. But after weeks, something tenuous had begun to form between them.

He'd given her so much: stories about his family, his goals, his business. Her tongue ached from all the times she'd bitten it to avoid revealing too much. She wanted to tell him about Tal and the long road north and the dreams she'd lost along the way.

This had gone too far.

She looked up at the clouded glass as the noise dropped away. "The rain's letting up."

"I should get back."

She knew what she needed to do—what was best for them both. She couldn't afford any grand romantic gestures. But at the pond, she hesitated.

He spoke first. "Next week's pretty slammed, getting set up for the construction crew."

Something in her chest she hadn't known existed shattered, even as she saw this was the best way. *Better that it is his idea. Better that he does not chase after you, long for you, wonder.*

The knowledge didn't stop the raw, tearing sensation in her chest. Years spent wearing masks closed around her. She gripped the handle of her basket so hard she would bear the imprint and the marks of her fractured nails breaking the skin after.

She kept her expression even, light. "No time for swimming?"

"Probably not." The muscle in his jaw flexed. "But, uh—"

"I understand." She pressed onto her toes, kissed him lightly on the corner of the mouth, and tasted rain. "No promises. No plans. Thank you. For everything."

His eyes darkened, surprised. "You're welcome?"

"I hope the rest of your time in Jevany goes well," she said, unable to keep the rasp from her voice or the tenderness. "With the job."

"You too?" He fumbled. "Not the job. I mean. I think?"

She smiled, benign and forgiving. Without another word, she turned to go.

For the first time, she felt his gaze on her back when she entered the trees. She knew when she looked over her shoulder, she would find him standing where she had left him. The starlight had dimmed, the moon faded. *Walk away, Evie girl. Let him go. Keep him safe.*

"If this heat keeps up, a daily swim doesn't sound like a terrible idea," she said anyway, a thread of hope in the words. "You know where to find me."

She wished she could read his expression, understand if the flex of his jaw was anger or regret.

And then he was there, moving so fast there was no time for reaction except the gasping breath that he swallowed.

It wasn't a gentle kiss, none of the sweetness or the teasing. There was only heat and need and pressure. Longing. One of them cut a lip in the process. She tasted blood.

"I won't be coming back." He backed away, his eyes locked on her. He licked his split lip. "Bye, Evergreen."

"Goodbye, Markus." Evie walked away.

It turned out that not looking back didn't make it hurt less.

# CHAPTER EIGHT

MARK FLUNG the last of the rubbish—a dilapidated washer—onto the pile.

The rest of his crew was focused on cleanup—sweeping, checking for tools, deciding on a bar to meet up at later—but Fresh Meat just stood there, staring.

The kid had been mostly useless all day as his excitement at the job being close to done grew.

Mark had been fresh meat too, even if he'd thought he'd known his shit at the time. He still hadn't stood around with his mouth open like a netted carp.

The growl rose in his chest, the wolf unusually irritable. *That's not how we get things done, Big Guy, and you know it.*

The wolf huffed.

"You just *threw*…" Ondrej's voice dropped off in wonder.

On the slab of the porch, Pavel paused his efficient strokes with the push broom. "You got a job besides standing there and keeping me from my beer or what?"

The boy hurried off, nodding.

Pavel leaned on the broom handle, grinning at Mark. "Quit showing off, boss."

"I'm trying to get you to your beer, gramps." Mark stripped off his gloves.

"Gramps." Pavel snorted and went back to sweeping. "Who taught you everything you know? No gratitude."

Mark hopped off the rubbish pile, kicking a few old pieces of tile in with the rest. They'd brought the job in on deadline. After today, he'd have no other reason to return to Jevany.

All week he'd avoided the lake. A few times, he'd broken his promise to himself and wolfed out, going back to the villa. Evie's scent in the woods around the walls had faded. He wished he could have given her more warning, but perhaps breaking it off had been enough. Good.

He made one final pass through the demo site, surveying their work with pride. He pressed his hand against the rough-hewn surface. A few hundred years of history pushed back. The house would be a pleasant place to spend the hot summers. He saw children in the yard and a small dog with tufted fur chasing them. A trip to the lake, gelato for the children, and a bitingly chilled beer for their parents in the local restaurant. People would be happy here. That filled him with a subtle joy that settled even his restless wolf.

He found Sam packing the last of his tools in the van. Before he could ask what bar they'd decided on, Sam began swearing.

"Mouth, Sam, mouth." Mark followed his gaze and groaned. "Fuck me."

A flatbed loaded with building supplies trundled up the gravel road, kicking up clouds of dust. Unloading at the end of the day was an invitation for trouble. As construction boomed, theft from jobsites rose, with supplies resold on the black market. Often the presence of security was enough to dissuade an attempt, but Anton didn't put anyone on-site until construction started.

Mark stalked down the driveway with Sam in his wake.

"Is that what I think it is?" Pavel called after him, setting down the broom.

"Call Anton, see if he can get somebody out here tonight," Mark barked. "Let me talk to these knuckleheads."

The truck ground to a stop at the front, and a clown car full of paunchy men tumbled out of the cab, ready to unload. Mark went to the driver's side.

"You can't unload now," Mark shouted.

The driver put the truck in park, grabbing his clipboard. He leaped out. "Order is here now. We unload now."

"No, you don't," Mark said.

The driver turned his back to Mark, giving orders to his crew.

*Okay, Big Guy, let them have it.* Mark raised his voice. "Everybody stop."

All motion in the yard halted. Even the driver took a half step back. They heard, if not understood, the command of the ancient predator beneath his voice.

A few men looked uneasily between Mark and their boss.

Pavel turned back to his phone call.

"This is what I got." The driver shrugged, rattled. "Order says today."

"Give me five minutes." Mark held up a hand. "Please."

The man jerked a nod to his crew.

Mark jogged back to Pavel. The older man was frowning.

Pavel disconnected the call. "Anton can't get anyone here until tomorrow."

*Fuck.*

"I'll stay," Pavel murmured. "It's been a while since I did an overnight, but I can manage."

They'd all done it a time or two until Anton had regularly started adding security patrols to his jobsites. Increasingly, the thieves had been more than just opportunists—they'd been organized and occasionally armed.

Pavel was smart and good with harmonizing the different personalities on a crew, but in all the time Mark had known him, he had never been a young man. Mark didn't like the idea of his mentor facing off against a couple of young jackasses with their eyes on an easy payday.

Mark gritted his teeth. He jerked his head, and the driver followed him warily to the front of the rig.

Out of sight of the others, Mark reached for his wallet. "I need you to come back tomorrow. How much to make that happen?"

The driver shook his head. "You don't take it now, you'll be lucky if we get back before September."

Mark sighed, calculating. "At least leave it out of sight of the road?"

"Orders are to leave it in front." The driver's shoulders eased as he sensed victory.

Mark fought the urge to take the man by the throat and shake him a few times for good measure. "One thousand crowns and you unload it in the back."

"Make it fifteen hundred."

"Twelve fifty, final." Mark growled.

"Fine." The driver licked his chapped lips. "That's fine."

There went his beer money. He strolled back to his crew clustered by the refuse pile as the delivery guys went about their work. He was glad he'd driven his car up this morning to get an early start. He kept a camping kit in the back with all his personal tools.

"Here's the plan," he said. "Take the van back to town. See you in the morning."

Pavel and Sam started arguing immediately over who would stay with him.

"It's not a negotiation," Mark said. "I'll stay."

"By yourself?" Ondrej added.

Pavel started for the company van, shaking his head and muttering to himself. Sam scuffed his boots in the dirt, unhappy but resigned.

An hour later, the delivery truck trundled away as the sun sank toward the tree-lined horizon.

Mark dragged out the sleeping bag and rummaged through the glove box. His stomach was already gnawing a hole in his organs. He'd relied on the wolf's strength to keep the pace up. He'd been counting on being able to load up on a plate of dumplings after.

He came up with a pack of peanuts and a bag of desiccated Haribo gummies. "Fan-fucking-tastic."

Maybe the wolf would get lucky on some dinner. Of course, transitioning while digesting raw meat wouldn't be the most pleasant way to spend an evening, but he'd survive.

Mark checked the rig, ensured the tools were loaded and secured and that Fresh Meat wore his seat belt. "Nice work, Ondrej."

The boy flushed, grinning. "Thanks, boss."

"Markus," Pavel called over the rattle of the van.

He paused at the driver-side window.

"I don't like this," Pavel said, shaking his head. "They knew it was too late for a delivery this big."

Mark rubbed the back of his head. He'd had the same thought too many times over the past hour. Even more reason someone ought to stick around. It didn't matter how on schedule he'd kept his team. If the load got stolen, it would take weeks to replace.

Plus he was the demo lead. Technically the site was still his responsibility until the foreman came on in the morning. He could handle the foreman's attempt to pin it on him if something happened. It would be much harder to live with letting Anton down.

When Anton had started running small jobs for his family's company decades ago, one of his first had been a run-down building in Vyšehrad owned by Mark's parents. Anton and Lukas Vogel found friendship and a shared passion for renovating the old building, and with no sons of his own, Anton treated Mark like a nephew. Even when more prestigious jobs came along, he consulted and managed work outside of Lukas's capabilities.

When Mark had left secondary school for a trade, Anton was waiting. *Come work for me, just for the summer. See what you think. All my crew starts on demo—dirty work, but beer money in your pocket. If you stick around, smart guy like you will be running jobs before long, mark my words. Miler and Vogel. Nice ring, eh?*

Mark never forgot the chance Anton had taken, bringing on a surly teenager all those years ago, even when they had bumped heads a time or two over the years.

"Nobody's coming way the fuck out here on the chance for supplies." Sam came around the van, a plastic shopping back in one hand. "Come on. Spartans are playing. We're done on deadline. When does that happen? Let's celebrate."

"Eh, I gave all my beer money to those assholes to unload somewhere less obvious." Mark sighed. "Might as well hang out."

"Spend the whole night out here, getting eaten alive by mosquitos while you jerk off." Sam shrugged. *Your loss.*

"Probably." Mark sighed. "Without the jerking-off bit. I'm not as entirely hopeless as you are, Sam."

Sam rolled his eyes. "The guys and I made this up for you." Sam held out the bag. "I know we're not supposed to have beer on-site, but seeing as we're done today…"

Mark inspected it. A couple of sticks of dried jerky, peanuts, a bag of paprika chips, and a liter can of Staropramen. Practically a meal.

Mark cleared his throat, wiping his palm over his dusty face. "Samuel, you shouldn't have."

This shrug was a bit less cavalier. Sam might have even flushed.

"Rigged up a shower off the back porch," Sam said, clapping an arm around his shoulder. "Ondrej left clean—mostly clean—towels. Do us all a favor and take a shower, 'cause you stink, boss."

"Go fuck yourself." Mark shoved him away.

"Thankfully, I'm so good-looking I don't have to," Sam said, wandering away.

It felt good to laugh. "Thanks, Sam."

Sam's shoulders lifted and fell. Resignation. "Night, boss."

"Night, guys."

When the dust from the van's tires settled on the road, Mark set himself up in what had been the kitchen. He polished off the peanuts and the jerky to quiet the dull ache in his belly.

The wolf rose at the scent of animals stirring in the coming night. *In a little bit, Big Guy.*

The July heat cooled only slightly as the sun fell. He stripped out of his filthy work overalls and sweaty T-shirt and jeans beneath. Then he grabbed the lukewarm beer and a long shower, gazing over the darkening forest between sips.

As the moon rose, a waning crescent and dusky orange in the thick summer air, Mark decided to run before spending the rest of the night on guard duty. He jogged out of the house.

The wolf rose before he made it to the tree line, yipping like a pup and gathering his hind legs beneath him to fling himself skyward in celebration. The breeze stirred the long hairs on his spine and his tail, bringing the distant scent of a village. He turned away from the smell of humans and burned meat and loped into the trees.

He ran over the hills, moving like a shadow between the trees, more spirit than man or beast, made flesh by the air and the damp and the wind. Unleashed by the bone and the sinew and blood that pumped lightning hot through veins to muscle.

Which was a man, the wolf wondered as they dodged roads and houses until only the scent of forest and wild filled his nose. Which was a wolf, the man marveled as his paws fled and met the earth and lungs filled with wind.

Usually Mark stayed close to the surface of their awareness, but tonight belonged to the wolf, and he surrendered himself completely.

Around midnight, the wolf circled back to the jobsite. He settled in the sleeping bag, flopping onto his side and panting in the heat. There was a fix for that too. Bare skin cooled faster than the dense coat of fur.

The wolf eased back, retreating into the pit of Mark's belly and the marrow in his bones and the ancient hindbrain that functioned without his input.

Mark rolled onto his back, pillowing his head on his forearm.

There was still too much moonlight and the city light too close for a clear view of the Milky Way. Still, the little glimpse of patchy brightness, like a seam had opened in the ceaseless dark and spilled tiny grains of light, resonated with something deep in his chest. A whispered response to a distant calling.

On a night like this just over two years ago, Mark and his brothers had saved a witch from a possessed book. In gratitude, Libuše, the city's patron spirit, had given each brother a blessing in their wolf form. He remembered the sensation, like a cool meteor shower, settling into his coat and slipping beneath. It stung too, with the fleeting pinch of a sparkler, because magic wasn't always pleasant even in reward.

Her blessing coalesced in his chest, fused with the essence of the wolf and the spirit of the man. Heart full of starlight.

It heightened the resilience he had always shared with his wolf. Even after a full day of demo, a few hours of sleep were all he needed to recover. If he could surrender to the wolf, not even that. In either form, he was stronger and recovered faster from injury. Not quite invincible, but close enough most days. He'd only just begun to explore the added strength and speed.

Mark didn't realize he was dozing until the approaching rumble of an engine woke him. He entertained the drowsy Pollyanna thought that maybe it was Anton coming to relieve him with a security guard.

Then he came to his senses. *Ah fuck.*

The wolf rolled onto four paws, and the man's consciousness stayed close. He slipped into the tree line as the noise of the rare diesel engine drew closer, keeping low as he moved toward the front of the building. The brakes protested as the truck drew up to the front of the house, headlights cutting vast swathes in the darkness.

The wolf kept his gaze down to avoid blowing his night vision. The motor switched off, but the lights remained. He circled the site, gathering information for the man to interpret with each inhale—four men, maybe five. Three of them were drunk. All of them nervous. One of them armed.

*Shit.*

The armed man jumped out first, barking loading orders.

*Shit, shit.*

He rumbled annoyance. It must have been louder than he'd intended. The conversation stopped.

A question, hesitantly issued in a squeaky voice, rose in the silence. At the answering snap of instructions, the movement resumed. If not for the gunpowder, the wolf would have been on them, but Mark wasn't ready to test his new healing ability with a gunshot.

For a second, Mark wished for his brothers—this kind of thing would have been easy dealings for the pack. But he'd never risk their safety with this shit.

He started at the fringes, picking off two drunk men and one of the most terrified. Their screams before they fled to the truck with bloody tears in their clothes and flesh should have been enough. He spat out blood and cloth, slinking around the edge of the headlights.

He picked up the word for dog and snorted. *Try again, asshole.*

They circled up, backs to each other, making it harder to pick off the weaker members.

All Mark needed was to give them enough of a scare to take off.

He darted through the headlight glare, letting yellow eyes flash in the light before he vanished back into the shadows. The high-pitched scream sounded like a child's. He chuffed a laugh.

Now the word *wolf* passed among them, and one he liked even better —*demon.* The advantage of necromancers being in charge was that most people were far more likely to believe in the supernatural than they were before the godswar, even if they wanted to pretend it didn't exist most days.

He let a low growl build in his chest, echoing around the demolished structure and bouncing off the truck. The echoes made it hard to distinguish the source.

The scent of fear spiked, the hurried footsteps and swinging flashlight beams betraying panic. In the darkness, thousands of years of civilization gave way to the primitive instincts that had kept humans alive in a world of animals with teeth and claws.

One more good scare and he'd break them. They'd run.

The chorus of screams satisfied the wolf more than Mark wanted to admit. It liked being the biggest, baddest, scariest thing in the woods. A lot. Too much maybe.

He leaped into the headlights, his lips curled back, revealing his teeth.

The click of a hammer stopped him.

The boss stepped between him and the men with hands clenched firmly around the grip of a .357 Magnum revolver. Mark allowed himself a split second to wonder where on earth a thief had picked up the legendary weapon of Hollywood icons before considering he was staring down the barrel of the thing.

*Ah fuckety, fuck, fuck.*

The wolf coiled his haunches and unleashed a snarl. Too late to back down. The thief grinned.

The wolf sprang. The gun went off.

The wolf sank his teeth into the man's biceps and squeezed. The bone snapped satisfyingly before a sharp burn registered in his chest. His weight hit the man full force. The man buckled, finally emitting panicked screams in chorus with his fellows.

The wolf whipped his head back and forth, yanking the man across the dirt and gravel like a rag doll with the force of the powerful muscles in his neck.

*Let go, Big Guy.* The last thing Mark needed was a dead man on-site in the morning.

He put his forepaw down, and pain drove a spike into his shoulder, accompanied by a hot wash of thick liquid. The blood in the air wasn't just human anymore.

The wolf released his jaws and slipped out of the light. He managed to hide his limp until he was back in the shadows, watching as the men broke and ran, dragging their wounded leader to the truck. The diesel engine roared to life, gravel kicking up streams under the tires as the truck reversed and lunged into gear, bouncing down the road.

Mark watched the taillights with satisfaction. Then his front leg gave, and he tumbled into the dirt. A low, keening whimper escaped him.

Wet heat soaked his dense fur and pain spiked in his shoulder, running to his spine. Tremors shook him. Instinct took over, and he overrode the fresh lance of pain to find the wound with his tongue. He lapped with long, even strokes, panting with the taste of his blood flooding his mouth. He coughed.

*Fuck. Fuck. Fuck.*

Who knew what shifting when he was injured would do, especially if a bullet was still lodged somewhere inside him? It was too hot to be shivering as hard as he was. Thirsty. He was so thirsty.

The witch's blessing words rang somewhere in the distant back of his human brain amid its desperate scrounging for the best chance of survival. *Wherever you go, the wild places will restore you.*

Each breath was a nail in his lungs.

*Water, Big Guy.*

The wolf picked the path as the man surrendered into darkness. He pushed through the brush, driven by instinct, trusting the man's guidance as he always had. Once, he thought he smelled their witch, but with the stench of gunpowder and blood in his nose, he couldn't be sure it wasn't just because he'd crossed her old trail through the woods.

A brush of cold air startled him, and he snapped at nothing, whimpering when the motion drove spikes into his side.

Gradually he was aware he was being watched. He lowered his ears and tail even as he swayed, trying to make himself less noticeable. Cool stroked over the back of his neck, down his flank. He was too weak to move away this time.

Ahead, a decayed structure rose from the forest. In the thin moonlight, it was the skeleton of a great beast brought low.

The smell of humanity was old here, but he caught a whisper of lavender and familiar magic. On the other side of the ruined building, a creek ran through the garden reclaimed by the forest. He collapsed in a shallow eddy.

Nothing magical happened, no sudden restoration of strength, ebbing of blood flow, ease of the ragged throbbing in his chest. He opened his jaws. At least it washed the blood out of his mouth.

He rolled onto his side, catching a glimpse of the night sky between the tree branches. He searched for stars above but found only darkness.

# CHAPTER NINE

Evie had always adored the sight of the graceful waning moon. Tonight she saw only the bright edge of a scythe and hooded death in that shadowed face.

She told herself her inability to sleep was due to her earlier call with Nikolai. She'd checked and rechecked her work before she made the call. She might very well be handing down death sentences with each name, amount, and date. More blood on her hands.

The work Valentin had brought her here to do was complete but she was still no closer to determining what new operation Valentin had begun. In a few days she would return to the city and the club, and figuring it all out would begin.

No more flitting about the woods, making love to a strange man in secret glades and falling asleep in the safety of his arms.

Tired of lying awake with her ghosts, she dressed and slipped out the back door to the garden. A quick walk to clear her head, to quiet her heart… and to collect the money she'd left by the pond. Added to her cache, it would be a nice cushion.

At the garden gate, she looked back once. The property was silent, still. For the last time she opened the gate and charmed the brambles away. The practice had done her well. Both moved easily, as if anticipating her call.

She headed for the pond. Under the low light, the forest closed around her with a foreboding she hadn't noticed in the daylight hours. Or perhaps that had just been Mark's presence beside her, turning it into something safe and familiar. A chill struck her despite the heat.

A branch snapped and she spun to face the sound, her breath coming far too hard. Something large moved through the trees in the darkness, still distant. She tensed, readying herself to run. The branches rustled, accompanied by another crunch of leaves. It was moving away from her.

She should turn back now. For once, the idea of being enclosed in walls felt safe.

But a low, labored groan froze her in place. Whatever it was, it was in pain.

*What could* you *possibly do to help it?* The sensible part of her screamed for her to run.

She followed the noise instead.

Even moving slowly, it outpaced her and she had to run, tripping in the darkness over logs. She stumbled once, and her palm connected with the ground to break her fall. When she stood up again, her hand was covered in sticky wet dirt with a peculiar metallic aroma. Her notion twinged at the faint presence of iron. Blood.

It was wounded.

She picked up her pace. Her teeth clacked together, goose bumps rising on her arms and legs. Ahead, between the trees, loomed a gorgeous, decayed old villa she had never seen before. Abandoned, most humans would naturally avoid the chill that swept them in the place. Some great tragedy had befallen here.

As she stepped onto the property, the dead swept around her. Evie, who saw death masks in living human faces, rarely saw the dead so clearly. Their soft, muzzy faces flickered between happier times in life and the instants of their death.

An entire family, their faith an excuse for murder fueled by greed. They closed in but did not touch her. She could feel the eyes on her, their awareness of her presence.

A necromancer should have released them, or a godsdancer should have been engaged. But whatever had happened here was before the godswar. The property abandoned, they had been forgotten.

Grief took her to her knees like the blow from a fist. She dug her fingers in the soil and detritus, flattened her palms, and let the horror escape her in a muted howl.

"I'm sorry," she whispered when she was spent. "I can't even help myself."

Closer now, an answering howl rose, wavered, and fell.

The cool, weightless dark settled on the back of her neck. In it, a comforting silence, bathed in the robust sweetness of lavender, seeped into her skin.

Evie searched their faces again.

Another witch had been here and recently, or their work.

It was said that only necromancers could touch those beyond death. But the witch had tried to help anyway. The shades were softened around the edges. Perhaps they were less aware of themselves than they had once been. Not enough to release them, but it granted a measure of peace.

She rose when they parted for her, creating an opening toward the dark wood near the back of the property.

A small boy of about twelve in short pants and a bow tie was the most solid of the bunch. He turned, taking a few steps toward the garden, then hesitated, and when he glanced back at her, the expression flickered to an urgent grimace.

She followed.

Her footsteps squelched in the boggy ground as they grew close to water. Her guide flowed effortlessly ahead, and she focused on not losing a shoe in her effort to keep up.

A cloud passed over the moon, stealing what little light filtered through the trees. She almost tripped over the body of a dog.

Not a body. Not a dog either.

The cloud moved on, revealing an animal lying in the muddy stream bank as if it had been conjured by the moonlight.

If night itself chose a form and features, she imagined it would be this. The shaggy layers of midnight-colored coat rose and fell. She'd never seen a wolf this large. It must have weighed over two hundred pounds and had paws like teacup saucers.

Whatever darkness had spawned it, the labored breath, uneven and interspersed with whimpers, convinced her the creature was mortal enough. The iron tang of blood combined with an ugly sour, acrid odor.

It opened eyes the color of late summer full moons, yellow-gold and bright as coins, and watched her, then lowered its head to the ground, exposing the column of his throat. Beneath its chin, the fur was a paler shade of black silk. Her fingers twitched with a longing to touch.

She lowered herself just out of reach. Even caked in peat and blood, that fur looked like it was made of rough silk, shining softy in the low light. "Who is guarding Hades' gate in your absence?"

When she hovered her hand over the beast's chest, the sense memory of impact flickered against her skin. The inaudible whine of a cartridge traveling through the air and fur and flesh echoed beneath the fur clumped with blood and dirt.

Gunshot.

She sang and the bullet whined back, a hard, shrill noise only she could hear. The wounded animal groaned. She released the bullet from her notion, not wanting to cause the animal any more pain.

An idea bloomed in her, one born of her worst memory. She dismissed it.

*Try.*

She started at the command from a high, ringing voice. The boy stood attentive, but his mouth was closed. The beast's yellow eyes were fixed on a spot between the trees, staring at something even she could not see. It panted softly between low whimpers of pain.

She clenched her fingers against her chest to keep from stroking the beast, shaking herself out of the stupor. *Don't be a fool, Eves, the wounded wolf will bite first.*

"I can help you." Even if she could remove the bullet and repair the ruptured flesh, it had lost so much blood. It might die anyway. "I can try."

Moon-yellow eyes followed her briefly before lowering to slits.

She ripped a strip of her dress free and used it to bind the massive muzzle. The back of her hand brushed the long hairs of its jaw, rough silk that made her shiver.

The beast didn't even twitch at the contact, only blinked one yellow eye at her and sighed.

She didn't need to see a death mask to know it didn't have much time.

She hovered her fingertips over the beast's chest, following the echo of the bullet's passage inward. It had stopped somewhere behind the shoulder —she felt the ache of bone and stress in the surrounding tissues.

Her fingertips prickled with the sensation of metal so close.

"This is going to hurt," she warned them both.

And then she began to sing. The beast tensed and released a long mournful howl, muffled by the binding cloth. Flesh resisted and the beast jerked, paws thrashing. Bright yellow eyes fixed on her, teeth baring as the cloth strained.

She flung herself away, her eyes blurring. This was worse, not better.

"I'm sorry." The words left her in a chant, fierce and desperate.

The beast slid back onto its side, landing with a thud and a low cry.

*Try again,* the woman's voice insisted.

"I can't." She whimpered, rocking.

*You must.*

"I am killing him."

*He will die if you do not.*

Evie sat back. Did animals linger as unrested spirits? The thought of him trapped here with the rest broke her heart.

Her heartbeat quickened. She'd never attempted to heal anything. She imagined that kind of work took a tremendous amount of skill and energy. More of each than she possessed.

Her gaze settled on the flickering boy appearing and disappearing at her side. Unrested dead were a remnant of life they'd left behind. Energy.

"I call you, and all those left restless and bereft," she summoned softly. The boy fixed his eyes on her, and his face did not flicker.

"I may have a way out for you. I need your help, but I cannot make any promises."

His death mask appeared again, but when his living face retuned, it was smiling.

She took that as permission. Then she turned her attention to the wolf. The others would come, or they would not.

She would try anyway.

She saw the mistake in her first effort. This time she sang to soften the metal, to bend it. She felt it pull apart, thousands of tiny little liquid globes that flowed through tissue and around broken bits of bone. The wolf released a small groan this time.

She cupped her palm under his chest, and the tiny flow of pieces danced merrily into it, re-forming as they settled. They were followed by a rush of dark fluid. She didn't have time to celebrate.

For this to work, she was going to need touch. And intention. And luck.

"Please be still," she whispered, more prayer than command. "I cannot be responsible for what happens if you try to bite me. The last time someone tried to hurt me, I killed him."

With a wary eye on his bound muzzle, she buried her hands in the fur at the base of his neck. The yellow eye opened but didn't stir.

The temperature dropped around them, turning the humid summer night into something better suited for November. She didn't need to look to see the suggestions of human shapes clustering close, chilling the air so much even the great dark creature before her shuddered.

"Use me to restore what was once whole," she whispered. "To set to right all that is broken and to free yourself from the pain that remains."

Every exhale clouded before her face and left the wolf's nostrils in short, visible puffs.

"It's good," she whispered, reassuring them both. "It will constrict the veins and slow the blood."

The icy sensation of touch settled over her, a hand, fingertips, thumb stroking her cheek. She fought the urge to gasp as the sensation sank into her flesh. Her tears ran freely at first, soaking into his jet-black coat until they froze on her cheeks. Flecks of ice fluttered to the ground, and she fought the urge to pull away though her skin burned with cold.

She channeled the flow, following the iron in his blood to the ragged tears in muscle and tissue, shards of bone and bits of cartilage massed like the jumbled pieces of a puzzle.

Frost dusted the long tips of his fur, and the creek around them began to harden until it cracked. She gave up her fear and lay down beside him to share whatever warmth might remain.

She shivered in the dark. "Can I tell you a story?"

The beast moaned, and the broad fan of his tail settled over her thighs.

"Once upon a time, there was a girl," she said. "She arrived in a new city with a dear friend after a long journey. She had plans for her life in this city —they would open a shop and become famous clothiers. But she found even holding a needle made her shake, and any more than a stitch or two and she descended into a state of near madness. She'd wake hours later with her throat raw from screaming and her hands torn open again from trying to dig through rubble."

She swallowed. "Life in the city was hard and expensive," she said thickly. "One day she met a woman who told her she was young and pretty enough that if she covered her scars with enough makeup, she could make good money serving drinks in an exclusive club. She wouldn't have to take off her clothes or sleep with anyone if she didn't want to. And the girl thought, well that is fine, I can do one better. She made herself even more beautiful than the woman imagined, and she got the job."

After a few seconds, she continued. "Her dear friend begged her not to take it because the man who owned this club was a dangerous one connected to even worse men. But the girl thought if she could just make enough money, perhaps they could still go into business on their own somehow. She took classes so that she could learn to keep their books instead of sew."

The wolf grunted.

"But when she discovered the bartender and one of the bouncers were stealing from the club, she was stupid. She should have ignored it. But she saw their deaths in their faces, bright and close. She tried to warn them. They thought she was threatening to reveal them, so they set her up with a client, one who was known for being hard on girls he patronized."

A low growl settled in his chest.

She stroked his shoulder. "Shh. It turned out okay, I promise."

The air around them warmed.

Her voice broke, and she forgot the distance between herself and the story. The rest came out in a rush. "He tried to hurt me, and I... I panicked. I screamed and the metal answered. It all came out of him—the fillings in his teeth, the metal plate, the screws in his arm, maybe the iron in his blood. I think that's why... At last I came to myself, covered in his blood."

She no longer saw her breath. The wolf's eyes were closed, but his breathing was steady. She hummed and his blood whispered back, its course unbroken.

Evie sobbed, grief for the girl and the woman she had become. Relief for the unrested dead and despair for the beast left to die in the woods. When she was spent, all that remained was the boy in short pants, and he, too, faded before her eyes. She no longer saw his death mask. Only his smile. He touched his heart.

And he vanished.

Evie dreamed of her sister and brother laughing at one of their father's jokes and woke with dried tears on her face. The birds called to the dawn in the trees overhead, banishing a night's long silence. There was no sign of the great beast, only the churned-up mud and dirt. She might have dreamed the whole thing except for her ruined dress and the crumpled metal in her palm. The bullet.

She made it back to the cottage by sheer will and collapsed into the bathtub. It was almost an hour before she found the strength to run the showerhead over her body, dress, and all. When the water was clear of dirt and blood and she'd done the best she could with her skin and hair, she wrapped herself in a towel and crawled into the bed. This time she did not dream.

When Nikolai arrived to take her back to the city, he appraised her. "What has changed? You have done something to your hair. I preferred it as it was."

She'd barely had any glamour to pull on. It was the first time since she'd discovered her notion that its response was muted, sluggish. Whatever she'd done in the forest had tapped her dry, even with the aid of the unrested dead. She hadn't even seen Sergei's death mask when he came to say goodbye. After hating her notions for so long, she expected it would be a relief to be without them, but their absence terrified her.

"I've spent a month in the middle of nowhere, Kolya," she said, pulling on oversized sunglasses and leaving her bag at his feet. "My roots need to be touched up. Can we please go now?"

As the city grew in the windshield, she regarded it like a former lover.

For a time she had loved Prague—in the foolish way young girls newly arrived in cities in movies did, their eyes on the sky, laughing with joy. She'd imagined a life for herself in it. But her notions had irreparably ruined her chance at any kind of stability. Happiness. Again. Leaving was the only option she had. But she would carry the memory of giant wolves and men with stars beneath their skin forever.

# CHAPTER TEN

ANTON'S OFFICE was shoved into the back corner of the building that had served as a warehouse for wine barrels from the king's vineyard, a Nazi youth training camp, and a communist stockpile of art and valuables before the godswar hastened a revolution to a more ostensibly democratic system.

His father and uncles had started their construction business here, and no matter how successful he became, Anton refused nicer offices, better spaces. *My family tended the vineyards and survived every wave of invaders,* he'd told Mark too often. *You don't tear up a floor because a few dirty boots have stomped across it.*

The man himself was on the phone when Mark finally finished recounting the story to Pavel and Sam and headed in to settle with Anton. At least the version of the story he'd told the construction crew when they arrived and the cops shortly after.

Truth was, he had no idea how he made it back to the jobsite. Only that he staggered back before dawn, naked and clutching a length of fabric so filthy and stained with blood he couldn't tell what color it had been.

Waiting for a break in the conversation to make himself known, Mark splayed a hand on his T-shirt, over the new pucker of a scar on his chest, just below the shoulder. The wolf had been shot and staggered off to die. But he'd survived. How?

The wolf had gotten him out of a scrape a time or two over the years when he'd lost consciousness, and the memories were always difficult to sort. This time they were even more fractured than usual. The wolf had been unable to make sense of something important, and the confusion only muddled the chaotic assembly of images and impressions.

The crew arrived before he could clean up the mess, and he was too tired to put much effort into it anyway. They took one look at the site and at him, concerned, but the freaking out started when one of the guys found the gun in the grass. Anton had been called, then the police.

Mark'd made a statement about the attempted robbery.

No, he had no idea they were armed. They'd taken off without anything. No, he hadn't seen their faces. No, he didn't recognize them.

Adrenaline surged through him as he remembered the gun. He'd been shot by a weapon designed to blow a crater in anything it hit, and he'd survived.

The wolf memories pressed against him, clamoring for attention.

"Come in, Markus, Come in."

*Not now, Big Guy. Let's just get through this.*

The wolf picked up the sour tang of the older man's scent first. It matched the hunched shoulders, the thick fingers and palm splaying reflexively over his thinning hair. As the youngest son, Anton had come up through the ranks, trained on jobsites, same as so many of the hired employees, in spite of the fact that his father had built the place. These days he seemed to have a phone surgically implanted in his palm and glued to his ear.

He was doing a lot more listening than speaking, his grunts cut off before he could manage more.

Mark hesitated in the doorway. Watching Anton capitulate to the unseen caller made him uneasy. He started to turn around and give the proud man privacy, but Anton looked up and waved him in.

Mark sank into the chair across from the battered metal desk, taking in the small office full of paperwork and file cabinets. His chest ached, and he was tired as hell. After this, he was going back to bed. He'd earned a couple of days off.

At last Anton hung up the phone with a sigh.

"Things okay, boss?" Mark asked in Czech. "None of the supplies were damaged."

Anton held up a hand.

Mark waited for a couple of breaths. "There was really no point filing a report. They won't catch them—"

"What were you thinking!"

"I? What?" Startled, Mark sat back in his chair. "The supplies came early. I couldn't leave all that stuff out there unprotected to get poached overnight—"

"You leave Pavel to handle it," Anton said.

"Pavel?" Mark coughed in disbelief. "*He* would have gotten killed."

"He knows how to handle men like these, they… respect—"

"Respect?" Mark exhaled sharply in disbelief.

Anton waved his hands. "The foreman told me there was blood—everywhere. A fight."

Little snitch had hopped on the phone at the first sight of blood.

"I didn't start it." Mark sighed. "I warned them, told them to clear out."

In a manner of speaking.

"It's not all gunslingers and outlaws and Wild West." Anton's face turned a mottled shade of red. "There's a code—"

"You mean they wouldn't beat Pavel into a bloody pulp—". Mark sputtered.

Anton's voice rose over his. "—many things could be resolved with a conversation—"

"—because he's not Black."

The mottling disappeared, and Anton turned a solid shade of red. "This isn't about the color of your skin."

Mark let the sharpness of the man's anger roll around high in his nose, stinging the edges of his tongue with a particular sharpness. "You gonna tell me it's because I don't speak the language?"

About time they had this conversation. He didn't want to burn a bridge, but he was done putting up with this unspoken bullshit. Getting shot made everything clearer, more urgent. If now was the moment, so be it. He was done pretending everything was okay.

"And how would I face your father?" Anton snapped.

Mark set his jaw to cover his surprise. It took all his control not to touch the puckered scar under his shirt.

"I'm not a kid anymore." He hated how surly he sounded. Exactly like the kid he had been when he'd started and had gotten called into this office for mouthing off to his crew boss.

"You wanna know why I keep you on the demolitions, Markus?" Anton switched to fractured English as though that would somehow get it through Mark's thick skull.

This should be interesting. Mark folded his arms over his chest and met the older man's eyes.

"You're strong and you're fast and you can outwork ninety percent of the guys I got here."

The compliments galled him. Too little, too late. "Then why—?"

"You don't think." Anton jabbed at his own temple with his index finger. "You don't plan. You don't use your *crew*. You try to take on the whole job all by yourself. You charge in with your guns firing like this Clint Eastwood, and that fucking chipper on the neck—"

"Chip." Mark bit back a grin. "On the shoulder."

He was sure Anton might throw something at him. The older man sighed and braced his hands on the desk.

Mark swallowed the gleeful cheer. Anton was getting older, and he was under a ton of stress. Pumping his blood pressure up like this was no good.

"I couldn't let those guys rip you off like that." Mark sighed.

Anton spread his hands. "You think I don't know how much you are part of *this*—"

"Well, not this shitty office, I hope." Mark grinned.

"Your fucking mouth," Anton said, but the irritation had gone out of him. He slipped him a paper full of his own chicken-scratch handwriting. "I have a job for Full Moon Construction."

Mark ducked his head. Anton even knew the name Mark had picked out.

Anton confirmed his knowledge that Mark hadn't just been pulling side gigs for extra money. "I'm surprised it's taken you so long."

Mark swallowed hard. His throat burned. "I don't want to—"

"Go see this man," Anton ordered. "Tomorrow, day after. When you look less kicked around. Today go home. Get some rest."

"Thanks, boss."

"You are a smart guy with a big appetite. I also had a big appetite once. But I was never as smart. And I had all this to step into." He held up a hand when Mark would have interrupted. "My demo schedule is light for the next month or so. Should give your crew plenty of extra time to do this job."

Pavel had experience but not strength. Sam was a plumbing guy at heart, but he could fill in when needed. But they were a start.

"Ondrej work out?" Anton asked.

"He's a good kid."

"Take him with you," Anton said. "I'll cover his pay. Call it an apprenticeship. He learns from the best, he maybe becomes halfway decent. His mother forgives me for marrying her sister. Everyone is happy."

That was generous. With one less salary to cover, Mark could afford to bring on Chris too. Keeping his little brother busy meant keeping him out of trouble. And Mark could use the hands.

"This gig will lead to more if you do the job I know you have in you," Anton warned.

Mark grinned. "I sure as shit hope so."

"Get out of here." Anton threw a balled-up scrap of paper at him, and his laughter followed Mark all the way out the door.

Ondrej was hanging around while the other guys smoked at the end of the loading dock, trying to look like part of the conversation. Interesting that he didn't join them in the cigarette. Mark liked this kid more and more.

Pavel ground out his, knowing how much Mark hated the smell. He nodded toward the office. "Things good?"

"Better than good." Mark slapped the paper on his palm. "Take a few days off. Get rest. Because we've got a job."

"Job, job?" Sam perked up.

Mark grinned. "Build, baby."

"Fuck yes." Sam pumped his fist at his side. "About damn time." He slapped Mark's shoulder, wincing when Mark flinched. "Sorry, boss. Sorry."

"Ondrej," Mark barked. "You want in?"

The boy's face lit up. He stuffed his hands in his pockets and tried to contain his smile. "Okay, yeah. I'm in."

Sam rolled his eyes.

"But first, lunch," Mark said. "I could eat a horse."

"It's ten thirty." Pavel's brows rose.

"Late breakfast?" Mark grinned. "My treat."

Sam dropped his tool bag without ceremony. "Let's go."

Mark took them to a place that served big plates of food at odd hours —American-style, they called it—and he ate until Ondrej started staring again. The wolf slept, content.

As Mark settled the bill, Sam asked, "What's the job? Who's it for?"

Mark paused, embarrassed that in his enthusiasm, he hadn't even checked. He squinted at Anton's scribbles, then groaned. "The fuck."

Pavel leaned in to get a look. The older man began to laugh, wiping his hand over his face.

Sam looked between them, then took his own glance. "What's so—? Oh."

Mark shook his head.

"What is wrong?" Ondrej scanned their faces.

"Absolutely nothing." Sam grinned and threw an arm around the boy's shoulders, leading him toward the door. "Little Blossoms, eh? You're about to get an education."

Mark stuffed the paper in his pocket with a sigh. He'd asked for just one. If he'd wanted a certain kind of job, he should have been more specific.

But a job was a job was a job. And this one was now his.

At home later, Mark tried to rest but couldn't relax. Healing took a lot out of him, but he was shit at lying down. While he waited for the microwave to finish warming up the half dozen burritos he'd stuffed inside, he tackled the overgrown pile of laundry.

The duffel bag from his disastrous overnight in Jevany lay on the bottom, under the accumulation of socks and sweaty T-shirts. He dumped the whole load into the machine and started a cycle.

An hour later he'd polished off the burritos and started on another round when the washer timer went off. He dragged his laundry out of the wash, setting up the drying rack on his balcony at the back of the building. The afternoon sun lit Vyšehrad fortress, shadows lingering on the street below doing little to cool the hot air refracted off the sun-drenched hill. He was sweating as soon as he stepped onto the balcony. He shook out his clothes and hung them carefully, taking pains to smooth out the wrinkles and match the socks. In the bottom of the basket was a crumpled piece of fabric that didn't match anything else.

A scrap really, of a material that never should have gone through the machine. It was hopelessly wrinkled now. But it had already been ruined, one long edge ragged.

The wolf surged hard into his chest in recognition. Mark staggered back onto his haunches, leaning against the wall as his breath came short and fast. He knew this fabric—had bunched it in his hands many times on his way to pushing it up her hips or down her shoulders. Navy so blue it was nearly black and tiny white polka dots.

Evie's dress.

She had used this to bind the wolf's muzzle. A silk so fine the wolf could have ripped it apart with one flex of his jaws. But he hadn't because she was trying to save his life.

When he pressed a hand to the scar on his chest, the lingering tingle, like a blessing, rose back.

The wolf howled in his chest. He owed Evie his life.

"Okay, Big Guy," Mark pleaded. "We'll get to her. I promise."

That evening he hopped in his battered Škoda wagon and drove hard for Jevany. He parked off the road on a hiking trailhead and set off into the trees. When he was a good distance off the trail, he shed his clothes and let the wolf take control.

At the Russian villa, silence ruled. The guardhouse was empty, the gate locked. He loped the perimeter, staying wide of the cameras, sniffing. Her scent was so faint he almost missed it. She'd been gone for days, maybe longer.

He had no way to find her.

# CHAPTER ELEVEN

"You come very highly recommended." The pale, shark-eyed dude in a perfect suit spread his palms. "Due to our reputation, we need a small crew, a discreet one. The work must be done quickly and to an exceptional standard."

The guy didn't even blink as a half-naked young woman sauntered to their table and deposited a small tray and tea.

Mark did his best not to look. It was easier now than when he'd arrived at Prague's most prestigious gentlemen's club an hour ago. He focused instead on the oily coating in his nostrils that only seemed to thicken with every minute spent in the other man's presence.

Mark thought he might have recognized the man from the news feeds, though he'd introduced himself only as Nikolai. He was often seen with Valentin Dimitrov, the wealthy businessman whose portfolio included some of the most expensive real estate in the city as well as a handful of exclusive clubs. This one, Little Blossoms, was the crown jewel, the finest one of its kind in Prague, known to be a place visited by the most influential players in business. People didn't even get in without a sponsor these days. The women here all looked well treated, each prettier than the last and perfectly content to play their part in fleecing wealthy patrons of their cash. He couldn't blame them.

Situated in the north end of the city, where the river curved back on itself to form a substantial peninsula, the building had been one of the many shipping warehouses this part of town was known for. The conversion was well done. The cavernous main floor had been closed off just enough to provide a feeling of intimacy while staying large enough to retain a stately grandness.

It was dominated by a main stage, nearly 360 degrees with old-time lighting, rigging for aerial work, and a pair of brass poles. Tables, now set for lunch, circled the stage. The far edge of the room was the bar, discreet enough to be unnoticeable but still plenty accessible to those who didn't want, or couldn't afford, the full table experience.

Much of the exposed brick and wood beams had been preserved along with the original windows and ironworks. The rest was a study in sumptuous materials and rich jewel tones. Vinyl masquerading as something more expensive on the main floor would hold up under dim scrutiny. He doubted anyone was checking out the furniture anyway. The overstuffed leather was reserved for the curtained booths lining the west edge of the room, each designed to give privacy, ending in a smaller passageway for even more private shows. Backstage dressing rooms, prop rooms, kitchens, and their prep. A couple of adjoining banquet halls hosted special events.

On his way in, he'd clocked the narrow passage and stairs to a second floor. If the building was anything like the other warehouses in this part of town, it also had a basement—that would have been the original floor. He wouldn't know; he hadn't yet seen it. Mark expected to find out specifics, but Nikolai had shown him only the main floor of the club and seated him at a generously appointed stage-side table. And that fact added to his growing unease.

It was just before lunch, and the club was coming alive around them as staff prepared for the rush. Still, Nikolai seemed in no hurry, steering the conversation away from the details of the job repeatedly and back to politics and current events.

Mark stifled his impatience, resisting the urge to so much as bounce his knee under the table. Maybe the guy was just stringing him along until he could issue a polite dismissal. Then Mark could have some words with Anton about sending him out on a wild-goose chase.

He caught himself. Anton trusted him with this, had sent him here. His ass was on the line too. Mark couldn't go whining back to HQ that he hadn't gotten the job because the guy didn't like him. Time to make himself likable.

The woman depositing the tea winked at him, her hair in an elaborately curled pile that smelled of roses. For a human, the scent would have been pleasant, but he took a shallow breath to avoid being overwhelmed.

"Thank you." Mark met the woman's eyes, ignoring the generously displayed cleavage. The gentleman's club was the part of the ecosystem that troubled him the least.

"You understand that there will be no exchange of… services," Nikolai went on with his oily smirk. "We are not that kind of establishment."

Mark kept his face even. "We're not interested in any exchange, sir. My guys are good men. Been in the business a long time. They keep their noses clean and their eyes on their job. And I'll make sure they do."

"Glad to hear it." Nikolai showed his teeth, his gaze fixed on Mark in that steady, strange way he had done the entire time they waited.

"Just here to see to your job." Markus tapped his pen on his open portfolio, which was turned to his project notes. So far the page was blank. "Are there any questions you have for me about my qualifications?"

It was a bluff—he was going to have to make some shit up, but it was better when the guy was talking. He didn't get that creepy, stared-into vibe.

Mark wondered if Nikolai was somehow sensitive to shifters. It would make sense that that kind of empathy would be useful for someone like Dimitrov to keep close. Mark trusted his mom's charm to protect him as it always had, but this guy was officially weirding him out.

At the silence, he looked up to find Nikolai fixed on him again. Mark stared back.

At last the other man blinked and smiled. "All right then. Let me introduce you to Mr. Dimitrov, and we will give you the specifics."

Mark's chair scraped the floor with a bit more force than necessary. He'd expected his only contact would be Nikolai, or a club manager. His surprise must have shown.

Nikolai clapped him on the shoulder with a toothy grin. "Mr. Dimitrov likes to be involved in every aspect of his properties. And this is a particular project of his. He would like to make your acquaintance."

Mark was no good with flattery—he hoped Dimitrov wasn't hoping for a good ass kissing.

A guard opened the door to the elevator, nodding a greeting to Nikolai and taking in Mark impassively. The upstairs office was as lavish as the club below, if smaller.

The aroma of a spice he couldn't name tickled his nose. Faint but familiar. He managed to stifle his sneeze just in time. The smell came from an empty desk by the front door. It had been empty for some time, each item stacked neatly as though it were waiting for its occupant to return. He caught sight of a stack of glossy magazines tucked under some paperwork and a makeup compact.

The wolf turned over under his breastbone, suddenly alert and wary.

Nikolai followed his gaze. "You will run all your purchase orders, supply and payroll requests by the secretary when she returns from her vacation."

Mark nodded, suddenly irritated that Nikolai assumed he would take the job. He hadn't even seen it.

Who was he kidding? Of course he was going to take it. He just liked feeling that he had some options.

"I'd love to hear more about the project," Mark said. "I'm sure you have better things to do with your day than babysit me."

Nikolai's lips curled beneath the mustache. "It has been a pleasure. Please, Mr. Dimitrov will see you now."

"This is the man Anton speaks of like a son." Valentin Dimitrov threw open the door and emerged with hands outstretched. "Strong as an ox, wily as a bear, handsome as the devil. Welcome. Come."

"Anton's better at talking these days than building." Mark grinned, giving a carefully firm handshake. No good breaking the guy's fingers.

"He's a busy man, and so he compliments me by sending his best." Valentin laughed, escorting him up into the office. Nikolai closed the door behind them.

Gregarious and personable, Valentin seemed far too delighted with himself and his empire to be the one holding ties to the mob.

Mark reconfigured his view of the two men—the rumors linking Dimitrov to the mob must be hiding the real connection. Nikolai fit the part, down to the rings and the sheer menace. The illusion of legitimate business must serve them well, and Valentin's fortune couldn't have hurt either.

After introductions and more small talk, they took him to the basement.

He was right. The club was built over an old shipping warehouse that had been raised after a flood, leaving a basement hundreds of square meters unused. They showed him the space. Mostly old props and busted equipment and a portioned-off area that had been floored for dancers.

"They rehearse here, my girls," Valentin offered. "Before they blossom above. Our choreographer once taught at the Praha Dance Academy, you know. Before she got too old for it. We picked her up for a song. She whips all my girls into shape. Have you seen a show?"

"No, sir," Mark said. He didn't begin to have the kind of connections that would even get him in the front doors.

"Ah, you must see." Valentin slapped Nikolai's arm with the kind of thoughtlessness that made Mark wonder how he hadn't lost a hand pulling some shit like that. "Kolya, get the man on the list for Saturday night. Bring a friend. Boys' night out and all that."

"Thank you, sir," Mark said. "But that's not necessary."

"What is necessary?" Valentin waved away his protest. "Breathing, eating, sex. This is a bonus."

It was Nikolai who saved him. "Let's walk you through the plans."

It was simple enough—finish sealing and reinforcing the basement, and a build-out into a series of rooms to be used for private entertainment.

He saw it as Nikolai spoke—walls rising around them, a small entryway with the broad wooden barn doors leading down the long, wide hallway to individual rooms. Two wet rooms—showers and changing areas. He assumed the decor would be much like the above spaces—lush, decadent, dark. Too heavy for his taste, but what the client wanted. And that was the designer's problem anyway.

Mark had no fundamental objection to people making money however they saw fit. Sex work was work. It wasn't for him, but he didn't judge it either.

There was no prohibition against prostitution, only abuse. The necromancer Azrael enforced codes barring slavery and trafficking with the same ruthlessness that kept supernatural creatures confined to the shadows. Valentin probably made way too much money to risk it by stepping over the necromancer's line.

And Mark could make sure everything went to code—ventilation, lighting—so that people were safe doing whatever they were going to be doing down here.

The job was solid. And the connections. The Dimitrov family had made its money building the metro after World War II, and Valentin had folded it into real estate. There might be more projects too small for Anton that he wanted to throw money at, and he could introduce Mark to others who might be in the same situation. A couple of referrals would set Mark up. He was loyal to Anton, but he wasn't stupid. And he'd practically gotten the man's blessing to go out on his own.

At the end of the conversation, they looked at him, clearly expecting he would jump on the opportunity. He knew he should.

Except the wolf kept shifting in the pit of his stomach, rising to his hindbrain and sinking again repeatedly, on the verge of a snarl. For the first time in his adult life, Mark clamped down on the animal he shared a form with. *Enough, Big Guy.*

The wolf pushed back, startled and angry, before retreating.

Mark rocked from toe to heel, wanting suddenly to be clear of this cavernous underground. Nikolai was focusing a steady, penetrating gaze on him, making Mark even more suspicious that he was somehow able to pick up on Mark's dual nature.

"I'd like to run the numbers in some detail and get back to you with a better estimate of the costs," Mark said, stalling. "And consult with someone familiar with water encroachment in these old buildings. Can't have you spring a leak after the work's done. I can get back to you by the end of the week."

Valentin's expression tightened before he grinned. "A detail-oriented man. Measure twice, cut once, my mother liked to say. A seamstress, you know. I come from the ground up, just like you. I like him already, Kolya."

But that tension was enough to convince Mark he'd made the right decision. Something about this stank.

"Appreciate it. Thanks for your time, sir." He swung his focus back to Nikolai. "If that's all?"

Nikolai held a palm out toward the door they came in. "We will wait to hear from you."

# CHAPTER TWELVE

"AND YOU HAVE no idea where he went or where he came from?"

Evie braced her forehead on her palms, listening to the sound of Tal bustling about the depths of his shop in search of chalk. "The creature?"

She could tell his eyebrows were raised when he spoke next. "Not the wolf, Eves. Your *lover*. The construction worker."

Evie rolled her eyes, unable to keep the smile off her face. "He's the boss."

"Oh, the boss!" Tal cackled dramatically.

Evie sipped the coffee he'd made when she arrived at the small shop tucked away among the warren-lined tunnels below Wenceslas Square. It was almost cold.

"It's about time you turned up," he said finally. "You're overdue for a wardrobe refresh. Valentin is going to get suspicious about where his money is going."

Evie waved a hand. "Valentin is oblivious. But Nikolai keeps track I'm sure—"

"Nikolai." Tal rounded the forms with his tape and pins. He looked older —the fine lines bracketing his eyes deeper. He had always been angular, but his features seemed more pronounced. "He delivered your note himself. And three times what you owed me."

"I hope you spent it on something delightful," she chirped, refusing to be chilled at the image of him here, in one of her safest spaces.

"Best date night ever," he said. "Nice work on the shoes, by the way. Are those—?"

She nodded, flashing the bright purple bottoms. She'd paid full price for them, blanching a bit at the register. But Tal was right, they were worth it. They always were.

Looking the part of a well-kept woman came down to the shoes. A perfect outfit would be ruined without them. With them, even the most unremarkable would be elevated to something extraordinary. The shoes she bought new and on her lunch break—the large shopping bags from high-end stores fueled the club gossip mill.

The real work was done away from prying eyes.

Every couple of weeks, on Sunday mornings, she left her apartment early for a series of appointments. She dressed simply, her hair secured at the nape of her neck and a touch of refined, carefully applied makeup but no glamour.

At each home, she rang the bell and was welcomed in for tea. In some cases, an affluent matron had died, in others a family business had soured and the woman of the house had to divest of her wardrobe. Evie played the assistant of a discrete and wealthy woman who preferred to remain anonymous. Most were happy to see her privately to save face and too uncomfortable in the presence of her scar to ask many questions. They tsked briefly over the ruination of an otherwise striking appearance and quickly showed her to their back rooms and closets.

She went through the clothes hung and folded and gathered carefully, plucking exclusive labels for a fraction of what she would spend on the high street. When she'd concluded her morning appointments, she took the metro into the city, disembarking underground at Můstek station. She weaved her way through the crowds by the platforms to the shop level and a tailor's unassuming storefront.

The reinforced door always gave reluctantly under her weight, and she always almost tumbled inside the tiny front room packed full of threads, fabric, and completed pieces on mannequins and racks.

Today Tal had been puttering around, trying too hard to look busy. When she arrived, he'd dropped what was in his hands and taken her by the shoulders. The rare direct physical contact betrayed his worry. They bussed cheeks.

"I thought you'd forgotten me down here, up among all your high rollers."

Evie laughed shakily—it was better than crying, which was what she really wanted to do. "Bullshit. You got my note. I came as soon as I could. I missed you."

"Who are you fooling?" He grinned. "You only want me for the clothes."

He flipped the CLOSED sign and herded her into the back room, disappearing to make coffee.

The back room was an unexpectedly expansive workshop. Evie deposited her finds on the empty rack near his worktable and toured the half-finished garments draped over mannequins around the room.

When he returned with coffee, bread, and jam, she told him everything. By the time she finished recounting her tryst with Mark and the strange income she'd discovered on the books, he'd abandoned puttering around the coffee service and collapsed into the chair across from her, rapt.

She marked the years they'd known each other—over half her life. They were both getting older. And he was at least ten years her senior.

She blinked hard to overlook the death mask that appeared—bloated and graying with the first signs of decay just overlaying the contented face.

"You're seeing it again," he said somberly.

She frowned, annoyed that she hadn't been able to hide it.

"I know you." He shook his head. "Your eyelashes twitch like you're fighting to keep your eyes from closing. Am I the same in it?"

She lowered her chin once and steeled herself to speak over emotion. She owed him the truth. "An old man. Probably in the shop, judging by the tape draped around your neck."

"You're better at hiding that wobble in your voice."

She rolled her eyes, sniffing once.

Tal returned to his seat across from her, his hands clasped and dangling between his knees. She knew how hard it was for him to keep from reaching out to comfort. She had never told him the specifics of what had happened at the club, but he must have had his suspicions when she began avoiding touch.

Funny that it hadn't bothered her with Mark. But then again, she had been so focused on that energy between them when they made contact. She hadn't had the chance to recoil, and then they'd been all over each other. The irony of playing Valentin's lover was that she'd been celibate the whole time, too afraid to even risk word getting around. No wonder she'd been so responsive every time she'd been with Mark. That was all it was. Deprivation had a way of heightening everything.

"You never have to look," Tal said quietly, drawing her back to the conversation. "If you don't want to. I won't be offended."

"People expect eye contact." She shook her head, staring him in the face. After all they'd been through together, she would see him as he was. "It's good practice. It only lasts a few seconds."

He smiled, going to the garment bags she'd brought. "Let's see what you've found."

"Just a few things."

"Eat. The bread is fresh."

Evie slathered extra jam on the soft bread and bit off a chunk, chewing and swallowing to push the lump of emotion down her throat.

The bread was fine, but the jam sparkled against her tongue, sweet fig with a touch of tart. "Calvin?"

He nodded, beaming with pride. "This is the last of last year's jars. Balsamic fig."

"He's a wonder."

"He's like you." His brow ticked up. He made a slight rapping noise on the tabletop with his knuckles, an old symbol between them when one of them spotted a person they suspected of having a notion like Evie's, one they must be extra careful around.

Now it was a slow, fond gesture, a military salute between veterans.

"You seem to have a notion of your own," Evie said, grinning. "Finding us."

"Putting up with your strangeness is more like it," he grumbled, pleased. "He is my heart. I never thought... after Malia."

Evie nodded, reaching out tentatively. He stayed very still, and she squeezed his arm. "And as long as he keeps sending you to work with jam, I'm happy for you both."

He rested his fingertips lightly on hers. When she didn't pull away, he patted the back of her hand. "Wretched imp."

"Old goat."

He let go when she did, but his smile remained. Tal rifled through the bags, laying out her purchases on the table.

"Oh, very nice," Tal murmured as he went, checking labels and hems. "Excellent taste. This is lovely. A size too big, but we can work with that. Your color. Nice work, Evie girl."

Then he waved her off to the fitting booth. They spent the next hour with chalk and pins, arguing about hemlines and sleeve length while trading the latest gossip from the club and news: politics, celebrities, and the Allegiance.

This had been Tal's idea, a way to stretch the allowance Valentin gave her so that she could put most aside to fund her vanishing act.

At last she returned to her simple wrap dress, tying it at her waist.

He eyed it skeptically over the half glasses perched on his nose, and she couldn't remember when he'd started needing them.

How far they'd come from her family's small tailoring shop.

Tal had started out as what her father called a special client. The kind who required the shop to be closed and Mama to assist with the more intimate details of the fitting.

*Do you know why Papa loves clothes?* Mama asked one night. Evie'd never thought to question why. It had always seemed a part of him. *Clothing is possibility. We discover who we can be in what we wear. It can speak volumes about us before we open our mouths. He has a way of seeing it in people—who they are, what they can be—that is his true notion. He would have made a fine designer. You have his eye, Evie girl.*

As word of mouth spread that the small family shop was a safe space for those who needed special care, their clientele grew.

Eventually Tal had asked to apprentice with her father. He cooked and shared faith with her mother, and her father treated him like a brother. Her siblings grew up with Uncle Tal.

When he completed his apprenticeship, he moved to a larger city to build his own shop, though he and her parents remained close. They made the rare trip for his wedding.

When they got word that Tal's neighborhood had been bombed, her father went to search for news. He returned empty-handed and hollow-eyed. Her parents mourned quietly, each in their own way. They talked about leaving contested territory.

If they'd left, maybe they would have lived.

After discharge from the field hospital, Evie was sent east, away from the river and the sea, to a camp for refugees in the foothills. A week in, she was caught fighting with another orphan over a rare pair of trousers.

The guards separated them, and it would have been a trip to the camp administrator, but a familiar voice called out from the crowd. "Evie girl, there you are. What trouble have you made?"

For a minute she thought him a ghost, and the guard must have mistaken the fear on her face for recognition of the trouble she was in and gave her a good shake. *This one yours?*

*My sister's child.* Tal nodded, speaking before she could. His hair was longer, still unruly and his skin was hard and tan from exposure. But he wore a well-tailored suit as she remembered. *She is my responsibility.*

She stumbled when the guard released her suddenly, pushing her at him.

When the guard was out of sight, Tal grasped her shoulders, jaw working mutely. Finally he jerked his head for her to follow. *Come with me.*

His tent was one of the older canvas models, larger but drafty from cracks in the seams. He had been here a while. When he lowered the tent flap, he sank to his knees, tears streaming down his face with prayers of thanks on his lips.

She threw her arms around him. *How did you get here, Tal? We thought... We heard you were dead.*

The story came haltingly as he rebandaged her hands and made her a cup of weak tea. He'd been unconscious for weeks, then spent months in a medical treatment center before being released to a camp up north. The camp'd had bad luck—flooding, then influenza—and they'd been moved several times. He'd been trying to get ahold of her parents before news of the latest round of bombing reached him.

*I've got no spleen.* He laughed. *No sense left either. But why are you alone? Where is your mother? Omar? Menno?*

It was the only time she'd cried since coming to the camp. He held her, rocking softly until the tears ran out. Then he held her at arm's length, his own eyes and face wet again. *God sent us each other then, Evie girl.*

The solid knot of grief built up in her belly over the weeks since the bombs fell seemed to take up too much space. No room for food, though the hunger never went away. What use did she have for any god, what of her remained for faith?

For the first time, she registered the scraps of fabric and half-constructed garments. *You are tailoring here?*

He shrugged. *I lost everything. They cut the beautiful binder your mama made for me. They would only give me dresses at first. By the third camp, I'd finished a suit. Nothing as fine as your father's work. But it turns out even refugees appreciate well-fitting clothes, and my skill has been profitable even here. Imagine what we could do together, Evie girl.*

He ventured deeper into the little tent and returned with a folded piece of deep brown cloth. *These should fit. You're taller than I remember.*

She inspected the pants. They had been repaired with his fine, even stitches.

*The best stories are a shade away from the truth,* he said. *A man and his orphan niece might have an easier time than two useless refugees.* Families got bigger space, more assistance. But it was still a refugee camp, and no one left without family or a sponsor to speak for them. *It's a start. But we need a plan.*

*A plan.*

*I was thinking of heading to Prague. I had some family there once.*

A city thousands of miles from the refugee camp in the shadow of an ancient horseman rearing over a fallen lion carved out of a cliff face. It might as well have been another planet. With no money, no identification, and only the clothes on their backs, reaching it seemed impossible.

She'd wanted to lie down and die in the ruins of the building that was her family's tomb. Instead, she'd been found, treated. She ate when they fed her, submitted to the ministrations of her wounds. The will to survive was a curious thing.

*We are all animals,* Tal murmured her father's words. *Survival is our nature. Hope is a more complicated thing.*

*A more dangerous thing,* she finished.

Tal's shoulders rose one more time, but in acceptance.

Her father's words stirred something in her. He would never accept this as his future. Her future. *Is it better than here?*

*I'd say anywhere is better than here, wouldn't you?* Tal smiled fully for the first time.

Escaping the camp was their first con. Years spent on the on the road had taught Evie to survive on her wits, her ability to observe and plan, and to play the role that suited to get what she wanted. They traveled between jobs, passing the dream of the tailor's shop between them along the way.

She'd never known how fragile dreams could be and how broken they could leave the dreamer once they fled.

In the years since they'd come to Prague, Evie had gone to work for Valentin, but Tal found a way to make their dream a reality, and his tailoring shop had become the best-kept secret in the city.

She sometimes imagined his shop as her parents'. She would have sacrificed the dream of a brightly lit, windowed storefront for this tiny, underground cubbyhole any day if it meant having her family beside her. But she would not imagine Tal out of her life or think of where she would be without him.

"I've just taken some work for the national theater." Tal lowered his voice, gesturing at the costumes on the dress forms. "A certain star who shall not be named has found herself in a delicate condition and needs to keep it discreet until the end of the season. I suppose I have you to thank for the referral."

"Me?" Evie shrugged off his gratitude. "I've been out of the city for weeks."

"She found out about me from one of your girls at Blossoms. The baby's father is her lover, and they are patrons of your establishment. Your blossom is overjoyed. They intend to raise the child together, all of them. It's quite a progressive arrangement. They seem happy."

Business had really taken off when he began working for Blossoms dancers. They incorporated the flower of their stage name into their costumes and routine choreography. When one girl retired—whether through carefully managed assets, marriage, or a bargain with a wealthy client—she sold her persona. The most successful ones went for small fortunes. Having a tailor to resize or re-create the costumes was essential.

Some tailors turned up their noses at the business and the scanty costumes, or they groped and propositioned the dancers. Tal embraced the new clientele, his enthusiasm for the costumes and the drama of life backstage paired with respect for the performers and a shrewd business sense. He did the work for all Little Blossoms performers.

That was because he was a fair man, and a good one, she told him as often as she could. He used the income to help others afford to customize wardrobes to suit the stages of their transitions.

Tal eyed her over the blouse he was pinning. "So you're back in Prague."

"I go back to the office on Monday. Construction starts on the basement. They're turning it into private rooms—"

"And how goes your plan?"

"Valentin and Kolya are up to something. I need to find out what. It could be useful to have the information. Evidence."

"That's not part of the plan." He frowned, hands slowing.

"I know, Tal. I know," she said. "I must ask you for a favor."

He halted work entirely, staring at her. "You're going to want me to keep your evidence safe?"

He knew her too well.

"I wouldn't ask." She rushed on. "But someone searched my apartment while I was in Jevany. Probably Nikolai, but I can't be sure."

The job had been well done. She wouldn't have noticed except for a few items she'd intentionally left askew being returned to orientations that should have been proper. Whoever it was hadn't found her savings cache and no one had been back, but she couldn't be too cautious.

She misread his silence. "I'll only come by when I have clothes, the way we always have. I promise I'd never endanger you—"

"It's not danger to me I'm worried about, Evie girl." He looked grim. "They don't search apartments unless they suspect something. If he finds out you're looking… Or that you even know something is amiss…"

"I'll be careful."

He jabbed a pin into place, realized his mistake, and swore. "You have the money, what more do you need?"

She thought of the expensive bird in the cage. "I'm beginning to suspect that Nikolai would follow no matter how far I went."

"I know, dearest." His knuckles rapped the drafting table softly but with a more ominous rhythm.

"I need leverage." She spoke quickly. "Something I can hold against Valentin if needed. Nikolai would stop if Valentin called him off."

"And if they catch you?"

She closed her eyes, steeling herself. "When I leave, I'll get word to you in three days, as we planned. If you don't hear from me, get it to the press. Anonymously. He won't get away with it."

"A lot of good it will do you in a shallow grave," he said grimly.

"Then I'll just have to stay on this side of it." Her vision blurred before she blinked away tears.

The door rattled as a customer shook it repeatedly. Tal hummed under his breath. "What about the damned sign don't they understand, you think?"

"Go," she said. "I can't be your only customer."

Evie listened to the joyful rise and fall of voices, the sound of the register. By the time his familiar footsteps sounded on the tile, she had mostly collected herself.

"What do I owe you for today?" she asked, hoping to change the subject.

"Just pay on delivery, as usual." He sighed. It would be a fraction of what he was due. But he always gave her an absurd rate, knowing whatever money she saved from this operation went straight into her getaway fund. "Do you have anything else for me?"

"One thing," she said hopefully. She rummaged through her bag, carefully removing a smaller sack containing the remains of her silk dress. She'd washed it by hand and gotten it clean, but the tear…

"Oh, Evie," Tal groaned. "Is that a Rebekah Cerny original? I think I saw this in her shop window a few weeks ago."

She grimaced. "It was?"

"What have you done?" he said, pained as he spread the navy dress on his worktable, fingers touching the ragged hem as gingerly as an open wound.

"It was an accident." She pinched her fingertips worriedly.

He exhaled long and low before looking up at her. "Is it important to you?"

"It has sentimental value." She thought of the beast's bound muzzle and the paler, softer fur beneath. When she woke, the scrap had been gone.

"I'll see what I can do." Tal shook his head sadly, folding it up. She started to take it back, but he held on, peering into her bag. "And what else is it you have there? You're sketching again."

Evie flushed, reaching for the bag, but he beat her there. "I was just bored in Jevany until I started working. I was killing time!"

But it was too late. He had the sketchbook open, flipping through it.

"This is very strong," he murmured. "Clean lines and a nice silhouette. Your sense of balance is growing with every design, Evelia. You should be quite pleased. If you tighten up the bodice, perhaps a dart or two. Yes, here. Do you see it?"

She peered carefully over his shoulder. She did see it—it was a subtle change but a good one. He flipped a page and gasped.

"Oh, saints and angels, this is perfection." He touched the page almost reverently. "What fabric?"

"A tulle," she murmured. "Maybe with satin beneath, or crepe. Depends on how it moves, I think."

"And the color, I'd imagine."

She bobbed her head, eager for the first time. "And the lady, of course. Some will prefer more shine, other a more subtle effect."

He sucked his teeth, glaring at her. "You are the artist. *You* make the choice. Your patron will obey your sense of style."

"My patron." She rolled her eyes at him. "This is a gown for a business-woman or a politician. Not a performer."

He shook his head at her. "We are all dancing to the tune of one player or another. And this will elevate and enchant. Your talent is nothing compared to the work you have put in."

"My current occupation does leave a lot of my brain for designs," she murmured softly.

"And traipsing about the woods with a mystery lover?"

She rolled her eyes. "It was…"

"It's about time if you ask me," he muttered. "It's time you stopped just surviving and started living, Evie."

"You can't run forever." Tal held up a hand before she could interrupt. "It breaks my heart, but leaving Prague is for the best. That doesn't mean—"

"Mean what, Tal?" she said, hating the emotion in her voice and the tears she wasn't quite able to contain.

"What do you want, Evie—really want—for your life?"

The image of Markus, five years, ten years, twenty years from now, face creased with smiles, his broad hands on her waist, her hair, her cheek, flashed quickly through her mind. Images that weren't hers to imagine in the first place.

Her gaze returned to the sketch pad. Once this had been their dream, together. Her fingers smudged the delicate sketches. She was glad he had achieved it even if her heart ached not to be a part of it.

"I want to see the world," she said lightly. "We've come this far, why stop here?"

"You are a terrible liar."

"I just want to find a place," she said softly. "My place."

"Then you need to stop running," he said. "Plant your feet and not let anything knock you aside."

It wasn't as simple as all that. Settling anywhere for too long was danger-ous. "You know what happens, what always happens."

More than once on the road when she stayed too long in a place, got too attached, her notion would get in the way. She would try to warn someone of their impending death, or she would use her affinity for metal to help, and someone would notice.

The godswar had not only revealed the wonder of a world full of magic but the horror and death it could bring. People were frightened or threatened. Then she and Tal had to move on, usually in a hurry. She shouldn't have been surprised that even Prague had ended in disaster.

"Not always, Evie," he said. "Maybe not here, but not always."

"Speaking of running." Evie rose, checking her watch. "I should go. I've been here too long already."

"Never long enough." He slipped a small jar of homemade jam into her bag. "The anniversary is coming."

The last thing she could take right now was the reminder of her family's death. Every year, no matter how lean or unpredictable things had been, they had always marked the death of their loved ones together. Until she'd begun working for Valentin.

Tal mistook her silence for openness to the idea. "We could make meldado—"

"And what good is scripture?" Evie snorted. "I don't even believe—"

"It's not about belief." His voice rose. "It's about memory. Honoring their lives."

She stuffed the sketchbook into her bag. "It's not safe—"

"We don't have to go to synagogue—"

She was being unfair. It wasn't about the scripture or the tradition. This might be the last chance they had to mourn together. But she wouldn't risk it, not after everything she'd done to protect him.

"If they know you're more than my tailor, they'll come looking around here, asking questions when I'm gone. It's too dangerous," she said. "I have to work anyway. Don't be mad. I'll fast, okay?"

He shook his head. "You don't eat enough as is."

"I'm sorry," she murmured, her smile wavering. "Don't be angry at me please."

Tal studied her and settled his hands on her shoulders. "The first of these will be done next Saturday. Bring your insurance here. I'll keep it safe, and I'll see that it gets into the right hands if you cannot. I promise."

She hugged him hard, so spontaneously they both gasped. She breathed in his scent, coffee and jam and the spicy aftershave he favored. "I love you, Uncle Tal."

"My heart."

On her way to the tram, she stopped in a stationery shop. She stood for a long time, contemplating the simple composition books. The whisper-thin, lined paper should be used to record innocent thoughts, first stories, perhaps love letters. Her use for them—recording Valentin's sins to be used as leverage—seemed too dark, too ugly. But they were also a common thing, sold in many stationery shops, bookstores, and even among limited school supplies in some larger grocery stores.

She bought three, stuffed them into her bag behind her sketchbook, and ran to catch the train.

As the tram wound up the steep hill between the castle and the river, she slipped her hand into the bag, finding the soft worn leather of her sketch pad and the harder, crisper covers of the composition books, and beneath both, the warped metal stub of a spent bullet.

She closed her eyes and ran her fingertips over the rough edge, remembering how they felt in fur. She hoped the beast from the forest was all right, but she wished she had seen it whole. It must be magnificent.

Wishes were nothing but heartbreak. Her plan would keep her safe. *Stick to the plan, Evie girl. It's too late for anything else.*

# CHAPTER THIRTEEN

LATE SUNDAY AFTERNOON, Lukas Vogel left his study on a mission. The smells coming from the kitchen for the past few hours had made focusing on his newest puzzle harder than usual. He eyed the massive Crock-Pot with glee. Chili night. Which also meant cornbread and spaetzle. He preferred the mac and cheese, but Beryl refused to make it without proper cheddar.

The apartment was quiet. He never thought he'd see the day where he missed the noise of the kids. Any number or combination of the four moving around the space generated an energy he enjoyed. They were all adults now with lives of their own. One was even married—to a brilliant, delightful woman with steel in her spine and a smile like pure sunshine.

Most days Lukas Vogel could forget his wife and daughter-in-law were witches and his three sons were werewolves. It had been much simpler when it was just him and Beryl and little charms hung about their apartment and candles lit in specific orders in accordance with the phases of the moon.

But as their family grew, he became increasingly aware that what his wife and his sons were put them on a knife's edge. He could move through humanity as one of the mundane, the secret in his own blood hidden. But if they slipped—big or small—or were discovered and exposed for what they were, the danger was very real.

He knew only that he must protect them, as best he could, in whatever way he could.

At least the boys were under one roof. His only daughter, Isela, was just across town at the Dance Academy where she worked and now seemed to prefer living. He tried not to let that hurt too much.

In the kitchen, his lovely bride was perched over her journal by the kitchen sink, her pen in hand and the soft, shadowed afternoon light pouring over her from the window facing the hillside.

He'd never stop thinking of her that way. The day she'd chosen him above all others.

The thing no one told you when you were starting out was that the choosing didn't end that day. She'd had to keep choosing him, and he her, every day over the years, through the sleepless nights and the struggles and the pain.

*I've always wanted a big family,* she'd said to him over their first coffee.

In hindsight, he should probably have been glad she didn't say, *I've always wanted to rob a bank.* He would have made a terrible getaway driver.

Every time he looked at her, he remembered the choice she made that day and every day after. He kissed her temple, enjoying the pleasure of her weight leaning into him before she returned to her work. The light from the kitchen window fell evenly on her careful scrawl. Not that he could read it. He squinted, but that didn't help. He wasn't even sure what language it was in.

"Are you heading down to the workshop?" Beryl asked without looking up.

"I was hoping to get the shelves done by the weekend," he said, switching languages. "Wie lange dauert es, bis das Abendessen fertig ist?"

"Don't test me, Vogel." She sucked her teeth lightly. "We eat in an hour tops, just waiting to hear back from the boys."

He was starving, but he knew better than to complain. Skipping lunch to argue with some arrogant know-it-all on his cryptographer's forum was his own damn fault.

Beryl slid a basket of peaches that smelled like sunlit heaven his way from beside the sink.

"Farmers' market?"

She hummed.

He finished one in two quick bites and then headed for the fridge.

He grabbed a beer, leaning back against the counter. It had been a while since they'd spent more than a few minutes in the same room not related to sleep or a meal.

Beryl always seemed to be coming and going lately, and not just to her classes in the studio downstairs. She wasn't sleeping well either.

Though they'd promised each other honesty, he knew she didn't tell him everything in the moment. He tried to be okay with that. She'd told him the whole story of saving Barbara—after the fact—and he'd aged a decade just thinking about how while he was escorting Isela to some upscale party, his wife was battling ghost witches. That was when he'd extracted the promise that she would talk to him before launching off to save the day alone.

He didn't know how to ask. "How are they?"

"Markus had a big job interview today," she murmured idly. "Isela had something come up at the academy. And Christof is out being Christof, running in the street with a cute little something-something no doubt."

Lukas was proud of himself for avoiding the temptation of defending their youngest son. It was an argument they'd had a few too many times to be helpful. "Tobias and Barbara?"

"Dinner with the dean."

"I told you they were going to make him head of the department." Lukas grinned.

Beryl cocked her head, looking at him sideways.

"You were right," Lukas added.

Now that she was looking at him, he could see the exhaustion in her face. Worry etched the corners of her mouth, her usually flawless brow wrinkled.

"You've been… busy lately," he said quietly, holding up a hand before she could protest. "Maybe time to take a break?"

Irritation flashed on her face, and he regretted the words. But they'd promised to tell each other the truth. As much of it as they could. Always.

"Teaching Bebe everything you know doesn't have to happen all at once," he said.

"It's not," she said with a long sigh. "Are you sure you want to know?"

He didn't hesitate, setting down the unopened bottle.

"There have been stories… of supernaturals, others… us… disappearing."

"Practitioners?" It was what she preferred to call them. Safer.

She shook her head. "Mostly those who can't hide. Can't pass."

For human.

She threw down her pen. "I didn't even give it much weight at first. It's hard to make it in the city when you have to hide. Life is tenuous. Some just quit trying. There are plenty of abandoned villages in the countryside. It seemed so random. But then…"

She slipped away from him without moving, her gaze going a thousand yards over his left shoulder. He waited patiently. When she came back, her eyes were fathomless, dark, and full of stories.

The air left his lungs. He recovered quickly, feeling the heat in his face, the thunder of his own heart. "You've been investigating these disappearances. Beryl, of all the— dangerous, foolish. Dangerous."

"You already said that one." She smiled wryly.

"When? How? Alone?"

"They aren't even permitted to show themselves to humans. Should we file a missing person's report?" She looked away, guilty. When her eyes fixed on him again, more alarming than the distance were the tears making them shine. "They have families, friends, lovers. Some of whom can't leave the shadows they must survive in. Who else was going to do it?"

Lukas exhaled one long breath. Anxiety still clawed at the inside of his rib cage, but his heart beat hard against it now, loving this woman even if he sometimes wanted to lock her in her yoga studio for her own good.

It was no use railing at her or, gods forbid, trying to stop her. That would only drive her on. He said the only thing he could. "Any idea who is responsible?"

"Necromancers that need fodder. Some kind of predator that preys on others. Human anti-supernatural splinter group?"

"What did you find out?"

"The first was a vodník that used to frequent the Kampa. Then a couple of imps. Nightmares. No one would have missed them, but a few days later a homunculus got grabbed in the same alley. It hadn't acquired a voice, but a minor clairvoyant in the neighborhood heard the screams. And then nothing."

His mind was already turning over the details, looking for any similarities. "Patterns?"

"None that I can see." She held up her hands, frustrated. "Different species, different times of day—mostly at night though, which makes sense. And except for the imp and the homunculus, different locations."

He caught her fingertips lightly in his own. "Beryl—"

"But this could be an early sign of something bigger," she rushed on, tension making her breathless. "They start on the fringes, perfect the technique with the most vulnerable. The ones no one would miss, and then they move on to the rest of us."

"Beryl." He squeezed her fingers to get her attention, drawing a fallen twist of hair from her brow to join the locs behind her ear. "I need you to promise me something—"

She smiled, lopsided. "I won't do anything dangerous. Or foolish. Or dangerous."

He raised a brow.

"Anything more than I already have," she said, and his heart stuttered but he bit his tongue. He hated this feeling, like there was so much going on around him. How could he protect any of them when he couldn't even see all the danger?

"Beryl, I can't be your Mary Jane," he announced.

She stared, blinking at him. To her credit she didn't laugh, though her mouth twitched with delight. "Are you comparing yourself to Spider-Man's girlfriend?"

"Yes. No. I don't know." He threw up his hands, frustration getting the best of him. "You are all out there saving the world while I—"

"I know this is hard." She wrapped her arms around his waist and pressed her cheek into his collar.

He'd known the scent of her longer than anything else in his life. Breathing her in wasn't just natural, it was a necessity. Air was useless without her. "I can help. I did break the code in Tobias's journal."

She leaned away from his chest, brows up. "I thought he—"

"I pointed him in the right direction." He tugged her back.

"Of course you did, lover." She smiled, dimples puckering her cheeks.

"Don't patronize me, Beryl Gilman-Vogel."

"Never, my love."

"Don't leave me out, that's all I'm asking," He shook his head, fighting the urge to stamp a foot like a petulant child. She could be so reckless. What would he do—how would any of them make it without her? "This isn't about me. It's just—"

"I promise not to leave you out," she said. "I will tell you what I know when I know it."

"And we decide what to do together?"

She nodded once, but Lukas wasn't a fool. "Your word."

"What I can, when I can."

It was the best he was going to get, and they both knew it. She hummed, looking toward the door. "Markus is here."

"You don't still have that tracker on him, do you?" Lukas frowned.

She pursed her lips, tilting her chin up at him. He obliged her with a kiss.

"Beryl," he warned. "The tracker?"

She lifted one shoulder, tugging him back for another kiss. "Something must be wrong with it anyway. It went out again the night he got—"

"Ma, that smells amazing, I can smell all the way down the street— Uh..." Mark rounded the corner and stopped. "I can come back."

"That's because you have your father's nose." Beryl laughed, hopping off her stool with the ease of someone half her age to greet their oldest son. "Come in. We were just finishing."

"Ugh, Ma." Mark winced. "Don't ever say... that. Hey, Pop."

"Hallo, mein Kind," Lukas said.

"How on earth do you imagine the four of you got here?" Beryl put her hands on her hips. "There was a lot more than a few smooches, and you are old enough—"

Mark shuddered exaggeratedly. "Can we not, ever, talk about it?"

She rolled her eyes, and he let her drag him down for a kiss on the cheek and brushed off her worries that he wasn't eating enough.

Watching them together, Lukas reveled in how alike they were, down to the facial expressions and sense of humor. Growing up an only child, Lukas hadn't understood how different each child's relationship could be with their parents. And as much as he'd tried to be everything for his first-born son, it was hard to watch the ease he'd never achieved play out before him.

Lukas reclaimed his beer, heading for the door.

"Where are you off to?" Beryl called.

"Workshop," he said. "Finishing the shelves for Barbara's shop."

"I can help," Mark offered.

She hooked the back of his shirt. "You stay right here. I want to have a look at your shoulder. How is it?"

He rolled it both directions. "Good, just stiff."

"I'll be downstairs until dinner," Lukas called over his shoulder.

"Vogel." She eyed him. "If there's a saw involved, I want you sober as a monk."

He sighed and deposited the beer back in the fridge.

Downstairs, he threw himself into the work until he caught motion on the edge of his peripheral vision. Mark waved again, a half smile on his face and a pair of beers in one hand.

"Mein schatz," Lukas shouted, perching his work glasses on top of his head. Mark tapped his ears, and Lukas slid the ear protection away. He grinned, lowering his voice. "Überprüfung meiner Arbeit?"

"Somebody has to make sure you still know what you're doing." Mark shrugged, pushing himself off the door to cross the room.

"Auf Deutsch, Kind," Lukas said, chastising his choice of language.

Mark groaned. "Eigentlich?"

"Ja." Lukas stretched the word, beckoning impatiently.

The switch in language didn't come as easy to Markus as it did for the others, but Lukas was patient.

"Ich kann nicht zulassen, dass du etwas verpasst, alter mann," Mark said.

*Old man.* Lukas scoffed. Still, he checked the plans surreptitiously. Had he missed something?

"Essen ist fertig," Mark delivered the news on dinner, sticking to German. "Mom sent me down to let you know."

Lukas checked his watch, surprised to see the hour had flown by. He stretched his spine—leaning over the bench for long periods wasn't so easy these days.

"But you know for Mom that means another half hour." Mark lifted the beers. He opened one with his multi-tool and handed it over. "And Chris still isn't home, so how about I sub in for a bit?"

"Mein Sohn." Lukas hugged the younger man.

He enjoyed a few long pulls on the beer while they went over details before Mark got to work.

It hadn't always been easy for them to find each other.

After the move, something had shifted between them. Maybe part of it was being here, a place where Lukas blended in and Mark never would. Lukas knew his son's life became difficult in ways he couldn't imagine. And though he'd always tried to understand, Mark seemed to resent even that. Resentment and puberty had made life hard for them both for a long time. But building and repairing things had always been common ground.

When the saw was put away for the night, Lukas popped the second bottle and held it out. Mark took it back to the worktable, going over the plans. He seemed restless, bothered by something.

Ordinarily, Lukas might have left it to Beryl to suss out what concerned him. But he was tired of playing second. Plus Mark was unfailingly prag-matic. Whatever was bothering him wouldn't be supernatural in nature and certainly not as dangerous as any trouble Beryl would wander into. Lukas could handle it.

"When are you installing these?" Mark asked at the same time Lukas said, "I heard you got a big job."

Lukas drank instead of answering.

"Big," Mark said, "for me. Anton gave it to me, you know. The whole thing. Says I'm ready."

"You've been ready—" Lukas dropped off at Mark's sour expression, changing direction. "Who's it for?"

"Guy named Dimitrov," Mark said, "Businessman, owns a few clubs?"

"Valentin Dimitrov." All Lukas's alarm bells went off at once. "*Anton* gave you this job?"

Mark shrugged, tension creeping into his shoulders. "That's just what they say. Valentin seems okay to me. He's got a guy working for him who definitely gives off a mafia vibe, but the job seems legit."

Lukas tried to keep his expression mild and interested but was probably failing. "What's the job?"

"VIP client rooms," Mark said, hesitating a little bit. He took a drink, considering. Then he grimaced. "A brothel, I'm pretty sure."

Lukas choked on his beer.

Mark winced. "You okay, Pop?"

"You cannot take this job."

Mark leaned back, arms folded over his chest. "What?"

"This is absurd." Lukas didn't think about his words, just let the protest come as his voice rose. "You can't work for this man, doing this *job*. Markus. What are you thinking?"

"I'm thinking it's a solid gig that can lead to more good gigs," Markus snapped. "This guy, Dimitrov, he rubs elbows with the right kind of people to get more work from."

"The mob?"

"Ah fuck, Dad." Markus threw up his free hand. "Anton is your friend. He wouldn't—"

"I'm beginning to wonder about that." He grunted.

He might not be able to help Beryl figure out the mystery disappearances, but this? This he could handle. He was going to find out what the hell Anton was thinking, getting his *son* involved with mobsters.

"What is going on down here?" Beryl appeared around the corner. "I sent you down to get your father forty-five minutes ago. Why are you shouting?"

"Sorry, Ma. Just got caught up," Mark said, shoving off the worktable with enough force to make it rock backward.

Beryl watched him stalk out of the room, then turned wide eyes on Lukas. She mouthed, "What was *that*?"

Lukas shook his head. She didn't need anything else to worry about, and he wasn't ready to talk about it. But when he was, his first words were going to be with Anton.

◆

As FAR AS Mark was concerned, dinner didn't improve much. It didn't help that it was just the three of them.

"Isela is where?" Mark asked again.

"She canceled last minute." His mother shrugged, passing the cornbread. "Something at work."

"Work," he scoffed. "She makes her own schedule."

"And sometimes things come up." Mom nodded.

"Ma, you asked us to start doing dinners together. You said it was important," Mark said.

"Maybe weekly is too much to ask," she said with a little shrug. "It is the quality, not the quantity, Markus."

"We live in the same building—most of us—and some in this apartment. Speaking of… Where is Chris anyway?"

"Christof is out," she said, unperturbed. "He's twenty."

"It's rude. Disrespectful."

They'd all agreed at equinox to make an effort. Tobias was back for good,

Barbara was part of the family, Isela had graduated and could make her own schedule. All their mother had asked for was *one* meal together a week. And yet they were all being selfish little assholes. He reached for his phone.

Dad spoke up. "Eat your mac and cheese."

"It's spaetzle, which you don't even like," Mark said.

Mom glared at him as his father flushed.

"I think I can get some American cheddar." Dad brightened and lifted his fork. "I met a guy on the cryptographer's forum. Well, we got into it with this upstart in Milan over whether the Beale papers are a hoax—"

Mom cleared her throat.

"Anyway, his family repatriated from Wisconsin after the war. They've got a farm down south, and they've been working on some artisan cheeses. Imagine that. Good old yellow cheddar is artisanal now."

Mark stabbed his spoon into the bowl. He felt twelve again, before his wolf, watching his siblings act like idiots while their poor, exhausted parents tried to create normalcy. He was going to talk to each one of the ungrateful little shits.

"Markus." His mother sighed, her laser gaze fixing on him. "It's none of *your* business. Let it go."

He looked up, accusing. "You let them get away with—"

"I was thinking we could borrow Barbara's Citroën and make a road trip out of it." Dad carried on as if Markus hadn't even spoken. "They invited us down to 'meet the cows.'"

"Sounds wonderful, my love." Mom squeezed his hand, smiling.

"Tobias and Bebe are schmoozing," Markus said, "Isela is fucking off with those bobbleheaded friends of hers. And Chris is—"

"Right here, brother," Christof breezed into the room, carrying a bakery box. "Hey, Mom, sorry I'm late. I brought dessert. You look gorgeous. And you made spaetzle. It smells amazing."

Mom softened instantly, accepting his kiss on the cheek like a queen and stroking the pale brown hair out of his face. "It's fine, sweetheart. Grab a bowl."

The tallest and fairest of the siblings, Chris was a genetic throwback to some distant Scandinavian ancestor. He bore the least resemblance to either of their parents and seemed to come into the family complete, his own bubble of easygoing self-reliance. Born after they'd immigrated and life had stabilized again, he'd grown up speaking Czech like a native, and had never known anything but this building and their lives here. Nothing bothered him, but he didn't seem to feel particularly passionate about anything either.

"Where the hell were you?" Markus snapped.

Mom scowled.

"Out." Chris shrugged, plopping into his seat next to their father. "Hey, Dad, did you see the Slav Epic is at the national museum? I was gonna go tomorrow, wanna?"

Dad nodded eagerly. "We could stop at the academy, see if Isela would get us in to see the Mayor's Hall. Mucha's best work."

"It's the dancing ring now." Chris grimaced. "Nobody gets up there but dancers."

"We'll talk to your sister. She and the headmaster are close." Dad reassured him.

Mark growled. "Dinner started a half hour ago—"

"When does the job start?" Their mother cut him off. "Markus? Your job. When are you starting?"

"He's not taking it," Dad said firmly.

"What job?" Chris asked.

Mark glared at them all. "Chris, you're with me. I'm gonna need some hands, and I'm guessing you need a paycheck again?"

Chris reddened. "The barber-apprentice gig isn't working out. But hey, I got us covered at least—I could clean you up this weekend, save you some cash."

"You need figure your shit out." Mark pointed a fork at him. "At least pay these guys some rent for fuck's sake."

Their father flushed hard, mouth tight. "I won't have you—either of you —anywhere near the mob."

Mark scoffed as their mother's eyes went to him, wide.

"Markus Vogel, what are you involved in?"

"This city is full of gossips," Mark said. "He's a businessman who has a few shady connections. Which of them doesn't? Anyway, Anton's done work for him before and he's—"

"In over his head," Dad roared. "And he's not taking you with him."

"Pop, I got this," Mark snapped.

His father had always treated him like an adult. It was too late to go back now.

"Lukas," Mom began, rallying to his side, "I'm sure Markus knows what he's doing."

"Does he?" He turned to her. "Do *you*? Investigating disappearing creatures. What if whoever is behind it finds out?"

Mark froze. "What's going on, Ma?"

Chris looked up from shoveling spaetzle into his mouth like it was running off his plate. "What did you find out at the Specials Office?"

"*You* went to the Office of Special Citizen Concerns?" Mark's stomach dropped out from beneath him.

The necromancer's public-facing department handled reports of the supernatural. It managed everything from dispatching minor necromancers for unrested-dead sightings to following up on supernaturals that had revealed themselves in some way. The latter often ended up never heard from again.

Everyone knew the penalty for revealing themselves to humans was death.

"I needed to report the villa in Jevany," she said, not quite looking at him.

"Mom." Markus took a long breath. "If you had been detected…"

"She was careful." Chris went on shoveling, looking between Mark and their father. His jaw slowed and he swallowed a mouthful. "Right, Ma?"

"You knew about this?" Mark and Lukas spoke at once, English and German, just for good measure.

"I'm obeying the codes," she said. "I didn't bewitch myself—not so much as a minor glamour. The form was anonymous."

Mark speared his father, then his brother, with accusation in the long silence.

Mom pushed her fork around her plate without looking at any of them before saying, "I spoke to an information officer."

"Beryl." Lukas sighed.

"Just asked if there was an official channel for reporting missing creatures." Her voice wavered when she spoke again. "She laughed in my face. 'Who would miss them?' was what she said to me."

Chris growled. "She didn't."

"No one cares, Lukas." Mom wiped her cheek, clearing her throat. "What if it were one of the boys?"

Chris threw himself into the seat beside her and wrapped an arm around her shoulders. "You're doing the right thing."

Dad sighed in resignation. He reached across the table and took her hand. "I understand why you're doing it. I just need you to be careful. If anything happened to you—"

Mark looked between them. Was his father out of his mind? How could he let her—?

"You'd go on." She smiled, her watery eyes twisting Mark's heart in his chest. "Barbara can do all the important things now."

"She needs you as much as we do," Dad said. "And you see, this is the kind of thing I can help with."

She frowned. "You think they would have given *you* more information?"

"Of course not." Dad pushed back from the table, patting his belly with a contented laugh. "Before I retired, I trained a kid, a brilliant hacker we caught trying to break into the national health system. I hired him. Then we got that contract for the necromancer's network and he wound up building the database and working their security for a while. He owes me a few favors. There's no way they don't keep records of *some* kind—we just must get to them. We can cross-reference, see if any were picked up by the necromancer's people or if they're truly missing."

"That's fucking brilliant, Papa." Chris grinned.

Their father had the nerve to look proud of himself. Mom squeezed his hand and said the most nonsensical thing Mark had ever heard. "Good thinking, Mary Jane."

Their father laughed and brought her knuckles to his lips. "Together."

Mark slammed his fork down. This was the kind of shit that made him feel like he couldn't turn his back on them for five minutes. Not only did his mother not have the good sense to keep her head down, she walked right into the worst possible place for people like them. And his brother and father wanted to help her. It was only a matter of time before things got out of control.

"This is insane," Mark said. "All of you. Mom. You can't—"

"Be careful, Markus, with what you say next." She met his eyes, and the crackle of energy left the faintest scent of electricity in the air between them.

He rose from his seat and collected his plate. "I'm taking the job. Chris, we start on Monday."

# CHAPTER FOURTEEN

EVIE WAITED ALMOST an entire week before going down to the basement to see what all the fuss was about. She'd expected Anton with his apologetic smile and wary eyes but gossip flowed behind the scenes at the club like liquor at the bar, and by Thursday the rumors of the new foreman reached her desk on the third floor.

The men Valentin had assigned to help clear the basement in preparation for work to begin complained about how hands-on he was. Not hands-on enough according to the girls, who found the new crew—foreman included —immune to their attempts at seduction.

*Can't please everyone.* Evie'd laughed when her quick run-in with one of the dancers backstage had brought that last piece of news.

She needed to check in with the dancers anyway—she might as well get a look for herself.

When she arrived at the club on Friday, the barbacks were prepping for the lunch crowd. It was still too early for the air-conditioning, and all the young men were sweating in the T-shirts that would be replaced with button-downs right before the doors opened. She hurried past them on her way to the service elevator, keeping her gaze low to avoid the death masks that appeared and vanished over their living faces like flickers of light over water.

Evie was used to the club's subterranean level being full of crap: old props and broken equipment from the club floor or the restaurant framing a rectangular taped off square of floor for the dancers. But the corner designated as a rehearsal stage looked even smaller in the nearly empty room. The back freight doors were open, the noise of trucks being loaded and orders shouted in multiple languages a distant din from the other side.

She headed for the stage.

Thin strains of music greeted her, the makeshift seating area composed of a few battered tables and chairs drawn around a stage, marked off in tape on the wood floor. The dancers lounged, waiting their turn.

Unlike some of the other clubs in town, Little Blossoms maintained an air of respectability due in part to the elaborately choreographed routines. The performers may have left the stage wearing less than they did entering, but their routines were always choreographed to highlight the strength, beauty, and flexibility of dance. It kept everyone happy.

At this hour, most wore leggings and sweatshirts. But a few had put more effort into their rehearsal wear. She saw more low-cut shirts and postage-stamp shorts over tights or leg warmers than usual. Must be part of the effort to catch the eye of one of Anton's new guys. Some stretched or marked routines, but the bulk collected at the discarded tables and chairs, passing cigarettes and filling the air with hushed gossip.

Laureline, the head of show, commanded the area between seats and stage. With her fair skin under layers of even paler stage makeup, she looked almost spirit-like. Until she tapped her hawk's-head cane on the stone floor, her thin frame hunched at the shoulders, and roared a few commands.

"*Boudou!*" Laureline barked and her words continued a steady, songlike stream of praise and correction. "More power, more sensuualiteee."

Evie had learned the hard way never to distract Madame while she picked at choreography until it was flawless. Near the back, a veteran dancer who went by Sweet Pea occupied a lopsided café table with an extra chair.

The club was known for the variety of performers—a scent for every nose —each named for a particular blossom. It was safer to think of them by their stage names. A good reminder not to make friends.

Evie slid into the seat and the other woman beamed at her, blowing her a kiss. "Welcome back, Evie. Vacation good?"

"In a manner of speaking," Evie murmured, smiling.

Violet had the stage, her dark skin glowing even under the improvised stage lighting as she practiced peeling away the multicolored handkerchiefs that served as stand-ins for her costume's layers of aubergine and gold. She let her petals flutter to the floor as she slunk and spun between them.

"Gar, she's amazing." Peony leaned over from the neighboring table to whisper in awe, staring at the stage. Peony's wild curls had been cut to emphasize the petallike curves, but her mouth rested in a constant down-turn. "You can't even tell she's knocked up."

"Hush." Sweet Pea was older than she looked, rose and cream cheeks accented with blush these days, but her blue eyes were bright and doll-like, and her ample curves kept her popularity high.

"I heard he proposed." Peony's lowered voice was her only concession to the demand. "Violet turned him down."

"Proposed or *proposed*?" Sweet Pea frowned.

Peony sniffed. "You guess."

The other women within earshot nodded at the distinction. Proposals came in two forms: romantics and pragmatics. The first were the fools who envisioned themselves saviors for all their bent knees, and the others offered security in exchange for exclusive access.

Evie had never been one of the dancers, but she understood what it was to have your life controlled by a man who could always claim to have your best interests at heart as he built a cage around you. And whatever else she would have said about Valentin's operations, enough top-performing Blossoms had retired into a tidy but respectable fortune for Evie to know that a well-managed career was its own escape plan.

"A proposal's not part of her *plan*." Sunflower joined the conversation seamlessly.

Just when Evie had thought the stage names could get a bit ridiculous, she'd met a woman who embodied hers so perfectly that Evie was forced to reconsider. With golden hair and long limbs, when Sunflower smiled, the six-foot-tall Dane looked like she'd been born to play her namesake.

Sunflower slid onto Sweet Pea's lap, curling her legs around the thicker woman's calf and draping her arms over her shoulders. Sweet Pea circled her waist. They folded into each other, a perfect bouquet.

Sunflower sighed in affectionate frustration. "That woman has the perfect package."

"Perfect for some is an airless room for others," Evie said. Enough gossip. Of all the dancers, it was Violet she thought she understood the best. It was as close to friendship as she was going to get.

Sunflower's pale brows rose. "Who scarred your heart, Miss Evelia Acaz?"

Evie's heart clenched at the sound of her mother's surname. She'd taken it when she arrived in Prague. When she disappeared again, the trail to Evelia Acaz would end in rubble thousands of miles away.

Evie pitched her own darker brows in answer. "I never give anyone that chance."

"Heart of ice, our Evie." Sweet Pea laughed. "Fortress of one."

"What about romance?" Sunflower seemed to be personally offended and not a little bit sad.

Evie winked. "I've got plans to see through, and none of them involve romance."

They all watched Violet in silence.

Peony scratched her nail lightly on the back of her chair, canting her head to look at Evie from the corner of one eye. "And things with Valentin are going well?"

Evie had enough practice hiding her reaction to the repulsive and shocking. She'd grown good at ignoring flickers of Peony's bloated face, geriatric Sunflower's deep wrinkles. Still, she could not lie to them. She respected them too much for that.

"Nothing lasts forever, particularly with a man like Valentin Dimitrov," she said lightly.

"Heart of ice," Sweet Pea repeated firmly.

"Wise," Peony said, considering her.

"Madame is in a terrific mood today," Evie noted as Laureline hobbled to the stage, thrusting her cane around her as she gesticulated her corrections. She'd slipped entirely into French to do it.

"You know how she abhors distraction," Iris said from another table, rolling her eyes. Built like the stalk of her namesake, with elegant cheekbones and large dark eyes, she played waif and seductress with equal skill.

"Distraction." Sunflower thrust her slim, pointy chin in the direction of the open basement doors. "I like having the fresh air for once."

Evie spared a glance toward the freight doors. The voices had risen in a creole of English, Russian, and Czech.

Laureline summoned Peony to the makeshift stage.

Her rehearsal complete, Violet collected her things. Weaving her way through the tables, she grinned when she saw Evie. British born, the Ghanaian dancer's accent was a musical seduction of its own. "Welcome home."

"I wouldn't say *that*." Evie laughed ruefully. She felt herself a bit under Violet's sway every time they were close.

"Good to have you back then." They bussed cheeks.

"Good to be back," Evie said and meant it. Not even the occasional petty squabble could disrupt the easy acceptance and camaraderie she'd found among these women. She'd miss them no matter what.

"You see we have new entertainment," Violet said, glancing over at the men.

From the back of the room, something crashed, followed by a chorus of shouting men. The startled dancers jumped. Peony missed a step and crashed to the floor, holding her knee. A former nurse, Sunflower leaped into action.

Madame Laureline's mouth set into an even tighter line. She let loose a stream of curses.

"Always something around here." Violet's eyes widened as she grinned.

Evie sighed and rose. "Madame, if I may."

"If you *would*," the aged dancer demanded with the dignity of a queen.

Evie strode across the floor, steeling herself to make eye contact without flinching. She wondered briefly why Anton sent another foreman—he usually supervised all the work himself. In any case, she always handled the invoices and supply orders. She was going to have to work with the new guy anyway.

She was grateful she'd spent extra time on her glamour this morning. It highlighted her cheekbones and lightened her hair to a honeyed gold, made her eyes larger and more innocent, though she could not have made them blue if she bled for it.

Valentin said she should dress sexier, more revealing. Evie compromised —the high-necked blouse might have gone to her wrists, but it was made of a silk so fine it settled over her breasts like liquid tissue paper. Her pencil skirt ended just below the knee, but Tal tailored it to fit like a second skin, working her curves for all they were worth. The shock of red stilettos drew attention to her legs, plumping her calves.

Sweet Pea loosed a low wolf whistle in her wake; the others giggled.

Evie shot her middle finger at them behind her back. She approached the circle of men, glaring down at the mess of an old dressing table. Broken glass and cracked wood shattered everywhere. She recognized Valentin's men. The youngest, the cousin or younger brother of a relation of Valentin's, looked up at her approach. Solidly built but unable to read, his job prospects were limited. But he was unflaggingly kind to the girls who worked in the club and always referred to her respectfully as *Slecna Evie*, something the others wasted no time teasing him about. He did it anyway.

She made the mistake of meeting his smile, and her vision of his battered, swollen face was eclipsed by the shy joy of that expression. The small gold cross—a gift from his mother—aligned in her vision and in the gap formed by his ill-fitting collared shirt. She'd long ago given up trying to save people from their fates, but no amount of will or practice could stop the visions from appearing.

She froze the smile on her face and scanned the rest. The usual suspects, useless for doing much besides heavy lifting and cleanup.

Three of the men were new. Those must be Anton's. A weathered Czech man, a young one—gaping like a fish—and one man her mind simply refused to see for long moment.

Mark.

Then shock and alarm jangled through her like a tray of dropped plates.

The familiar low tones of his voice in reply to something one of his crew said shifted the world on its axis in some critical, unseen way. That voice existed only in forests on warm summer afternoons, breathing words of appreciation into her ear as he moved inside her. It didn't belong in this place, among these people.He did not belong here.

*Think, Evie girl.* She prayed her glamour was enough to throw him off and knew it wouldn't be. If he recognized her now, it would raise questions, bring scrutiny she couldn't afford.

It was too late to turn around—they were all looking at her now.

When she could no longer avoid him, she plastered on a cruel, assessing stare, daring him to recognize her. *Remind him he dumped you.*

In a sky-blue collared shirt and gray work pants, his copper eyes lit as his gaze passed over her face. The starlight beneath his skin was distant now, mostly hints and shadows that flattered his deep brown skin. He was so beautiful it hurt to look at him.

He began to smile. "Ev—"

"Is all this racket necessary?" She demanded.

Valentin's men looked suitably chagrined, or at least avoided her glare.

Mark stared. She knew he registered everything: her battered hands, the glamour, the scar on her face. His smile faltered.

The old Czech guy on his crew mistook Mark's staring for ogling and cleared his throat. "Sorry, Miss—"

Mark held up a hand, and the older man went quiet, rubbing his palm over his face.

Mark began again. "Miss—"

"Are you the new foreman?"

After a long pause, he nodded. "And you are?"

"May I have a word?" She needed to get him away from the others, needed to run this shock out of their systems and buy time to figure out how to get him the hell out of here.

❧

"You can't be here."

Mark looked up at Evie's low hiss. He'd spent the short walk trying to make sense of what his forest witch was doing here and why she looked like... like she'd been dipped in Barbie paint. All while he fought the wolf to a standstill.

Wolfing out on a jobsite in front of a dozen people was a definite no-no. One the wolf had never questioned until now. For a second or two he was sure he was losing it because the wolf was freaking out in his chest, and when Mark looked at Evie, he could still see the scar that bisected her brow and ran to her jawline, the darker hair beneath the overlay that made her skin and hair even and bright. It wasn't *just* makeup.

The scent of magic coming off her was stronger than he remembered. She wore some kind of illusion on her skin like a mask. He didn't know more about it than it was possible. And more than anything, he wanted to bury his nose in the soft place under her ear and breathe her in.

It had been over between them for weeks. He shouldn't still want her this much.

The part of him that wanted to kiss her battled the one that saw this job as the gateway to his future. By the time they stopped in the no-man's-land between the two groups, he still hadn't figured out how to play this.

She clearly didn't want anyone to find out they knew each other. Her eyes were the same, and he focused on them. Today they seemed a creamier version of the chocolate he remembered, larger in her foxlike face. When they fixed on him, heat crept up the back of his neck.

"What are you doing here?" she repeated, a demand.

"My job," Mark said, suddenly irate. How was this his fault?

The loss of Evie's gaze seemed to make the air cool again as she took in the basement around them.

The crews—all of them—were busy, or at least attempting to appear that way. Across the room, the old woman spared no effort in her determination to carry on rehearsals. She pounded the floor with her cane. His guys—Russians included—kept sneaking not-so-subtle glances at the curvaceous, spiky-haired dancer currently shimmying around the stage. It was impossible to tell which group was more distracted by the other.

"I'm *trying* to do my job," Mark admitted reluctantly. "What are *you* doing here?"

"I work here," she said, sounding so miserable he forgot his anger.

"Dancer?" But she wasn't dressed like she was rehearsing with the others. She hadn't gotten that outfit off a rack either.

"I manage the office." Her words stopped abruptly like there was something else she wanted to say but couldn't. He knew the feeling. "You work for Anton."

"Yeah, but this job is mine," he said. "I negotiated the contract; I'm the boss."

Her brows drew together in alarm. "You have to find a reason to quit. Whatever he's paying you, it's not worth it."

"I can guarantee you it is," Mark snapped. He finally had a chance to build something of his own, and it seemed like everyone was so damn against him taking control of his future.

He gave her a good head-to-toe sweep with his glare. The hair, the shoes, the dress, the artfully applied makeup, the nails. Part might have been glamour, but the rest was a well-funded woman. That was not on a secretary's salary. When he'd passed the desk in the office—her desk—Nikolai said she was on vacation. What kind of arrangement did she have that she vacationed at her boss's summer villa? Did the white BMW belong to Nikolai or Valentin?

He bit his tongue to keep from asking. It wasn't his business. Breaking it off had been the right thing to do—this only confirmed it. Except he had a wolf in his throat, threatening to howl its fool head off, and his heart was pounding.

They had to settle this. He couldn't risk this job. No matter how much he wanted— What? They weren't anything to each other anymore. It didn't matter what he wanted.

He lowered his voice. "I need this job. We had a... thing. But it's over, and when I'm done, you never have to see me again. I won't step in whatever you have going for yourself. I promise."

A subtle rose flushed her cheeks and above the collar of her blouse. He hated his memory for reminding him that she flushed to the tops of her nipples.

"I'm not judging," he murmured. "I'm here for the money, same as you."

Unhappiness settled in the corners of her mouth, her large eyes shining. "It's not what it looks like, Markus."

He took a breath, wiping a hand over his face. The plea in her voice rattled him. What did she want from him? "I just want to do the job. Let's just pretend Jevany didn't happen."

He hated himself for saying the words out loud. More so when her face pinched tight and her chin wobbled. He fought the urge to reach out to her.

"I'm sorry about all the racket," he said, setting his shoulders with a deep breath. "I'm catching the looks from your battle-ax. But we've got to get this space cleared out so we can start demo."

"This is their rehearsal space."

"They can't keep rehearsing down here once the real work gets started. It's noisy and dangerous—and I need my guys focused on the work. I'll talk to Nikolai—"

As if summoned, the man appeared at the far end of the room by the elevator doors. He scanned the room before his eyes settled on them.

By the time he reached them, Mark felt almost under control.

"Everything going well?" Nikolai asked, his shoulder too close to Evie for Mark's comfort. His wolf started up again, baying like a chained hound.

"It would be easier without the distraction," Mark said, brows up as he canted his gaze to the makeshift stage.

Nikolai glowered, but Evie spoke first. "I'll take care of it."

His eyes flickered over her, searching in that inscrutable way. Then he smiled—a soft, predatory thing. "Of course you will."

A sudden, irrational jealousy flared in Mark as he watched this slimeball fawn over her. And then he registered the tension in Evie's neck.

Who was she truly?

Nikolai's dark eyes flicked to him suddenly, and the small hairs rose on Mark's neck. Mark's suspicion that Nikolai was somehow sensitive to supernaturals grew.

"If that's it," Mark said, excusing himself. "I should get back to it. Miss—"

"Acaz." Her chin lifted in challenge.

"Acaz." The shape of her name in his mouth felt right. He forced himself to look at the man who was, for all intents and purposes, his client. "Sir."

"You must call me Nikolai, Markus." The smile was too wide. "I insist."

"I'll work on it," Mark said.

He walked away, certain Nikolai's dark eyes never left him. It was time to get some backup.

◆

"Good day, Evelia," Nikolai said, his voice a dark syrup of warning as he escorted her to the elevator. "We expected you earlier."

Alarm stiffened Evie's shoulders. That was new. It wasn't a bookkeeping day. There was no reason Nikolai should mark her coming and going. A trickle of unease bumped along her spine.

"I had an appointment, Kolya." She pouted, flashing freshly glamoured hands. "For a manicure."

She'd done them the night before herself. She was proud of how good she'd gotten with the glamour. It was impossible to tell they were an illusion.

"And then I stopped to check in on the girls," she went on innocently. "They can't stay down here in all this chaos. I was thinking we could move them to the French garden. It's so dated they aren't renting it for banquets until Karla decides on the decor."

Valentin's wife liked to oversee the decor of all the clubs. Evie had met her only once—a woman as unforgiving as a Russian winter and twice as beautiful. They had four daughters, to Valentin's dismay, but her family's money was heavily tied into his business, so she inserted herself wherever she saw fit.

Evie prattled on about relocating the dancers, letting her mind churn over possible reasons Nikolai might be extra alert to her comings and goings. Since she always managed the finances for any construction work, it shouldn't have been a surprise that she talked to the new foreman.

Except the new foreman wasn't Anton.

By the time they reached the upstairs office, she still hadn't come up with anything else. She dumped her purse on her desk and drew out a compact to touch up her deep carmine lipstick.

"Valentin doesn't like to be kept waiting." Nikolai stood at the edge of her desk, watching.

She focused on her reflection.

"Evelia, Kolya." Valentin summoned them to his office.

She snapped the compact shut and quirked her mouth in a pouty grin. "Duty calls."

In his suite, Valentin prepared to leave for afternoon appointments. "Evie, at last. What do you think of our new foreman?"

She made a show of confusion and shrugged. "If Anton recommended him..."

She didn't like the way Nikolai watched Mark. Or that they'd brought a stranger in at all.

Anton knew what he had gotten into when he'd come to Valentin so many years ago, begging for help. She might not have understood entirely, but she'd learned to swim among sharks, knowing the deeper she got, the more difficult it would be to surface again.

Mark didn't stand a chance.

"Anton owes us too much to screw this up," Nikolai said.

Valentin's striking blue eyes settled on her again. The three bullet holes of his death mask were still there. Did they seem brighter? *Focus on his words, Evie.*

"You will watch him, my dove." Valentin's orders always came out like a plea, a command wrapped in velvet. It made her skin crawl. "He seems like the kind who will be honest. But if he tries to take advantage—"

"I will alert Nikolai." Evie nodded firmly, relief flooding her. Perhaps this was all Nikolai meant by expecting her—Valentin wanted to speak to her before he headed out for the afternoon.

Valentin exhaled sharply, and she wondered if she'd overstepped by cutting him off.

He opened the top drawer of the desk. She knew the contents of that drawer, the small but effective pistol he always kept close.

The skin between her shoulder blades tightened and her stomach dropped. *This is it. He knows.*

Somehow they'd figured out she was going to run. Stupid mistake.

Hadn't Tal always warned her she had less time than she thought? Her brain cycled uselessly, counting the books on the wall and the number of flowers in the field of the painting behind his desk.

"I think you enjoy the prospect of sending men to their deaths," he said. The reminder of the last time she caught someone skimming off his business hovered between the three of them. "Wouldn't you say, Kolya?"

Behind her, Nikolai shifted, but her focus had tunneled to Valentin's hand reaching into that drawer. She would have liked to think she would be coming up with a plan, some way to spare herself one more time, but all she had was this voiceless panic and her numbers.

"I supposed I should count my lucky stars I have you on my side." He withdrew an envelope.

She blinked hard and tried not to wobble on unsteady knees.

Oblivious, Valentin closed the distance between them, encroaching on her personal space so deeply she shivered to resist the urge to move away. "I understand your stay in Jevany was no small inconvenience to you."

Nikolai cleared his throat.

"It may not have been as bad as all that." Evie restored her pout, and his smile grew. "Maybe next year a little warning."

He wagged the envelope. "A bonus. Fine work."

Evie matched Valentin's smile, clapping her hands. "Oh good—I've got a new wardrobe coming and my tailoring bill is due."

"Again?" Nikolai raised a brow.

"Quiet," Valentin snapped at him before bathing Evie in his benign smile. "Good girl. We have a game to play, do we not? And people seeing you in the same clothes gives me a bad reputation."

As her fingers closed on the stack of money within, the amount appeared in her mind's eye. She shut the thought down. She hadn't counted it yet. She refused to let her notion creep into her skill with numbers. "Thank you, Mr. Dimitrov."

Valentin sighed as if even her voice exhausted him. "You are expected to address me informally. Why on the gods' unholy earth can you not?"

"In public," she murmured before she could bite her tongue.

He had already turned away, shrugging on his suit jacket. "You do as you are supposed to, I know. But after all this time." He spread his hands, taking in his second. "Kolya, you'd think..."

Nikolai shrugged, the edge of his gaze on her heavy with censure though he replied to their boss. "Our Evie has been a peculiar one always. But the books are tighter than ever. Worth putting up with a bit of peculiarity, don't you think?"

"And with the new venture..." Valentin hummed and his nostrils flared when he returned his attention to Evie. "Our little ruse has served us well the past two years—be careful no one sees through it, no?"

"Da, Valyusha." Evie mumbled the endearment distractedly. *The new business. She was certain it had something to do with the strange entries in the ledger.*

"Much better." He beamed. "Now, Kolya, we have a meeting with the minister of transport. I need to encourage him to stop delaying our shipments."

"The car was delivered this morning," Nikolai said.

"That should sweeten the pot." Valentin's smile grew to almost comic proportions. He scanned the office. "Evie, straighten up in here before you go, would you?"

This time her endearment had a bit more enthusiasm behind it. It was rare these days to have Valentin and Nikolai out of the office at the same time.

When they were gone, she moved around the room, gathering papers and nudging the furniture. Sometimes it took Valentin longer than expected to make it out the door. Everyone wanted his ear. It would do her no good to get caught now. She schooled herself to patience and found the cleaning supplies in the main office closet. She even dusted.

After fifteen minutes ticked by in her head, she hurried to the safe hidden behind a set of false books—Dostoyevsky. Her first attempt at the code failed.

Valentin must have been taking Nikolai's advice for once. On the birthday of his second daughter, the lock slipped open. She pitied Nikolai. He really was the brains of the operation.

That just made him the more dangerous of the two.

She searched the contents, looking for anything that might shed light on Valentin's new pursuit. She flipped through the ledger and the stacks of bills and papers. Nothing. Frustrated, she replaced everything as she'd found it and locked the safe.

She had half hoped it would be that easy. The clock was ticking. Having Mark here made everything feel more dangerous. Her time was coming. She needed to run.

No one knew the inside of a business like the hands that kept the books, and even more so one as slippery as Valentin's. She knew exactly how much of the income came from what sources. He or Nikolai always gave her notice when there would be something new for her to handle creatively. They were all things that would threaten his work but not endanger him.

Except this time. And if he was doing something illegal enough to hide even from her, she'd have something solid to hold over him, something that could guarantee her freedom. She just needed to find it.

# CHAPTER FIFTEEN

THEY'D BEEN HAULING crap out of that stupid basement all week. Demo yet again. At least this time he could see beyond it. Every time he entered that cavernous underground space, he could see the image of what it would be now. What he would build.

Only now he could see her there too, emerging from the pack of dancers like a Valkyrie in a pencil skirt and sky-high heels. On her, they looked like armor, completing the image that started in whatever altered her appearance. He could see beneath that too.

He'd lied to her face. He could no sooner forget Jevany than his own name. Putting her out of his mind would have been for the best. It was also impossible. He wanted to know why she was there and hiding beneath all that illusion. Did Valentin or Nikolai know what she was?

That night he wolfed out in the park, an attempt to settle the wolf. The entire time, the wolf kept turning his attention north toward the club.

*She said no, Big Guy. We back off.*

The wolf took its frustration out on a couple of city rats, but Mark refused to eat them. He had to draw the line somewhere.

Mark resolved to strengthen whatever charm kept him from being detected. He just needed to get his job done. Evie knew what she was and what she was doing there. It wasn't his problem to solve. He could walk away.

Asking his mother for help was out of the question. After the last family dinner, they'd tacitly agreed not to talk about any activities the other disapproved of—his job, her investigation. It led to a lot more silence than he was used to. But he certainly couldn't go in now, asking to have his charm boosted because he thought his creepy client might be on to his dual nature.

That left him with one option.

Climbing the stairs to his apartment, he hesitated on the landing and stared at the door opposite his. Neither Tobias nor Barbara would probably take to having Mark dragging them from the marital bed before dawn.

One night not long after they'd moved in, he'd passed by their door on his way to his own flat to the sound of raised voices. He'd paused, falling into the wolf senses out of an instinct for trouble. He wasn't sure who he'd be protecting—Tobias would rather chew off his own arm than hurt Barbara, and Barbara was five foot two of pure powder behind a long, patient fuse. It took Mark a minute to determine they were arguing about a book and that she was winning.

The argument ended with her shriek of laughter, the squeal of furniture, and a set of yipping growls that were just human enough to make Mark retreat into his own flat and turn up the television for the fourth time in five days. Who knew two academics could be so damn horny? When did they sleep?

Newlyweds. Having wolf-sharp ears came with downsides.

He'd wait for a reasonable hour, preferably when Tobias was gone so he wouldn't have to deal with his too-smart little brother asking questions. His business was with the witch anyway.

Inside, he showered, sat down at the drafting table and his architectural drawings, and grabbed a pencil.

Valentin had insisted the plans remain in the building and that Mark and his crew remain silent about the job's specifics. Competitors, he'd said in explanation and shrugged. Valentin promised glowing recommendations and future work. Mark had agreed. It wasn't like he would put building a brothel for Prague's largest gentleman's club on his website. Most of the work he'd be hoping to get happened by referral.

But he liked having a set of drawings of his own, so he'd simply re-created them. He had a good memory, and it helped that he could visualize a project. He cleaned up his copy, fixing lines and making corrections after a week spent working in the space. He kept a notepad nearby, adding changes he thought would suit.

When the knock on the door called his attention back, dawn had come and gone. He opened the door to see his bland middle brother in his standard three-piece suit.

"You forgot dinner last night," Tobias announced, holding out a foil-wrapped plate. "Bebe sent you leftovers."

"Ah fuck," Mark muttered. They'd invited him to join them. "I'm sorry."

"More for me." Tobias handed off his burden and needlessly adjusted his glasses. "You went for a run."

Of course Tobias would know he'd wolfed out.

In the past, Mark always knew when his brother *hadn't* for too long. Something in the air around him seemed tense, strained. Their mother would say it was aura or some shit. Mark knew Tobias just needed to let his wolf run.

"You headed to work?"

"New exhibition opening next week." Tobias was excessively cheerful to be headed into a library on what promised to be a sweltering day. "Everything okay?"

"Big job. Crashed hard. I'll make it up to you guys."

"You'd better. Bebe finally heard back from her dad's family. She has two great-aunts. They sent her family recipes." His expression softened, warm with excitement and a tenderness that was as strange as this new contentment. Love. "It's like she's always known them, and after her dad... did what he did... Well, it's like getting a piece of her family back. Anyway... She's trying everything out. I never thought I'd say it, but—"

"Careful, Professor Vogel," a female voice called from behind him. Barbara stepped out onto the landing in her sunny yellow robe, curls escaping a matching scarf.

She waved at Mark. "Morning, Jerk."

"Hey, Baby Witch."

"Forgot something?" She lifted a familiar travel mug.

Tobias bounded across the distance with a smile and a guilty shrug, snagging it. "Thanks, Dr. Svobodová."

She made that little squeaky noise of surprise and delight when he swept her up for a kiss.

It was bad enough that centuries-old walls were barely a match for all the matrimonial bliss in that apartment. Now he had to watch all *this* before coffee.

"I only meant there's just so much food even I can't eat it all," Tobias said when he let her go. He leaned in for one final kiss. "Gotta get my tram."

She made some sort of unnecessary adjustment to his tie. Repeat.

This could go on all morning.

"Go," she purred at last.

Tobias trotted down the stairs, whistling like the lovestruck fool he was.

Markus met his sister-in-law's eyes and lifted the plate. "Thanks."

"It *is* a lot of food." She waved off his gratitude and turned to go, yawning.

"Hey, can I talk to you about something?" he said impulsively, lowering his voice with a glance up the stairwell. His parents' flat occupied the entire top floor of the building, and some witches also had pretty sharp ears. "Something witchy."

Her gaze shuttered, but she went completely alert. "Sure. I think Toby left some coffee. Come in?"

He nodded, grabbing his key and shutting his door.

"Don't you dare try to seduce my wife," Tobias shouted cheerily up the stairs.

"Go to work!" Mark and Barbara called in unison.

Barbara rolled her eyes, grinning like the lovestruck fool *she* was.

He'd only been in their apartment a handful of times since he and Chris had put in the bookshelves that were their wedding present from the family. Almost two years later, he was struck by how claustrophobic it felt, stuffed to the gills with books and papers and nooks and crannies for reading both. The terrible cat snarling at him from its perch on the windowsill didn't help the feeling that he was closed in. Plus the scent of Tobias's wolf was everywhere.

But for all that, it felt like a home.

She poured him the last cup of coffee from the french press and collected her tea in the kitchen. He scented jasmine and orange peel and a bit of bergamot, or maybe that was just her.

She smiled, a bit more shyly than he was used to seeing. "Have a seat."

The compact farm table he'd helped Tobias haul across town from her apartment sat by the window overlooking the river. It was currently covered in a massive book, a notepad full of her neat little script, odds and ends, and a sticky note or two.

"Just put all that stuff over"—she scanned the room before shrugging helplessly—"wherever you find a spot."

"Witchy stuff?" He eyed the book warily. He respected the practice too much to charge into a witch's home and start touching things at random. He might inadvertently curse himself or give himself a rash.

"It's a dictionary, Jerk." She rolled her eyes, and then excitement brightened her features. "A first edition Samuel Johnson to be exact. Though your brother thinks it's a misprint or a fake. I'm going to prove that big know-it-all wrong if I have to summon Johnson from the—" His disinterest must have shown because she sighed. "Never mind, it's just not… witchy stuff, as you so elegantly put it."

He obediently cleared the table. They sat. Barbara watched him over the rim of her cup.

He struggled to get comfortable in the little metal café chair and passed his palms over his thighs. He cleared his throat. Smiled.

She looked out over the river, sipping her tea.

He ran a hand over his hair and contemplated his cup.

"No offense, but I have to go into the shop in about"—she glanced at the clock in the kitchen—"three hours. So if you could..." She waved a hand in a move-along gesture.

He growled.

"That bad, huh?" Her brows rose. "Must be a girl."

He froze.

Barbara had been working with their mother for a little while, but he hadn't expected so much progress so soon.

"Process of elimination." She laughed. "You have a problem that requires a witch and you don't want to talk to Beryl, so you came to me even though I've got a quarter of the experience and an eighth of the expertise. You worried about getting Beryl's hopes up?"

Mark laughed and rubbed his palm over his face. *Witches.* "Are you sure?"

She tilted her head in question.

"That you don't read minds."

"Drink your coffee before it gets cold," she said primly, tugging her lips down on an answering smile. Mark eyed the cup. "I never put anything in the coffee."

"Not even something for Toby?" He lifted his index finger in slow motion. "To, you know, keep things moving."

"You are a scurrilous wretch. You know that, Markus Vogel?" She glared at him. "What do you *want*?"

At least she wasn't shy anymore. He had no idea what it said about him that he liked her better when she was fierce and a little irritated with him. It was her home after all, and he had come into it for a favor. She should learn to be more witchy and a little less agreeable.

"And there *is* a girl, but it's not what you think." He took a sip. It was still the best coffee he'd ever had. "It's not about her. She's just... there. Look, I need you to strengthen my charm."

"The charm your mom put on you boys to keep your natures hidden?" She shook her head, sitting back. "Dabbling in another witch's craft is fraught."

"You do Toby's."

"Your mom thought it would be better since we're..." She flushed a little.

"Shacked up in your book cave making babies." He lifted a brow.

"Careful, Jerk." Barbara narrowed her eyes. "It's not too late for me to hex that coffee."

Mark sighed, exasperated. He had no idea why he'd thought this would be easier than going to his mother. "Look, I don't want you to change it. Or alter it in any way. I just need... a little more of it is all."

His sister-in-law leaned back in her chair and watched him with a patient knowing beyond her years.

There it was—a glimpse of the witch she was becoming. Perfect. His timing couldn't have been better.

Her eyes narrowed at him. "Who do you have to hide from?"

"There's a guy on the jobsite. He's weird." He scraped his feet on the floor.

She started to take a sip of tea, but a wrinkle formed above her nose. The words she spoke ghosted over his ears, eluding him. Steam rose from her cup again.

He sneezed, and her gaze snapped back to him in wonder. "Are you allergic to magic?"

"It's just that it has a scent—this close it's like strong perfume," He shook his head, struggling with an explanation. "I've always been most sensitive to it, of all of us."

"That's a rare talent." She was looking at him like he were a bug she'd like to pin to a board.

"Yeah, well, seeing as I don't need to detect witches before they try to kill me—I hope—" He cleared his throat. "It's more of a nuisance than anything."

"You would have been a formidable enemy." She sipped her tea. "It's a good thing we're family."

Now she was just scaring him. Mark eyed her warily, and she watched back, but this time her thousand-yard stare was focused internally.

The noise of the tram and traffic on the street below increased with the morning commute. He wondered what was taking her so long. Was she still stuck on his sneezing thing?

"You mentioned having a shop to open."

Barbara held up a hand. "I'm thinking. Be quiet."

He drank to keep from smiling. *Witches.*

"Shifters like you and your brothers—able to change at will—are rare and incredibly special, but lots of people have a little bit of magic in their blood. Maybe the trick isn't to strengthen the charm but make it seem like whatever the charm is hiding is more pedestrian. Less... wolfy," she said, humor playing around the corners of her eyes.

"And you can do that?"

"It will only be temporary, and you're going to need me to recharge it, maybe once a week," she warned. "And it might make you a little dizzy."

Mark waved his hand. "It's only a couple of weeks till this job is done. It's just… we can't get Mom involved."

"And we should probably leave Toby out of it for now."

He tilted his head in question.

"How long do you think it will take Beryl to figure out something is up once Toby knows?"

*Point.*

He drained his cup. He'd had just about enough of witches for one day. Barbara walked him to the door. "I need a couple of days."

"I've got to bring those shelves by your shop. Wednesday?"

"That works. We can use the office."

In the doorway, he hesitated.

Belatedly, she seemed to realize he was still standing there and caught the door before it hit him. Her chin tilted in question.

"Why are you gonna help me?"

Intelligence sharpened her gaze, and she pressed her lips tight. "There's a girl involved—a *woman*. And if you're involved, it means you're going to try to help her. That's what you do."

"It's not like that. She's… It's none of my business."

She gazed into the hallway. "Goodbye, Jerk."

He took the hint. The door closed sharply behind him. Through it, he heard a heavy sigh and the slap of her hands against her thighs with the muttered protest: "Wolves."

# CHAPTER SIXTEEN

THE SOLID WEIGHT of worry rested under Lukas's breastbone like granite. He had known Anton for a long time. He'd felt lucky to have a friend who could help his own son where Lukas could not. Give him a trade and be a mentor to him. To fill a space that Lukas had somehow created.

The idea that Anton might have somehow, even inadvertently, endangered his firstborn son changed worry to something much sharper.

They met at the same little bar in Nusle where they'd been drinking beer for almost twenty years. Anton was already there when he arrived. And he flinched when Lukas patted his shoulder in greeting.

Anton grunted a little, and the smile that rose fled all too quickly.

The bartender drifted over with Lukas's regular pilsner. They caught up a bit over projects—the reconstruction of the cabin after a fire two years ago, one of Anton's latest bids on an apartment building development outside the city.

"And you've got my son working with the mob?" Lukas said, too lightly.

Anton choked on a swallow of beer. "I wouldn't say…"

Anton had begun to work with Valentin Dimitrov a decade ago. Small jobs at first, but increasingly as the money rolled in, Lukas had watched his friend become more anxious and unhappy. It seemed to make sense at first. He was busier, expanding the company that he'd saved from ruin. But it never eased. Then his wife left, taking their children back to her village north of Budapest on a visit to family that seemed permanent.

Now, sitting with his old friend, Lukas wondered that he hadn't noticed Anton was afraid before now. He had been for some time.

Anton's shoulders rose and fell. "Well, you know, it's just a one-off. He's trying to start his business up. The money is good."

Lukas nodded in agreement. He took another sip of beer.

Anton focused on his empty shot glass beside the liter. How long had he been here, drinking like this? Even in the old days, when they were both younger men, neither had been one for hard liquor.

"We've been friends for a long time," Lukas said finally. "I value that."

Anton's head bobbed, he opened his mouth, but Lukas held up a hand.

"And I am grateful for all that you've done for us," he said. "The building. Taking on Markus."

"He is like my own son." Anton beamed uncertainly. "I tell him this all the time."

Lukas's smile flattened out. "Then you know that a father must do his best by his son."

Anton bobbed his head anxiously. "I've tried to advise him, to guide him. Like we talked about."

"Good, that's good." Lukas showed his teeth with none of the warmth of a smile. "But *I* am his father."

He closed the distance, lowering his voice to a whisper. "And if anything happens to *my* son because of a bad association you have brought to him, I hold you personally responsible. And I will stop at nothing to undo you, brick by brick. If that's what it takes."

He rose, abandoning his beer with enough money to cover both their tabs. He walked out.

Much like Beryl, Markus was impossible to shift once he'd decided on a course. Worse, Lukas knew if he tried to, it would drive a wedge between them he'd never bridge. He might have to sit aside and watch, but he would be ready to make good on his threat if came to it.

# CHAPTER SEVENTEEN

BY THE TIME Evie left Tal's on Sunday with her newly altered wardrobe, a muggy golden dusk had settled over the city. She'd left two notebooks—the meticulous transfer of everything she could remember from Jevany—with Tal. None of it alone would be enough. But it was a start. She was determined to track down the source of the income. She'd already begun to formulate a plan for the week ahead—five more days.

She got off the tram early to make a quick stop at the grocery store. The skin between her shoulder blades prickled in warning until she stepped between the sliding glass doors. When she emerged, she was certain someone was watching her.

She should call Nikolai. She had strict instructions to use the direct line he'd given her. He would send the car for her and station a guard outside her apartment. But if that began, it would end only when she was relocated to one of Valentin's fancy new apartment buildings and under lock and key.

And curiously, awareness of something familiar tugged at her notion. She pushed on, sweating under the burden of garment bags and groceries as she weaved her way off the main street and into the neighborhood. A stolen glimpse of yellow and black in the shadows confirmed her suspicion.

Evie stopped at the edge of a narrow city greenbelt, shifting the groceries to relieve her overburdened arm.

She faced the shadows and the shape within. When the street was hers, she put steel in her voice. "I know you're there."

Only recognition stopped her from fleeing when the beast slid into a puddle of streetlight on the greenbelt. It was canine-shaped and the right size to be mistaken for a dog at a glance—albeit one carefully bred to monstrosity. It carried its head low, spine hunched and tail curled around its hind paws in an attempt to look less threatening. Still, one look into yellow eyes served as a reminder that once, humans were prey.

The ancient part of her hindbrain registered only mortal danger even as she recognized the wolf from the forest. Fur, the color of midnight between the stars, was unbroken, though she supposed it would cover a scar. When it lifted its muzzle to scent the air, the paler fur flashed at its throat.

Evie's fingers twitched with a phantom memory of touch. "I'd wondered what had become of you."

At the echo of conversation from the far end of the street, it slid back into darkness. No sign of a limp. The last of the stubborn insistence that it had been only a wild animal she'd saved that night vanished. This was no natural wolf.

From deep within the shadow, yellow eyes reflected the light from the streetlamp like twin licks of flame in the darkness. When they closed, it was as if the creature had never been there. A pair of chatty teen girls came down the sidewalk, a burst of laughter from one sharp enough to startle her.

Evie kept her eyes lowered and stepped aside to let them pass.

When they were gone, Evie stared into the shadow, trying to determine where it ended and animal begin. The creature's eyes opened and she jumped.

"You're terrifying, you know that?" Her laugh shook around the edges. "What are you doing here?"

Yellow eyes fixed on her, unblinking.

"I'm flattered that you've come all this way to see me." For the moment, they had the street to themselves. That wouldn't last long. "But this isn't the best time or place."

She turned and continued walking. The soft click of nails on cobblestones trailed her, then stopped. When she turned, the wolf-not-a-wolf stood at the edge of the shadow. It loosed a low, mournful whine.

"Well, come then," she said, not sure whether it was sillier to talk to it or pat her leg. "I'm just a few more blocks away."

She took a longer route that didn't involve crossing streets or brightly lit storefronts. The wolf stuck to the growing shadows and might have been made of the same stuff except for the occasional glimpse of tail or paw or flicking ear.

Home was the ground floor in a villa that had been subdivided into apartments. Her entrance was in the back, separate from the main building entrance. The impenetrable hedges framed a small garden in front of her tiny flat, a haven in shades of green.

At the gate, she stepped inside, half certain that like any good ghost story, her companion would vanish before the certainty of home and hearth. But it slipped past her into the garden, as real as any animal in the harsh porch-light glare. She closed the high gate, shut out the world. The bright light on its coat seemed wrong, and she turned it off as soon as she opened the door inside, returning the garden to twilight's shadows.

She left the door ajar.

Out of habit, she checked the small rooms: kitchen, bedroom, bath, living area. Empty. Everything as she'd left it.

She shucked out of her clothes and into a knee-length cotton slip with a lace racerback that settled like petals between her shoulder blades. Her stomach burbled complaint. Sweat pooled under her arms and on her belly.

Her visitor remained on the porch, paws on the edge of the doorframe, panting. Wolves in the zoo had narrow faces and lean bodies. This one had jaws like a mastiff, wider ears at the base, and broader shoulders. In the gloaming, its burnished yellow eyes glowed.

Necromancers might have been the most visible supernatural creatures, but many others had slipped into human awareness as myth and superstition. In both, where the black dog went, death followed.

They had that in common.

"I'd have thought you'd be used to this heat." She pulled an old bowl out from under the sink, rinsed and filled it. "Or has hell frozen over?"

She liked the image of this magnificent, fearsome creature guarding the gate to an underworld and answering to no one but death itself. Hellhound it was.

As she approached, it slid away, moving with an economy that was both refined and graceful. She set the bowl on the porch.

"I doubted I'd see you again." She sighed, returning to the kitchen. "Are you hungry?"

The eggs she'd set to boil on the stove had just begun to rap gently against one another when she registered water being lapped outside the door. As she passed the mirror in the entryway, the sight of her reflected smile startled her.

In the kitchen, she wilted spinach on a piece of bread smeared with fresh goat cheese, blanched fresh asparagus. When the eggs finished, she sliced one atop the bread and dusted the whole thing with pepper and salt. She peeled the remaining eggs for her guest and set them in a bowl with a heel of bread.

Hellhound lowered his hind leg from the far bushes when she stepped onto the porch, head low.

"So this is your place now."

His tongue lolled, and she had to remind herself he probably was not smiling. He did not show doglike alertness at the presence of food, though his nostrils wrinkled at the scent. She set the bowl of egg and bread close enough to the table that he must join her but far enough that she wouldn't give in to the temptation to touch him.

"Go ahead. Bon appétit." She waved her fork. He watched without moving. She shook her head. "Fine. Bon appétit to me."

Hellhound sidled toward the bowl when she took her first bite. She expected the contents to disappear in a few massive swallows. Instead, he reminded her of nothing so much as a genteel old man, drawing small, polite bites and chewing thoroughly before swallowing. The sweep of his tongue collecting the egg on his whiskers resembled a tidy napkin tap against a dignified mouth. He nosed the empty bowl, searching.

It *was* delicious. The textures mixed, cool and warm on her tongue. There had been no shortage of days without food on the road, and for years she hadn't had even this small luxury of cooking a simple meal of fresh ingredients for herself. She treasured each one.

She slipped her heels onto the seat across from her and leaned back in her chair to look up at the stars. She must have dozed because she was awakened by the soft, questioning rumble of an animal. The hellhound had stretched out on the stone path between her and the gate. On the other side of the high hedges, low voices carried on a conversation, accompanied by footsteps and the faintest whiff of smoke.

Hellhound rose deliberately, nostrils flaring. Beneath that coat of liquid night moved ridges of muscle. His hackles rose, and he huffed deep in his chest.

"Shh." Her cheeks warmed at the foolish idea that he would obey. "Please."

As the voices drew closer, he lowered his head, but the passersby moved on without incident, and he settled back onto the cool stones.

"Thank you."

He flicked an ear back at her.

Evie gathered the dishes and headed inside.

She pulled the loose floorboard from under her sofa and slipped a plain metal box free. Then she carefully double-counted the remainder of the money Valentin had given her. She put less than a quarter in her purse for expenses during the week, tucking the bulk of it into the box. It joined the rows of bills, stacked neatly and counted.

The math came to her before she consciously began a calculation, the amount formed in her mind. It put her over the top.

She rocked back on her heels. Maybe Tal was right. Screw the evidence.

She could grab the go bag stashed behind the refrigerator and the stacks of bills. She ran through the transit timings. Leaving at night wasn't ideal. Fewer options made her route more traceable. She kept as many possible routes and connections active in her brain as she could. It was best not to be locked into anything.

An overnight train to Zurich or Milan would be her best bet. Otherwise she'd have to spend the night in Paris or Berlin, and she didn't want to risk that much time waiting for her next connection. If she went north, she would try Helsinki or Edinburgh. South she could continue on the coast to Barcelona or Valencia.

Nikolai was one man, and whatever perceptive ability he possessed, he was neither psychic nor supernatural. Valentin wouldn't spare him to pursue her indefinitely. She knew how to go to ground. With her glamour, she could change her appearance and disappear. The fitful dreams in which she rode a train, and no matter what station it stopped in, Nikolai was always waiting were just that—dreams.

Her hands shook anyway. She tried out the words. "Just go. Go now."

And what about Mark? How could she make him understand how dangerous it was to get tied into Valentin's empire? She had no idea how to convince him to leave, but she couldn't abandon him to the sharks.

"Not yet," she whispered. "I need a little more time."

Five days. If Evie didn't find it by Friday, she would go.

When she returned to the doorstep, her eyes met the unearthly yellow glow.

"Thank you for the company," she said. "But you owe me nothing. I did it for those poor souls. You are free to return to wherever—whatever—it is you do. Please don't get shot again. I'd like to think of you healthy and happy in whatever realm you reside."

That night she dreamed of walking through the trees, her fingers threaded through the hairs behind the dark ears. In the morning, her visitor was gone.

Monday evening, Hellhound was waiting in the shadows when she finished her quick pass through the farmers' market for produce. She'd spent the entire day at work, going through old club invoices, searching for any clue of the new income. That and negotiating alternate rehearsal space with the club manager—a headache she preferred not to think too much about.

When she rounded the corner, out of the flow of pedestrians, she paused, aware of eyes on her. She scanned the shadows and locked on a flash of yellow. "You'd better come along then."

Hellhound fell into step with her, shortening his stride to match hers. Unlike the previous day, he didn't disappear when they met oncoming pedestrians. The few people they passed did a double take. Without thinking, she extended her glamour over him, feeling the slight tug of strain in the effort.

He looked at her at the same moment she looked down.

"It's just not good to attract too much attention," she said apologetically. "You understand?"

He sniffed his fur and sneezed. She caught a glimpse of the biggest black German shepherd reflected the shop window as they passed. Just another dog in a city full of dog lovers.

As soon as they entered the garden gate, surrounded by high hedges, she let the glamour fall.

He shook his coat hard anyway with another sneeze, as if to rid himself of the last touches. He grumbled and flopped onto the grass, rolling a few times for good measure.

"It is best to rethink your plan to walk me home." She thrust the key into the lock with more force than was required. The key stuck, and she jerked it against the lock, surprised. "I don't need that kind of attention, and in a city this close to a necromancer, you shouldn't either. All it takes is one wagging tongue."

She dismissed the idea of using her notion. It was a stuck door, not a rusted-shut fence. All it needed was a little human effort.

"I'm arguing with a hellhound." She wrenched the key in the lock once more, harder this time. The key snapped. She groaned.

She rested her forehead on the door with a series of bumps.

She could call her landlord. But how would she explain the dog—hellhound—or convince him to leave before the man arrived?

When Hellhound slid close to her, long hairs brushing on her elbow, a startled gasp escaped her. He drew back, lowering his head and tail.

She stretched out a hand, fingers curled.

He pushed his muzzle into her palm. The fur texture was a curious sensation against her scars—stiff outer hairs a distant tickle on the thickened skin.

She splayed her fingers along the side of his muzzle, sliding to the broad space between his ears before dipping into the thick ruff at the back of his neck. She curled her fingers and scratched until he loosed a low sigh and shut his eyes.

She set down her purse and a small bag of groceries and lowered herself to the front step next to him. "Am I forgiven for the glamour?"

He bumped his muzzle under the hand that had gone still on her own thigh, and she obliged with long strokes down his spine. His eyes closed to thin slits in what she imagined was pleasure.

She started to rise, but he leaned against her. "Oh, not ready for dinner just yet?"

She released her weight, and her head settled against his shoulder. His tongue lolled between his canines, panting in the heat.

It was time to stop being stubborn. Fixing a key was nothing compared to healing a gunshot wound.

"I could use a drink of water." She pushed off his shoulder, rising.

She slipped her fingers over the lock and hummed. The tumblers grumbled softly in response before the dead bolt slid back. When she pulled her fingers away, the broken end of the key slipped into her palm with her key chain. She closed her hand around it. When she twisted the handle, the latch opened. She set the repaired key on the table with her groceries.

They ate under the faint dance of new stars in the growing twilight. When she said good night on the porch, she reminded him of his lack of obligation and wished him well.

Tuesday she rescued an old fan from the heap that had come out of the basement. It was an industrial thing and weighed a ton, with a cage more decorative than built to keep out fingers. She told herself she wasn't thinking how hot the wolf must be in all that fur.

This time Hellhound was waiting in the garden when she arrived. She was getting better at spotting him in the shadows. The fabric-wrapped cord was short, so she placed it as close to the door as she could in her kitchen and flipped it on. He hesitated in her doorway.

"You can come in."

He crossed the doorway and sprawled on the floorboards. Cool air ruffled the long hairs of his coat. His eyes slid partway shut.

Evie made a simple dinner of fried egg and boiled potatoes. She set the table with silverware on a cloth napkin. Her serving was slid over a bed of arugula. She placed his bowl just inside the front door.

When her own plate was clean, she pulled a plastic bag of frozen peas from the freezer. For a few seconds, she pressed the frozen peas to her neck and just breathed in the cool air. Then she slit it open along the seam and withdrew the composition book wrapped in another sheet of plastic. At the table, she opened to the last entry.

Today had been tithing day: a day when the people and businesses who owed Valentin money came to make installments on the debt. Once the office had closed down and the last of the briefcase-carrying men had come and gone, Nikolai escorted her to the table in Valentin's office where stacks of cash were kept beside notes of debt. Then she began the real work, recording the sums against debts and making the money disappear into Valentin's operation.

She sharpened a pencil and set about meticulously copying each figure she'd written into the ledger in Valentin's office earlier that day from memory. It didn't take her as long: she was merely regurgitating. The calculations had already been made. When she was done, she sat back, content. She replaced the book carefully, sealing the bag and settling it among other frozen food.

She found the candescent yellow eyes watching her with eerie clarity. She rose, turning off the fan. "Good night."

Hellhound slid obediently out the door.

Wednesday, Evie steeled herself for a perfunctory check-in with Mark and his crew. The first of the supplies had arrived. She needed to make sure everything was according to spec.

A rail-thin, sad-eyed Czech who had not been there the first day—Samuel—met her instead. He walked her through the supplies, confirming the order was as expected. It was all she could do not to peer around him into the framework that had mushroomed into the space over the past few days, searching for Mark.

"You speak Russian well," she said, trying to delay her departure.

"My grandmother was born near Odessa," he said. "She raised me after the war. You?"

She shook her head. "Here and there. A bit from my father, a bit on the road."

A new face on the crew caught her eye. Painfully handsome but as gangly as a young colt, he wore sweats and a T-shirt, a tool belt slung low on his hips. He was young, fair-skinned with wavy hair, but familiar in a way she couldn't place.

If the dancers were disappointed that they could no longer flirt with the crew during rehearsal, all they needed was to catch wind of this one and the tentative separation she'd brokered would be wrecked.

He caught her staring. The corner of his mouth tipped up, blueish-gray eyes lightening.

She did not return the smile.

"Boss isn't going to be thrilled with these switches," Samuel said.

"Oh?" She dragged her focus back.

Samuel shrugged. "Not as reliable as the Denmans, ma'am. Replaced an entire set after install more than once."

Evie nodded, feigning concern. "Show me?"

Samuel walked her through the difference. Still no sign of Mark. "And where is he, your boss?"

"Called on another job." Samuel smiled, regretful. "He will be back soon."

He kept watching her with that curious, patient expression. She wondered if he had been on Mark's crew in Jevany and what had Mark said about his absent afternoons. She fled.

Hellhound met her in the garden that night, nosing the brown bag in her hand.

"Yes, I brought you something." She'd stopped at a butcher known to carry game meat. He'd wanted to know how big her dog was, and it was all she could do not to correct him. She said only *very*, and he returned with what looked like the leg bones of a small dinosaur. The gamey scent had cleared her a nice space on the tram ride home.

Hellhound's jaws snapped lightly, and the broom of his tail swept the paving stones. While she finished her dinner, he scraped the long bone clean, too distracted by the tickle of her toes against his ribs to pursue the marrow. When she rose to take in the dishes, he set his molars to the thickest part of the bone. It split with a deep crack she heard from the kitchen.

She peered into the dark and met his gleaming eyes. One eye closed with deliberate slowness.

"Showoff."

The bugs were out, and as she closed the door, he grabbed the biggest chunk and jogged inside, flopping onto the floor in front of the fan.

"Make yourself at home." Her apartment was going to smell like a butcher the next day, but she didn't have the heart to kick him out.

She ran a bath. The water felt delicious against her sticky skin, and she sank under the surface, watching the ceiling through the gently rippling current as she contemplated Valentin's new income source. And she still had no idea what to do about Mark.

She surfaced when the ache in her lungs became too great. When she emerged, Hellhound had moved closer, the bone forgotten, his chin between his paws.

She flicked a few beads of water off her fingertips at him. They sparkled on his coat like stars when they caught the light from the vanity mirrors.

She was mesmerized, thinking of Mark's constellations.

"What kind of notion does he have, I wonder..." She slid through the cool water, folding her forearms on the edge closest to him, and rested her chin. "...with starlight under his skin?"

On Thursday, Hellhound was waiting in her garden, nose on his paws. After dinner, she retrieved her surprise.

She'd bought the ice tray on her way home when it became apparent that he might become a regular visitor. A foolish purchase. A whim. Her tiny freezer barely fit the tray and a couple of bags of frozen food.

But it was worth it when she gently flexed the tray and Hellhound's ears twitched attentively at the crackle. She popped the neat, pineapple-shaped ice cubes into a bowl and settled onto the floor.

He leaped back and away like a puppy from the first piece she slid toward him, nose and ears tuned to the sliding shape. Then he pounced. The ice cube disappeared beneath his massive paws. His nose dove in after and jaws crunched a half second later.

He looked up expectantly.

Evie slid him another one.

The great ice cube hunt had begun. She was glad her place was minimally furnished. Even then, he knocked over a chair and a side table. She hurried to push her kitchen table out of the way before that too went over in a crash. She prayed her neighbors were out or watching television while the supernatural beast crashed around her apartment in pursuit of pineapple-shaped ice.

She tried not to laugh. But when he executed a wild dive and twist ending with him on his back with four legs splayed and tongue dangling as he crunched ice, it escaped her in a gasp.

She slid him another cube as a distraction. He caught it easily, barely moving and without taking his eyes from her.

"So all the theater was for my benefit."

He winked.

"You sneaky beast." She laughed outright.

He rolled onto his side, stretching his forelegs so hard the pads of his paws splayed wide in a move that exposed the velvet soft expanse of fur from throat to belly. It was an invitation too great to resist even though her heart picked up a bit when she closed the distance. He'd cracked that elk thighbone without effort. The thought of his teeth around her neck should have terrified her.

She pushed a sliver of ice at his muzzle. He slurped it up with surprising acuity.

She stretched out her fingers and he lifted his chin, the invitation as clear as if placed on a silver platter.

The fur at his throat was her new favorite texture, soft under the dense ruff of guard hairs and a shade or two lighter than the rest of him. She stroked the fluffy strands, buried her fingers until she reached the skin. With the next ice cube, the smooth rise and fall of his swallow rose along the muscled column. She shivered.

They ended up nearly nose to nose on the kitchen floor. Evie lay belly down with her chin stacked on one forearm as she slowly slid the last ice cubes across the distance between them. He caught them one by one with an elegant maneuver of tongue and canines, and they disappeared into a cool gust of his breath. The last thing she remembered was the long tongue brushing her fingers over the smaller pieces.

It the morning she woke in her bed, the melted slurry on the kitchen floor cleaned up, the furniture replaced, her doors locked safely from the inside with no trace of Hellhound.

By Friday she was too restless to stay in the garden. She'd made no progress with Valentin's secret. She added five more days to her plan and tried to convince herself she wasn't looking forward to the chance to see Mark again.

When full dark had settled over the city, leaving behind the sweltering heat of another record-setting day, she rose. "Come on. Let's go."

Hellhound looked up from his customary place on the paving stones without moving his head.

"It's too hot to sit around," she said, collecting the dirty dishes.

One long, furred ear flicked. His eyes closed. When she looked up, he was still lying there, sprawled on the stone.

"I'm going for a walk."

His eyes opened again, lazy yellow moons low in a summer sky.

"No glamour, I promise," she said. "It's so late most wouldn't notice you anyway."

The hellhound exhaled.

"They'll be more likely to mistake you for a dog."

He growled.

"Fine then," she said, grabbing her key. "You can see yourself out."

He rose, shaking nose to tail. But he was waiting at the gate when she'd finished locking her door.

There were more than a few people out, mostly clustered around gelato stands and restaurants. She avoided them, winding her way through the streets on the slope below the castle before turning toward the river on a familiar route from the days after she and Tal had arrived in Prague.

They'd stayed in a hostel for a few weeks, and every night she would leave to walk, driven by the sense that her journey wasn't finished. Later, it was how she planned her escape routes and worked out her timings. She'd never had a companion before.

As soon as she left the brightly lit main streets, Hellhound appeared at her side, a yellow-eyed phantom made flesh.

Her fingers brushed the long, stiff hairs of his outer coat as they walked. The wide wedge of his head rose under her palm, connecting them more directly. He tipped his chin, and her palm slid down to rest above his shoulder. Beneath the rough silk threads of fur, muscle rippled against her hand.

The streetlights faded, replaced by the more distantly spaced fixtures in the hillside park. At this hour, there were a few packs of kids clustered at the viewpoints, couples strolling, and dogs being walked or run on the grass. Hellhound attracted a few awed glances and, once, the growling charge of a pugnacious terrier.

When the terrier was a meter away, Hellhound turned his head and fixed the smaller dog in its silent yellow gaze. The terrier nearly backflipped, shrieking in its hurry to get away. Hellhound didn't bother to glance at the dog again as he continued at her side.

Its owner yelled after it, apologizing to Evie.

"Miss," the man called after her. "What kind of dog...?"

She splayed a hand over her companion's withers. "South Aidonian Tor Hund."

She left the man puzzling over the name.

After dodging a pack of skateboarders five minutes later, she sighed. "When I used to come here, it was empty this time of night. Perhaps another time."

Hellhound slid away from her hand, moving toward the shadows where a side trail led into the shadowed heart of the park. He looked back once, tail swinging in invitation.

Each subsequent turn took them deeper into the trees and gave the park the dreamlike quality of a moonlit forest. The city's lights twinkled below them on the hill, where only the brightest managed to reflect on the darkness of the slow-moving Vltava. Bridges formed rows of light that carried over the ribbon of dark water, binding the city together. She wondered at the darkness they crossed.

At last they came to the ruins of a wall. Evie settled in a forgotten lookout with a view of the south end of the city between the bent barrier railing. Most people, including city maintenance, seemed to have abandoned it. She tucked her legs beneath the rail and let them dangle, arms braced on the bit still secured against the old stone wall.

Hellhound patrolled the space, marking and sniffing about before joining her. It was cooler here. The breeze came off the river, carried high up the hill.

He flopped his massive head into her lap and rolled onto his side.

"Shameless." She laughed, rubbing his ears.

One paw settled on her thigh, the long hair between the pads tickling her skin. The broad expanse of his rib cage heaved with a long exhale beneath her palm. The steady thump of his heart made the long hairs quiver.

"I miss Mark." Confessions were always easier in the dark. Doubly so when your confessor was guaranteed not to reply. "And I have no right to."

Beneath her hand, the massive creature went perfectly still.

"Someone coming?" she murmured, glancing back toward the path.

But the park was silent around them.

"No, just you and me," she said. "And I'm talking for the both of us now."

A low whine sounded in his throat.

"What we had, whatever it was... I know what I said. I know what we agreed to. But when I saw Mark..." She hadn't known she'd held any hope she would see him again until that moment. "I thought the worst thing that could happen was that he would recognize me in front of Valentin and Kolya and that there would be questions I couldn't answer. But the worst thing is pretending it meant nothing. Pretending he means nothing. The worst thing is knowing I don't deserve anything as good as he is and wanting him anyway."

# CHAPTER EIGHTEEN

By the time Mark finished the additional support beams on Monday afternoon, he'd missed three calls. Two were Anton, curiously enough. Anton never called him. The third was one he'd been half dreading all week. Mark shut off the circular saw and stripped off his ear protection and glasses. He hit Redial, then glared at his silent phone.

A tap on the shoulder startled him—Chris, grinning like an idiot and pointing at his ears.

Shit. Mark had forgotten about his earplugs.

Over-ear protection often wasn't enough for hearing as sensitive as theirs. He chalked forgetfulness up to being busy, not just excited.

"Thanks, man."

Chris's grin widened. He patted Mark on the shoulder, blew a bubble with his chewing gum, and returned to installing switches. They were a day behind on the switches—but he counted that as a plus. When he'd gotten in Thursday and seen the order, he was so pissed he wasn't able to deal with it. The next day, inexplicably, a new order arrived, with higher-quality switches and an apologetic-looking delivery driver.

He ordered his crew to quit on the crap switches and get started with the new set. So they were half a day behind, but nothing he couldn't take care of, especially with Chris on to work most of the week.

The guys Nikolai had sent seemed more like bruisers than construction, and they worked like it. For all their size and bulk, they tired quickly and needed smoke breaks to "recover the wind." They seemed only to answer to Nikolai, so they refused to learn anything. Mark mostly kept them busy with small jobs that wouldn't break anything or ones his guys could pick up once they abandoned.

"Smoke break" became an inside joke on Mark's crew—the only answer to the question of where any of Nikolai's guys were.

As he fished the earplug free, he scanned the site. It was coming along. A flare of pride lit his chest. He knew he could do this. He pressed the phone to his ear. It was still buzzing with a ringtone.

He hurried up a set of side stairs as the cacophony resumed behind him. The stairs spit him out into an alley behind the club. He recoiled at the olfactory slap of piss and stale beer.

"Dobry," Mark said when the line picked up. "You called about my custom order. Vogel. Markus Vogel."

The clerk took extra time looking him up. Mark rolled his eyes. He hadn't missed the call that long ago.

"Yes, it's complete," the man said. "This is the third call. You will pick it up today?"

Mark checked his watch. Cutting out early wouldn't be doing them any favors, but he had been putting it off too long and it had to be done. He hung up the phone, checking the missed calls. What the hell did Anton want? He didn't have time to get stuck on the phone reassuring his boss. Especially since Anton wasn't his boss on this job because it wasn't his job. Fuck him. He could wait.

He pocketed the phone and ducked back inside.

This thing with Evie couldn't go on. And after that confession Friday night, it had been hard to leave her after their walk in the park. He'd still felt woozy from whatever hex Baby Witch had put on him, but just being around Evie settled him. The wolf might be happy playing midnight hellhound, but it wasn't nearly as satisfying for Mark. She spoke to him. He wanted to reply. She stroked him. He ached to touch her back.

As if he'd conjured her with the intensity of wanting, she was standing at the edge of the site when he returned, a hard hat perched on her head, talking to Sam.

Today she wore an aquamarine dress tailored to fit her curves. The shallow scoop of the neckline revealed her collarbones from shoulder to shoulder, which was startlingly more arousing than loads of cleavage. A little gold scarf was tied around her neck below the chin, the trailing edges at a jaunty angle. The bit of silk highlighted the long column of her neck, bare of jewelry and hair. From what he could see under the ridiculous hard hat, her hair was secured at the nape of her neck in one of those complicated twists that looked like it was held with a single pin but probably took several hundred to achieve. He knew: he'd helped his little sister with her buns more than once since junior ballet class.

The almost full-length sleeves exposed her wrists and forearms, and the skirt fell to just below the knee, the slit at the back offering a peek at one long thigh as she shifted her weight on another pair of heels that looked like death traps for ankles.

He was used to seeing her barefoot at home or in the woods, so these stilts hooked his eye. It wasn't that he didn't appreciate the view. Not at all. But each pair was flashier than the last, clearly expensive.

The eager lurch in his chest when she turned to him didn't give a shit who she was to anyone else. Even the wolf bucked in recognition. If he wasn't careful, he was going to wag his goddamn tail.

Smiling, Sam looked almost shy, but he sobered up quickly at the sight of Mark.

"Miss Acaz," Mark said. "I got this, Sam."

"Yeah, boss," Sam mumbled and hurried back on-site.

Alone—or at least out of hearing range of the others—he tried not to stare. Tried not to remind himself that the makeup and the nails were an illusion. That he had seen her, the real her, in a way that none of them would. And that they had once been something good to each other before it had been complicated by all the rest.

She seemed speechless, searching his face with a tiny furrow in her brow, as though she wasn't sure about something she once had been.

*She missed him.*

He wasn't going to be throwing himself at her feet belly up, like a pup. He'd broken things off, but she hadn't protested much. And she'd all but begged him to quit. No matter what she told the wolf, she didn't want him here.

"Did you come down for something specific or just to ogle my guys like the rest of your friends?"

"My friends?" She frowned.

"Yeah, we had a couple of 'forgotten wraps' from the rehearsal space." He made air quotes. "One water bottle, a missing hair tie, a scarf." He resisted the urge to tug the trailing end of the one at her throat. "They're getting creative."

"I'll talk to Madame Laureline later."

Mark scoffed. "She's the worst of the lot. And at least she pretends to be interested in the work. Mostly whatever Pavel is working on, but hey, no accounting for taste."

Evie laughed outright.

Well, damn, that sounded good. He grinned.

She bowed her head to collect herself as her shoulders trembled.

"Well, perhaps you should hire a less attractive crew." She smoothed her dress, but the remnants of the smile were harder to repress.

"Attractive, huh?" He shifted his weight toward her. "You think so?"

She rolled her eyes. "As these things go."

"How do they go?" he taunted in a low voice.

The rosy flush kept up her neck. "The Czech with the sad poet eyes, and is the boy Anton's nephew or cousin? Then you brought in that new, lanky one—"

"Chris," he supplied, not daring to look over his shoulder at that moment where his little brother was probably not minding his business based on the fact that the drill had gone quiet a bit ago. "What about me?"

"What about *you*?" Her brow skated up with her smirk.

He fought the urge to growl. "Woman."

The curve of her lips became one he knew too well: an invitation. *He missed her too.* The knowledge exploded in him, undoing all the rational reasons why they should maintain any distance at all. He wanted to get her someplace private, where he could extract how attractive she found him out of her while he put some wrinkles in that dress.

"I like that dress," he said, for her ears only. "The neck and the sleeves. And the scarf."

He almost groaned. *Really dude? Where did your game go?*

The corner of her mouth quirked upward, and he didn't imagine the way her eyes crinkled a little bit when the smile reached them, brightening her expression in a way that had nothing to do with illusion.

"Boat neck," she murmured. "Three-quarter sleeves. And thank you. You look…"

"Like a guy who's been hauling bricks all day?" he finished. "It's okay. You don't have to—"

"I'm not." A flush rose in her cheeks. "I like how you look, working… Anyway."

*He* liked her a little flustered. That flush reminded him of how she looked when they'd forgotten to come up for air, the sound of that first breathless gasp as he slid into her.

He shifted forward a half step. "We need to talk—"

"Mr. Vogel, may I have a moment of your time?" Nikolai was suddenly there.

Mark twitched. He'd been so focused on Evie, he'd missed the man's entrance. Even the wolf had been caught off guard.

But Evie turned smoothly, the slight smile on her face a little cooler. "Problem, Kolya?"

"I just got off the phone with our suppliers. I have some questions about the orders."

Mark's hackles rose in answer to the challenge in that tone. "Sure, I'd be happy to go over them with you. Should we take a walk?"

"This will suffice," Nikolai said, letting his voice carry.

Whatever remaining work had been going on came to a stop. Out of the corner of his eye, Mark caught one of Valentin's guys elbow another with a satisfied leer. Oh, so this was supposed to be that kind of thing. The real boss was bringing the outsider to heel. They planned to enjoy it. The wolf bristled under his collarbones, prowling restlessly.

"The switches are not what we ordered," Nikolai said, gaze sweeping the crew. "Who authorized—?"

"I did," Evie said.

Nikolai turned that flat stare on her. Mark stared too.

"Samuel, if you would." She raised her voice. "Bring both. Kolya, day mne ruchku, pozhaluysta."

The enforcer slipped a thin, expensive pen from his pocket and handed it over.

Mark watched, stunned as she explained in exquisite detail the difference of the wiring systems in both and the advantage of the second, in Russian. Nikolai followed the point of the pen tip moving between parts with the occasional glance up at Mark.

Mark caught every third word, but the authority and confidence in her tone were unmistakable. And erotic as hell.

Sam nodded along, supplying a technical term or two when she faltered.

"I'm sorry." Evie slipped back into English for an apology to Mark. "It was easier for me to explain... Did you understand?"

Sam's brows ticked a fraction in appreciation. That was all Mark needed. "Enough."

"So you see." Evie offered the pen to Nikolai. "In three to six months, half of these would be shorting out. At best, they would need replacing, at worst, a fire waiting to happen."

"And you know all of this?"

"Samuel was kind enough to explain to me," she said. "Last week when the supplies were delivered. I wanted to save you and Valentin the headache."

Nikolai glanced between them. "I see. Are you finished here?"

"Not quite," Evie said without looking at Mark. "I'm headed to lunch after, but I'll be back in time to record notes for the meeting with the city."

"I will have something from the kitchen sent up for you," Nikolai said, sliding the pen back into his pocket. "To your desk when you've done."

"You are too thoughtful, Kolya." Evie inclined her head, regal as a queen, but her lips tightened as he stalked away.

EVIE LET the exhale leave her in a long, measured breath before she smiled at Samuel. "Spasibo za pomoshch."

"Vam tozhe spasibo." He accepted the switches and her gratitude with a little tuck of his chin.

He gave Mark a look that might have been a warning or appreciation before returning to his work.

This was not keeping her head down and focusing on her plan. Nor was it allowing Mark to do his job without interference. She should have left it alone. She braced herself for Mark's response.

Startled by silence, she met his eyes. Humor warmed the copper. But as before, the galaxy she'd once seen in his face was gone.

"What's wrong?" he said, amusement fading.

"Nothing." She forced a smile. "If that's all, I should go."

She left him flat-footed. Not for long. He caught her in the hall on the way to the elevator, hooking her elbow lightly with his fingertips. "Wait. Please. Evergreen."

Evie froze.

The hall was empty, but any number of kitchen and waitstaff passed through this place. Even some of the girls entered the building this way at the start of their shift. They could have an audience any second. She told herself concern was the reason her heart kicked into triple time, that it wasn't the simple contact.

As if reading her mind, he looked down the hallway before dropping his hand and lowering his voice. "Thank you for what you did in there."

She shook her head. "You could have handled it."

"It meant something," Mark said. "You going to bat for us."

The tension escaped her in a single outgoing wave. A budding warmth filled the void. It meant something that he'd fed her almost every day they met, caught her when she fell, protected her from anyone they came across with no explanation.

"It was nothing."

"It *was* something." He frowned. "You were something."

"I don't need Kolya telling me how to do my job any more than you do." Nikolai had no right to attempt to humiliate him. It had roused a protective instinct she didn't know she had—and affection she couldn't afford to feel.

"I hope it won't make life difficult for you." He pointed at the floors above.

She fought the little shiver of physical need at the sight of that long, dexterous finger to a draw, letting the answering smile tug at her lips. "When one swims with sharks, one must learn to avoid teeth."

"Or get eaten." He leaned close enough for the clean sweat scent of him to reach her.

It would not do to angle in and sniff him no matter how much she wanted that aroma to fill her lungs. She hummed softly. "That's not always the worst thing."

His cheeks darkened. She almost laughed. He'd always seemed the uninhibited one. Maybe it was the context—in the woods, he had been less restrained. They both had. And she should definitely not be flirting with him in the hallway where anyone could come across them.

Because once she'd started, she could not stop, she searched his face once more for unfamiliar constellations. She found only leagues of deep brown skin, small freckles dotting the landscape like island chains, making him look younger. Still handsome as sin. Even without the stars, she could have watched him all day.

He lowered his voice. "Are you in trouble?"

"Never more than I can get myself out of." Unspent emotion roughened her throat. She'd done nothing but push him away, and he still seemed to care about her well-being.

He seemed to consider his next words carefully, though they came out in a rush. "Can I see you again sometime?"

Her breath stopped.

"It doesn't have to be... what we were," he said. "It could be... a decent meal. A real one. At a table with chairs. A walk after, or a cocktail?"

A date. He was asking her out on a date.

"It's not a good idea." The shadow of disappointment on his face made a mess of logic and all the reasons she should definitely not see him outside this building or for any reason unrelated to this project.

"Some of my best memories come from my worst ideas." He swallowed hard. "I've missed you."

She closed her eyes against an emotion she could not bear. Hope.

"It cannot be, you and I." Behind them, the elevator pinged before the doors jerked open. A busser wheeled a hand truck of bottles toward them. Pale, Evie drew away. "I must go."

She slipped away, the hand truck between them, and fled to the elevator.

# CHAPTER NINETEEN

THAT MORNING he'd headed in early to get started before the crew showed up and almost crashed into Toby.

"Bebe says hi." His younger brother offered a second coffee mug.

Mark took it. The first sip scalded his tongue, but it was worth it. "Ever heard of a South Aidonian Tor Hund?"

Toby's eyes did that glazed thing behind his glasses, signaling he was indexing that big brain of his for an answer. "South Aidonian— Where did you—? Never mind." Then that fucker laughed. "A dog breeder with knowledge of antiquities and a sense of humor?"

Mark tried not to be impatient as his brother amused himself with his own book-nerd inside jokes.

Finally Toby felt like explaining. "Aidoneus is a name for Hades—lord of the underworld—and the German, *Tor Hund*, translated terribly literally?"

"Gate dog?"

"I'm not a *dog* expert, but as far as mythology goes—"

"Hellhound." Evie's nickname for the wolf.

"Cerberus, technically." Tobias stared at him for too long. "Mark, who's calling you a hellhound?"

"Nobody." Mark jogged down the steps. "Thanks for clearing that up. Gotta go. Have a great day."

After Evie stood up to Nikolai for him—his very own knight in shining armor with a pen for a sword—with her large cocoa eyes fixed on him, he'd known he'd fight lost souls and demons for her. Most inconvenient because he was not, in fact, a hellhound. Just a werewolf. One with bills to pay and an ever-expanding family of witches and wolves to protect in a world that forced them to live in hiding.

The way she'd looked at him in the hallway, searching for something she hoped she'd see, made him think maybe Nikolai wasn't the only one capable of perceiving him as more than human and Barbara's charm was working. His mistake had been thinking it meant he still had a chance with her. She'd shot him down. No matter how big her pupils were or how her scent warmed and deepened. Interest wasn't permission. Hell, even arousal wasn't permission. Evie had *said* no.

But she always welcomed the wolf. So he spent another night chasing ice cubes on her kitchen floor.

*Hope you enjoyed making a fool of yourself,* Mark told the wolf. He might as well have been talking to himself.

Guilt flickered and he quashed it petulantly. It wasn't like Evie had been entirely honest with him. What did he really know about her? Certainly not where she'd come from or how she'd chosen this life.

The wolf memories tugged at him, but he could make no more sense of them weeks after he'd been shot. The wolf's sense of obligation to her was tied up in knots with his just plain wanting her, and he couldn't see a way out of either one.

Tonight she managed to catch herself before falling asleep. She walked him to the gate, but the wolf waited in the shadows beyond until he heard the locks of her door slide shut and saw the last light wink out in her window.

A pang of something like longing passed through Mark. She'd fallen asleep on him once in Jevany. He had the sense she did not rest often or easily. The feel of her going slack, voice softening midsentence, had made him want to crow with victory. When she was *really* gone, she snored—a low, deep breath followed by a huffing exhale. He smiled at the memory of her peeling her cheek from his chest and self-consciously wiping at the corner of her mouth when she woke.

Mark had perfected a route he could take in wolf form from her place on the north side of town. Going wide of the castle, he curved south through the park at Petřín and into the less well-lit streets of Smíchov. Avoiding the mall —lights still flashing even at this hour—he followed the old tramlines to the train station and down the tracks. Then it was a slightly harrowing race across the train bridge to cross the river before he was back in Vyšehrad, moving in a long, efficient lupine jog to the foot of his apartment building.

His battered old Škoda was parked out front, the doors unlocked. He snagged a pair of cargo shorts, not bothering with a shirt, and let himself into the building. He took the stairs by twos up to his apartment.

Maybe he shouldn't have gone to her apartment in the first place. He'd thought letting the wolf see her would be reassurance. But she'd called him out of the dark and the wolf came, helpless to resist. She told it her secrets, welcomed it into her space, trusted it enough to fall asleep within reach of those massive jaws. The wolf had known that kind of affection only from its pack and their mother. From everyone else it was a hidden, secret thing. It liked being seen. It liked the way she saw it.

Mark knew the feeling.

*Why now*, he'd begged anyone listening—gods, demons, or otherwise—as he stepped into the shower. *Why her?*

The only answer came from deep within his chest. *She sees starlight when she looks at me.*

Her words from the bath. Was that why she'd looked at him the first day as if she'd been struck with wonder, why she'd kept coming back?

Finally cool but still restless, Mark collapsed into his bed and grabbed the first book within reach on his nightstand. His fingers bumped the velvet box he'd picked up from the jeweler. He resisted the urge to open it. He should have just given her the divinestone in the woods. Divinestone provided good protection, but it was best when worn close to the body. For those of the witchy persuasion, it could be charged and used to focus their practice. Jewelry was always a bad idea. At least he hadn't been stupid enough to get a ring.

But he'd missed his chance. There was no way it wouldn't be awkward and weird now. He'd give it to his mother—or to help Tobias earn some points with Barbara.

He spent the next day looking up every time he thought he got a whiff of her and trying to convince himself he wasn't going to her place tonight. He'd been too lenient with the wolf. Time to set some limits.

As they finished packing tools, Chris passed a hand over the back of Mark's head. "Looking a little shaggy, brother."

"You gonna give me another one of those busted fades again?" Mark rolled his head away irritably, but his brother had a point. "I don't want to wait for the forklift. Help me move this pallet."

Chris put his hand over his heart as if wounded. "It was the best one you ever had."

"Here? Yeah," Mark admitted, grabbing his end of the wooden pallet. "But a bit longer this time, huh?"

"Yes, boss." Chris flexed his knees, squatting to get under the opposite end.

When Mark nodded, they lifted together. "Tapered, you know?"

"Okay, boss," Chris said, his voice thick with sarcasm. "Where do you want this?"

"Back left corner." Mark jerked his chin in the general direction before eyeing his brother sternly. "No skin this time."

"I got it." Chris began the slow shuffle sideways.

"Tonight?" Mark was pushing it probably. But it would keep him from showing up uninvited at the door of a witch who didn't want him after all.

"Ask nicely." Chris relaxed the grip on his end, leaving Mark scrambling not to drop the whole thing.

"You little shit—" Mark grunted under strain, eyes flashing yellow. Chris raised an eyebrow. Mark exhaled and felt the wolf retreat. "Please."

Chris tightened his grip, and they finished relocating the pallet to the far end of the room. No forklift required. "Fine."

Mark tossed his brother the keys and squatted to grab the two stout boxes of assorted tools on the way to the door. "But just longer on the top."

Chris took one of the boxes. "Dinner's on you."

Which would probably mean this haircut would cost three times as much as a trip to a barber, Mark calculated later as he sat down in the bathroom and let his younger brother drape him in a smock.

Chris showed no signs of hitting the end of his latest growth spurt. He could outeat Toby and Mark in a single sitting—and still look for dessert.

"I'm surprised Mom doesn't just throw you raw chickens," Mark grumbled after watching Chris devour two pizzas from the takeaway booth down the street. It was a good thing he'd ordered three or he'd starve. "Do you even taste anything?"

The same easygoing nature that made Chris seem content to float through life like dandelion fluff kept him affable and unruffled.

Case in point: Tobias would have bristled at the hint of a scolding.

Chris beamed like a star student. "Oh man, Woof loves them raw. Do you think that's okay? I mean, it hasn't made me sick or anything."

*Woof.* An animal capable of running down a bull elk lived in his bones, and he called it *Woof.* It was like someone had allowed the toddler to name the family dog.

Chris laid out his clippers, brush, and a sponge with a precision Mark grudgingly admired. For a few minutes, Chris worked in silence, angling Mark's head this way and that as he began putting in the guidelines over his ear. When he began the delicate process of creating an even gradient in earnest, he started to hum, dance a little, rolling his hips side to side and feeling some invisible beat.

"Are you high?" Maybe Mark should have asked for another buzz.

Chris squinted at him. "I don't do that shit anymore. Just enjoying my vibe."

*His vibe.* But Chris had started cleaning himself up. He was still out late, running in the streets with that pack of no-good, raving lunatic techno-heads. But he was home before dawn more often than not and, based on the increased size of his biceps, spending time in the gym. "Somebody giving you trouble?"

"Man, why are you riding me?" Chris raised his hands to the sky as if praying for patience. His little brother was starting to fill out, gangling limbs taking on solidity.

"You're bulking up," Mark said. The last time he'd picked up a weight with any regularity was after he'd gotten beat up defending some girl from bullies. The girl had left school, and Mark had dealt with the bullies. "So either somebody's giving you a hard time or somebody's somebody is giving you a hard time."

Chris laughed. "You gonna go bust somebody's ass for me?"

"Do I need to?"

Even looking like an awkward scarecrow postpuberty hadn't scared off an endless train of hopeful partners. From the dubious to the desperate, they came, and Chris couldn't help himself. He was too open-minded, too curious for his own good.

"I can take care of my own business, Markus." Chris turned his focus to Mark's forehead, lining up his hairline in neat, quick strokes. "I'm just trying to put some muscle on. You know. In case I need to—"

"Bust somebody's ass?" Mark resisted the urge to admire his younger brother's work.

Finding anyone in the city who knew how to handle the Vogel range of textures—from their father's fine waves to Mark's coils—had been impossible. Then, sometime before he'd hit secondary school, Chris had picked up clippers and figured it out.

This apprenticeship thing was a formality. Chris had been trimming their dad for years after Dad's favorite barber retired. He pitched in to help Mom groom and form up her locs. Even Tobias had eased off that textureless Caesar and let Chris shape it into something more natural that still suited his bespectacled-professor persona.

Things "not working out" with the apprenticeship obviously had nothing to do with his skill. Chris could figure it out most anything. It was his ability to stick with it that Mark worried about.

"You are so single-minded." Chris rolled his eyes and moved to Mark's temples, the pressure of his fingertips light but direct. "I am not a kid anymore."

Mark snorted. "When you quit living on Mom and Dad's dime and cleaning out their refrigerator, you won't be a kid anymore."

"Toby's married to a badass witch." Chris pulled away to check his work. "Dad's retired. Mom's business is doing great. Issy is making bank dancing at the academy—hey, didn't she loan *you* money? We're all *fine.* We don't need you sniffing around and cleaning up our messes. Get a life already."

"What messes?"

Chris exhaled sharply. Mark was glad to know he could still annoy his youngest brother. He might be the only one in the family capable of it.

Chris finished his nape and grabbed the sponge.

"How are things going with Mom's missing supernaturals?" Mark said.

Chris shrugged, avoiding his eyes as he brushed counterclockwise circles. "Just let it go, man. Mom can take care of herself. Unlike you."

"Unlike me what?"

"The cute blonde at the club," Chris said. "The fancy one who smells like expensive perfume."

"She works for Dimitrov." Mark replayed the memory of the envelope full of cash in her hands. "I don't know what—"

"You know good and godsdamn well." Chris hooted laughter. "And the look on your face when she took that cute little ass out of the room."

"Have some respect," Mark snapped.

His little brother crowed in victory. "You are so easy to push. Man, get some chill or something."

Mark aimed a knuckle at the spot guaranteed to give Chris a charley horse and was rewarded by his little brother's yelp.

"You know she and Valentin are... right?" Chris said. "That's what the dancer said. The pretty one with the flower name."

"They *all* have flower names, Chris. It's the theme of the fucking club... Little Blossoms. Get it?"

"You're an asshole, Markus. You know that?" Chris showed his teeth. "You have a lot of nerve talking about Mom while you're sniffing around some mobster's girlfriend."

Mark's wolf bristled in response. "I am not sniffing—"

"Where have you been the past couple of nights, eh?"

"Mom asked for family dinner one night a week. You can't even get your ass out of the club long enough—"

"You're done." Chris ripped off the towel. "Get out of here."

"It's my apartment." Mark countered, petulant.

Chris stomped out of the bathroom.

Mark knew what it looked like, Evie and Valentin. He'd wondered at first. But she spent every night alone in her apartment. He never saw

Valentin or Nikolai, and she never went to them. If either man had touched her, the wolf would have smelled it. And yet she was bound to them in some way he couldn't explain.

The night he'd watched her hide her money, the expression she wore troubled him. Resignation, determination, and something too close to fear. The stash might have been just an eccentricity. After the instability of the godswar, mistrust of banks was common, especially among older folks. Lots of people took payment in cash. And depending on whatever her arrangement was with Valentin, it might be expected—getting paid off the books wouldn't have been a surprise.

But there was something in the hidden nature: the loose floorboard, carefully disguised among the others. Taken with the notebooks she kept in a freezer bag and her simple, too-spare apartment, it didn't seem to complete the picture of a kept woman she was trying to project with the fancy clothes and expensive shoes.

He thought of the camera outside the villa, the single dark lens as curiously penetrating as Nikolai's steady gaze. Who was she hiding from?

He found Chris in the kitchen, polishing off the last slices of pizza.

Chris sighed, chin lowered, and gazed at him sideways. In wolf form, it would have been as submissive as it came, a juvenile wolf asking for comfort from a senior member of the pack.

Mark spread a palm over his youngest brother's neck and squeezed with strength but without force. At the contact, he felt Chris's wolf settle as his own reached out. "You did a good job. This is a fresh cut."

Chris's smile was a ghost of its usual carefree ease. "Look, after that business with Bebe and the witch. It just seems like—"

"Like what?"

"I don't fucking know, Markus," Chris snapped, irritable. "I'm a wolf, not a fortune-teller."

"Your wolf has an instinct."

Chris had always been kin to their mother's practice. He collected her wild herbs when they were at the cabin, had a nose for when whatever she was brewing up was done, and was the only one who understood some of the unintelligible chants she used to soothe them as children.

Mark recognized the distant look on his face.

"We've had a long time to grow up, figure ourselves out—you know, with the wolves," Chris began. "But what's it for? So we can keep trying to live like normal people and hide out in the woods on the weekend?"

"Nothing is normal in this world," Mark said. "I mean, the city is ruled by a necromancer and has a ghost witch looking after it—"

"Libuše wasn't a ghost." Chris sounded too certain to argue with. "She... it's like she *is* the city now. She gave us her blessing for a reason."

"What reason?"

"Like we're about to get called to do something bigger." As a child, Chris talked in his sleep. About the time his wolf came on, he quit, but Mark recognized the timbre of his voice as the same.

"When?" Mark pitched his voice low so as not to break the spell.

Chris's brow furrowed as if the uncertainty upset him. "Don't know, maybe later?"

Mark changed tack. Asking logical questions of a dreamer never worked. "What does it feel like?"

"Like trouble is coming."

Mark's hackles rose as a chill went through him. Trouble. The last time trouble came, it had taken all of them and their mother to free Barbara. They'd gotten lucky—no one had been hurt. More importantly, Azrael hadn't come down from his castle on the hill to check out what magical drama was going on on the opposite side of the city.

Luck ran out.

And now another witch was in a bind. But this time it appeared to be a bunch of mundane bullshit—mobsters weren't vengeful ghosts.

He thanked Chris, slipped some money in his gear bag, and sent him on his way with the rest of the last pizza.

Alone, he contemplated the velvet box.

He popped the lid open. The setting alone, a silver bezel on a simple clasp bail and a delicate spiga chain, long enough to hang low in the valley of her breasts, was art and had been just as expensive. But once he'd seen it, he hadn't been able to resist. The silver caught the rainbow of metallic flecks in the dark stone.

It would offer her some protection against whatever Nikolai's deal was.

The time she usually came home had come and gone. But at least Mark wouldn't have fading daylight to contend with. He could let the wolf make the gesture. It wouldn't mean anything then. One supernatural creature to another. A token of gratitude for a life saved. He was out of his apartment and down the hall before he'd made the decision, the wolf cramming itself up his spine and into his chest. One more night.

# CHAPTER TWENTY

THE HEATWAVE SEEMED to have finally broken. Still warm, but a breeze had begun to come up, stirring the small damp hairs on the back of Evie's neck and raising goose bumps as she stepped off the tram. She contemplated the almost empty streets ahead of her. On the weekends, most people left the city for a countryside cottage if they had one. Others headed into the Old Town for the bars or a walk beside the river. The emptied-out neighborhood was an echo of its usual constant thrum of activity.

The streetlamps were on, and the humidity had formed an orange haze around them.

Today was the anniversary of the bombing. She was looking forward to nothing so much as breaking her fast and maybe a walk in the park with her hellhound. She would sleep in all weekend and drink too much wine and lose the war with memory. She quickened her step.

The garden was empty when she arrived. Her flat was cool and dark. She left the front door open with the screen locked, keeping most of the lights off as she went about unpacking her groceries. The day's glamour slid away with the rest—she freed her feet from her shoes, stepped out of the dress to the light cotton slip beneath, and released her hair.

Unable to wait, she ate a cold dinner alone to quiet the rumble in her stomach, and then retrieved her sketchbook from the high shelf.

As she had done every year, she drew the faces she remembered, focusing on the shapes and the eyes, the expression. She was getting better. This year's sketches looked like they would breathe and speak—her father's thinning hair, his wise dancing eyes, his long chin. Her mother, focused on the day's accounting, curls escaping the scarf she used to bind her hair during the day.

When she looked up again the low buzz of dusk had surrendered to night's stillness. Evie closed the door with a final check of the garden for the unearthly yellow eyes of a supernatural creature masquerading as an over-sized wolf. She refused to worry. Just because he'd been at her doorstep or the tram stop almost every night didn't mean it would continue indefinitely. He certainly had some responsibilities to attend to as the keeper of hell's gates. He was running down errant souls perhaps, or catching rats. Did rats dare trouble the underworld?

Smiling, she turned her attention to her sketches. It was better that she spend this night alone, in quiet contemplation of all that she had lost. She picked up her pencil. The second two faces were harder. Menno, his mouth open and laughing, uneven teeth and eyes squeezed shut. Laila's tiny mouth an echo but pursed in focus as she practiced her slip stitch. Their faces were nearly identical. Distinguishing them became a devotion.

She'd lost track of her surroundings when the soft scratch of claws on wood and a low whine startled her. She closed the sketchbook and stashed it on the high shelf.

She did not run to the door exactly, though she didn't bother to dampen her enthusiasm as she flipped the latch.

Hellhound slipped into the space like a shadow, his coat swallowing the dim light of the room. He huffed.

She switched on the big fan near the door and refilled the bowl of water, setting it in its usual place beside her chair.

A muffled whine drifted out of his throat. His mouth was full.

She crouched to get a better look. "What's this?"

Massive jaws cradled a fist-sized package wrapped in thick brown paper. One paw tugged lightly on the back of Evie's hand.

Obediently, she held out her palm.

He dropped the package. His hips and elbows thumped to the ground as his broad tail stirred dust bunnies from beneath the counters.

She stared at the slightly damp butcher paper.

It had been tied with twine, well and securely knotted. Evie inspected the knots, running her palm over the threads.

At last she rose and dug a short knife out of a kitchen drawer. The knots gave easily under the blade she always kept sharp. She peeled away the outer layers of paper to reveal a bit of gold and red fabric beneath, satiny to the touch, and within a little velvet box. She rubbed her fingers over the soft nap.

Watching her intently, Hellhound gave a sharp whine and yawned. She glared at him.

"Patience," she scolded, opening the lid. "It's not every day a girl gets…"

The air left her in a rush. It was all she could do to catch herself when her knees gave, free hand clutching for the counter as she slid to the floor with a muted sob. Her vision blurred.

After all these years stifling grief beneath the day-to-day of survival, the inferno rose in her chest. It flowed into her mouth, an ocean of salt and heat fighting its way free.

Once upon a time, the night had rained stars and destroyed everything she loved. They fell like stars at least, with rainbows for tails, and screamed like missiles. On impact they didn't so much explode as shatter the surrounding buildings and people and cars, seeming to rend the air itself.

Not stars at all, or bombs, but the power of gods turned to destruction.

Where they struck, the energy fused to chunks like glittering glass: obsidian fused with rainbows. Strikes like this had been common during the godswar, and the resulting material had come to be known as gods' bones. But those days were supposed to have passed when the necromancers ended the war. Until that night.

She'd been covered in the dust of it after hours spent digging through the rubble where her family's shop and the small apartment over it had once stood. The glitter on her skin, obsidian and rainbows, was how the relief workers had found her as their searchlights swept for survivors.

A decade later and a thousand miles away, the same rainbow-flecked obsidian glittered against her palm. She didn't remember picking it up, but the slender chain tangled around her fingers, prickles of a familiar energy racing up her wrists and into her arms. She sucked in a hard breath when her lungs screamed for air.

She didn't have the strength to throw it, to run from it. And so she curled up around her hand, face pressed to the floor as her body wrung sobs from her core.

Gradually she became aware of another animal noise in the room.

Hellhound's eyes were wide and stark, flames in the low kitchen light. His ears were back, tail tucked under him, the muscles in his face taut. A low, keening whine rolled out of his throat. The pale black ruff beneath his chin trembled.

She closed her eyes and willed herself into oblivion. Stars bloomed and swirled behind her eyelids.

"Breathe, Evie, you have to breathe. Please."

She was hearing voices.

"Evergreen."

She must have passed out or been hallucinating. How else could she explain the naked man sitting on her kitchen floor where a hellhound had just been?

She closed her eyes again. When she opened them, he was still there. "Mark?"

◆

USE YOUR POWERS FOR GOOD, *Markus.* Their mother had often teased him as a child, tapping one of the wrinkled comic books on his bed, *And put away your laundry.*

Growing up, he'd always thought villains were much more interesting than the heroes. He didn't want to *be* one. But the best ones pushed the heroes beyond their limits and forced them to rise to their best.

Heroes were nothing without their opposition. There was a place in the universe for pressure.

In that realization, Mark had found his purpose in the world. He was more than happy to bust up a relationship between his youngest brother and some shady gold digger. Or shatter Toby's rose-colored glasses about how far their mother would go to interfere in their love lives. Or pull his sister off her high horse for forgetting where she'd come from.

But he always knew what he was doing when he was doing it. He knew what buttons to press and when and exactly how hard. He never went too far.

And now, without even knowing how or why, he'd crossed a line.

Evie's pleasure at seeing the wolf sent waves of relief though him. She'd had another hard day. Dark hollows swept beneath her eyes, and strain tightened her mouth. But it fell away when she opened the door for him.

All around her apartment were the little signs that he was welcome here: the fan, a bowl of cool water. She cooked for him, played with him, talked to him, made space in her life for him.

Mark had been so proud of himself for devising a good way to get the necklace to her without having it covered in wolf slobber—even if it meant running across town in the heat, unable to pant most of the way to cool himself. The wolf had been tickled to get to make the presentation, to be the hero for once.

And then something had gone wrong.

The soft velvet box tumbled to the floor as she dropped to her knees. The wolf tried to cushion her fall and was flung backward, end over end. He lay on the floor, body juddering with the remaining tremors of whatever force had come from her.

She folded in on herself, clenching in mute spasms of pain he would have done anything to relieve.

Anything, like reveal himself. Damn the consequences.

*I think we need words for this one, Big Guy. And arms.*

The wolf subsided reluctantly, leaving Mark clammy with sweat on her kitchen floor.

Evie had turned inward—her eyes glazed and her mouth open in a mute wail. And she wasn't breathing.

He hung back in case she accidentally zapped him again. Wolves had a natural resistance to attack by witch magic, but he had no idea how much of that carried over when he was in human skin.

"Evie, you have to breathe," he repeated. "Please."

After a scary long moment in which she seemed too still, she found her voice.

Deep brown eyes fixed on him. "Mark?"

"I'm here." He lay down across from her, pillowing his head on his forearm to meet her gaze.

Salty pearls raced over the bridge of her nose before puddling on the floor beneath her. Splotches of red bloomed on her cheeks and neck. She was flushed as though she'd run full out to collapse. Feverish.

Mark slipped his fingers across the floor toward her, only to feel the sharp crackle of static race between them, stinging him.

"Okay, not yet," he murmured, drawing back but not away. "But I'm not leaving. I'm right here."

Last night they lay on the floor just like this, his wolf licking melting ice cubes from her fingertips. Inspired, he leaped up. He grabbed a kitchen towel and opened the freezer. She'd refilled the tray of tiny pineapples, and he cracked them into the towel. When he returned to the floor, her eyes opened briefly, surprise breaking through pain.

"You're really here." Her voice scraped raw, rasped at the end.

He settled back down onto the floor across from her. "I have something for you. Put it on your wrists. The back of your neck would be better. Will help cool you down."

He reached out, slow and steady. When his skin didn't snap with a jolt of pain, he settled the icy bundle in front of her. But as he reached for the glint of rainbow-flecked obsidian in her opposite hand, her fingers closed around it reflexively. Needles shot through his extending fingertips.

"I just thought maybe I'd make it go away." He withdrew, returning to the towel. "How about I help with this?"

She nodded, eyes never leaving his face as he settled the cool towel against the base of her neck.

Almost immediately, the towel was soaked, water leaking down her neck into a puddle on the floor beneath her. The flush staining her cheeks had gone to a mottled red over her neck to bare shoulders. He passed a hand close to her neck. His skin snapped with tingles. Her eyes slid shut.

"Evie," he murmured. No response. "Evergreen?" Nothing. "Love." Where had that come from? "Please. You're burning up."

"I saw them, and it was too late." The words left her in a stream. "They were already dead. They just didn't know."

"Who, Evie?"

"My mother served the soup, and my father was teasing and trying to make the best of it because Menno hated onion soup, but with the delays, it was all we could get. When I looked up, they were gone."

"Gone?"

Her voice broke. "They wore their deaths like masks."

A chill prickled the back of his skull, raising hair down his spine. Had her family been turned into undead by necromancers? It was one of their more effective—and cruel—punishments. "Zomb—undead?"

She shook her head, the sob wrung from her, and she curled tight, knees to chest. The flush had spread, beads of sweat forming at her temples, the hollows of her throat. Her eyes slid back and forth beneath the lids.

He couldn't touch her, but he could keep her talking. "What happened then?"

"I ran, and when I looked back, the stars were falling, and they were gone." Evie's eyes snapped open, glazed with heat and memory. "Where did *your* stars go?"

"My stars?" The night of her bath, she had asked the wolf about a man with starlight in his skin.

A bath. The overheating had to be related to her abilities, and the rock was making it worse. Water purified, it cleansed, and if he was lucky, it could help bleed off some of this excess energy that was causing her to overheat.

He scrambled to his feet. "I'm coming right back. I promise."

In the bathroom, he paused. He had no idea how this enormous old tub had managed to survive so many of the modern era remodels that mostly ended in shower stalls or smaller inset tubs. It had probably been too heavy to lift and maneuver. But bless the cheap-ass souls who had left a bathtub big enough for two.

He turned on the taps, scanned the room. The fluorescent light was hard and bright. Candles lined the windowsill. "Matches."

A quick search turned up a box of matches and a few more candle stubs, also a box of salt. He grabbed all of it. When he was done, he hit the lights.

The glow of candlelight was an improvement. He added a few tablespoons of salt, stirred the water. Warm enough not to shock but cool enough to counter the heat, he hoped.

Evie hadn't moved from where he'd left her. Her breath came in little pants.

"I think I can help with the heat thing." He dropped to his heels, reaching out but recoiling when the live wire sensation snapped painfully against his palm. He had no idea how he would get her into the tub without giving himself a coronary.

A low moan escaped her. He thought he made out the words stars in it.

"I'll tell you what happened to my stars, where they went." He had no idea what he was going to tell her, but it sounded good. "I just need you to come with me. Can you stand up?"

Evie tried, he gave her that. But unsteady arms wouldn't hold her weight, and she wouldn't let go of the rock long enough to splay her palm for better support. She sank back onto the tile with a weary sigh, as though she bore the weight of a building on her shoulders.

In the end, Mark grabbed the throw blanket off the couch and steeled himself with a deep breath. Then he wrapped Evie in it and picked her up. The material did nothing to dull the electrified sting of a hundred tattoo needles between them. He wobbled, gripping her tightly. His heart stuttered in his chest, the blood thrashing erratically in his veins.

There was something critical about why it hurt so much to touch her that he should remember. But those memories were the wolf's from the night he'd been shot and out of reach.

By the time he reached the bathroom, waves of nausea swept him. Getting her into the water took some doing. In the end, he climbed in first. It was impossible to avoid her touch entirely. The water took the edge off the pain, but not enough to keep his vision from dimming at the edges.

He gripped the side of the tub, willing himself to remain conscious. *Help.*

The spike of a burn where his protection charm had been shot out to his skin. Barbara's work tangled with it, rising and falling to settle into harmony that formed a shield against the worst of it.

This was all Evie. Divinestone was known for channeling power, not creating it. But getting it out of her hand would help. "Hey, that death grip can't be comfortable."

Grief shadowed her face in old pain. She stared at her own fist. He cupped his shaking palm beneath it. "Just let's put it aside for a minute. Okay?"

She opened her fingers. What tumbled free was no longer a pendant and necklace. He grunted at the residual shock as the bare stone touched his skin, followed by a twisted lump of metal.

Light-headed, he dumped it on the edge of the sink. Immediately the needling live wire sensation dulled to a tolerable ache. He braced his head on his stacked forearms and focused on his breathing until the shaking stopped.

He started to wiggle out from beneath her, but she clenched his wrist. The soft magnetic tingle was back, and the fractured rattle of his heart eased as nausea fell away. She touched his arm, fingers climbing an unsteady path to his face.

"You're hurt." Tears spilled over her lashes as her palm settled on his cheek. "What were you thinking? I could have killed you."

Cold fear washed over him belatedly, but he stuffed it down. "I told you I'm tough to kill."

"I hurt you."

"Nah. That was just a tickle." He pressed his mouth to her open palm, the tingle warming his lips. "This is nice though—great big tub. Cool water. Like the lake, eh?"

A rusty, tired laugh left her. "Would you mind— Can you hold me?"

It was no country pond, and it took a bit of sliding and splashing and a muttered apology or two, but he wound up reasonably comfortable behind her.

She eased into his chest, and the last of the tension slid from her.

He grabbed the washcloth hanging off the side of the tub and soaked it. The scent of clean, crisp soap like fir trees and wildflowers settled over the water as he ran it over the knob at the base of her spine, down the long column, the taut stretches of skin over joint and bone, the coin-sized birthmark on her back, the sloping flesh at her navel. It was all too easy to remember how it had felt to be fitted against her like key and lock. He worked her clawed fingers open, rubbing the red imprint on her palm.

"I'm so sorry," she said. "The setting looked expensive."

He laughed. "It really was. How did you do that?"

The silence stretched between them. He let the question go unanswered. It was asking for a lot—the kind of trust they'd barely earned of one another.

"I have an affinity for metal," she said, resolute. "Since I was a kid. It responds to me."

The gate. That was how she'd turned a rusted old gate into an escape route. Also repaired a broken key and the lock. "That's amazing."

She scoffed. "As amazing as what you just did on my kitchen floor."

"You're right." He lifted a shoulder. "It's pretty mediocre compared to that."

"Mark, what are you?"

He cleared his throat, bracing for the worst. "You were right about most people being willing to see a big dog— A what did you call it? Aidonian..."

"South Aidonian Tor Hund," she finished.

"You scored major points with my brother—the other one, the brainiac. He got a real kick out of it." He was babbling—must be the afterburn of adrenaline. He'd gotten too used to being more resilient than most humans. He hadn't stopped to think she might actually do damage. A witch might be the only one who could. "He wanted to know who calls me—"

"Hellhound," she said. "Papa loved mythology from all over. He said we were foolish to forget how dangerous gods could be when we tried to use them to destroy each other."

"I'm not a hellhound. I guess werewolf is closer." He hurried to add, "But I'm not bound, not by the moon or emotion."

Her brows lifted. "That sounds…"

"Crazy?"

"Special," she said, chiding him. "Like it would be rare."

"W— I haven't met anyone like me. Like this." He narrowly kept himself from implicating his entire family. He wasn't ready to give that up yet.

"Lonely then?"

"Not exactly."

She stared, the question she didn't seem to know how to ask hovering on her lips.

"I have him. The big guy."

Her brow rose. "As nicknames go, my vote is for Hellhound."

He couldn't help himself—he laughed. "I was twelve. It seemed like a good idea at the time."

It was such a relief to say the words out loud. All his life, he'd lived a double existence. Being revealed was the only thing that really scared him. Until her. Knowing she saw all of him set him free.

Evie stiffened, splashing water over the sides of the tub in her hurry to face him. The slip clung to her as she sat up in the water, outlining her breasts in stark relief.

The glimpse of curving flesh and dark nipples beneath the wet cloth stirred his blood. Her, flushed and damp and cradled between his thighs, was a short maneuver away from being between hers. When her fingertips settled on the keloid scar on his chest, arousal rippled through him.

Her gaze jolted up to his with alarm. "Who shot you?"

"Some guys came to rip off the jobsite," he said. "I chased them off, but one was armed."

He watched her search the scar, probing and poking at it with wonder.

"You saved my life." He flattened her hand on his chest, covering the scar. "Our lives. I shouldn't have left you. He goes into protective mode when we get wounded badly. It's all instinct, no thought. If I had been in charge—"

"You shouldn't have come back." The humidity had curled the hair closest to her face, the natural waves emerging as he remembered them after a swim, or a particularly enthusiastic round of sex.

"Then you shouldn't have fed me." With his gaze locked on hers, he delighted in watching the flush bloom, her pupils swell. "Don't you know anything about strays?"

"That was you. All this time. Lying on my kitchen floor. Here in the garden. The walk to Petřín Tower." She buried her face in her hands, and he thought he heard embarrassment in her muffled words. Feeding you like a dog... and ice cubes—"

He tugged her hands free. "Not a dog, like a guest. You made him welcome. He doesn't get that a lot. Most people are just afraid. You're a good cook. And the ice cubes... The big guy loved them. And being a dumb idiot to make you laugh."

"Him?"

He knew this was going to be impossible to explain rationally. If she hadn't seen him go from one to the other, he'd probably sound like was out of his mind. "We're different, he and I. He's got his own sense of the world. He cooperates because I give him a lot of rein, and I think he gets how dangerous it is in the city for us. But he's not... strictly me."

"I like... him."

"Maybe you like him more?" He cupped the slope of her throat below her jaw.

Her pulse beat, steady and warm against his palm.

The fresh tears clumping her already-damp lashes tore something loose in his chest. "Seeing you in the office and having to pretend to be strangers, that you mean nothing to me. I thought I could do it, Mark. But it tears at me. Every time, I lose control a little bit more."

Reservations fell away, doubts too. Whatever they had been in Jevany, whatever they would be moving forward, they would figure it out together.

"It's not so bad." He grinned, understanding the wolf's urge to do anything to make her laugh. He rolled his eyes skyward, one hand over his heart. "I get to see you almost every day in one insane pair of shoes after another. I have no idea how you stay upright in them, but you look— Damn. They make your ass look edible."

The hint of a smile rippled her cheek as she swatted at him half-heartedly.

He caught her hand, savoring the roughness of her fingertips and the warmth of her palm. How long had he craved being skin to skin again? He'd wanted to lose himself in her. He knew how she responded to his touch, his kiss. Having her just out of reach had been unbearable. Her eyes closed again, chin drooping toward her chest. The shadows fell hard in the hollows beneath her lashes, the cups formed in the base of her neck and her collarbones.

"I'm sorry I snuck around like that." Their fingers tangled. He kissed hers one by one. "It was only supposed to be once, just to make sure you were okay and to let you know he was okay. And then I couldn't keep him away. *I* didn't want to stay away."

"I'm glad you didn't, either of you."

When his thumb brushed her cheek and the pale line that puckered the skin, she turned her face away.

He wanted to tell her that a few scars changed nothing, but he wasn't going to pretend they didn't exist either or act like their presence didn't affect the way she moved through the world. "Is what you can do to your face and your hands tied to the metal affinity?"

"In that they're two things I can do, I suppose yes, they're alike." A flush rode high on her cheekbones. "But they're not related. I don't really know. The metal was first. The glamour—I saw a man do it at a checkpoint. A pickpocket. He stole a wallet and made himself look like the man inside. Something just resonated in me when I saw it. I asked him—well, I threatened to reveal him if he didn't tell me—and he taught me the basics. I figured out the rest myself."

"Blackmail." He laughed. "Should I be worried?"

Her ribs expanded against his in a sigh. "I would have done whatever it took to survive. But I wouldn't have betrayed one of us. Ever. Anyway, I think he liked bragging about it."

"Who wouldn't—a beautiful young woman comes asking."

Her laugh hardened into a sharp sound. "A skinny girl with a scarred face and hands that look like they've been through a meat grinder? He pitied me. I've just gotten used to people treating me a sort of way when they're visible. They make assumptions. I'm damaged, or broken, or dangerous somehow."

He understood that very well. "If it makes you uncomfortable, I won't touch them. But they're just part of who you are. Not even the most important part."

"It feels strange, being seen. But good." She met his eyes, her mouth close enough to taste.

The skin dimpled, tiny bumps rising on her shoulders and her arms. She eased herself back against him, resting her temple against his cheek.

"You're cold," he murmured, relief swamping him.

"That's good?"

"Considering I thought you were going to fry me? Yes." He exhaled, laughing softly. "Let's get out."

He helped her to stand. When she had cleared the tub's edge and had her balance, she extended her palm back to him, open. Scars and all. He took it.

He gave her credit for trying, but in the end, he levered himself to his feet. "You asked about stars in my skin... No, beneath. What did that mean?"

"When we met, I saw stars." She plucked at the wet slip. "Like you were a window into another universe. I've never seen anything like it. Usually I only see..."

He offered her a towel and grabbed a second for himself as the silence grew. "What do you see?"

"How people die." She met his gaze steadily for her next words. "It covers their faces, like a mask."

"When?"

"All the time. Every day." She shrugged, wrapping a towel around her hair. "The violent ones are obvious—gunshots, stabbing, bludgeoning, drowning—there are too many of those at the club. But there are a million ways to die that look identical from just the face. I do know that if the color is vivid, it means soon. And if faded, later."

*They wore their deaths like masks.*

"And you saw your entire family..." He couldn't imagine that terror and the fear it must have instilled. Like wolves, most witches got their abilities around adolescence. "You were how old?"

"Fourteen. Old enough to help in the shop, to look after my brother and sister. I panicked. I ran." Her chin jutted at the sink where the twisted metal and the divinestone sat. "I was outside when it happened. It was so beautiful. Shining stars come to earth. I didn't move. I just watched."

"You were a kid."

"I let them to die." The conviction in her voice spoke of years of self-blame that had hardened around the story like a shell, protecting it and wounding her at the same time. "I should have gone back. I could have gotten them out."

"There wouldn't have been time." He tried anyway. "And you would have died with them."

"I should have." A humorless smile did not meet her eyes. "Now I am stuck. Death follows wherever I go. So you see why I mistook you for a hellhound—it seemed fitting."

He tried briefly to imagine what it would be like to see death everywhere he looked. Nothing she'd ever done would have given it away. Even her tendency to avoid eye contact just made her seem aloof, added to the mystique of the persona she'd created. She lived beneath layers of illusion, not all of it glamour, a woman in control, untouchable.

He pulled the plug on the tub, staring at the soaked throw blanket in the water and wondering what he could possibly say to make up for the well of grief he'd plunged her into. After a long silence, he felt her watching and looked up.

She'd traded a towel for a cotton robe and sat on the edge of the closed toilet with a tube of sweet-smelling lotion. "You haven't asked."

"Asked what?"

"About your crew. Your brother—the young one—is your brother?"

"Chris." He nodded. "I don't understand."

"About the death masks," she said patiently. "People want to know if I see them. Themselves. Their friends, their family. It doesn't help. But they always want to know. You haven't asked."

He exhaled, rescuing the blanket before it blocked the drain.

"That's because I don't believe it." At her startled expression, he hurried on. "You see what you see. I don't doubt that. But I just don't think that's all there is. Our futures aren't determined. You see... a possibility. If you tell me, maybe it becomes a certainty because two people see it instead of just one. Possibilities can be changed. And death isn't something to be afraid of anyway. It's just a transition, not always pleasant, but a stop on the way to something else."

She stared at him, hands slowing as she warmed the lotion between her palms.

Maybe he'd said something wrong. He changed the subject. "Any idea why I'm different?"

"I've never seen anything like you." The smile in her voice warmed him. "Your stars. So many, I couldn't even count them. But they're gone now. What changed?"

*Maybe the trick isn't to strengthen the charm but throw them off, make it seem like whatever the charm is hiding is more pedestrian. Less... wolfy.* Barbara's words. He owed Evie some explanation to know it wasn't something wrong with her. But it was a fine line, protecting those closest to him from a woman who'd begun to mean everything.

She began smoothing cream up her calves, over her knees, and his blood thickened in his veins. To distract himself, he fished out the wet blanket.

"I got a bad vibe about that guy, Nikolai. He gives me the creeps. So I had a... friend do something to make me less obvious. The wolf part. It must have also dulled whatever you saw."

"A friend?"

"Yeah." He kept his focus on wringing the water out of the blanket in steady twists. It was mostly the truth and the lies only in omission. It sat poorly with him anyway. When he looked up, her gaze darted away from his hands and her lip pinched between her teeth—checking him out and trying to be sly about it.

He liked knowing she still felt something for him because watching her smooth lotion over her legs beneath the towel ruined him for keeping his head on straight.

He changed the subject. "This must be the cruelest thing anyone has done to you, and I never meant—I found it at the jobsite in Jevany. Well, Ondrej did. The other guys cashed in, I traded my share for this. I thought…" He exhaled, looking up at the ceiling. "Divinestone is good at channeling power and storing it. It makes a good vessel for protection charms. I knew you were… I knew there was something about you that was different, maybe like me. I thought if you were in trouble, it might come in handy."

Her eyes went watery again, but this time accompanied by a rueful smile. "You're right about Nikolai. He's not to be trusted."

"And Valentin?"

"Valentin helped me, got me out of some trouble." The warmth leached from her gaze as she capped the tube and swiped the last bit over her elbows and shoulders.

The words sank like they led to the pit of his belly. A story in glimpses and flashes of pain tangled up in wolf memories. He couldn't make sense of them.

"Do you love him?" It felt like the sensible question to ask in the situation, even if speaking it left him in knots of emotion he'd rather not deal with right now.

Evie paused in attacking the snarls in her hair with her fingers. "Are you serious?"

"We never promised each other anything." He squeezed harder, hearing the blanket fibers stretch as water dripped into the tub. "That was the arrangement—"

"I run the books for Valentin's operations," Evie said with a shaky laugh. "I have for almost two years. I told you it wasn't how it looks. He lets everyone believe I'm his mistress—we both do—so no one knows what I really am to him. Please don't tear my blanket in half."

He looked down at the tortured bit of fabric in his hands, sheepish. He hadn't judged her. It didn't seem fair, all things considered, but he'd be lying if he said the thought of either man with his hands on her—in any context— didn't make him want to take throats in his teeth. Every memory and interaction turned over in his brain, coming together in a new way.

"And Nikolai?" He met her eyes.

"Nikolai doesn't like it." She reached to the high shelf for a comb, giving him a tantalizing glimpse of damp skin at the top of her thighs. "The Saints are family, blood. I'm an outsider."

Mark had a hard time imagining she could be so oblivious. "That's not how he looks at you."

She stopped with a wide-toothed comb halfway to her hair. "What?"

"Like he's one step away from marking his territory."

"Valentin comes first, always. Kolya's loyal. I belong to Valentin, so he protects me like the rest of Valentin's assets." Her eyes fell away from his for the first time. She lowered her hands into her lap. With her shoulders closed and spine rounded, she looked small.

He tried to imagine what the years of living a lie this big was like. So big it took over her whole life.

"You don't belong to Valentin," he said, firmly enough to make her gaze sharpen with alarm. "You belong to yourself."

She attacked the length of her hair again, combing and braiding quickly. She tied off the end and pushed it over her shoulder. When she rose, her spine was unbowed again, her shoulders back. The curl of heat in her eyes sang to him. "I don't want to talk about those men anymore."

She came at the softest tug, her lips parted and turned up to his. His fingertip slipped down the line of her nose, outlining her lower lip. Anticipation charged the air between them. He tasted her on his next inhale—salty and sweet.

His stomach rumbled. Physical recovery always cost calories. Apparently, resisting powerful witch magic did as well.

"You're hungry," she said, tugging his arm.

"Not for food." He allowed himself to be led, mourning the sight of her cozy bedroom as she dragged him back into the kitchen. "But let me cook for you, okay? It's been a rough night, and I turn up naked, with the world's worst gift. It's the least I can do."

# CHAPTER TWENTY-ONE

EVIE WATCHED Mark putter around her kitchen from the chair at the battered table. Her pantry was embarrassingly bare. "We can call—"

Mark emerged from the cupboards, a towel around his hips and big hands full of potatoes. "This is perfect. Potato pancakes, you know them?"

"You know how to make latkes?" She tried not to laugh—not wanting him to think it was at his expense. But everything about this improbable, beautiful man filled her with surprise and delight. The towel hanging off his hips wasn't hurting either.

"Exactly. My downstairs neighbor made some for us once. I liked them, so she taught me." He reached around her to snag the carton of eggs. He shuffled a grater free of the cabinet and grabbed a kitchen towel. "This clean?" When she nodded, he frowned. "You don't mind, do you?"

She produced bowls and a whisk. "That your neighbor taught you to make latkes?"

"That I show up naked and eat all your food?"

That was stupid. Feeding him was the least Evie could do for the pleasure of all this seminakedness. But about this woman. "Your neighbor. She cooks for you often?"

Mark didn't seem to notice. Or maybe he knew exactly what he was doing. He loosed a sly smile. "Jealous?"

"I am only trying to get to know you." She had no claim on him and no right to begrudge anyone who saw him for what he was and tried any path to his heart they dared. Still.

His smile grew, the direct gaze making her squirm. Finally he took mercy on her. "When we were kids, she used to watch us sometimes so our mother could get a little sanity break."

"Your babysitter?" The flush of envy that had heated her chest flared into embarrassment.

"In her book, learning to cook for myself was the way to stave off becoming an 'inveterate rake.' And when I finally did meet the woman I was ready to settle down with, it might convince her I wasn't a hopeless old bachelor." He paused as if hearing the words tumbling out of his mouth at the same time she did. He made a detailed study of the eggs on the counter. "She taught both of us, Chris and me. I think she was just thinking... Well. They keep me from starving to death in my own apartment. They're fast. And cheap. And mostly dummy-proof. Anyway... one thing I learned was that every family has their recipe."

"They do." Evie joined him at the counter. They stood shoulder to shoulder, eyeing the potatoes and salt and egg. "Mama made hers with cheese. Ricotta is best."

"Ricotta." His words held a reverent wonder she appreciated. "Sweet, savory?"

"A bit like a blintz." The sweet ache of memory tangled the words in her throat.

"Sounds amazing." He kept his voice low, a quiet rumble that plucked at the warm, growing tension in the pit of her belly every time he spoke.

It was different than hearing him around the jobsite, barking orders at his crew, or talking to Nikolai. This voice was hers. It was all she could do not to lean against his shoulder, soften her ear to the place under his chin and bring that sound right into her.

Her body flushed again, comfortably this time. "My mother was an incredible cook. I'm named after her. Evelia—they called me Evie. Acaz was her family name. Wine?"

"Definitely." When she returned with the bottle, he had retrieved glasses. He poured generously and nudged her out of the way. There wasn't much counter space, but she found a perch that left him plenty of room to operate around the stove. "I didn't learn the potato way until... Well, as you say, potatoes are cheap."

"Acaz," he mused when she was quiet. "Is that Spanish?"

She listened to the soft shredding of potatoes on the grater, appreciating the slope of his shoulders, the ripple of his back and forearm. In profile, focus settled in the line of his brow and the way his lips flattened slightly. "My mother's family came from Cordoba. After the expulsion, they followed many others to Constantinople, but they got accused of witchcraft—again—

and had to leave. They wound up north, on the Black Sea, where they met my father's family during the godswar. When rumors started that the Necromancer Kadijah would conscript people like us to her service, my parents packed up everything and crossed the border into Azrael's territory before it closed for good. I grew up near Dobruja."

If he had been a wolf, one ear would have tipped toward her, though the rest of him seemed perfectly focused on his task. It was impossible not to see them both when she looked at him and the indirect focus made it easy to talk.

"Contested territory," he said. "What was that like?"

"It was all I knew." She took a big swallow of wine to wash the knot out of her throat. "They tried to keep life normal for us. We lived between the river and the sea, in a town where children of a Sephardi and a Turk were no more remarkable than any other family. Except that she was a witch and he was descended from sorcerers—but we hid that, of course. We took trips to the beach in summer. The news reports of fighting in the north felt distant. Maybe they should have left. But they were already so far away from their families, and they'd built up the business from nothing. To start again, with three children..."

Her voice shook but didn't break. "I used to think about them every day. But sometimes, I forget too. A day or a week will go by, and it's always just been like this. And then something will remind me—"

"Like some jerk brings you a piece of jewelry made of the same material that destroyed your home?"

How wondrous that he could make her want to laugh, even at this moment. "That was a new one. You called it divinestone?"

"What do you call them?"

"Gods' bones."

"My dad says the Allegiance takeover didn't settle all of humanity's differences," Mark said carefully. "In some places, the godswar only added a layer to old conflicts."

Her chin jut stubbornly. "When Azrael claimed the western borders of the Black Sea, Vanka funded splinter groups in the locals to oppose his claim. A resistance fought to be part of his territory rather than hers, and he backed them. The only ones able to call down something like this are necromancers."

She shook her head, trying to strip the vitriol from her voice and failing miserably. "I spent hours in the rubble, trying to find my brother and sister. My parents. Because two necromancers let extremists fight a proxy war over *their* border. For their *peace*."

Mark reached for her.

Evie drew away. She didn't deserve his affection. His pity. Necromancers might have been responsible, but she had let her entire family die when a warning might have saved them. If only she had been able to keep her head.

He lowered his hands but didn't withdraw. "Wanna hug or hit something?"

Her gaze snapped up to his face in surprise.

"I'm the oldest of four. I know how to take a punch."

"You fought with your brothers?"

"I'm good at pissing off my little sister and *she* can throw a punch. Come on. Give me what you've got."

He straightened, bracing.

When she reached for him, it seemed to take him a breath to realize her arms were open. He caught on quick though, dragging her into his chest and squeezing with a strength that promised to hold her up no matter what. "I would have figured you for a puncher."

She laughed. He felt good against her, warm and familiar. When she pressed her face into the space between his jaw and his collarbone and drew a deep breath, it was unquestionably right. She'd never been much of a dancer, but she might like to try, especially the slow kind that had them holding on to each other like this.

"I bet they'd be glad to know you survived. Proud of you for making it this far." His voice vibrated through her, his lips moving against her hair. "Forgive that little girl for running away. She was scared, and she didn't know any better. She saved your life."

A hard, sharp sound left her. He held on until the tension became tears, and those too subsided. She'd never been held like this. The world faded outside the circle of his arms, the wall of his chest. She surrendered. He didn't let go until she did.

She accepted the wineglass he offered with his next question. "How'd you get to Prague?"

She told him everything, about the camps and Tal and the years on the road. Before her eyes, ingredients came together in the glass bowl. He caught her watching his hands as he worked the onions and potatoes into salt, pepper, and starch. His eyes locked on her lower lip when her teeth sank into it. Low tension simmered at the base of her spine.

She looked away, flushing at the memory of those solid and dexterous fingers moving over her skin.

He set the bowl aside and draped a kitchen towel over it. "That's gotta rest for ten minutes or so."

A sly smile curved her lips. "What should we do with ourselves?"

"We're gonna need more than ten minutes for that." He smirked. "Do you have any pictures of them?"

"Everything was destroyed." She hopped down and returned from the bookshelf with a bound sketchbook, flipping through it. "Tal warned me that I would forget their faces, so he got me a sketchbook when we had a little money. I do one every year on the anniversary. These are today's."

"Just when I thought my timing couldn't have been any worse." He dried his hands, taking the book with a wince. He continued flipping. "These are amazing."

She peered around his biceps to the delicately shaded rendering of a small, light-skinned man bent over a workstation, a stretch of fabric in one hand and a needle in the other. The single lamp illuminated the dark space on the page. That was two years ago when she had been grieving the loss of her ability to work with fabric without breaking into a sweat, to touch a needle without weeping.

She grabbed at the notebook. "That's it. Really. That's all..."

He held it out of reach as he flipped the pages. She watched him thumb backward through the dresses and ball gowns until she couldn't bear it. Her heartbeat was deafening in the silence.

When he offered the sketchbook, she grabbed it.

"You're a designer," he said without a hint of mockery.

"It's old stuff. I was still learning. I *am* still learning." Her gaze came up hard and a little wary. "I never went to school or apprenticed—"

"Do you have more?"

"You want to see more?"

He scowled. "Think a meathead that works construction can't appreciate good design when he sees it?"

"That's not what I meant." She hurried to the bookshelf. She returned with an armful of notebooks, took one look at his grin, and loosed a goofy one of her own. "Oh. You are terrible."

"It worked, didn't it? Come on, give me a tour." He dragged her into the chair beside him. "I promise I won't ask too many stupid questions."

Mark asked good questions and many of them. What he didn't know about the finer points of garment construction he made up for in enthusiasm.

While she talked, he turned the burner on beneath the pan and set the oil to heating, then washed his hands and started portioning out thick patties.

By the time they moved to the table, the plan she and Tal had once nurtured on the long road to Prague was spilling from her. She ate until she wanted to burst, amused as he continued to pack it in. But his last question brought her crashing back through euphoria to reality. "Tal has a shop, right? Why didn't you go into business with him?"

"It's complicated."

"Because of what you do for Valentin?"

Evie started to clear the plates.

"Is it the money?" Mark joined her at the sink. "Because I get it. Trust me. The money is good."

She laughed, but the sound was brittle. "It's not that simple."

The unexpected domesticity of them standing shoulder to shoulder at the sink infuriated her. It was so easy with him—having him in her space, being within touching distance. She hated loving it as much as she did. After everything, the fact that he had come into her life now burned hollow below her breastbone.

"You cook. I clean up," she snapped, snatching the plates from his hand. "Go sit down."

He lifted his palms with a grin, backing slowly away. When he settled in his chair, he rocked back on the rear legs. "Help me understand why you're all tangled up in the mob instead of tailoring with your best friend."

She studied him in wonder, waiting for some sign that he was leading her on. "You don't remember, do you?"

"Remember what?" He looked genuinely confused.

His fingertips beat out a pattern on the worn surface of the table. She'd gotten it at the flea market a week after moving in. It had taken as long to refinish it, stain, and seal it. But she loved the way the old wood grain had been battered but still shone under the kitchen lamp. It looked even more beautiful with its scars. She was going to miss it.

She was going to miss him.

"Turns out I couldn't touch them—needle and thread. I had these attacks." She closed her eyes against the memory of being pulled down into the darkness for days and the knowledge that she'd failed to fulfill her end of the dream. "I started serving at Little Blossoms because I had to pay my share of the rent, put food on the table."

"Your friend, Tal, was okay with that?"

"Tal is not my keeper." She pushed the sponge across the plates with more force than was necessary. Tal had been decidedly against it. "I needed to not be a burden."

"And you stayed because?"

She sighed, keeping her back to him so he wouldn't read the omission in her face. "I was too good at my job."

"They know about your thing with metal?"

"I may have convinced them I'm just really good with numbers." She eyed the bowls and the pan and decided that would have to wait until the morning.

"So quit now."

Even in the earliest days, Tal had never presumed to tell her how to handle a situation. No, Tal wouldn't have let her get into it in the first place. This mess—and the blood on her hands—had been all her own doing. And she was the only one who could get herself out of it.

"Mark, how do you think this ends for me—Valentin lets me retire to a nice villa in the countryside?" Tension sharpened her voice. She was in a cage. Couldn't he see that? "Maybe he'll rent me the cottage in Jevany, and you can come to visit me on the weekends. I know his entire operation, income, sources. He doesn't just let me go. If a rival gang found out what I was to him, or the authorities..."

Mark didn't rise to her anger, his voice unconcerned. "The money in the floorboards. You're going to run."

Startled, she opened her eyes and glanced over her shoulder at him. She'd hardly ever said the words out loud. It solidified something, made it real. The knot in the pit of her stomach became an ache.

Guilt lowered his gaze. "He saw you—the big guy. And the books, the ones in your freezer. In the peas. What are they?"

"Copies of the ledgers." A chill washed through her. She hadn't even considered what she'd done in front of the hellhound—er, wolf. She thought she had been so careful. What else had she missed?

"What are you waiting for?"

She weighed her options. She'd already told him so much, too much. He knew her plan and her stash. But he'd trusted her with his secret. She dragged the pan into the soapy water and attacked the oily residue. "I need to figure out what Valentin's up to."

His head snapped up. "What does that matter?"

"Valentin is planning... something big. Maybe something I can hold over him if I need it. There's a lot of money involved, whatever it is."

While she scrubbed bowls and rinsed everything, she told him about the strange warning Nikolai had given her, leaving out the offer of his protection. In the following silence, she watched the dwindling suds circle the drain.

"I don't like it, Evie." Mark's voice rumbled with warning. "Nikolai is too perceptive. If he catches you poking around..."

"I'm not poking." She spun to face him, leaning back on the counter.

His raised brow told her what he thought of that.

"I'm just keeping my eyes open. But you don't want to be caught up in it. And this job has something to do with it. I feel it in my gut."

He laughed, rocking so far back on the old chair she was sure he would lose his balance. But he hung there, eyes going yellow. "I *know* working with shady mobsters comes with a risk—but I'm just here for a job."

"It starts off that way. But then they get their hooks in you and it's not so easy to go."

"Is that what happened with you?"

She growled, fighting the urge to run her fingers through her hair and tug hard. "That is how it started for Anton. One job, two jobs. A loan to keep the business afloat. I track the money. One minute he's doing jobs, the next, Valentin owns him. Do you know how many bodies are in the foundations Anton's poured for Valentin?"

"Between five and ten?" Mark's brows rose. "More?"

"This isn't a joke."

"I'm not joking. Give me a ballpark."

"I'm beginning to understand why your sister punched you." Evie shoved herself away from the counter and turned her back to him, smoothing the dishtowel under her palms.

"You picked hug. Too late to change up now."

His ability to stay calm was annoying as hell. This was life and death. He seemed to have no sense of self-preservation.

"I can't worry about you," she said. "I have to stay focused. Please."

"Who's going to worry about you?"

She buried her face in her hands. "Mark."

"Yes, *Evergreen*?"

"Don't call me that." The words came out hard. She sucked in a surprisingly unsteady breath and met his eyes. "The girl you met in the woods doesn't exist here. I don't need you to look out for me. I have a plan."

Behind her came the soft sound of wine sloshing into a glass. "Make you a deal: you go, I'll go. You've got enough cash in there to float for what—six months?"

"Years," she said. His eyes widened, and she shrugged. "It's not all here. I didn't want to take any chances. If I go, I need to disappear. You're not in danger yet, but you have to quit. Make up an excuse. Pawn the job off to Anton. Nikolai is dangerous, but Valentin... I don't trust him."

"I'm not leaving." Mark crossed an arm over his chest, palming the wine-glass in his free hand and contemplating her in a way that made her skin prickle with a warmth that would only be relieved by his touch.

When she glared at him, he took a big sip from the full glass before setting it on the edge of the table close to her, as if reading her thoughts and issuing a formal invitation to debauchery. A drop caught in the corner of his mouth. He dragged his thumb over the edge of one full lip to his tongue.

"Don't be mad." His voice lowered to gravel and silk. "Come 'ere."

"You are frustrating, you know that?"

"I get that a lot."

She refused to look at him, not ready to give up yet even if he was making her all mushy and hopeless just calling to her in that sexy voice. "Unsurprising."

He waited, brows lifted, and now the corner of his mouth nudged his cheek. Those remarkable copper eyes warmed. The tension that had been building inside her all night—drawing her eyes back to his mouth, his hands, his shoulders—spilled over.

"We are going to talk about this later." She stalked toward him and rested her foot on one of the lifted legs, giving it a bit of a push.

"Does that mean we can move on to more pleasurable activities?" He grinned, counterbalancing easily. "Please kiss me."

"Why should I?"

"Because I asked nicely."

When she straddled his thighs, he let all four chair legs hit the floor, hitching her closer to the bulge pressing the towel tight across his hips. The heat of him reached her through the layers of cloth.

Kissing him was even better than she remembered. He was playful, baiting her with licks and nibbles until he'd enticed her tongue into a game of chase and seek that left her gasping for air. While she tried to get her breath under control, he dropped kisses from her ear to her jaw. His teeth grazed her throat, not with enough pressure to leave a mark, before he soothed the skin with his tongue.

"Are we going to have to go back in the tub?" He grinned, palms clenching her hips hard. "You can ride me just like this."

"Mark, we can't start up again." She wasn't sure who she was trying to convince because it didn't stop her from winding her arms around his shoulders, squeezing her breasts between them as if that would somehow alleviate the pressure building from inside. "Nikolai doesn't have the place watched regularly anymore, but what if he did? If they find out... If they catch us..."

What they could do to her, she would survive. But if anything happened to Mark, it would break her. She would tell him that as soon as he stopped kissing her, branding her mouth with his own, tugging the small hairs at the base of her neck in a way that made arousal slip down her spine to her hips.

◆

SHE WAS in deep with Valentin, and Nikolai already thought of her as his.

No plans and promises be damned. He would see her through this. He just needed to make sure she was clear, and then he would get out too. One job.

"You should know that whatever this is between us, there's been no one else for me since the woods." He took her hands, unwinding them from around his neck and cradling them between their chests. Her fingers curled in. The tension in her wrists made him think she would pull away. He didn't let her go, but he kept his hands loose enough that she could break his hold easily.

She snagged the lower corner of her mouth with one crooked canine. "When would you have time, between work and being sprawled on my kitchen floor?"

"Minx." He ground himself up against her.

"Since utterly aggravating and absurdly hot are an impossible combination," she said, breath coming in rugged little pants, "I never even tried."

He'd come to associate her with the woods and the wild things. But in hindsight, she belonged here as much as there, maybe more so. And wherever she was, she made space for him. He belonged, too.

He gathered her hands up—the moon swallowed by night—and brought them to his lips. The kisses landed lightly, fingertips first, then knuckles, his own hands drawing back to her wrists as he kissed her palms, the fleshy pads of her thumbs, the valley at the heels.

The moon emerged. When he dared look into her face again, it was open with wonder, stained with tears. She made a little noise of surprise and delight. Her fingertips settled on his jaw, tentatively at first as her eyes seemed unable to rest on one spot on his face. "What do you see now?"

"They're back." The words rasped softly through emotion. "Your stars."

"Ah, Evie." His thumbs coaxed tears from her cheeks. His body buzzed with excitement and anticipation. It knew how good what came next could be, hungered for it. Only his big stupid brain wouldn't shut off for some reason. He still needed to convince her that he meant it. He was all in. He reached for the right words. "Guess I gotta go talk to the witch who did the spell about a top off."

She blinked at him, still. "The witch."

He cupped the base of her skull, fingers stroking the fine hairs as though they were new feathers. "My mother is a witch. It's not the word she uses— she calls it her practice, like her yoga or something, but that's what the world calls it, so let's go with that for now."

"Your *mother*…"

"My brothers—you met Chris, and the other one, Tobias—are like me. Wolves." He ticked their names off on his fingers. "And Tobias married a witch, so that's two now in the family. She's the one who hid my stars. My dad and my sister are the only normal ones, but the wolf thing runs on his side of the family. It's just recessive. And Issy—well, she's a godsdancer—but

I'm fairly sure she's only dancing for real estate deals these days, but you should know that."

"Why are you telling me this?"

"You told me about your gifts, and I've seen them," he said, as reasonably as if she'd revealed being double-jointed. "Now you know mine. We're even. We're in this together. If I'm on the job, I have a good excuse to ask questions you can't. I'm going to help you find out what Valentin's up to."

"You can't—"

"We've dealt with a lot worse than the mob," he said. "The longer you stay, the harder it's going to be to get out. And I'm going to be there when you do, just in case. I'll make sure you get clear of this."

"You are so stubborn." Her voice wobbled.

"I am."

"Of all the foolish, reckless..."

"Dangerous." He nodded. "You forgot dangerous. But you also said I was hot."

She rolled her hips in a deep, grinding circle, and his eyes lost the ability to focus entirely. "Absurdly. But Markus?"

He made a wordless noise.

"This doesn't change anything." The towel tuck came apart under her impatient fingers, and when she touched him for the first time, his hips bucked with impatience.

He parted the robe, drawing her close. "I know."

"I have to go." Her exhale stuttered as they came together.

"I'll put you on the train myself."

Everything he'd remembered about her sweetness remained, grown more potent in their time apart. Or maybe that was just his longing for it. Because he'd forgotten how deliciously sharp she could be—urgent and demanding. Playful too, the way she fought back against his attempts to slow himself down, to sustain each delicious moment until its edges honed to sharpness. That too sweetened everything.

But when she finally came apart in his arms, each clench and tremble felt like the tick of a clock, counting down to an end.

The chair beneath him creaked with protest. He lurched to his feet a second before it gave.

Their eyes met, his round with surprise, hers alive with mirth. She pressed her forehead into his neck, laughter hot on his collar. "It was an ancient chair."

"I'll take a look at it in the morning. Maybe I can fix it."

Her gaze went over his shoulder and to the floor. She winced.

"That bad, huh?" He laughed.

"Firewood," she pronounced with a wry grin.

"What a way for it to go." He adjusted her effortlessly, striding down the hall. "Hey, you still have those red patent leather heels, the ones with ankle straps?"

# CHAPTER TWENTY-TWO

ON MONDAY MORNING, the immortal known as the Amazon strode into the office.

No one *knew* she was immortal, but in the decades since Azrael had taken over the territory, she and the rest of his inner circle had not aged. Since they also seemed impervious to human weapons, it might as well have been a deathless existence—perks of serving necromancers.

Every member of the Allegiance of Necromancers had at least one companion that seemed to function as both guard and enforcer, though their level of public interaction varied. In North America, the leader of the Nightfeather's immortals was a dual-sword-wielding enforcer with her own action figure and a comic book. But that seemed quintessentially American—Hollywood or it didn't happen.

Azrael's group seemed to be the largest and their application the most mixed. While at least one always appeared at his side in public, they had also been spotted moving independently through the territory—likely his eyes and ears—and in some cases acted as his proxy.

This woman, Elise Le Seppe, did not often appear in his public detail, but when the necromancer did not deign to speak, he made it clear she was his voice. Le Seppe managed Yan Petrov's arrangement with the necromancer. But visiting Petrov's lieutenant was odd.

Now she stood without comment as the two men on guard duty began to argue over a pat-down neither man seemed willing to attempt. Evie had never seen either of the two men sweat before, but they were visibly anxious.

Evie tried to gauge Le Seppe as she would have in the old days on the road. She was of average height with cool brown skin and full lips. She didn't appear to be a day over twenty, though she carried herself like a regent, crowned with only the thick braids of her hair. Her expression was placid but unyielding. Nothing that would have given Evie an in to the kind of empathy that might have gotten a meal, or a ride, or someone to vouch for them at a checkpoint.

Expensive clothes, insanely precise tailoring, and the casual air of one who didn't need a gun or a knife to wreak deadly havoc. Le Seppe was not even armed as far as Evie could tell. Her hands rested in her pockets before she slid one free and checked the chunky silver watch cuffing her slim wrist.

"Peredayte bossu, chto ya zdes'." Le Seppe addressed the two men in flawless Russian. "I will wait."

Both men started, the whites of their eyes showing like children who'd been told a convincing ghost story.

Faddei broke first. "Yes, madame."

Evie returned her gaze to her desk as the gust of air from the big man's passing on his way to retrieve Valentine moved over her. She contemplated the quickest way to get herself out of the room against the value of staying. The mystery of the woman's presence was a powerful lure. It left holes that Evie scrambled to fill with possibilities.

If the relationship with Yan had soured, perhaps Le Seppe—and the necromancer—were aware of Valentin's move against Yan. That might be why he was emboldened to make an attempt.

If so, Evie was in bigger trouble than she'd anticipated. She might have to jump territories to escape Valentin's grasp. She needed to know so she could change her plan.

"I have not seen you before." The Amazon's voice came from too close.

Evie jumped, dropping her pen, and her eyes snapped up before she could catch herself.

Elise Le Seppe stood before her desk, though Evie hadn't heard her move. She wasn't the only one. The remaining guard sputtered and shuffled across the room in her wake.

Who knew what abilities Azrael's inner circle possessed? The inhuman-speed rumor was true apparently—physical strength, healing, perception? Perhaps she was able to see through the glamour to Evie's notion.

From her end, Evie saw nothing but the woman's living face. No death mask.

"Madame," the guard said, voice edging toward a plea.

She ignored him, fixing Evie in her curious, impassive gaze. There was nothing welcoming in her expression, but Evie felt no outright enmity either.

"Pardon?" Evie said politely, giving only uncertain curiosity in her answering smile.

Le Seppe's head angled, a little smile on her face. "You are new?"

Evie tried to sort her accent—a touch of the familiar Arabic around the edges in the long vowels and the gently rolling r—but perhaps complicated by time and other languages. Evie wondered briefly how old this woman truly was.

"I've been here only two years," Evie said.

The woman studied her, silent.

"Welcome, Madame Le Seppe. To what do we owe the favor of your visit?" Nikolai filled in smoothly as he strode toward them, excusing Evie with a nod before giving his attention entirely to their visitor.

Elise Le Seppe, whoever she was, smiled, and the casual ease fell away. It was a terrible thing, full of the promise of violence. The kind a heralded soldier made before first contact on the battlefield. This is why she was called Amazon—no tailoring could hide that she was born a warrior when fighting was a way of life.

Even Nikolai had nothing on that smile. To his credit, he didn't flinch, only folded his hands in front of himself and lowered his head like the penitent. "I see."

"I would have words with your head man," Le Seppe said with an unspoken warning—*continue to delay me at your peril.*

Nikolai cleared the path to the door.

Evie had to get herself in that room. She jerked to her feet. "Tea. I'll bring up some refreshments."

Nikolai seemed to have forgotten her until she spoke. He nodded.

In the kitchen, Evie stilled her shaking hands by gripping the countertop as she waited, the busboy and chef she'd harried into service hustling around the kitchen, preparing tea and a plate of delicacies worthy of a dignitary. "On the good service. The silver and crystal."

"Is it true?" the busboy asked, wide-eyed beneath the visage of an old man with eyes closed and smiling peacefully in death. Evie reached for the tray, but he held on. "They say she's a thousand years old."

Evie shivered but cut him with a look. "It's rude to ask a woman her age. The tea."

She took a deep breath outside Valentin's office, settled a polite smile on her face, and entered without knocking.

"—engaging in a public war with the Croats in violation of our arrangement." The Amazon finished her sentence, a glance up at Evie as casual as a sated tiger. Her posture managed to make the uncomfortable seat across from the desk appear luxurious as she ignored Evie's progress with the tray, accustomed to such service. "Two weeks ago, one of their clubs was hit after closing."

In his great chair behind the desk, Valentin squirmed, wretched. Fair as he was, now he looked like his own ghost. She couldn't tell if his death mask had gotten more vivid or not in a glance, but the future bruises on his jaw and chin and dark holes above remained.

"My kitten," Valentin said, with forced cheer. "An excellent hostess this one, yes, Kolya?"

Nikolai looked up from his phone screen, darkening it and slipping it into his pocket. "Yes."

Evie served, reading the woman's signal for two sugars and arranging a small plate based on the Amazon's subtle gestures.

"Imported from Solokh-Aul," Valentin offered expansively. "The caviar arrives fresh from the Black Sea. Beluga."

Evie served Nikolai next. From his post at the end of the room, a quarter turn toward the window but with an excellent view, he continued the conversation. "It was perhaps a misunderstanding, madame. There is old bad blood between us. But in accordance with the generosity of your master" —he seemed to realize it was the wrong word a half second before her lips flattened into a line—"we uphold our agreement. Yan Petrov is *our* master. We would no more defy him than—"

"Three died," she said. "six wounded. Interviews conducted have identified your men."

"They have had it out for us since we took over the club in Smíchov, claiming it is their territory." Valentin added, "False claims."

"Wounded men panic," Nikolai offered generously.

"The dead cannot." She sipped her tea.

For once, Nikolai clamped his mouth shut.

"The dead?" Valentin's voice trembled.

"Did you think my *master*"—she mocked the word—"would not make the time to speak with those who died that night? He is very hands-on, you know. Likes to be involved in all our business unlike, it seems, yours."

"Petrov—"

"Not Petrov's men," she said. "This is why I come to you directly. Because if Petrov were to learn you were violating our agreement…"

Valentin's face purpled.

The rush of relief Evie felt was immediately ratcheted back up to tension. Going against Petrov was one thing—violating the necromancer's laws was a quick way to becoming an undead servant while everything you'd built was burned to the ground. Sometimes literally.

"If we have an understanding?" The Amazon rose, surveying both men and setting down her untouched plate.

Nikolai bowed his head in respect.

Valentin shuffled out of his seat, but his chin jutted out petulantly.

Standing with Valentin's tea and small plate in hand, Evie resisted the urge to slap his shoulder in demand of the necessary obedience. Was he too stupid to realize what danger he was in?

Whatever Elise Le Seppe saw seemed to satisfy her.

"I can see myself out." She paused with her hand on the door. "There is something else I find curious about that night."

Nikolai's head lifted.

"You know what they were running?" Le Seppe asked idly. "The Croats."

Valentin spread his hands, a little chuckle dying rapidly when her gaze settled on him.

"A circus of sorts." The ghost of a smile lifted her mouth. "Supernaturals, all of them, disguising their blood as sleight of hand and costume."

Valentin sputtered. Sweat beaded on his brow. "I am not aware—"

"I'm fond of circuses," she mused, apropos of nothing. "A clever way to skirt the rules for the ones who cannot truly hide. An old-fashioned one."

He spread his hands.

"I know because two were among the dead," Le Seppe went on as though answering the unspoken question. She faced Valentin. "But it appears others are missing. Fled perhaps. We are still looking for them."

"For those unaccustomed to gunfire, it can induce panic," Nikolai said lightly. "I'm sure you will find what you look for, madame."

"I will." She smiled, taking them all in.

*Not me!* Evie wanted to scream. *I have nothing to do with whatever nonsense these two are up to.*

Defying Azrael's laws.

This wasn't a power play. It was the kind of suicide that didn't end in death.

"As delightful as this little visit has been," Le Seppe said, "I cannot promise my the next one will be so pleasant. Our arrangement with your boss and offers you limited protection."

Le Seppe left the room.

Evie slid into the recently vacated seat. The chair was warm. The rumors that Azrael's guard was undead were not true then. She drained the tea intended for Valentin in a single gulp.

"Well, immortals before noon." The smell of caviar turned her stomach and she fought the urge to flee. On a good day, Valentine couldn't hold his tongue. Pressed like this, he might very well reveal the whole scheme in a fit of anger at having it threatened. She set the plate aside with a weary sigh and extended her fingertips toward Nikolai. "Ne pomeshalo by zakurit'."

Nikolai obliged, freeing the slim silver cigarette case from his pocket, a match for the flask, and offering it.

It had been years since she'd smoked, a habit picked up in camp and on the road, a way to infuse warmth on an otherwise frigid night or settle restless nerves before a big border crossing or to fool an empty belly. And an essential part of the first trick she'd ever taught herself, using her notion.

Now she clung to the slim, high-quality cigarette, pressing it to her lips, and Nikolai produced the corresponding lighter.

His eyes met hers as he thumbed the flint wheel. His jaw was tight, a muscle flexing below his temple. Did she read a subtle warning in his dark gaze? Evie watched his face for a long minute before leaning in.

She exhaled when he turned away, focusing on the smoke and the little mental chantey that went with it. The one that made her fade, to slide beneath notice. She tried to make herself insubstantial, holding as still and silent as a deer catching wind of a hunter.

"That bitch," Valentin hissed, his eyes skating over Evie to the door.

Nikolai turned from the closed door, the look of censure unmistakable.

Valentin flushed. "How dare she come here... asking of me—?"

"Another reason to have left the freak show alone," Nikolai added as if to himself.

Valentin fixed him with a heated look that Nikolai shrugged off easily as he decanted vodka and poured a few fingers. He brought it to Valentin.

At his cup, he slipped a flask from his jacket and spiked his tea liberally.

"Hell, what were the Croats doing?" Valentin sulked, draining his glass. "Wasting an opportunity—staged fights, acrobatics, and fortune-telling. I offered them a sizable cut. I didn't expect them to put up so much of a fight."

Nikolai snapped, "And if we had let them be, *she* wouldn't be showing up here."

"Even with the shipment from Valencia, we were under the number we promised." Valentin's eyes skated away from his second-in-command.

"The holding facilities are barely able to contain what we have they're—"

"Adequate," Valentin barked.

"For now." Nikolai faced him, eyes hard. He lowered his gaze first. "We get this shipment off, and we take a little break. We do what she says. Keep quiet, yes? Like church mice. Let the heat die down and resume in a couple of months."

Alarm juddered through Evie's limbs. *Shipment.* The sudden movement drew too much attention to her. They remembered her, their glances skating over her as though they'd forgotten she was there. She covered it by searching for an ashtray. Nikolai slid one under her elbow.

She put out her cigarette languorously, as though nothing she'd just heard had been said out loud. "If you don't need me for anything, darling...?"

Valentin waved a hand without looking at her. "Of course, my dove, of course."

Nikolai's arm was waiting when she rose.

"What you heard in there today," he said when they were at her desk.

"Nothing," she assured him. "I heard nothing but my heart racing. That woman is terrifying."

His hand settled over hers before she could withdraw, the solid weight pressing a rough palm into her skin. "Our conversation in Jevany would also be good to remember. Nothing here is certain."

She knew better, but the spark of fury in her rose with her gaze. She met his eyes, unable to keep the wry cant from her mouth at the irony. "Nothing?"

A slight flush colored his cheekbones, and for once he looked a bit taken aback.

Evie wondered if she had misjudged him. Maybe all his watching her had been just this—a schoolboy crush. A man unused to such feelings.

Then his hand tightened sharply on her wrist, the compression sending arcs of protest through the small bones to her elbow.

"It is a dangerous game for one such as you to play," he said, bowing his head toward her.

"Such as me?" Her throat dried.

His smile glinted with certainty. "I believe we both know you are more than you seem."

"I am exactly as I seem." She shook her head slightly, closing her eyes against pain that had nothing to do with her hand and letting the bitterness bleed into her voice. "A bird in a cage."

"Kolya," Valentin barked from within the office.

Nikolai released her with a rueful smile. Then he pulled up his shoulders and tugged his lapels, rolling his neck like a boxer before heading into the ring.

The numbers scrolled through her head again. Captured supernatural creatures. He was selling them. What use for them, Evie didn't want to imagine. And what could she do about it?

⬥

"YOU CAN'T RUSH THIS. This kind of spell is not like placing an order in a restaurant." The woman's husky voice was tight.

Mark had returned to the jobsite at the end of the day because he'd left his hammer drill and that thing cost a small fortune. He trusted his guys not to fuck with his shit implicitly, but Nikolai's goons hardly knew which end of the hammer was for the nail, and he had no doubt they'd pick it up and do something foolish, not knowing how to use it or how expensive it was.

The site was coming along nicely. It was amazing how few issues Mark had with shipping and supplies—he was sure he had Evie to thank for that. Sam and Pavel were midway through plumbing and wiring, and apparently Ondrej showed an aptitude for electrical. Good—he needed an electrical guy. He wondered how much it would cost to get the kid apprenticed to a master electrician or if he could get Anton to sponsor it in exchange for some work.

Mark was so busy thinking of his crew that he almost walked into the middle of a conversation. The basement was dark. New shadows formed by the walls and the construction equipment interfered with his visibility. He leaned back into the stairwell where it entered the basement, hoping the shadows would be enough to hide him from casual view.

In the space that would one day be a lounge area, Nikolai stood with his back to Mark, blocking the view of his companion. Mark tried to figure out what the hell they were doing down here.

"I need confirmation that you can manage the entire space." Nikolai leaned back, smooth and unhurried as if he were discussing the latest news in the markets.

Mark inhaled, the wolf sorting scents as familiar—Nikolai's cologne—and new—powder, perfume, and sweat. One of the dancers. And something else. He inhaled deeper, ignoring the wolf's irritation.

*Just do it, Big Guy.*

The wolf hated to be second-guessed. Mark knew the feeling. But it was such an unexpected scent, he needed to be one hundred percent sure.

She was pregnant, and she was afraid.

Mark's nose twitched at the faint whiff of magic. He held his breath to avoid sneezing.

"What choice do I have?" She hid both well, her voice conveying irritation and annoyance, but he knew that metallic tang.

"Trust me. It is better to find out that you are incapable now than later," Nikolai drawled. "The consequences will be much lower."

Mark bristled. That ass was threatening a pregnant woman.

"I can do it." She gave up the words like a surrender.

"Good," Nikolai snapped. "Let me know the minute it's done."

Mark listened as the sound of Nikolai's heel strikes faded into the building. The elevator doors slid open, groaning a little with age. He waited, hoping she would follow. He checked his watch. Almost seven. He could come back for the hammer drill tomorrow. He'd planned to be on-site first thing for the flooring guys anyway.

But the soft sound of a stifled sob and the scent of salt reached his nose. He swore under his breath. He couldn't leave her here alone. He wasn't sure what the hell he was going to do for her, but he'd figure something out. He always did.

He stepped out of the shadows slowly, making his footsteps loud so as not to startle whoever she was.

All the dancers had names like flowers, which he supposed fit the club but made them sound a lot more delicate than he assumed the lot of them were. He had a professional dancer as a sister—he recognized the strength hidden behind grace and serene expressions in those routines. Dancers were athletes. The performance was about making the skill look effortless.

This one, a lean, dark-skinned woman with her hair artfully arranged in a row of delicate cloudlike puffs down the center of her skull, seemed to be the de facto leader of the performers. The only person they deferred to more was their choreographer.

"I'm sorry." He lifted his palms when her startled, wet eyes rose to him. "I didn't know—"

She waved him off, hastily dabbing at her cheeks with the backs of her hands. "We're not supposed to be down here. It's just I've forgotten my—" She looked around.

He gave her an out with a smile. "I left my drill. Mark, by the way." He offered a hand.

"Violet." She took it with a little smile, composed again. "You're the foreman."

"Yes, ma'am."

Her brows lifted. "Am I that old?"

"Just meant to be respectful."

"You talk like a cowboy." A faint smile lit her face, deepened the creases around her eyes and mouth. She was older than she looked. "You are American?"

"We left when I was a kid."

The music had started upstairs, the sound of the early-evening crowd a dull clamor above their heads. He'd stayed late enough a few nights to know it would only get worse from here. His shoulders drew tight. Unlike Chris, he hadn't figured out a way to comfortably tolerate the loud music in night-clubs and avoided them as much as possible.

"It's none of my business, but are you okay here?"

Violet stared at him, her brows knit as if preparing to break bad news.

"No one is okay here. Don't let them convince you otherwise. Surviving in this place is a poker game—you know the song? When to hold."

"And when to fold 'em?"

A ghost of a smile lit her eyes. Her hand went to her belly where her unborn child rested, hidden beneath the generous empire waist of her otherwise slinky dress. "When to cash in your chips and run like hell."

A chill went through him at the thought of Evie and her hidden money.

"I appreciate your concern, but I am playing the hand I was dealt." Violet peered at him with an intense gaze. "I suggest you finish the work you were given here and do the same. Excuse me."

He stepped aside before their shoulders would have brushed. Again the whiff of powder and perfume and baby, and beneath it something familiar. He sniffed lightly, confirming.

And sneezed.

Not as strong as Evie, which was why it took him being up close, but it was there.

Nikolai knew what she was, and he planned to use it. How long before he uncovered Evie's secret? Maybe he had already and he was just waiting for the right time to turn the screw.

Mark retrieved his drill and headed back up the basement stairs. The stairwell opened up into the alley where he'd parked his battered Škoda near the street. Once in the driver's seat, he stared at himself in the rearview mirror, the flash of human hazel irises to a very lupine yellow almost too quick to notice. "Finish the job and get Evie the fuck out of here."

# CHAPTER TWENTY-THREE

THE NEXT DAY, Evie made her presence known by dropping off her purse and checking her makeup at her desk. She needed to get down to the basement as quickly as possible. Hellhound—Mark—hadn't come by last night.

She needed to talk to him about Le Seppe's visit.

Nikolai's and Valentin's voices, muffled by the office door, gave her the excuse she needed to grab a pile of papers and head out.

"I'm missing invoices," she snapped irritably at Faddei. "Tell Kolya I've gone down to the basement if he looks for me?"

The doorman grunted.

When she reached the basement, the sputtering Czech boy, Ondrej, informed her that Mark was upstairs, in the French garden.

Evie stalked back upstairs to the banquet room turned rehearsal space she'd negotiated for the dancers, far away from the basement—and Mark's crew. Memories of the weekend coated her belly in honeyed warmth. She could get used to that heady feeling of him in her space—hands never far from her hips, her thighs, the curve of her ass—his smiling mouth, soft on hers, breath on her neck, teeth on her skin.

When she'd woken in the predawn hours, he'd already been awake, watching her. He had to leave before daylight. She understood, but she wanted to see the morning sun in his eyes. He was intoxicating.

She pulled open the door with a deep breath. No time for this. Inside, a cluster of women had accumulated at the stage. She slowed, unable to fight amusement at the sight of Mark and Chris Vogel neatly flanked by dancers while working on the stage.

"Fancy a wager, Evie girl?" Sweet Pea called gaily from one of the banquet tables near the door with Violet and Sunflower.

"I've got Peony with three-to-one odds on the young one." Sunflower cackled. "She's got her hook in him, and he doesn't even realize it."

Peony sat on the stage, legs dangling over the edge right between the two men. Braced on her hands, she leaned forward, displaying an impressive amount of cleavage.

Evie gave Chris credit—even with the blush riding high on his cheekbones, he kept his eyes on the job—mostly. "I think I'd take that. Put me down for two hundred."

Sweet Pea laughed. "Sunny?"

"Noted."

But Evie's eyes had already moved on to the second figure at the center of the orbit of flirting dancers.

Mark's easy focus didn't break even as he flashed the occasional grin in response to some—probably salacious—comment from one of the girls.

*Not yours.*

"What are they doing here?" Evie said, unable to keep the edge out of her voice. She ignored Violet's sharp gaze. "The whole point of moving you all up here was so that they could focus on the renovation downstairs."

Sweet Pea chuckled. "And here we were thinking you did it to improve our working conditions."

"Nikolai sent them this morning," Sunny filled in helpfully. "One of the stage supports broke during rehearsal yesterday, and Madame is not willing to have us risk our lives and limbs."

"Lives and limbs?" Evie frowned.

"I heard she suggested he ask them." The petite contortionist who went by Lily parked her elbows on the back of Violet's chair, bending her leg up and behind her until she could grip her toes over her shoulder. "Too bad for her they didn't send up the old one. I hear she's got a boner for him."

Sweet Pea wheezed laughter.

"What about the other one, the foreman?" Violet purred, not taking her eyes off Evie. "Where are your odds, Sunny?"

Sunny contemplated her nails, looking carefully away. "I'd say his mind is elsewhere. Long shot on that one. Eh, Evie?"

"I'm sorry?" Evie blinked, unlocking her teeth.

Sweet Pea waved her off, laughing. "Nothing, precious."

"Janek saw you two in the hallway the other day, 'arguing' over an invoice," Sunny said with a proactive hint of mocking.

Evie raised a brow, refusing to look at the papers in her hand. "Janek is a gossip. It's my job to keep track of the money—"

"Her job." Sunny winked. "What've you got there, Eves?"

"More invoices." Sweet Pea leaned over the table, plucking at the pages.

Evie snatched them away, giving her best glare.

"Uh-oh, looks like Peony's decided to move up the chain," Lily cooed, switching legs. "She's after much bigger game."

Evie's gaze snapped up before she could stop herself. It was a subtle shift, but Peony's attention was now on Mark, her blue eyes narrow and calculating.

When Evie turned her eyes back to the table, all four women were watching her carefully.

Sunny picked an imaginary bit of lint from beneath her nail. "Interesting."

"I'd say." Sweet Pea coughed lightly.

Evie turned her back on the whole scene. *No promises.*

Sweet Pea reached for her hand anyway. "We mean nothing by it. We know you're loyal to Valentin. And we're grateful for the stage—and the air-conditioning."

"And there's no harm in a flirtation," Sunny added with a little grin.

"We wish you had warned us you were going to be away for a few weeks. We worried about you." Sweet Pea pouted. "If it wasn't for Violet going up there and demanding some answers—"

Evie stared at Violet. "You did— Why?"

Violet would not meet her eyes.

"You're one of us," Sunny said, grasping her other hand. "Well, you may not be one of us, but you always take care of the girls, especially the younger ones. The stage isn't the first time you've interjected on our behalves, Eves. We all know it."

Evie's nose warmed. The distant prickle in the back of her throat was an emotion she refused to name. Guilt that she hadn't factored in what they would think when she disappeared entirely tugged at her. She forced a teasing smile. "You'd think I negotiated a swampy gulag for all the gratitude you lot show."

"Can you blame us?" Sweet Pea beamed. "I mean, look at the view."

She expected she would feel the same if deprived of the magnificent view of Markus Vogel every day. "It's not terrible."

While she was here, it couldn't hurt to ask. "Has Nikolai talked to any of you about making some extra cash in the new rooms?"

Entertaining clients privately wasn't a requirement for the dancers at Little Blossoms as it was in some clubs. Valentin thought it added an air of forbidden fruit. Some girls simply weren't available at any price. But many of them liked the money, and the clients were mostly tolerable. The main floor had rooms for that kind of thing, but if Valentin was trying to branch out—maybe Mark's job really was a brothel and the supernatural trafficking was unconnected. She couldn't help hoping.

Sweet Pea frowned. "What rooms?"

Violet studied her hands on the table in a way that made Evie certain she knew something. She wasn't going to be able to hide her pregnancy on stage for much longer. Evie wondered what the dancer had decided to do about her lover's proposal.

"I think it's nothing we should concern ourselves with," Violet said, meeting Evie's eyes. "Any of us."

"Ladies." The familiar shadowed-silk voice rolled through her, sending every nerve ending into a state of heightened awareness.

Evie looked up a second after her companions. "Yes, Mr. Vogel?"

At least one person at the table sighed when his mouth curved upward into a smirk.

Peony floated in his wake, forgotten. His stars were obscured again today. Even without them, he practically twinkled.

"It's Markus," he said as though ending a long argument. "Mark is fine."

"What can I do for you, Mr. Vogel?" Evie straightened her spine, frowning.

He gestured at the papers in her hand. "I needed to speak with you about some of the invoices when you have the time. Miss Acaz."

One of the girls coughed, choking on a laugh. She ignored them.

Peony cooed something from his elbow, but his gaze never left Evie.

"Now is fine. I have delivery updates for you as well." She rose, gesturing toward the quiet space at the back of the hall.

"Excuse me." Mark removed his elbow from Peony's searching fingers.

Peony sucked her teeth before stalking back to the stage.

Evie rose from her seat and led him away from the table, aware of their audience. It would be worse to leave the room. It would start all-too-eager tongues wagging that wouldn't easily stop.

Her early years serving drinks on the floor among these women had put the finishing touches on her ability to read a room and the people in it. There was so much beyond the awareness of danger—so many nuances to attraction and interest—that had helped her increase her tips when she served, made her one of the most popular servers with the VIPs, and helped keep her on Valentin's good side.

Well, if she could fake attraction to a mob boss, she could fake disinterest in an actual lover. And this was more important. She picked the banquet table next to the kitchen door under a bright, unflattering light.

With the noise from the kitchen a wall away to keep her focused on where they were, she took a deep breath, steadying herself.

She watched Mark's brother. "Is he going to be all right?"

Chris reached for his hammer, and Fuchsia was there with it at the ready, her bright pink lashes—a perfect match to her glossy lipstick—fluttering. He looked like a kid in a candy shop.

Mark shrugged. "He knows we're on a look-don't-touch policy."

Evie glanced at the elder Vogel. "Look, don't—"

"Your buddy Nikolai was very clear." His brow twitched north.

"He's not my—"

"It's a figure of speech." Mark's voice lowered to a purr as he followed her gaze back to Chris. "They say he's the handsome one."

She kept her voice low and eyes on the younger man. "I suppose for some."

"Not you?" He might have been teasing, but she heard the old tension in it.

She met his eyes in the terrible light. "Not me."

The smile that followed usually came before he pressed a kiss to the hollow of her throat, the space behind her ear. She reflexively took a step back, knowing she wouldn't be able to stop him or resist the urge to reciprocate. But he didn't approach, only gave her a long, knowing look.

"The Amazon came by the office yesterday." She lowered her voice as she pointed out something unnecessary on an invoice. "Threatened Valentin and Nikolai."

Mark went still. "Not here."

She nodded. "I know. But it couldn't wait."

His voice hardened. "No. He's here."

Alarm raced through Evie.

"Be cool," Mark said, then raised his voice. "Nikolai, I just asked Ms. Acaz to let you know we're about finished here."

Evie coiled panic deep under her rib cage and lifted an annoyed gaze to Nikolai. "As I told Mr. Vogel, I am not a messenger."

"Forgive our Evie. She's got a big day ahead of her." He chuckled, palms spread and speared her with a look. "I'm surprised to not find you at your desk."

She heard the warning. "Invoices."

"Again?"

"I asked her to come down, Kolya," Violet announced, sliding between them to link arms with Evie. "My new costumes came back, and I wanted her opinion."

Nikolai's brows arched with opinions of what he thought of that.

"Are you two finished talking business? Mark, can I steal her?" Violet beamed, all flirt and invitation.

"Sure." He nodded, dismissing Evie with a glance. Nikolai opened his mouth, but Mark cut him off. "Actually, Nikolai, now that you're here, I've got a few suggestions about this stage if you've got a minute."

"For your thoughtful suggestions," Nikolai said dryly, "I make the time."

"Come on, Eves." Violet tugged at her arm.

Violet chatted brightly through the warren of the backstage areas as they passed other staff.

When the hall was empty, Evie whispered, "Your costumes aren't due back for another week or two."

She would know—Violet was one of Tal's first clients from the club.

"I have never known you to be a fool before, Evelia," Violet growled, all stage presence vanishing as she yanked Evie into the corner by the service elevator.

Evie's heart crashed against her ribs, the hammering thunder in her ears. "I don't know—"

"Making an idiot of yourself with that construction worker in front of the one man who doesn't miss anything," Violet said with more intensity than Evie thought it was worth.

Evie bit her tongue on excuses, lies. "What harm is a little flirtation?"

"You need to be keeping yourself on the right side of Nikolai and whatever it is you really do for Valentin." Violet jammed the button for the elevator.

"What I really do?" Evie echoed hollowly.

"Oh, you dress the part and you go through the right motions." Violet bullied her way into Evie's face, her voice low. "But we've seen every girl come through here that winds up with that idiot. For one, you're too old."

"I'm twenty-six?" Evie didn't mean it to be a question, but the words stuck in her throat.

"Valentin likes them young and flashy. Hopeful. Stupid. Not haunted and world-wise." Violet kept pressing. "You've been around too long. Usually he's replaced them by now."

The elevator doors slid open.

"Best you go back where you belong now." Violet stepped away.

Evie watched her go, willing her heart to stop racing. She'd never seen Violet so angry—or desperate. Something was wrong with the dancer. Evie didn't have time for another mystery to solve, but Violet was the closest thing to a friend she had. She couldn't let it go.

MARK RESISTED the urge to watch the two women leave.

After listening to Evie detail necklines and sleeve lengths at her place Saturday, he realized he needed to step up his game. After a few hours of poking around the net Sunday night, getting a crash course on women's fashion, he was becoming a shoe man.

Today's pair had been cobalt-blue d'Orsay heels. The cutout insoles revealed a tantalizing view of Evie's arches.

He stored that for later and gave his full attention to walking Nikolai through a few changes he thought would make the stage hold up better to all the gyrations it'd been put to use for recently. Nikolai left after authorizing changes with a perfunctory warning about cost and prioritizing the basement job.

It was easier than Mark expected to extract Chris from the bevy of gorgeous women. For once, his little brother almost looked relieved to be riding the elevator down to the basement and the rest of the crew.

"I don't know, man," Chris said. "That guy gives me a funky vibe."

"Nikolai," Mark said slowly, glancing at his brother with a little shake of his head. *Not here. Not now.* "You get used to guys like that. I'm new, and his ass is probably on the line for my work. So he's extra attentive. Just do your job and get out." He picked a few scraps of paper out of his brother's pocket, crumpling the numbers up. "And don't mess with any of these girls."

They stepped out of the elevator, and Chris groaned, laughing.

Mark dumped the paper into the nearest waste bin on the way into the jobsite. "The fuck you laughing at?"

"You need to take your own advice."

Mark liked closing up the site at the end of the day himself. It gave him a chance to look over the progress and make mental adjustments for the next day. Pavel and Ondrej were almost done with the floor prep. He stayed late to do a bit more work to make sure they were on track when the installers arrived.

"You take pride in your work. That is good."

Mark looked up as Nikolai strolled through the site, hands in his pockets, the very picture of an executive at the end of the long day save for the latent threat of violence.

Mark recognized guys who were a step or two away from throwing a punch or a shoving match, but this guy was the opposite. Nikolai would be quiet until the moment he went off, and somebody would wind up dead or close enough to it.

Bebe's refreshed charm flared on his skin, like the mark of a burn or a bruise. He thought she wouldn't have made it uncomfortable on purpose. Or maybe she would have, just to prove how ridiculous this whole thing was. At the moment, he had to agree with her. The wolf bristled.

"There's only one way to do a job," Mark said.

"What way is that?" Nikolai tilted his head, curious.

"The right way." Mark smiled, showing teeth.

Maybe it was the guy's eyes—so dark it was almost impossible to pick out pupil from iris—or the way it seemed he slipped on the easy smile like his expertly knotted tie and that what lay beneath it was far less civilized.

Nikolai appraised the framing and made a slow circuit of the room.

Mark slotted the last of his tools into place and shouldered his belt, box in one hand. "I'm happy to answer any of the questions you have about the job or my progress."

"You are a very smart man," Nikolai said. "No wonder Anton handed you a job this large."

"He didn't *hand* me anything." Mark bristled.

Nikolai held up his palms. "Forgive me. English is not my first language, you know. I sometimes make a bad choice of words."

"No, I'm sorry." Mark exhaled, forcing the tension out of his shoulders. "Anton's always telling me not to take everything so seriously…"

"I know what it's like to have to fight for everything you've earned. To know you deserve more chances than you are given." Nikolai smiled faintly. "I grew up in Valentin's shadow. My father was one of his father's closest, you know. Right-hand man. But he was injured on the job, and Valentin's father… Well, he left him behind. Overnight, my family's circumstances changed."

He began stacking Mark's plans, organizing papers as though he were a valet or secretary.

"My mother was not accustomed to the kind of work required to raise five squalling brats without the nannies my father's money had paid for. She left us. My grandmother raised us while my father went from calling shots to being a glorified delivery driver."

His hand squeezed on the rolled-up papers, and the sound seemed to rouse him from memory. He shook his head and sighed.

"When Valentin was coming up, I saw my chance," he said. "I fought men—older, stronger, more experienced than me—to stay at his side. Dirty work and hard work. You ran demos before this, correct?"

Mark shook himself out of imagining what kind of work Nikolai might have been involved in. "Yes… yes. Five years. But I've been with Anton since secondary school."

"Not university?"

"Not the university type." Mark shrugged.

"A man who works with his hands." Nikolai met his eyes. "Again, this I admire. Not afraid to get dirty. So many of the boys coming up these days are too soft. Too far removed from survival."

"Mr.—"

"Kolya." Nikolai smiled again. "Let us be just Mark and Kolya, yes?"

Mark lowered his chin once.

"Good." Nikolai beamed. "Friends. As it should be. And I should give you some friendly advice that may serve you."

Mark rose, preparing to brace against the blow. When it came, it almost caught him off guard anyway.

"She belongs to Valentin," Nikolai said quietly. "In every way that matters."

Mark cocked his head, feigning confusion. He knew exactly whom Nikolai was referring to.

"I see the way you look at her." Nikolai fanned his hand in front of his face briefly. "You're not the first to admire something that does not belong to him."

"I'm not sure what you think you saw, but—"

"She is a beautiful woman."

"And she's not the only one." Mark shrugged. *Be cool. He's just sniffing around for trouble.* "I was in a room full of them all day."

"And you handled yourself well," Nikolai admitted. "A consummate professional."

"That was a test?"

"I tell you this because I like you." If Nikolai heard the edge in Mark's voice, he ignored it, his tone just as offhand as before. "Mark and Kolya, remember? Friends."

Mark's brows rose.

"You seem like a good man," Nikolai went on. "An honest one. Clean. A thing not even your boss can claim any longer. It is a pleasure to see a good man succeed. It would be a shame for you to be derailed by a nice bit of ass."

"Is that what she is to you?" Mark's nostrils flared.

Nikolai tsked softly, shaking his head. "It is in your own interest."

"You threatening me?"

Nikolai's eyes widened. "Forgive me. I have been too evasive. I only mean to say Evie has made her choices. This life was one of them." He spread his palms to take in their surroundings. "And those of us who belong to it."

"Maybe she's ready to make different choices," Mark growled before he could bite back the words.

The wolf bristled under his collarbones, ready to fight, to defend. Nikolai's gaze had taken on that pointed, seeing look.

Mark had misunderstood the test. Nikolai had thrown him in the middle of a room of available women and caught him in the corner with the one he absolutely couldn't have.

Mark exhaled. It was a struggle to get the wolf to back down, but he had the sense that the closer it came to the surface, the more Nikolai could sense *something* there. He needed to walk away before exposing himself any further.

Nikolai's laugh raised the hairs on his arms. "She has everything she needs. More if she wills it. And some choices, once made, are not easily undone."

"Look, man," Mark said, voice tight. "I'm here for the job. You don't like the way I look at her, don't send her down here. If that's all?"

Nikolai nodded, stepping aside. "Good evening. Just. Mark."

Evie's warning stayed with him. He had to find out what she knew. He also had a call out to a guy in Paris who'd made a name doing dungeons and playrooms. Mark was hoping to get some answers about the peculiarity of the building materials and the plans. They had set up a time to talk tonight.

He wanted to have some answers before he saw Evie again. And she was right—going by her apartment was a bad idea, especially after the conversation with Nikolai. He had to come up with something else.

# CHAPTER TWENTY-FOUR

"HERE ARE THE WEEK'S INVOICES," Mark announced on Friday.

Evie looked up at him blankly from behind her desk, speaking her mind before she could catch herself. "We already—"

"Needed to check in with Nikolai, thought I'd save you the trip down," Mark said over her, setting a sheaf of papers on her desk.

She scanned the office. It was quiet and mostly empty on a midmorning save for the guard at the door. Both men watched Mark carefully.

"Nikolai is at the Anděl today."

Valentin's flagship casino was a two-hour drive outside the city in a wealthy spa town near the German border.

Mark angled his back to the door and winked with a muttered, "So I heard. Took the two goons downstairs with him."

Evie tightened her answering grin to a frown. "Is there anything I can help with downstairs?"

"Wouldn't want you to hurt yourself on the jobsite in those matchsticks." His expression was severe and a little smug as his glance skated down to the red patent leather stilettos with their thin ankle strap and up to where her knees disappeared beneath the desk surface.

"He won't be back in until Monday." Evie narrowed her eyes, feeling the flush rising in her chest. "I assure you, Mr. Vogel, I am quite capable—"

"Nah, I'll wait for the man himself." His index finger tapped the plain envelope on the top to draw her attention.

The office door opened, and Valentin appeared, beaming. "Markus, my boy. Nice to see you here."

"Just came to run some invoices to this one," Mark said, jerking his chin in her direction, "and to pick up our payroll."

She wanted to punch him. He was good at acting like an inconsiderate jerk.

"Your payroll will be delivered at the end of the day." She narrowed her eyes.

"Come, Evelia, give the man a break. It's Friday," Valentin chastised. "I'm sure his crew would like their pay to enjoy for the weekend a little early. You can do that, yes, darling?"

After a long, silent beat, she smiled prettily at Valentin. "*Da,* Valentinovich."

Evie slammed her hand on the paperwork, narrowing her gaze at Mark. That was when she saw the quick flash of yellow. He was no more comfortable with it than she was. But whatever he'd come for was important enough to risk being seen together. She splayed her palm over the papers, pressing the envelope flat.

"Good, my kitten." Valentin chucked her under the chin before turning to Mark. "Come, have a drink while you wait."

Evie fought the urge to snarl.

"And Evelia…" Valentin ushered Mark into the room. "Make it, eh, how do they say, Markus? Snappy? Yes. Snappy."

She tucked her chin in a nod, averting her face to hide the set of her jaw and the rage she wasn't quite sure she could hide in her eyes. "*Da.*"

She waited until the door had closed solidly before slipping the envelope to the bottom of the stack of papers and into her purse. Then she went to work on the payroll.

It wasn't until she was on the tram riding home that she took the envelope from her purse. She couldn't help a glance around to make sure there were no familiar faces. Inside was a scrap of paper with his neatly formed letters and a single theater ticket.

*Vyšehrad Amphitheater.*
*Saturday, 7:30.*
*Need to talk about your peas.*

She paused at the last line. Surely he didn't mean…? She shook her head, exhaling hard at the little frisson of excitement that sparked low in her core.

Saturday couldn't come soon enough.

It felt strange preparing to see him. A date. Is that what this was? Not a forest rendezvous or an illicit office flirtation or a midnight walk with a wolf. She changed her outfit twice.

Saturday afternoon, she boarded the metro into the Old Town, getting off at Můstek station and making her way through the warren of shops.

"Look at who finally turned up," Tal sang after the doorbell announced her entrance. "And just in time for coffee. Pull up a stool."

Evie slowed her chewing by her third slice of baguette and the thick herb spread, staring back at him.

Tal sipped from his cup, the smug smile barely visible over the rim. "So you and the foreman have rekindled your affair."

She cocked her head, blinking at him innocently.

"Nice try." Tal laughed.

She let the smile tug free, feeling the heat sting her cheeks.

"You deserve a little happiness." He contemplated the nearly emptied cup. "And perhaps—"

"Perhaps what?"

"A memorable send-off?" Tal finished without meeting her eyes.

"Precisely."

She and Mark weren't a couple. Their path wouldn't follow the usual route—dating, fucking, arguing, breaking up. Making up. One step led to a torrent of others, like tumblers in a lock she thought she'd sealed shut long ago.

A future spooled out before her. One in which she'd convince Tal to take a chance on a larger shop, something with better frontage. She'd meet Mark at the end of the day for drinks or a meal and walk home hand in hand along the cobbled streets.

A lifetime of impossible mornings. Parting at the doorstep for the day—him to a jobsite, her to the shop. Weekends in the woods, a little cabin of their own perhaps. She closed the door on those thoughts, turned the keys.

*Need to talk about your peas.*

The last line. The wolf knew where she kept her ledgers. This wasn't a date. Mark had found out something. And she needed to tell him about the Amazon and the circus.

"Why not leave town with a few good memories." She drained her mug.

Tal wasn't fooled. *"Evie."*

Now she'd given him another reason to worry about her. One more gray hair he didn't deserve. And maybe he was right to worry. She was losing her edge—the grasp of the plan she needed to hang on to. Instead of imagining snowflakes in Edinburgh or mild beach weather in Cascais, she saw small round faces with Mark's sharp ears and her dark eyes. Or his bright ones.

Which would they be—wolf or witch? She'd never heard of anything like Mark's family.

Tal began his next sentence carefully. "When are you leaving?"

A lump she hadn't known was forming hardened in her throat. *Oh no.*

She couldn't start feeling something now. Everything he'd taught her, and she was pitching it away after a big dick and a sly, wolfish smile.

She swallowed around it and forced an easy cadence in her voice that she didn't feel. "I'd think you're eager to get rid of me."

"I'm eager to see you free of this mess, my heart," he murmured.

"Soon, okay," she said, letting artifice fall away. "Soon."

"Evie, the enemy of a plan—"

"Is the failure to follow it," she finished, setting her plate down harder than she intended. She met his eyes. "I understand, Tal. Believe me. Things are getting strange. I know what I need to do."

"Strange?" A new furrow appeared on his brow.

She'd said too much.

"I didn't come here for a lecture," she snapped, harder than she'd intended.

She focused on digging in her bag to give herself time to regain her composure. When she emerged with the two slim, bound journals, Tal met her eyes. She set them on the table.

"Another set?"

"The last," she promised resolutely.

A flicker of relief softened his brow.

"But they come with a change of plans," she said, worrying the corner of her lip between her teeth.

His hand paused halfway. "That bad, huh?"

"Worse."

She held her breath. Would Tal think she was insane? Kick her out? If he was smart, he would. This would be asking too much.

"The best thing to do when one has a foul taste is to spit." Tal's expression tightened again.

"I need you to get these to Elise Le Seppe."

His face lost all color. "The Amazon."

She nodded once, a determined jut of her chin. Valentin and Kolya were fools to think they could match wits with the necromancer. And the necromancer was the only one who couldn't be bought or threatened.

"Valentin's got too many of the press and the police in his pocket," she said in a rush. "But the arrangement with the necromancer—his boss's arrangement—"

"His boss, *Yan Petrov*."

"They're frightened of her." A few minutes in Le Seppe's presence had convinced Evie that the woman was no fool—and her boss would not be either. With the ledgers, the immortal would have everything she needed to wipe Valentin from the map. "Whatever Valentin's up to is going to threaten

Petrov's arrangement with the necromancer. *She's* the one who enforces it. If something happens to me—" She stopped when the words stuck in her throat. "If I disappear and you don't hear from me, it is as we agreed except: get the journals to Le Seppe. Can you do that?"

"You could be dead by then, you know." His voice was blunt, meant to scare her. But Evie was past that. She would have freedom or nothing.

Evie closed her eyes, exhaling a long, slow breath. When she opened them again, she knew the fear was gone. "If I'm lucky. But I'm taking Valentin down with me. And maybe I live to see a miracle: he lets me go if I keep his secrets."

She slid the books across the table. Tal made them disappear under a few swatches of fabric. They would join the others, wherever he kept them. Better that she did not know.

"Now, I've got to go." She rose, clearing her throat and gathering her satchel and a light shawl in case the evening in the park cooled. "I have a date."

Evie rarely visited the southern part of the city, and it took her a moment to orient herself off the metro. In the end, she followed a group of tourists, chattering among themselves and pointing out signs. Once, she would have seen them as marks—a way to get a few extra crowns by offering a tour, or a sad story, depending on what they seemed ready to hear. Eventually the arched stone gate from the old fortress walls appeared, and she quickened her step to pass them.

"Excuse me, miss," one, red-faced and sweating, called out to her. "Do you speak English?"

Impatient, Evie almost mumbled an apologetic bit of nonsense and kept moving. But the memory of Mark's saying about strangers made her smile. She slowed down but thickened her accent so she wouldn't risk being drawn into conversation. "A little bit."

"You know this place?" They spoke loudly, enunciating as though Evie was hard of hearing. "Is there anything to see there?"

"The basilica is pretty in the afternoon." When that failed to impress, she tried again. "Smetana is buried beside it." Blank looks. "The composer?"

They nodded agreeably but seemed unimpressed.

"The beer garden just inside the gate." She smiled. "Great view."

That earned pleasant clucking and chattering as they thanked her, and she went on her way.

She left them to it and followed the shaded stone path and long strips of green, chasing the infinite quiet of the interior park. The ground seemed to hum contentedly beneath her feet, beneath the stone and the grass and the hill itself. She followed the signs north, along the rampart, toward the outdoor amphitheater nestled in the northeastern crook of the fortress walls.

She had given herself plenty of time. Now she found a bench that placed her back to the stone ramparts and opened a book. She didn't think Nikolai or Valentin had her followed, but she'd disrupted her routine just enough to be wary. She took in the parade of prams and packs of tourists—wondering at humanity's ability to insist on normalcy despite extraordinary circumstances—and kept an eye out for anyone she'd seen in the club.

"Is this seat free?" A tall young woman stopped at the edge of the bench. She was dressed in layers of black—a loose, nearly transparent mesh shirt over a tank top and tight jeans pegged where they met lug-soled boots.

Evie was so unused to being asked she fumbled before scooting over unnecessarily to make room. "*Prosim.*"

"No need, child," the woman said, though she could have been no older than Evie. "I won't be here long."

Something about the sound of her Czech made Evie—who was hardly an expert—stare. It sounded old. She steeled herself and looked above the woman's shoulders. Her hair was anachronistically styled in elaborate looping braids with a circular headpiece of dark fabric or leather. Her face rippled from a young girl to a mature woman to a crone and back.

Evie jerked away, her heart racing. "What are you?"

"I am a middle sister, a daughter, and I am like you," the woman said. "I see what lies ahead, behind, and within."

*A witch.*

"I took my castle on a hill, surrounded by women, far away." The woman surveyed the park. "My father settled this place, but my sister ruled it. This place belongs to her. It has taken much to send me here to this now. Time is not our ally. You must ask your questions and quickly."

*What questions* was going to be the first thing out of her mouth, but Evie knew better.

"Why does your face do that?" Evie dared another glance.

A small, approving smile followed the woman through the ages of her life. "Good. You see all that I was."

"Why can I see it?"

"If you are strong enough to see one aspect of time, then you are strong enough to see others."

"But I see death masks."

The witch frowned, looking disappointed in her.

Evie tried again. "Why can I only see death?"

"You see ghosts or the soon-to-be ghosts." The witch spoke patiently. "The unrested dead. That is *your* choice."

Evie coughed, her eyes smarting. "Why would I—? Why would anyone—?"

"Fear is a powerful tutor. If you're not vigilant, it shapes all that you see." The woman's expression seemed less indulgent than amused. "See the world as it is, and what is to come will appear to you."

Evie didn't like being laughed at, so she squared her shoulders and stared the woman down. The transitions slowed, gradually morphing from one to another until Evie could see all the details.

"Good."

Evie got the sense she didn't give praise frequently. "I can see the future?"

"Many things dark at first glance may not remain that way. Other things that are seen will disappear without the right choices."

*Possibilities can be changed*—Mark's words.

"He's my favorite," she replied as if Evie had spoken aloud. "He's smarter than he gives himself credit. Prettier too."

Evie gripped the bench beneath her to keep her hands from trembling. The metal bolts began to shift, vibrating.

"Why metal?" Evie said, holding back a sob.

"Like to like." The witch pulled out a soft linen cloth from her bag and slid it to Evie. "And power is changed by that which conducts it. We admired your use of the dead to heal the living. Very clever, little witch."

"Jevany?"

She nodded. "Your first boon. Two birds, one stone."

"I don't understand." Evie shook her head, barely feeling the tears streaking down her cheeks.

"Is there a question, my precious one?" Though the skin around them aged and renewed, the witch's eyes did not change, remaining as unbroken and blue as a summer sky.

"What were my boons?"

"The child, the man, and the crone who had a taste for a cool beer on a hot day. Can't say I blame her." The witch smiled again, pleased.

When Evie lowered her chin, the witch cupped her cheek in one hand, wiping away the salty tears with one thumb and dabbing at her cheeks with the cloth. The motion crackled energy against her skin, and where liquid connected them, prickles of energy flowed into Evie, sharp but invigorating. "I helped the ghost boy, and Mark, and the tourist, and that brought you here."

"That is not a question."

Evie frowned at her but took the cloth the witch offered. "I am trying to keep up."

The sharp peal of a laugh escaped her, like the bark of a crow. None of the park-goers seemed to notice. "You are doing wonderfully, darling. You haven't run screaming yet, which is an excellent sign."

Evie laughed. She couldn't help it.

The witch rose.

"Are you leaving?" Evie gaped.

"I've won the bet," she said mischievously.

"Bet?"

"My sisters said I could not make you laugh," the witch said. "And I have done so, which ends the spell that brought me to you."

"No!" Evie gasped.

The witch leaned forward and kissed her brow. She tucked the cloth firmly into Evie's fingers. "Keep it. It will help you to remember. That is the most important thing. What you remember, you believe."

"What do I do now about Valentin and the creatures?" Evie said in a rush.

Her face grew grim. "I see many possibilities. Too many. You must decide... Ask one more."

Evie thought frantically. Her heart raced, her mouth dry. One more question. "What do I need to know to access my power fully?"

The witch's smile was brilliant. The girl in the woman's face, youth in the crone, and the wisdom of age in a child's eyes. "What you long for is safety, but if you fight for your limitations, they will bind you. Be brave. Release them and set yourself free. And don't be late."

"Late?" Evie blinked.

She checked the time and sprang off the bench. When she looked up again, the witch had vanished, gone too quickly to have disappeared into the parade of slowly moving people.

Evie hurried to the theater, where a dozen people lingered in the waiting area, finishing conversations before taking their seats. Even this late, the sun-warmed stone emanated the heat of the day. She was glad she had gone with the linen maxi dress. She recognized no one, but she scanned their faces anyway. She didn't look away from the death masks. Instead, she observed them. Here and there, she could catch a glimpse of past youth.

She waited outside the ticket counter, gathering her nerve and scanning for Mark. The envelope had included her ticket, so perhaps he meant to meet her in the seat. It would make sense, could make it appear at a glance that they did not know each other.

The young woman at the counter's eyes lit up when she saw the ticket. "Please, this way."

The seats were near the back, which might have been bad except it was a lovely pocket of shade with nothing behind her and a perfect view of the castle peeking over the stage. The shade had already begun to creep over the seats, and Evie noted more than a few patrons eyed her curiously as she settled in. The usher returned with a small basket covered by blue silk. A scarf.

"For you," she said, placing it in the seat beside her.

Inside was a half bottle of wine, fresh baguette, and cheese slices with little glass pots of cheese and jam.

"Is he—?"

The usher shrugged with a bit of a smile, opening the wine and pouring her a glass. "I was only told to bring the basket."

Evie waited, fighting the urge to look up at every male voice. Gradually the shadows lengthened and the seats around her filled. The lights flicked twice, warning that the show would begin, and the crowd settled. The play was something local, charming, and absurd, but Evie hardly heard a word.

"Enjoying the show?" Warm skin brushed her arm.

Evie jumped, biting back a shout, and glared into familiar copper eyes. "You're lucky I didn't scream."

A few people glanced over their shoulders disapprovingly. Mark put a finger over his lips and winked.

"Come on, Evergreen." He took her hand. Evie began to argue, but he squeezed her fingers. "Trust me?"

Evie stood, and together they slipped along the back wall. The usher who had shown Evie to her seat silently brushed the curtain aside for them to exit the theater.

"I owe you one." Mark nodded gratefully as they slipped past.

The lobby area was empty, the voices of the performances following them as echoes bounced along the stone walls around them. Mark hurried her past the empty tables and dark, silent bar.

"Sorry I'm late," he said. "I was going to be here at the end of the first act, but I got held up."

"It's okay—but why are we leaving?"

"Did you want to see the rest?" Mark hesitated outside the gates, a pained look on his face.

"I barely understood it." Evie laughed when relief softened his expression. "I just thought—"

"It seemed like a good idea, just in case anyone is keeping an eye on us," he said, lacing their fingers together.

They walked along the tree-lined path inside the wall, dodging the glow of lamps. A flicker of memory rose between them—another night, another park, a death witch and her hellhound. Only they had never been that, had they? She tore her thoughts away from all they had become to each other. She would not waste energy on longing.

"And did you see anyone?"

"Not that I can tell." His eyes flashed yellow in the darkness. "Either of us."

"And now no one can follow us," she said. "You're good at this."

It was a good plan. A smart one. He would have been able to watch anyone going in after her or loitering after she entered. And because they'd left in the middle of the show, they would shake anyone who had been waiting.

"I watch a lot of spy movies." He laughed, drawing her close. "Hey, you."

"Hi. You." She tilted her mouth up to meet his.

The kiss sparked through her, tiny zaps and tickles of electricity that raced through her fingertips. And not just her imagination of the sensation either. Flickers of orange and yellow cascaded down around their locked hands.

"Ouch." Mark laughed.

"I'm sorry—"

"No, no." He pulled her in again. "Don't apologize. It was surprising, that's all. Kinda nice though."

"That's never happened before." She laughed when they parted.

His eyes narrowed, thin bands of yellow in the dark. "Never?"

She shook her head. There had been a few lovers over the years, but no sneaking around, kissing handsome men in moonlit parks. "Must be all the subterfuge."

"Must be." The corner of his mouth canted up. He sniffed. "You wearing a new perfume? You smell... different? It's good. Just different."

"I met a witch in the park," she blurted out. "She touched me. I feel different. I'm not sure she was alive."

He took it better than she expected. "She didn't offer you any too-good-to-be-true bargains? Promise you everything you wanted? Give you a mysterious spell book?"

"Do I look foolish enough to fall for that?" Evie's brow rose. She described the woman and the encounter, fighting the urge to make it all sound somehow rational. Only the scrap of linen tucked into her satchel beside a crumpled bullet kept her from thinking it a hallucination.

He laughed. "Witches."

"You're not surprised."

"You know the story. Prague was founded by a wise woman—a seer, maybe a witch—named Libuše."

"You think I saw—"

"Nah." He shook his head. Then he took a breath. "She had two sisters. The one with the castle far away—Tetin. That must have been Teta."

"You are very certain," Evie said, torn between laughter and disbelief.

Mark seemed to be at a loss for words. Finally he shrugged. "Libuše is a friend of the family. Sorta. It's a long story."

Before she could marshal her wits to ask, he peered into the vee of her dress. "Is that…?"

She'd spent the evenings with the ruined necklace, practicing imbuing the stone and metal with intention. It had taken all week—frustrating, headache-inducing work. Still, she'd finally gotten it exactly how she imagined—setting arranged as though it had grown out of the stone itself and a thin, filigreed chain almost invisible against her skin.

She fished the chain out of her dress, dropping the pendant into his palm. "I made a few changes. I hope you don't mind."

"Next time I'm just going to give you the silver and save myself a few crowns." He laughed before looking away.

"Next time?" She grinned, musing. Maybe she wasn't the only one having trouble with the future.

"You know you don't have to keep it."

"Regret giving to me?"

"Of course not."

"Good, because too late to take it back now." She tucked it away again. "It doesn't have to be a reminder of something terrible. It is beautiful. And rare. And it made you think of me. Gods only know why."

"I think you answered your question, gorgeous." His hand circled hers. "Come on."

The cemetery was locked, so they went wide around the church and down the stone walkway to the cliff's edge overlooking the river. Outside the manicured walls and arches, a winding path of switchbacks led through a forested hillside. Mark guided her off the main trail and into a dirt track, nearly straight downhill.

She pressed close to his shoulders. "Where are we going?"

"I wanted to take you someplace special," he said cryptically.

The path was steep, and he had to help her more than a few times over obstacles she could barely see in the absence of even streetlamps. His eyes had gone almost entirely yellow in the dark, more wolf than man. Which probably explained how surefooted and confident he was. That must come in handy.

But when they spilled out onto a narrow street before a big neoclassical building in shades of mint that warmed in the golden glow of streetlamps, she thought it wasn't just that he could see better. It was that he knew this place well because he was familiar with it. And she understood what he meant by "special."

She paused before the steps of the building, the weight in her heels forcing him to stop or let go of her hand. He refused to let go or draw her unwillingly, turning to face her on the step.

A torrent of emotion made it hard to keep her voice even. "This is your family's building."

"The Vogel compound," he agreed, hurrying on. "But, nothing weird, I promise. I have my own place. My parents are out—date night. I got the tickets from them; they're at the national theater—and my brother is probably at a club, and my brother and sister-in-law are holed up with their books if they're not at the cabin."

He huffed a little, shaking his head with a wry grin. The yellow had receded entirely, leaving only the warm golden brown flecked with freshly turned earth and the sparkle of starlight.

"Fuck me, I'm nervous." He laughed.

"I'm not the first girl you've brought here?" She didn't want to be his first anything, to taint that memory with her leaving.

He snorted.

"In that case," she drawled, biting down her laughter. "No need to be nervous if I'm just one of the masses."

"That's not what I meant." He shook his head, glaring at her. "Never mind. I thought you were right about not being at your place together. So I brought you to the safest place I know. Come up please?"

Evie glanced at the door and then the question on his face. "I've followed you everywhere so far. Why stop now?"

The flash of a smile he gave her was shooting-star brilliant. "Exactly."

# CHAPTER TWENTY-FIVE

HE WASN'T NERVOUS, just unsettled. Evie was connected to the mob. Bringing her home could expose his entire family. But he'd already done that when he told her what they were. And he'd taken all the steps to make tonight safe for everyone. He'd been late because he wanted to make one more lap of the park, sniffing out anyone who carried the familiar scent of Valentin's men. It would have been stupid to be nervous.

Evie looked beautiful, as usual, but more relaxed. She'd toned down the glamour to only conceal her scars. Her light brown hair shone through, and her eyes were their usual warm chocolate. Mark regretted leaving her alone for most of the night on their first date.

Anyway, this wasn't a *date* date. He and Evie had things to talk about. Important things. The call with the guy in Paris had been an eye-opener, and Evie had been vibrating with the story of the Amazon's visit.

He took her hand. Everyone was out, or busy, and they were going straight to his apartment and—

"Perfect timing." Tobias stood on the landing, his calm gray eyes steady on Mark. "Dinner's almost ready."

Behind Mark, Evie froze. Her glamour was back in force, and he almost did a double take.

Mark squeezed her hand.

Barbara bustled out onto the landing behind her much taller husband, elbowing her way to the front. "You didn't forget again, did you? And you brought a friend—good. I may have tripled the recipe, accidentally. It's not a perfect science...cooking. Honey, go get a chair from your brother's. This should be cozy."

Mark had not forgotten this time. There had been no dinner plans. He'd even told Tobias he planned to be out.

"We are…" Mark began, conflicting excuses fighting for dominance. *Busy. Headed out. Not free for whatever this shit is.*

Barbara started down the stairs, stretching out her hand to Evie. She was in on it too. "Maybe you can just stop in for a quick bite. No pressure."

Mark gave up all artifice. *"No—"*

"Problem," Evie finished, moving around Mark to meet Barbara. "We'd love that."

"Please come in." Toby ushered Evie inside as Barbara made introductions.

When the women were inside, Mark glared daggers at his brother. That awkward, lanky piece of shit didn't even flinch.

Mark paused on the doorstep, eyes yellow and teeth bared. In the old days, just a hint of Mark's wolf would have been enough for Toby to hunch and skitter off.

Toby squared his shoulders, eyes turning a shade smokier gray as tufts of dark hair sprang from his ears—his wolf responding to the asserted dominance. It didn't hurt that he was taller, making the subtle flex more pronounced.

Oh, that was *it*. Mark growled. Fuck *that*.

"Come on in, big brother." Toby smiled amiably, and his wolf retreated. He started down the hall, leaving Mark to follow. "Let's break some bread."

"I'm going to break your neck." Mark closed the door behind them.

They followed the women down the narrow hall into the separate dining room while Barbara chattered about the difficulty sourcing ingredients for an authentic American meal.

Inside, when Chris emerged from the kitchen, drawing off his cooking mitts, Mark was convinced. This wasn't a calendar mix-up. This was an ambush. The only thing missing was his sister's nosy ass bouncing around, demanding Evie's life story.

Tobias slipped past Evie. "Wine—red or white?"

Evie's voice was light and even as though she hadn't noticed them circling her. "Whatever you've opened is fine."

"I'll get you a glass." Tobias adjusted his glasses unnecessarily, once again the absentminded professor. He returned, reaching into no-man's-land to offer the wine but planting his feet beside his wife.

Gone was the meek baby witch. Her bright brown eyes were alight with fierce intelligence and a guardedness he'd never seen. Chris hadn't closed any distance, instead remaining at Barbara's shoulder.

"You work in the—establishment—at the site of Mark's job." Toby opened the conversation.

Mark stepped to Evie's side and rested his hand against the small of her back. One thing this was not going to be was an interrogation. The growl built in him—the wolf preparing to defend theirs. Whatever performance these three jokers thought they were putting on was done now.

"The gentleman's club, yes," Evie said before he could put his brothers and this upstart little witch in their places. "Though I'm not on the floor anymore. I'm in the office, upstairs all day. Answering phones and tracking down invoices for the bar and projects like Mark's. The hours are better, but the tips are lousy."

Mark coughed a laugh, and Barbara glared at him. He tried to keep the satisfied smirk off his face. *Back off, Baby Witch.*

Her brows lowered at him. *Make me, Jerk.*

"This is very good, thank you." Evie took a sip of wine. "I understand you own a bookstore and teach at the university. Do you two teach together?"

"She owns the store," Tobias supplied, apparently forgetting he was supposed to be the inquisition in his eagerness to humblebrag on his wife. "Mostly I stay in my lane, which is boring and academic. Her work focuses on appraisals. Authenticating books, working with collectors, and auctions. The really sexy stuff."

Mark would never have put *sexy* and *book appraisal* in the same sentence, but Barbara's face lit up, so somebody was getting laid later. The return of that shit-eating grin said he knew it.

"He's doing vital work—preserving history and items of immense cultural value," Barbara assured them.

Mark dared to meet Evie's eyes. The unruffled brown sparkled. The corner of her mouth crinkled. He didn't dare sigh relief. Something told him this was only the beginning.

Mark found himself steered to the end of the table, opposite Chris. Tobias sat to his left, Barbara to his right, with Evie between her and Chris. He tried to rearrange them, but Barbara waved him away as if he were a gnat. Tobias started chatting him up about some installation at the university that might be taking bids. By the time Mark got his head together, Evie was already seated as far away from him as the little dining alcove would allow.

The table and nearby surfaces had been cleared of books, but it was still a tight fit for five adults—three of whom were six-foot men.

"Tell me all about how you two met," Barbara said brightly.

"It was in Jevany," Evie said without looking at him. "A friend of mine has a cottage and offers it to me for a few weeks in the summer."

"Jevany," Chris said, reaching for her plate but looking at Mark. "Interesting."

Evie tilted her head. "How so?"

"You were the real reason this guy kept sneaking the off jobsite at lunchtime." Chris shrugged.

Tobias's eyebrows arched over the rims of his glasses. "Mark snuck off—"

"That was like two months ago," Chris said. "Sam told me all about it. *Hiking.*"

Mark added Samuel to his list.

"Try the cornbread," Barbara said. "I found a recipe with jalapeños. Exotic, yes?"

What business did cornbread have with jalapeños in it? Even a shallow whiff as the plates went around the table warned Mark this was going to be spicy.

"You two met in the village?" Barbara asked.

Evie sat, polite as a nun with her hands folded in her lap as the wide, shallow bowls of rice laden with chunks of stewed chicken, sausage, and shrimp in a thick, heady sauce made their way around the table. He didn't know what he expected when her gaze skated his, but bright with laughter wasn't it. His anger softened. Okay, they could play this game.

"One of the ponds, actually," Mark said. "I went for a swim."

"And I got caught admiring the view," Evie finished.

Barbara sniffed. "I'm sure."

"You've been seeing each other for a while," Tobias, wannabe Columbo, added, steepling his fingers. "That's practically a record, Markus."

The wolf hackled at his tone.

Before he could jump in, Evie spoke. "Not that long. I had to come back for work. We didn't even get a proper goodbye, and then a couple of weeks later, who turns up in the office to start the basement remodel?"

"Can we eat?" Mark jabbed his fork into his plate.

"Manners?" Tobias glared.

Barbara squeezed Tobias's hand. "We did promise them food, not the third degree. Well, bon appétit, you all."

"Yeah, right," Mark muttered, grabbing his beer.

He met Evie's eyes over the edge of the bottle as she lifted her own fork. He gave a little headshake. She subtly set it down again.

"So you two are…" Tobias dug in, all pretense of conversation lost as he shoveled in a mouthful and then doubled back for more.

"Just getting reacquainted," Evie said with a little smile for Mark. "Things are different here. And Mark is busy getting his business off the ground. That needs his focus right now."

"You hit the jackpot with this one, brother," Chris added unhelpfully before filling his craw.

Mark took a small bite, unable to keep the little smirk entirely from his lips as he began a silent countdown. Chris kept shoveling, silent now for the effort of stuffing his traitorous face.

"And your boss is okay with this," Barbara said around her own bite. "You two... getting to know each other?"

Evie's fork slowed, and for the first time, tension tightened her features.

"It's none of his damn business," Mark said. Nosy little witch. Mark resolved not to pity her one bit for what happened next.

Tobias was starting to feel it. The skin on his cheekbones and nose darkened with a decidedly red undertone as beads of sweat formed above his brows.

Mark put down his fork and took a long swallow of beer. Then he crossed his arms over his chest and rocked back on the legs of the chair. He winked at Evie.

She covered her mouth with the hand holding the fork, mirth dancing in her eyes.

Barbara coughed, blinking hard. "Oh."

"Oh?" Mark repeated innocently. "Something wrong?"

She shook her head, napkin to her lips as the skin above her collar turned a ripe strawberry-gold up to her freckles.

Tobias finally gasped. "Bebe, are there peppers in this too?"

"Followed the recipe." She coughed. "Mostly. The butcher had a spicy American-style sausage—a hot link?—I thought it would be authentic..."

Mark savored the next swallow, his eyes on Chris. Patient.

The fairest of the brothers, Chris went a shocking shade of red, and his eyes teared. He swallowed a lump and moaned pitifully. "Jesus Christ, Bebe."

He shoved a chunk of cornbread in his mouth a second before Barbara could cry out a warning. "Peppers."

Chris groaned as the heat hit him again.

Tobias downed his glass of water, wiped his forehead and then his streaming eyes.

Mark met Evie's wide eyes. He smirked.

She mouthed the words: "Do something."

He shrugged, content to let these meddling assholes suffer. But her mouth turned down, a glare forming. He sighed and turned to Barbara. "Bread?"

"Kitchen." She coughed.

He returned and set down a carton of milk and bread from the local farmers' market. It was his favorite. The caraway baked into the sourdough gave it an herby, pleasant flavor that went well with everything.

He took his time, methodically slicing the half loaf, snagging one for himself before handing down the board.

Bebe took hers with the decency to nod in gratitude.

Evie plucked one on its way past.

Chris snatched three slices, leaving Toby the heel. Toby grabbed a middle piece from Chris's plate and tossed the heel at his little brother.

While his siblings regained their composure, Mark lifted his glass to Evie. "*Buen provecho.*"

She shook her head at him, unable to stifle a grin. It might have been the first time he'd seen *this* smile. All ease and unexpected amusement, both so breathtaking he couldn't look away. The thrill of that sight raced through him, leaving him warm and tingling as that first kiss in the dark outside the theater, full of spark and promise.

He enjoyed the sight of it for a long time after she returned to her plate, balancing small bites of gumbo and bread and sneaking glances at him.

He resumed eating the same way, and for a while, it was as if they were at dinner alone.

Tobias recovered first, reaching out to Barbara. She finished wiping her eyes and set her fingers in his. "I may have taken some liberties..."

Mark wasn't sure who started laughing, only that Tobias broke first, dragging his glasses off to rub his eyes with his free hand while Barbara pressed her fist to her mouth, which did nothing to hide her grin.

"I don't think I've got any taste buds left." Chris groaned, lobster red and fanning the neckline of his sweaty T-shirt away from his chest.

That only made Barbara laugh harder. She exhaled for so long Mark worried she wasn't going to be able to inhale again, but she drew in a long snort.

That did it.

"This is a recipe for napalm," Chris said for emphasis.

"That's what you get for having the table manners of an adolescent chimpanzee," Tobias said before he lost his composure completely.

Barbara let out a high-pitched squeak and pushed the napkin against her face like she was trying to hide.

Mark guffawed, rubbing his face helplessly. But it was a new sound that caught him like a snare.

At the end of the table, Evie had wrapped an arm around her waist as though she could somehow hold it all in. The laughter escaped in fits and bursts, a sight like he'd never imagined. Her face contorted, the scar a ripple of mirth beneath the glamour. Most intriguing—she panted wheezy little gasps that made him think of the moment after she came really hard.

He'd had no idea it was possible to pop a massive boner while laughing his ass off—first time for everything.

It took everything in him to keep from sweeping her up from the table and taking her home to show her exactly how good this moment felt.

After dinner, Mark helped clear the table, leaving Tobias showing Evie his extensive collection of illuminated manuscript pages. Barbara was in the kitchen, scooping a surprising amount of leftovers into a reusable container.

"What the fuck did you think you're playing at, Baby Witch?" he muttered.

"Language." She sniffed.

"Fuck off."

She sighed and spun on him. The air crackled, and for a second, he was sure she was going to zap him just to see him hop. Then a sly smile spread over her face. "*This* is the woman you had me mess with your mom's charm for. And she's one of us."

He sighed.

"And you *like* her."

"You cook. You don't clean up. Those are the rules," he grumbled, snatching the sponge. "Even if you can't follow a recipe to save your life. If this is any indication of how your spell work is going, I should be grateful you didn't turn me into a jackrabbit."

"You're already a jack*ass*, that would have been too close," she sang merrily. "Don't change the subject. She knows what you are?"

He lowered his head once.

"And you know *she's* a fucking powerhouse, right?" Barbara said.

He blinked at her.

She wiggled her fingers in imitation of one of Beryl's many spells. "She pulled a bullet out of your ass *and* healed the wound. That's not an amateur move. What's her gift?"

"What the hell was tonight all about anyway?" Mark refused to give in.

"You've practically disappeared the past few weeks," she said. "You're never home. You don't go to the bar. You haven't been to the cabin with Toby and Chris in—"

An itch formed between Mark's shoulder blades. This was too much. So what if he'd been at Evie's a lot? He was a grown-ass man. He didn't need a babysitter. "And you figured since Mom's out for the night, you'd just step in and do the job for her?"

"Somebody has to make sure you don't get your ass in more trouble than we can get you out of."

"You should mind your business, nosy little witch."

"What else are you looking for, Markus? She's got her heart on her face when she looks at you."

The words hit Mark in the solar plexus, snatching his breath and cavorting around with it, taking it anywhere but his lungs. Was that the long look she gave him that heated him up like a bonfire? His chest ached, heart thumping. If he admitted it to himself, he'd brought her here because he was hoping she'd stay. He wanted to see what she looked like waking up in full morning sun. In his bed. Preferably naked.

Barbara looked concerned. "What—you guys have been telling each other it's casual and you're just having a good time?"

Mark froze, mouth open.

"It's a good thing you're strong, because you're an idiot."

"Go away, Baby Witch." He turned his attention to the dishes. For him, love was always an action: taking care of people, keeping them safe. He didn't have the capacity for all the hearts in the eyes and starry bullshit. Falling in love was something goofy people did in movies when they had nothing else to worry about. This was definitely not that. "Not that simple."

Mark sealed his lips and threw his energy into scrubbing the cooked-on sauce off the bottom of the pot.

Barbara laid a hand on his arm. "She's leaving."

Goose bumps sprang up on his arm under her touch. This witchy business was getting weirder and weirder.

"Don't look at me like that." She snorted. "Chris told us Valentin's crew is pretty thick with the mob. She's not stupid. If she's up there in that office all day, she probably knows more than she should."

Barbara had no idea. Still, the fact that his sister-in-law had put the situation together so quickly was a wake-up call, a stark reminder that this thing between them had an expiration date.

He was done with this conversation. He raised his voice, imbuing it with enough of the wolf to make it a command. "Christof Douglass Vogel, get your lazy ass in here and see about these dishes so your sister can entertain her guest."

Barbara glared at him, shaking her head. "Just be careful please."

"Ten-four, Baby Witch," Mark said as Chris trotted in, snagging a dishtowel.

"Jerk," she muttered, smiling as she grabbed her glass of wine and headed to the living room.

# CHAPTER TWENTY-SIX

THEY ADORED MARK.

It was clear in this little dinner party tribunal with their skeptical questions, their watchful expressions. His brothers and sister-in-law were looking out for him. And they were so blatantly obvious and awkward it was clear this was new to them.

However many women Mark had brought home, not one had warranted this level of intervention.

They were right to be wary. Evie was no good for him. One day she would be gone.

They remained, having each other's back and having Mark's back. Something she could never do. Something he deserved more than anyone she had ever met.

Evie told herself the pain in her chest was from laughter over the unexpectedly spicy meal. But she'd locked away how it felt to be surrounded by people who, even with their messy contradictions and a lifetime of memories, cared for each other absolutely. Their love made room for this moment —no blame, no anger, only a collective sense of *that didn't go as planned*. Now that lock had broken, leaving her aching with memories after what had been one of the best nights of her life.

She might never be part of the wall they formed at his back. But she would protect him from what they could not see.

"What is it?" Mark murmured after they'd finally said their good-nights and slipped across the hall to the opposite apartment. He slid his key into the lock and pushed the door open for her.

*Nothing.* The word was on her lips. Along with a pretty lie about being tired, or distracted, or surprised. But she was none of those things. Instead, she turned wordlessly to wait for him to close and lock the door behind him. He kicked off his shoes beside hers next to the doorstep and loosed a long sigh.

He met her eyes, head low with a rueful expression. "I have *no* idea what those jokers thought they were—"

She closed the distance between them and silenced him with a kiss. His arms closed around her, pressing her against the length of him. When they parted, his irises were thin bands of bright yellow in the dim light of the hallway.

"They're checking to make sure my intentions are pure."

He laughed. "I sure hope they aren't."

She tried again. "They want to make sure I'm not going to hurt you."

"*You* hurt *me*?" His expression turned wolfish.

She backed down the hall, feeling stalked and harried by the predator under the surface of the man. Her heart thundered, breath a taunting rasp in her throat. *Catch me. Catch me.*

He sniffed softly. "Gods, you smell good when you're turned on."

Heat flushed her body in a long pulsing wave. "You can smell…?"

His bared teeth only vaguely resembled a grin. The shiver of arousal turned into a low, pulsing ache.

When he lunged for her, she was ready. Instead of running, she flung herself at him, legs around his hips, hands gripping his shoulders. His hands settled under her ass, lifting her. She heard her dress rip at a great distance. More immediate was the pressure of teeth on her breast, her nipple, and the hot brush of a soothing tongue when he slid inside her.

They were in the hallway a few steps from his door. Across the hall from his family. She bit down hard to keep herself from crying out when he pinned her to the wall and set a pace that left her able to do little more than hang on and grind into him.

As if reading her mind, he paused, freed up one hand to grip the base of her neck, and sent them stumbling down the hall. They bounced off a door-frame and into another room, lit only by the reflection of streetlights off the river coming through the enormous picture windows.

Deeper into his lair, she thought, the den of the wolf that had claimed her. When the wall met her back again, he heaved her hips up higher, getting a better angle, and resumed their primal race. He set his teeth to the skin below her jaw. Not enough to mark but a sure, confident grip that sent shocks of desire raging against the base of her skull, radiating down her spine to where their bodies met. She wanted to feel his teeth on the back of her neck, the curve where it met her shoulder, the soft skin at her waist and her hip. She'd love to wake up wearing his marks all over her body, to see the unapologetically possessive heat in his eyes.

His fingers slipped between them, finding the rhythm she preferred, and the extra pressure sent her tumbling into her orgasm.

She couldn't stop the noise now, pleasure rippling from inside to her edges. She didn't even recognize the sound as coming from her own body until she made out the tangle of his name in her desperate cries.

"That's it," he crooned, slowing his pace.

He liked that—driving himself to the edge and then backing off—drawing out his own release until it must have been almost painful. She kept herself tight around him and felt his body ripple with restraint.

"Little vixen." He huffed, rhythm stuttering as he struggled for control.

"You love it," she crooned softly back at him, stroking the tip of one ear, sharp even in human form.

He groaned and planted himself deep. "I'm going wreck you."

"Promise?"

"If it's the last thing I do."

By the time she rode him to completion, she'd lost track of her own pleasure entirely and surrendered to complete satisfaction. She melted onto his chest, a senseless, panting lust puddle.

His pecs shook beneath her. "Lust puddle?"

"I said that out loud?"

"You did."

"You should come with a warning label, Markus Vogel."

"Would you have let it stop you?"

Her eyelids weighed a ton. She'd come here for more than just to have her body demolished by this unbearably sexy werewolf. For the life of her, she couldn't remember exactly what. She might as well make herself comfortable until the memory came back.

She snuggled in deeper, pressing her face to the skin under his jaw and inhaling.

A deep sound of contentment rumbled under her ear, and his hand splayed over her back, brushing extended circles from her shoulders to her tailbone. "Much as I'd love to let this be the end of the evening—"

"We need to talk." She loosed a groan fully intended to make him aware of the tortured agony he would be putting her through if he persisted. "I know."

"If we fall asleep here, we wake up cold and sore and stuck together."

Laughter bubbled up at the mental image. "You are a real killjoy."

"Three out of three people in the apartment across the hall would agree with you."

"You mean the world to them. They just want to keep you safe. And make sure you're happy." She shivered a little as his fingertips prodded the base of her skull, massaging down to her shoulder blades. She hadn't realized how much tension she was holding until his fingers settled there. All week the knowledge that Valentin was trafficking supernatural creatures had drawn her belly tight, brought bile rising to her throat. The steady chant to flee buzzed like a phantom mosquito.

"They need to mind their fucking businesses." Mark's smile faded as his gaze searched her face. "Come on. Shower, some water, maybe a snack, and then I wanna hear what you learned from the Amazon."

"We just had dinner." She ran her palm down his rib cage, distracting herself with the enjoyment of his shuddering squirm.

"Worked up an appetite," he said. "Let's get a move on, love. We get the business out of the way and maybe…"

Before she could register the words, he rolled them both up and scooped her off her feet. On the way through the apartment, this time she had a chance to pick up details she had missed.

Unlike his brother's cozy, book-lined haven, Mark's flat was almost spartan. But that didn't make it feel incomplete. The furniture all clung to low, clean lines but in soft, warm textures. More color than she expected too, and she liked that. Drawers and storage tucked under spaces left the exposed surfaces clear. Everything in its place. Aside from some rolls of paper on the table, it could have been a showcase home for an interior designer who favored modern, simple styles.

He ran the water for the shower, and her mind went back to the rolls of paper—architectural paper.

A half hour later, they were back at the table. She wore one of his T-shirts and a pair of light sweatpants that probably looked like leggings on her hips and thighs. She quit worrying when he groaned at the sight of her in them, adjusting the newly sprung hardness in his shorts.

"You're gonna be the death of me," he muttered in her ear as he palmed her ass on their way to the kitchen.

"I hope not." She grinned, wiggling into his hand.

"I'm trying to focus here!" He heaped a platter with an alarming amount of fruit and cheese and crackers and sliced meat. Then he grabbed a round of rye bread and led her to the table.

"What is this?" She exhaled as he started to unroll the papers, anchoring each corner with blown-glass paperweights full of tiny, luminous bubbles.

Then he went about stuffing his face, tapping the plate in her direction. She ignored it, focused on the drawings. Reproduced, exactly line for line, were the plans for the basement remodel.

"I thought you weren't allowed to take them out of the building?"

"I didn't." He grinned around a mouthful of a hastily constructed open-faced sandwich and tapped his temple. "You're not the only one who can hang on to things."

"Why?"

"Something wasn't right," he said, frowning. "Couldn't put my finger on it. But it kept jabbing at me anyway."

"Sounds uncomfortable."

He chewed in silence for a long minute.

Exasperated, she spun, leaning her weight on the table to stare over at him. She popped a grape in her mouth.

He met her eyes. "This project—it's expensive. *Way* expensive, even for a sex dungeon."

The grape exploded between her teeth, and she slapped a hand over her mouth to keep the juice from escaping. "Is that what they told you it was?"

"It was kind of inferred... I mean, I assumed it maybe, and Nikolai, he agreed." He looked a little embarrassed. "Anyway, I did some research. Anchors, for restraints, reinforced beams, maybe for suspension rigs. You know, for kinky stuff."

"Kinky stuff?"

His brows lifted hopefully. "You into that kind of thing, because I could definitely..."

Heat zapped her core, his look as solid as a touch to her most intimate places. "I could be. But maybe we can talk about that later?"

He nodded and shoved the rest of the sandwich into his mouth, returning his gaze to the papers. "I talked to someone in the business. Don't look at me like that. This is a serious business. There's real money in it—doing the job safely and correctly is important—I'd be an idiot not think about... Anyway. There are just things that don't match up. Materials that are not just too expensive, they're too much for this job—steel beams instead of laminated lumber. A new HVAC system—the club renovation already came with a robust one. Why duplicate it?"

He jabbed at the collection of lines and notations. "Look here—suspension bolts reinforced with steel fittings strong enough to hold a bull elephant. And the room isn't big enough to fit one. Soundproofing I get, but unless they're keeping a shitty metal band down there, these levels are just... excessive."

Evie listened, her gaze going back to his face until he stopped to point something out on the plans and then returned. After a moment, she realized he'd stopped talking.

"I'd think you were stuck on my pretty face, but you've got that witchy thousand-yard-stare thing going."

The corner of her mouth quirked involuntarily. "Witchy?"

His eyes took on an inward blankness though his gaze remained locked on her face. He was good.

"That's a bit… disconcerting."

"Told you." He smirked.

Connections thrummed deep in Evie's mind. "Can I see a calendar?"

Without hesitation, Mark disappeared into the kitchen. He returned with a thick portfolio. Once he had it on the table, he released the strained catch, then flipped through carefully organized sections, and she tried not to stare as words and numbers jumped at out her, all in his neat, ordered script. No flourishes, just utilitarian lines of communication. At last he stopped at the calendar pages and slid it to her. She hesitated.

"This is your—"

"Business planner," he said slowly. "I've wanted to go out on my own forever. I didn't want to blow my shot by not being prepared."

"This is a lot of preparation," she said, still not touching it. She'd come on an old book of poetry once that emanated with the kind of intention this one did and had been sick for a week after touching it. "I think you need to give me permission. It sounds foolish, but—"

"I get it. I do." He nodded. "A couple of months ago, I had dinner with those guys, and one of Bebe's old books zapped the shit out of me."

Barbara. His sister-in-law. The witch.

He shook his head. "But I'm not a witch, I'm—"

"Have you ever heard of any two of our kind… having a family?"

"Apparently it would have been pretty impossible considering our kind were sworn enemies before the inquisition wiped most of us out," he said, as reasonably as if they had been rival football leagues.

He knew so much more than she did—about his history, about what they were. A hunger for that knowledge gnawed at her. She popped another grape in a hopeless attempt to appease the ache.

"You're half-witch." Evie nodded at him and considered. Barbara hadn't seemed so bad once she'd let the tribunal act go. She was protective but not unkind. To study with another one of her kind—Evie didn't allow herself to imagine what that would be like. "And this book is full of so much intention and purpose it might as well be a grimoire, and I'm not touching it until you tell it I'm okay."

His laughing half smile always did her in, little dimples usually hidden in his serious expression flaring, bright as comets. All the brothers had them, she'd noted at dinner. Tobias, Chris, and Mark. She wondered fleetingly what his parents looked like. Probably absurdly good-looking.

"Fine." He waved his hands over the open pages theatrically. "Abracadabra, simsalabim, you're opened up. Now let her in."

Evie shook her head, fighting a giggle. "Spoken like a true storybook witch."

"Happy?"

"Very."

When their eyes met, the humor and warmth turned her to jelly. She looked away first. Tendrils of longing wound through her rib cage. Her heartbeat had become a clock, each beat closer to the end of this, whatever it was.

She dangled her fingers experimentally over the pages. When the book didn't snap closed around her hand—or zap her—she rested it on the creamy white page. After the initial tingling passed, it left behind the smooth, dense texture of the high-quality paper. He'd spared no expense.

She realized something else. "You write in German."

"It just came out that way." His shrug was self-conscious, a retreat. "It makes me more organized."

"That seems—"

"Cliché?"

"I was going to say fitting."

"Things seem more... orderly. Doable. It's a long story."

"I have time." She began flipping through the pages, scanning dates. "It's better if I don't focus too hard while I do this."

"My parents raised us in both English and German," he said on an exhale full of frustration and amusement, light with affection. "And Dad was pretty strict, especially when we were little. He refused to speak to us—or answer—in anything else. And if we wanted his attention, we had to try. He wasn't cruel about it, just determined."

"And that's been useful here?" She couldn't keep the skepticism out of her voice.

"Oh, they started before we got here—where it is absolutely *useless* because German is nothing like Czech. What are you looking for?"

"Following the money. Back in January, Valentin started selling something new. By May, the numbers increased significantly. Almost always the same amount, or near to it, for each code. And if this code follows form, it's single objects, something rare or expensive. By June, it's steady."

More money was coming in, equaling Little Blossoms' income. She softened her gaze, let her mind recall the ledger numbers. "Go on. So you speak both. And write. Read?"

"Enough to get by," he said, as though it was embarrassing. "Toby's got Dad's thing. He soaks up languages like a sponge. Issy and Chris were young enough that they figured out Czech early. I struggled. A lot. Especially in school. And this place isn't always great with dealing with kids like me."

"Like you?"

"*Blbec* was one of the first words I learned."

She winced, heart aching for the boy so far from home. So different from everyone around him, being told he was stupid for his struggle. After the ache came rage.

"Hey, easy on those pages, tiger," he said gently, settling a hand on hers. She hadn't realized she was gripping. "My mom's a real pain in the ass when she needs to be—probably hexed a few people. I got moved to another school with more international kids. But my dad said something to me. 'You have learned two languages before the age of ten. That is not the work of a stupid man. Let no one convince you otherwise.' In German, of course."

She smiled.

"There's the story. You've got something. Tell me."

She settled her finger on a date that corresponded with a blank entry in Valentin's ledger—a string of codes but no amount. Her heart stuttered at the date. Two weeks ago. That would be their most significant take yet.

What had Nikolai said—that their holding facilities were only adequate, but that would be resolved once Mark's job was complete? Valentin was trafficking supernatural creatures. And Mark was building the cages.

Her stomach turned over, fear spiking up her chest. "You have to quit."

He leaned away in surprise. "Quit what—?"

"It's not a sex dungeon," she said, hearing the tremble in her voice and hating it.

He cocked his head, waiting patiently.

"Two weeks ago, a Croatian club got attacked," she said. "That's why Elise Le Seppe came to Valentin's office. He's responsible for it, and she knows."

"I thought Petrov had an agreement with—"

"He does." Her heart was moving too fast. She pressed a hand to her chest as if she could slow it. "The Saints are a family organization first and always. All the more lucrative income streams go through the other bosses —they're all blood. Valentin's a cousin too many times removed, maybe related by marriage, not blood, so they gave him the business that's on balance the most carefully watched by Azrael and the least profitable— skin, real estate. I don't think anyone thought he would do as well had he has. But he's reached the ceiling. And the only thing I can think of that Valentin would risk both Petrov *and* Azrael over is the opportunity to"—

she reran the numbers quickly, double-checking—"double what he makes in a year."

"How was breaking into a club—"

"It wasn't a club." The words tumbled out of her, and she forced herself still, counting her breaths until they were steady again. She had to be strong. She needed to convince him. "It was an underground circus. Supernaturals disguised as performers."

Mark froze, his eyes wolf yellow.

"Le Seppe said several had been killed, but some were unaccounted for." Her fingertips were ice-cold, and time seemed to be crawling. "Disappeared." She noticed the rage filling his expression. "What?"

"You think the Saints went into that club specifically to take them." His gaze sharpened, locked onto something.

She walked him through the numbers, the codes, the amounts, and the destinations. He flipped back through pages, unknowingly tapping another set of dates a few weeks ago that corresponded with something from her ledger.

"What happened then?" she asked.

"Family dinner," he muttered.

"I'm sorry?"

"I warned her…," he began, then seemed to recognize the confusion on Evie's face and shook his head. "Somebody I know has been investigating supernaturals disappearing all over the city."

"Barbara?"

He shook his head.

"They're gone," Evie said, grim and certain. He blurred in her vision, but she met his eyes as best she could. "Valentin's shipping them out of the territory. Saint Petersburg and Moscow mostly."

"To the Red Death."

"You have to quit." The part of her that whispered she was a coward for turning away from creatures in need was drowned out by the desire to protect him. She wished she was strong enough to help them, that she could save anyone other than herself. And Mark. Valentin only went after creatures that could not hide. She and Mark were safe. For now.

"The ones that can't pass," he murmured as if to himself. "They live in hiding, and no one will notice them disappear."

The sick feeling returned, and she regretted eating anything at all.

"Their families." His shoulders slumped. "Their loved ones."

"I'm sorry," she said, knowing it meant nothing, changed nothing. "I didn't know, I swear. If I had known—"

"You could have stopped it?"

She shook her head, eyes sealing shut as she repeated her plea. "You have to quit."

"What does it matter?" he snarled.

She jerked away, startled at the burst of rage, but did not flee. "Mark, if he finds out what you are—"

"He'll just find somebody else to finish the job." Mark flung himself away from the table. "Anton probably. I have to stop him."

"It's too late. They're gone," she said, desperate.

"The ones from the club." He turned on her, but Evie refused to flinch. Whatever this was, it wasn't directed at her. There were many things she would run from in her life, but never from him. "He's holding them somewhere."

Tal's words slammed into her heart like a hammer. *You just have to decide to stop running. Plant your feet and not let anything knock you aside.*

Is that what it looked like—Mark refusing to save himself when there was a chance, no matter how small, to help the others?

"But we have no idea where or how," she said. "And after this shipment, he'll lie low for a while."

He caught the word before she did. His brow rose. "We?"

"You are a fool if you think I'm going to stand by while you go play white knight alone." She had lost her mind. The words coming out of her mouth didn't seem to come from the same place that had kept her alive all these years, the one she associated with survival. But a plan was forming, pieces coming together like numbers in an equation. "Especially when you don't need to."

That startled him out of fury. "If he ships them before—"

"He won't." She grinned, knowing it looked savage and not caring. "He didn't have enough of them. That's why he risked hitting the circus. That was his mistake. Le Seppe knows he's involved now. The plan is to take a break after this shipment until she loses the scent. But if we could find where they are and tip her off somehow…"

Mark considered her with the eyes of the wolf. She fought the urge to rub him behind the ears in reassurance. He huffed as if he could sense it. "You want to bring the necromancer down on him."

"If we can find where he's keeping them, maybe we could launch a rescue effort," she said reasonably. "But it won't stop Valentin from doing it again. The Amazon is the only one who can do that. But Mark…"

He waited, staring as though he'd never seen her, eyes flickering from yellow to pale brown and back.

"She thinks I'm with them." Her voice hitched with unspent emotion.

"For all she knows, I'm in on it. And she's right. I have been complicit in this—"

Sobs turned the rest of her sentence into an incomprehensible mess.

All the while she'd been scrimping and saving and looking the other way at the illegal activities Valentin was up to, supernatural creatures—like her—were being torn from their families and sold, likely to the most vicious necromancer in the Allegiance. Guilt slammed into her gut. She pressed it back down into the place where she lived with the knowledge that she'd lost her entire family because she ran when she should have planted her feet.

That didn't stop him from dragging her into his chest, circling her in one of the all-consuming hugs that seemed to shut out everything but them. She struggled to free herself, wiping her face. This was her mess. She had to face it. He refused to let her go.

"Come on, don't do that." His voice rumbled quietly through her. Concern knit his brows and netted the long fine lashes at the corners of his eyes.

"Do what?" She started to look away, but he caught her chin.

"You bury it," he said quietly. "Tuck it down so deeply inside yourself you can pretend everything is okay. That's what happened the other night, right? It builds up and builds up, and you overheat and nearly shock some poor werewolf to death."

She didn't have the luxury of wallowing in misery. She couldn't just emote all over people. And it served as a defense, protection from some of the ways people could hurt her.

"There's been something I'm trying to piece together about that night in the woods," he said. "Wolf memories are not like ours. He gets most of it, but it doesn't always make sense."

"He did get shot," she muttered.

"Stupid maniac lunged right at the damn gun. I'm lucky we still have a face."

"I'm so glad you do." She cupped his cheek.

He closed his eyes, resting against her palm and nuzzling softly. "I knew you just wanted me for my pretty face."

"It is so pretty." Flirtation sounded strange with a stuffy nose.

"You told him a story," he said, resting his fingertips over her heart. "About a man who tried to hurt you. And the ones who set you up to let him."

She chewed her lip, staring at the plans without seeing anything. Finally her eyes met his, haunted.

"The story of how you got roped into working for Valentin?"

She nodded.

"Evie, you don't have to hold this all by yourself."

His fingers rubbed the muscles below her shoulder blades. That did her in. It held nothing of the sexual charge that seemed to move between them like air and sunlight. His strength, yes, she didn't think he could help but imbue every touch with the core of who he was, but more than that, his presence.

*I'm here.*

The pressure in her chest cracked, spilling over into her rib cage with such sweet warmth the only way her body knew to counter it was with more tears.

"I count. When I'm nervous. I've always done it. And those guys—the bartender and the bouncer—they always made me nervous. I hated working with them." She could taste the bile in the back of her throat that always seemed to linger in those days. "They were always trying to get us servers to go with customers even though that wasn't our job. I think they were making money off it too. I counted to keep myself calm. That's how I knew something was off with the liquor when they were on shift. Then they started making whole bottles disappear, and parts of shipments were just 'lost.' I did the math. I saw their death masks, and I tried to warn them to stop. So they set me up with this guy in a private booth to teach me a lesson."

"You fought back."

"I killed him with my notion."

"You defended yourself." The yellow was back in his eyes. This close, she could feel the wolf under his skin, pressing toward her. "And Valentin used it to trap you. You've been in his cage for two years, Evie. You are not responsible for something you couldn't stop. Not your parents. Not this."

"Valentin had those men killed. We never saw them again. But their masks." She rubbed her own forehead. "It was probably Nikolai. He's a better shot. Their blood is on my hands too."

When she leaned into him, the weight left her as though it had been transferred. She rubbed her face against the ridge of muscle below his collar. The tension sighed out of her, the grief less sharp, less ragged.

"I doubt the Amazon is going to go for a good sob story. I keep the books. I'm complicit." Time for her to remember what she'd come here to do and her endgame. "I have to go. I can't stay. Not after that. Not even for—"

"You're not safe here," he murmured into her hair. "It doesn't matter what—nothing else matters."

Molten heat hardened and sank like iron into her guts. Mark wasn't going to beg her to stay, wasn't going to make promises he couldn't keep. Somewhere along the line, she'd forgotten to hope he wouldn't.

"But I won't leave, not knowing Valentin is preying on those who have no protection." This time he let her pull back. She met his eyes. "I can't live with it."

He searched her face, a half smile lurking in his concern.

"We need to figure out where he's keeping them," Mark said. "Any idea?"

"Valentin's got hundreds of properties all over the city—and beyond." Even as she spoke, Evie was calculating his portfolio, eliminating apartment buildings and office buildings and any of his legitimate developments. "Outside the city probably. As far away from Azrael's eyes as possible, but that's got to be inconvenient—keeping his guys out there, getting to the airport."

"Another club?"

Evie cocked her head. "Why do you say that?"

"Nikolai mentioned wanting some repairs done on work at Club Anděl."

"It's outside the city." She nodded. "Clubs make sense. No one lives there. There are people and shipments coming and going at all hours. Building out the basement at Blossoms makes sense—it's risky, that many supernaturals close to Azrael. But it's also a straight shot to the airport."

"How well do you know Violet?"

"What's Vi got to do with it?"

Mark ran down an encounter with Violet after hours that made the small hairs rise on the back of Evie's neck. Nikolai was holding something over her too. And Violet was a witch.

"I'll talk to her."

Mark squeezed her arm. "Be careful. I don't know what they've got on her, but if she's protecting her baby—she might be willing to give up anyone who's in their way."

"Violet and I are friends. Mostly."

"Mostly?"

"I trust her." She tried again. That didn't seem to reassure him. "I promise. I'll be subtle."

"I'll ask Nikolai if I can see the job at Anděl."

"How are you going to know if they're there?"

"Same way I knew you were a witch." He tapped his nose. "I'm sensitive to magic. Makes me sneeze when it's powerful or close enough."

The day they met at the pond. He knew even then.

The grin that lit his face replaced the air in her lungs with something light and sparkling that made her feel like she could float if she rose high enough onto her tiptoes. High enough to press her mouth to his.

Which she did. Because why not test the theory? And she might have floated away except his hands settled at her hips and drew her in, locking her to him and deepening the kiss.

"Done planning?" She sighed when they parted.

Mark nodded doggedly, lifting her onto the edge of the table. "For now."

A memorable send-off, she reminded herself. She lifted her hips so he could drag the sweatpants down her legs.

"Speaking of sex dungeons." She burst into laughter at his expression: alert and wary and incredibly turned on.

"I'm listening." He lowered himself to his knees and pressed a kiss to the inside of each thigh as he eased them apart.

"You know that thing you do," she said, struggling for words as his mouth continued its steady progress inward. "Near the end. Where you hold yourself back and then…"

All the air left her lungs in a long, low moan when he parted her, tasting.

"Go on."

"I'm trying," she panted, exasperated. "If you would just. Give me. A minute."

His laughter vibrated against her skin. "Sounds like you need to focus, Evergreen."

"Fuck," she hissed, curling her toes against his shoulder.

He sat back on his heels, smug mouth wet and pupils blown wide. "Better?"

"No," she whimpered. "Please. More."

"Hang on. I'm curious now." He bit down gently on the inside of her thigh.

Her spine bowed with something more potent than arousal. She panted. "Can we try that for me?"

His eyes went so dark she almost lost the line of his pupil and iris. He wiped his mouth with the back of his hand, and the slow smile that followed was all promise.

"Let me make sure I understand," he said, intensity graveling his voice. "You want me to get you close and back off a couple of times before I let you come."

*Let you.* Her insides fizzled to a warm goo of desire. She bit her lip, nodding, sure she looked like one of those bobblehead dolls on a dashboard.

He didn't laugh at her. Even the smile transformed into something more intense.

*Be careful what you ask for, Evie girl. You just might get it.*

"You got it."

# CHAPTER TWENTY-SEVEN

VIOLET ALWAYS ARRIVED before the other girls. No matter how popular her act had become or how comfortable her current patron had made her, she never took it for granted. And as one of the top acts, she had a closet-sized dressing room of her own.

When Violet opened the door to Evie's knock on Monday, the dancer jumped, hand over her chest. "Gods, Evie, you scared the shit out of me."

In the single unguarded moment, Evie glimpsed exhaustion and despair. With Mark's warning in mind, she had to play this carefully.

"I just thought I'd catch you before you got busy for the day. I brought tea." Evie focused on the tea service to give Violet time to collect herself. "It's your favorite, hibiscus."

Evie didn't wait for an invitation.

"You didn't need to do that." Violet closed the door behind her. The mask was back—cool, confident, unflappable.

The room was a mess. A single long clothing rack dominated the space, two folding chairs and a more comfortable reading chair in front of the lit mirror opposite. The counter was full of makeup and perfume. Headpieces hung haphazardly around, the lights catching sequins and rhinestones and sending glittering rainbows all over the walls. Evie had never known Violet to be disorganized. Something was definitely wrong.

Evie set the tea service on the edge of the dressing table as she cleared a space to settle it.

Violet hurried around the room, picking up bits of costumes.

Evie hefted the garment bag before Violet could reach it, depositing it on the rack. "New costumes?"

"No, just packing up some old things." Violet patted a stack of clothes, her eyes wary beneath the calm. "What are you doing here, Evie?"

Evie blinked, innocent, and gave her a bewildered smile. "I just came… to apologize for the other day."

"The other day?" Violet's wariness remained.

"I made you angry," Evie said, contrite. "I wanted to thank you."

Violet stared, eyes wide. She looked almost panicked. She blinked a few times, hard. "Thank?"

"For Mark," Evie said, lowering her eyes again. "You were right. I was stupid. He's just so… beautiful. I don't know what happens to me when he's in the room."

Violet eased, and the guardedness left her in a long sigh. "Oh, Eves. It happens to the best of us. I don't blame you. He's something to look at. Let's have a cup?"

Evie nodded, returning to the tea service. "You were right about so many things."

She poured two cups, light sugar for Violet, a bit more for herself, and wished for something with caffeine. She stifled a yawn of her own.

She and Mark had spent Sunday working out other ways to find out where the creatures were if Violet and the Anděl turned out to be dead ends. She planned to spend the rest of the day compiling a list of properties for him to check. There had been a heated argument over Mark doing that part alone until she managed to extract a promise to let her know as soon as he found something.

*What about your friend?* she suggested tentatively—*the one you said was looking into it?*

His face closed. *Absolutely not. They're not involved.*

Evie wanted to press. This was too much for the two of them, but Mark was firm. That was all the talking either could handle. Their time was short, and they had much to make of it.

While Mark slept, she went through his portfolio, running the numbers and revising his plan. When he found her sitting at the table, she was hesitant to show him her work, sure she'd overstepped her bounds, but he looked up, hopeful and focused on her with such intensity her breath tripped in her throat. What would she give to have him turn that look on her every day? Panic squeezed her chest. It was too late for this. The timing was all wrong, and this wasn't part of the plan.

She was in love with him.

Then his phone buzzed, a request for some ingredient for family dinner. It took all the strength she had left to refuse when the question appeared in his eyes. She announced her departure before he could ask.

Outside his building, she stood for a long moment, blinking back tears and assembling her glamour.

*A few deep breaths always help me get back to my center.* A petite Black woman with a crown of dreadlocks had spoken from the entrance to the basement shop. Not a shop. A studio. Yoga. *If you're here for class, it just ended, but I can get you a schedule if you like?*

*No. No, thank you.* Evie stared at her too long—no death mask, just the distant glimmer of stars.

Mark had this woman's eyes and skin. Her full, quirked mouth. Even her ears, small and delicately pointed. Evie resisted the urge to glance around self-consciously—had the woman seen her come out of the building? She should introduce herself... as what? No plans, no promises. She was nothing to him or his mother—just a lost stranger.

*Need directions to the fortress?* The woman asked.

Evie shook her head and felt the heat rising into her cheeks.

The woman smiled, and her variegated brown eyes glowed with the kind of energy that made Evie check her own hands to make sure they weren't sparking in response. When she met the woman's eyes again, Mark's mother lowered her voice conspiratorially. *It's terrific, your glamour. I wouldn't have known if I wasn't a little like you—more than a little.*

Evie touched her face self-consciously.

*There's a group of us, meets a couple of times of month down here. You'd be welcome. Look on the website for the special study session. It's free—come when you can.*

*Thank you.* Evie nodded, feeling like she needed to give her something in exchange. *I like... your hair. It's beautiful.*

The woman smiled, her age revealing itself when as a collection of small creases settled into familiar places. *Thanks, sweetheart. Take care, okay? It can be tough out there for us. But you're not alone. Remember that.*

Evie wasn't alone. As she looked at Violet in the tiny cramped space, she wondered who the dancer had on her side. Whatever blame she had fell away. Even if she was helping Valentin, Violet was on her own.

"I miss having someone to confide in," Evie said honestly. "I miss having a friend."

Violet gave a half smile. "I was in a mood, and I took it out on you."

"You were trying to look out for me," Evie said. "You've always done that since I started here. Why?"

At last Violet eased into her chair, and her smile lit the room. "You're a good kid, Evie. You have a big heart and not enough sense."

"A kid? You're not much older than me, and you look like a teenager!" Evie felt herself easing into the teasing behind that smile. She could curl her legs up on the chair beneath her, and they could talk about costumes and skincare routines as they had dozens of times over the years. Evie envied her smooth, glowing skin and bright eyes.

Violet was flawless. The dancer had a startling kind of beauty, perfect from every angle and with every expression. Her face drew the eye. It was almost unreal.

Unreal.

Alarm rocketed through Evie, adrenaline more effective than caffeine in leaving her wide awake. She caught the hitch in her breath before the realization gave her away, fixing her gaze on her own delicate cup and taking a small sip. But her attention was on Violet's face, searching for the signs she hadn't thought to notice before. Because how likely was it that she would meet someone with the same ability? It had never happened in all her travels, not since the man she'd learned the trick from.

*Now she knew what to look for.* The echo of the words spoken by Mark's mother flooded her.

Violet was glamoured. More, whatever she'd done was not just to improve her appearance. There was some sort of compulsion in it. It blurred previous concerns from the mind. Evie had almost forgotten why she came here.

She wished she knew more about what this was that they did and how it worked. Instead, she focused on seeing through the illusion, recalling the brief slip when Violet had opened the door.

"Are you all right, Vi?" It didn't take fakery to fill her voice with genuine concern.

Violet waved a hand. "It's just the morning sickness didn't ease like they said it would after the first trimester, and I'm not sleeping as much as I should."

Evie gave a sympathetic nod but let the silence linger. The other woman fidgeted. Now that she saw it, the compulsion slid away from her, unable to stick. Evie tried hard not to blame Violet for being part of this, responsible somehow.

"I'll catch up soon," Violet went on, too brightly. "Did I tell you I'm retiring?"

Evie let the surprise show. "When?"

"You thought I would still be on stage until I went into labor?" Violet's laugh was high-pitched, shrill. "Truth is, it's been on my mind for a while. This just accelerated things."

She waved a hand at her midsection, where the small bump was becoming obvious when she didn't sit just so.

"And you're ready," Evie said.

"I've never been more ready."

"You have a date."

"Two weeks," Violet said. "And then I'll spend the rest of this pregnancy on the couch eating bonbons and watching terrible movies."

Evie laughed. "You'd go crazy in a week."

"You're right," Violet said, a twinkle of her old self in her gaze. "But at least I'd have someone at home to rub my feet."

"You've decided to—"

"Yes," Violet said, hushed urgency in her voice. "It's a good offer. And we'd be together, raising this little sprout. I thought at one time that I should go on my own. But it's best, really. For us all to be together."

"I think you're going to make an amazing mother." Evie set down her cup, leaned in. "No matter how you decide to do it."

Violet blinked, staring at her. Her eyes filled with tears.

Evie grabbed for the nearest soft cloth, handing over one of the handkerchief-sized veils from the Dance of the Seven Veils.

"After everything I've done, I probably don't even deserve—" She sniffled violently. "These hormones make me so maudlin."

But Evie had already hooked on the words. Violet had never been ashamed of her work onstage or off. She was too pragmatic for that. "Violet, you've done what you needed to in order to survive, to provide for yourself. Nothing you've done on that stage—"

"Not on stage," Violet whispered, overcome again.

Certainty ringing that she was close to something important, Evie kept up the ruse of confusion. "Your patrons?"

"Just fools easily parted from their money." Violet shook her head fiercely.

Evie took a breath and a chance. "What are you running from, Vi?"

"You know good and godsdamn well what Valentin's gotten himself into," Violet said. "I heard you asking the girls about the rooms."

Violet went silent, watching her.

"You don't know." The dancer's eyes narrowed.

Evie exhaled slowly, too eager to be cautious at the prospect of finally getting some answers. "Are you a part of it?"

Violet closed her eyes, and for an instant, a rictus of pain passed over her face.

"We are all part of this, Evelia. You're the only one here looking to be *more* when you should be looking the other way," Violet muttered. She locked eyes with Evie. "I'm taking my bag of silver and getting out while I can. And you should too. Especially after they finish that basement."

Ice crept through Evie's veins. Her heartbeat pulsed for long beats in slow motion before she realized it was thundering. "My bag of silver?"

Violet smiled, a cold, cheerless thing. "We've served our purposes. And you know it. I'll live with what I've done for the rest of my life, but at least I'll live. More than I can say for the poor bastards that wind up in those cells."

Evie dropped the pretense. "What have you done?"

"What I had to," Violet said with grim certainty. "You'd better be ready to bargain. And hope you have something they want."

Evie pushed away. "Is that what you did?"

Violet coughed a hard laugh. The hand that slipped over her tiny bump trembled. "You will too. When the time comes."

"It's not too late to stop this," Evie hissed. "Do you know where they keep them?"

Violet shook her head once, decisively. "I'll do what they told me to do. That's the deal."

Evie opened her mouth to question what Violet meant and stopped. Before her eyes, a small, perfect hole appeared in the woman's forehead, a long dark line rolling down into her eyebrow and to the bridge of her nose. Violet should be blinking what with the way the burgundy ran into her eye, but of course she didn't because it wasn't really there. Yet.

The sight shocked Evie into silence. Violet was so sure she was safe. The death mask Violet was almost identical to the living one and vivid. It was soon then.

"Whatever you've done, it won't save you," Evie said urgently, casting off artifice, hoping beyond reason that this was the moment the other woman would choose to confide in her. "I can see it. A glimpse of it, at least. It's my —whatever this is—I can see it. You have to know you won't be safe even if you do what they want—"

"How dare you, you stupid little bitch," Violet shouted. "Get out. Now!"

◆

EVIE MANAGED to return the tea service to the kitchen and stagger to the bathroom before vomiting up the remains of her breakfast. It had been so stupid to say anything.

Nikolai was waiting outside when she emerged. His forehead creased when he saw her. "Are you well?"

She clamped down on sudden panic. "A little tired. I was up late reading."

"You need to take better care of yourself—no more of these foolish pursuits."

She forced a smile she prayed wasn't as ghastly as it felt on her face. How many women in her position would have taken advantage of his favor, gladly? Perhaps, in another life, she would have chosen him, chosen this.

"I heard you and Violet had a spat," he said.

The hair on Evie's arms rose to attention. How much had he heard?

"There was shouting at the end. I'm told." He waved a hand. "I don't have to remind you of the line between you and the dancers. And how important you remain—"

"Above it," she finished. "I just went to check on her and the baby, you know. She's emotional. Hormones."

"That situation will be resolved shortly."

"Resolved?" The memory of the single line of blood running down the bridge of Violet's nose made her stomach sway.

"Retirement." Nikolai shrugged. "A long and lucrative career. A flower rises and fades and another takes its place. Such is the way of pretty things."

Evie sealed her lips shut lest what she was thinking burst free before she could stop herself. She forced a breath. She needed to get back to her desk and start looking for potential properties.

"You needed something?" She pasted on her obedient smile.

"Valentin wants you to buy gifts for Karla and the girls. He's been away much lately."

"Me?" Evie frowned. It was a perfectly reasonable request for a secretary. Alarm screamed through her veins anyway.

"Something special is required. A woman's touch."

"I'll get started immediately," she said brightly. No time to get word to Mark. She'd have to get to the properties another time. "Let me grab my purse."

"Sergei will drive you."

"No need."

"Consider it a little perk for being tasked with such silly errands." He gave a half smile.

"I'm happy to help," she chided him. "But it *would* be lovely to have someone carry the bags."

He chucked her under the chin. "Good girl."

He walked her all the way to her desk and then down to the doors where Sergei had pulled up one of the sleek black Mercedes that Valentin used as company cars. The list was extensive. By the time she was done, there was no way she could plausibly return to the office for work.

Tuesday she managed to begin the search of properties when Nikolai informed her Karla was no longer interested in redecorating the banquet room and had hired a designer. Evie was to assist.

Evie could have shrieked frustration. But instead, she pasted on her smile and scheduled the walk-through appointments.

She and Mark wouldn't meet until the weekend unless one of them found something. Mark would slow the basement work down if needed—some delays were inevitable.

She just had to stick to the plan.

# CHAPTER TWENTY-EIGHT

"He's hot, but then his girlfriend opens the door." Chris loosed an incredulous laugh. "I thought, Oh shit, we're busted."

Mark smiled. This was what came of only half-listening to his little brother: his attention came back on the best—or worst—parts of a story with zero context.

Mark rubbed at his temple and tried to remember what it was like to be twenty and full of his wolf. For all his attempts to demonstrate confirmed bachelorhood, he certainly didn't have a backlog of stories like this was turning out to be. It was mildly horrifying to feel like his little brother had outpaced him.

"—all night," Chris went on. "God, I thought I wasn't going to be able to stand up in the morning."

"Rubbers?" Mark said hopefully.

Chris swung his head, perplexed. "Say what?"

"You used one... some... lots," Mark elaborated. "You and her and him and whoever else wandered through the door a half hour later."

Chris waved a hand. "No baby wolves running around from me."

"Good," Mark muttered, trying not to be extra horrified by that image. "Smart."

Why baby wolves made his thoughts go to Evie was another story. They had planned to keep it cool this week with no evening visits. It was Thursday, and his wolf bristled inside him, not at all in agreement with stupid human plans. It wanted Evie. It wanted to wake up beside her, her palm against the hollow below his throat. *Not part of the plan, Big Guy.*

The wolf huffed unhappily. Pouting.

Chris's story went on, and Mark allowed his thoughts to drift back to waking up on Sunday morning with the tickle of Evie's hair in his nose. He must have shifted at some point during the night because she'd laughed when she opened her eyes a few moments later. *You're back.*

*Sneaky fucker. Got me while I was out. Did it scare you?*

Her sleepy smile warmed him skin to bone. *No. It was a bit warm for summer. But cozy.*

He made her his signature egg scramble while she showered. The sound of her moving around in his space and singing to herself before emerging in the dress she'd cleverly knotted so it looked almost intentionally slit up to midthigh.

Four days and he was going to crawl out of his skin with wanting. Evie made everything warmer, brighter. Wandering around his apartment with all the lights on was no comparison to having her in the room. Her scent was starting to fade from his pillowcases. They didn't have a lot of time left. Every moment was one less.

"Phone." Chris's voice cut through his thoughts. "You gonna answer it?"

Mark fumbled with the sleek black square before Chris grabbed it.

"It's Pavel."

Mark glanced at the faded digital clock in the dash. The guys should be arriving on the jobsite now. He and Chris were almost at the casino. He'd poked around all week but so far seen nothing. He hoped Evie had a good list for him this weekend. He couldn't wait to see her.

Chris put the phone on speaker. "Dobry."

Pavel was agitated, his words clipped and fast. In the background, Sam argued with someone in Russian. Mark tried to interrupt, but Pavel wouldn't shut up.

Chris interjected smoothly in Czech, switching off the speaker and grabbing the phone. Mark listened, but Pavel was probably talking with a cigarette hanging out of his mouth, so even with wolf ears, he could barely make out the man's words. Mark tapped his brother impatiently.

"Hold up." Chris covered the mouthpiece and gave Mark the breakdown. They weren't being let onto the jobsite. Whatever personal tools they had left from the day before were locked in.

"This is why I tell you guys not to leave your shit at the end of the day," Mark muttered in English, not wanting to piss the old guy off any more than he already was with an "I told you so." He snatched the phone, took a deep breath, and focused on calming the older man down as he took the exit. "Go home. Take the day off. I'll take care of it. Gotta go."

He parked outside the back entrance to the casino and rested his hands on the steering wheel for a long moment, taking a few deep breaths.

Chris sat in silence as Mark tried to call Nikolai. "Voice mail."

He sent a text.

"What the hell is going on?"

Mark shook his head. "Let's get to work. Nikolai will call. I'll deal with it. But I want to be done with this ASAP."

Mark's unease grew all day. Finally, around lunch, his phone buzzed and he paused, waving Chris over. He kept the phone just off his ear so his brother could hear the conversation.

"I am so sorry for the mistake," Nikolai said. "You were to be told. The contract is canceled."

"But the job isn't done."

"We've decided to go in a new direction with the build-out," Nikolai sounded preoccupied. "The work so far will suffice."

Mark hesitated. He hated the confusion in his voice, the edge of desperation. "Is something not completed the way you wanted? We haven't made any substitutions. To spec, exactly—"

"Evie is transferring funds for the remainder of your fees, plus a little extra for this inconvenience, to your account."

"Our tools?" Mark said, too stunned to protest.

"We will have them delivered to Anton."

"I can come by—"

"That is not ideal," Nikolai said smoothly. "Next week, yes?"

Nikolai hung up after a few more meaningless assurances.

Mark found his brother staring. "Not here," he muttered. "Let's finish this and get home."

He'd lost his first real job. He'd have to break the news to Anton. But he couldn't seem to care. He'd rather spend a lifetime doing demo than build a career on cages for supernatural creatures. He would have happily burned it all down. Taking down Valentin Dimitrov was going to be a consolation prize.

As long as Evie was okay. Suppose she'd been caught poking around? But Nikolai had said she was transferring funds. That meant she was still working. It was cold comfort. He needed to see her.

On the way back from the casino, Mark mostly stared into traffic and hoped Evie was keeping her head down.

"So Evie, huh?" Chris supplied, snapping him out of his thoughts.

Mark stared before returning his eyes to the road. *Half-witch*, Evie had said. He'd never thought of it that way, and with no other werewolves in the city that they knew of, he had nothing to compare his family to. If he was inadvertently casting spells on his day planner, maybe Chris *was* a little bit of a mind reader.

That didn't mean he was going to let his little brother get away with it. Anything to keep his mind off the possibility that she was headed into trouble. "That shit you guys pulled on Saturday was not cool."

Chris didn't even have the decency to look chastised.

"Whose idea was it?" Mark pushed. "Toby minds his damn business like he should, but I can see Baby Witch sticking her nose in. And you—you must have told them about her."

Chris sucked his teeth. "Shows what you know about anything."

"Oh, you were the mastermind?" Mark lifted a brow.

"Toby was the one who put it together," Chris said, smug as fuck. "He is the smart one after all."

Mark rubbed his upper lip, trying not to laugh. "Don't sell yourself short, little asshole."

"You kept coming back to the jobsite in Jevany smelling like... I thought it was perfume, but it's just her," Chris said, lifting a finger. "And you got Bebe to double-juju Mom's masking spell. Which looks fucked up, by the way. When you got Toby to use his university pull to get box seats at the national theater and traded Mom and Dad for their Vyšehrad tickets, we put two and two and two together."

"And how many did that make?" Mark laughed.

Chris glared at him. "This isn't a math problem, you overgrown piece of shit."

"So you decided on a sneak attack?"

"I'm good." Chris shrugged. "She's cool, like how she defended you with that slimy guy in the suit. But *Bebe* had questions."

"Baby Witch?"

Chris nodded. "She's protective of you. Gods only know why. Probably because she thinks you're Mom's favorite and *she's* trying to stay on Mom's good side."

"Bullshit." Mark laughed. "But I *am* Mom's favorite."

"Nope, *I* am," Chris said, smug. "She told me."

"Mom's just trying to build your self-esteem."

"Tobi-ass, let Bebe get him all stirred up about this witch who happens to be the mistress of a Russian mobster. Way to pick them, brother. And so we decided to have you two over for dinner."

"An interrogation," Mark growled.

"Would you rather we let Mom have a go at her?"

Mark considered, scratched at his stubble with his thumbnail. "Fine. And?"

"And what?"

"Did you brainiacs decide, or were you too busy burning your tongues out?"

Chris stared at him for a long moment.

Mark rolled his shoulders back and glared at the road. "What the fuck *now?*"

"Just trying to figure out who *you* are and why you suddenly care?"

"Never mind." The question had slipped out, and he had no intention of submitting to another minute of this trash fire.

"I mean, we wish she wasn't also banging a mob boss and/or his side-kick, but..." Chris waved his hands elaborately. "We think you should keep her."

Mark weighed the risk of telling his brother the truth. And decided against it. "Look, what did I always tell you is the number one rule with girls —people?"

"Don't make any promises you can't keep," Chris parroted.

"Whatever this is isn't breaking any promises because no one's made any, little brother. So tell Baby Witch and that walking encyclopedia brother of ours to back off."

Chris snorted. "Have you met Bebe?"

"I'm not fucking around with any of you," Mark said, unable to keep the warning out of his voice. "I want you to stay away from Blossoms and anything that smells remotely Russian mob," Mark said over Chris's protest. "I'll figure out a way to get you the rest of the money I promised you for the work."

"It's not about the money," Chris said, surly now.

"Got another bad feeling?"

"I don't need a feeling." Chris shrugged him off. "We *care*, you asshole."

Mark didn't have anything to add to that, so he kept silent.

"About *you*," Chris said. "What is your damage?"

Mark parked in front of their building.

Chris was halfway out of the seat before he realized Mark hadn't shut the car off. "Want me to open the garage?"

"Nah, I gotta run an errand," Mark said. "I'll be back in a bit. Don't wait up."

"Going to see your mobster moll?"

"Goodbye, Christof."

Chris flipped him off.

Mark waited with a series of deep breaths until Chris was in the building. He fingered the newest key dangling from the key chain in the ignition. Maybe Nikolai had forgotten he had it. If he got caught, it might jeopardize whatever final payout they were going to get. But this job was a bust, and he sure as fuck wasn't working for the Russian mob again no matter how big the paycheck was. Burning a bridge meant nothing.

He wasn't walking away without his tools—and Evie. Fuck that guy.

On his way, he checked his phone. Anton. He dismissed the call. He might have to go crawling back for his old job. But maybe not. After all, Evie had shown him how he could pull off keeping his shingle hung with little more than the side jobs he was running now.

In the alley behind the club, he parked his car close enough to get to the door quickly. He had no idea how much shit the guys had left behind, but knowing Pavel, it could have been a trusted hammer or his entire kit. Mark planned to get in and out. A smash and grab—without the smash. He slipped the key off his ring and bounced it in his hand, tucking his keys under the seat.

He'd leave this somewhere. Nikolai would find it eventually.

The basement was dark but had a peculiar odor he recognized immediately. Fear.

His wolf bristled, and he let it come to the surface enough to sharpen his vision. Color leached away, and the space opened up before him. Most of the doors were closed. The guys had gotten to the fittings at least. But he didn't recognize them. These locks—heavy-duty prison-style—hadn't been on the plans. Cells.

The soundproofing was good, but wolf ears picked up soft shuffling inside some of the cells. The rest were silent. The doors were solid—he stalked through what would have been the reception area where a single screen was set up. Electronic must have been here already—a week ahead of schedule. He flipped on the monitor. The images came up, cells half full. In one, a bullheaded man paced as far as the chains on his neck would allow, unable to get close. In another, a man slumped, snapping his fingers until licks of fire rose from the tips. They sputtered out right away. Mark checked the HVAC status. Low oxygen. A woman curled around with a small figure that might have been a child in another. As if sensing she was being watched, she looked into the camera, bulbous eyes and skin glittering with what looked like scales through clumps of hair like riverweed.

Mark staggered back. Surprise gave way to rage. The circus creatures were here. He had to do something.

Why was his chest so fucking tight? The oxygen levels were fine everywhere but the incinerator man's room. Likely to keep him from starting a successful fire. Still though, breathing was getting hard.

Pavel's tools. He shoved off the counter, pacing to the spot that had been their base station for the past few weeks. He scanned for something useful. Crowbar. He hefted it, the wolf rising in his chest with a fury.

Walking back to the first cell seemed to take too long. It was like he was moving through water. He dragged in a hard breath, catching the familiar scent too late. Magic. He reached the first door and almost slid to his knees. He wedged the crowbar in place and threw all his weight on it. The frame cracked, but the door did not give. The crowbar groaned. He banged on the door.

"You in there, can you hear me?"

A voice rose, trembling. "Yes."

"I'm gonna get you out," Mark wheezed, trying again. "I swear."

"There's a ward on the place," the voice warned. "You have to go. Tell others."

Mark shook his head. There was a painter's mask in the pile of stuff. Suppose he could get to it? His lungs burned. His sinuses felt packed with cotton.

He went down in the tools, Pavel's kit clattering around everywhere. His world dimmed.

When he came back to his senses, a hand pressed to his forehead, cool and soft. The wolf bristled.

Violet.

"Don't fight," she whispered. "What are you doing here, you idiot? You were supposed to leave. You and Evie—I thought you'd run."

"I don't run," he snarled, low in his throat.

"Easy, beast," she snapped. "I mean you no harm. Valentin's security is crawling the place. How did you manage to get in here?"

"Had a key." His voice slurred away from his own ear.

He heard the footsteps on the stairs above before she did. "They're coming."

She swore, looking around. "You need to hide. They can't know you're in here."

She was strong, Mark gave her that. She levered him to his feet, and they staggered back toward the cells. He tried to resist, but all the effort had gone out of him. He was a puppet, and she pulled the strings.

"What'd you do?" he slurred.

"It's a compulsion," she said wearily. "Your willpower. It only affects those with any talent."

He tried again to run when she let him slump to the floor. His knees were rubber.

"Stay here." She snatched the key.

He did, even though she left the door open, and he could hear her footsteps retreating. He just needed one good breath. The wolf pressed against his collarbones but no farther.

"What are you doing here?" Nikolai's voice moved.

"Checking my work," Violet snapped back. "The seals will hold."

"How long?"

"As long as you need," she said wearily.

"Are you done?"

Violet hesitated a beat too long. Mark hard her gasp.

"Get your fucking hands off me!"

"Let's go."

Footsteps retreated at a great distance. A door slammed. If he could just get up, he could try again. He could get help. His mother would know how to counter this. He pushed to his hands and knees and slumped back to the floor almost immediately. His head struck the floor hard, his eyes finding the drain he'd installed on every floor. For cleaning up the mess, he'd bet. He'd had no idea.

Everything went dark.

# CHAPTER TWENTY-NINE

EVIE LOOKED up from packing her stash in the go bag at the knock on her door.

Mark's job had been canceled. She'd issued the kill fee earlier that day, hiding her alarm behind a respectful nod while Nikolai monitored every keystroke. She didn't know whether Valentin was on to them or if something in their plan had changed, but it was time to go. She had a list of properties. They would have to get the evidence to the Amazon and hope she sorted it out in time.

A driver had deposited her at her apartment that evening. A black car had been parked discreetly against the curb within view of her garden gate ever since. Her alarm grew. She unpacked one of her precious burner phones, dialing the number Mark had put on his paperwork. It went straight to voice mail. She risked a text, trying to keep it vague. *Thanks for the play. I'd hoped to see you soon. I'll try again.*

Another knock. The full bag would no longer fit in the space behind the refrigerator, so Evie shoved it and its contents in the tiny attic of her closet with the traveling jacket that was light enough for this time of year not to attract much attention. She'd already sewn money into the hidden pockets. She went to the door, smoothing her skirt and bringing up her glamour.

"I have the dresses you wanted. I won't be back at the club, so I thought I'd bring them to you." Violet pushed inside, handing her a garment bag. She wrapped Evie in a big hug, pressed her mouth to Evie's ear. "We don't have time. Don't ask questions. They have your boyfriend in the basement. He's— It's not supposed to hit them so hard. I don't know why it did."

"Mark?" Evie whispered before her eyes caught on the man standing at her gate. One of Valentin's, she was sure.

Violet glared at her.

Evie grabbed her hand, pitching her voice cheerily high. "Come in, have some tea."

The man at the gate started forward.

Evie turned to him, her glare hard. "You have not been invited."

"But Nikolai—"

She slammed the door in his face.

When the door closed, Violet hissed. "I heard what you said about me not making it out of this. I thought if I could change things. Does it change?"

Evie pulled back and knew Violet saw the truth on her face—the bullet hole still wept unnoticed blood. *Nothing is set in stone.*

Inside, she flipped on the radio, dragging Violet into the seat. She slapped teacups on the table, filled with cold kettle water. "Do you know how to give him the slip?"

"Of course." Violet canted her head, almost laughing at the absurdity of that question before her face turned grim. "For all the good it would do. I invested my money with Valentin. I didn't have a choice. He promised me high returns. And then he held it. Now it's gone."

Evie made up her mind. She fetched scissors from the cabinet and carefully cut out the sewn-in pockets in her jacket, removing stack after stack of carefully counted bills.

Violet's eyes widened when she returned.

Evie set the bills on the table between them. "You always talked about how much you missed home. Where's home?"

"Kumasi."

"You have family there. They'll take care of you?"

Violet nodded, her eyes tearing.

"This should be enough to get you there and to get by on for a while if you are smart." Evie infused her gaze with a dare and a challenge. "And you're smarter than I ever was, Vi."

"What about you?" Violet hugged her fiercely.

"I've gotten by on a lot less." Evie pulled away, wiped her own eyes. When they cleared, she only saw Violet's living face, luminous in the dim light. Hope surged, effervescent in her chest. She'd done it—changed the future.

At the door, they said their farewells.

"Come close." Evie touched the place where she had once seen a bullet hole, as if wiping at a smudge. "You had something there. Bit of lint. Gone now. Take care of both of you."

Violet's eyes brightened. "I'm off to dinner. Ta."

"Keep in touch," Evie said, clearing her throat. "Maybe we can go to coffee sometime?"

"Anytime, dearest." Violet pressed heavy kisses to her cheekbone near the hairline. "Be careful, Eves."

Evie watched her go, aware of the black Mercedes parked outside even after Violet's car had driven away.

Mark and Teta were right. The future wasn't fixed. It wasn't the warning that mattered. It was the action.

She carefully went about her nighttime routine. Panic would do nothing to help Mark.

This was to their advantage. Instead of having to look for the location of the supernaturals, all she had to do was point the finger. But Valentin having Mark changed everything. Time to change a few things herself.

She filled the last pages of the current notebook with the code and the dates of the disappearances Mark had remembered and the corresponding amounts. Then she gave the address of the club and scribbled a note. *I, too, enjoy the circus.*

She tucked the ledger into her cross-body bag and changed into her only pair of slacks and a long-sleeved black shirt with running shoes. She reduced the glamour, turning her hair dark but keeping her scars covered. She shut out the lights and retreated to the bedroom. Then she crawled out the back window, landing in the edge of the garden beside the refuse containers.

She slipped out. She had two stops and then she would be back at dawn.

It was late, but there were still plenty of people out. That didn't stop her from looking over her shoulder at every change. It was a short trip to the small up-and-coming neighborhood of Karlín. The bars and cafés were abuzz with activity, small clusters of people crowned by wreaths of cigarette smoke and heralded with laughter and rowdy conversation. She studied them as she stood outside the sand-colored building. They could have been her contemporaries. She felt decades older. She hit the buzzer.

"Hallo?" Tal's voice, confused and sleepy, crackled on the speaker.

"Only the angels are strong enough to withstand the price for vengeance." She spoke the words of their code from the old days, when things were going sideways and they needed to change plans.

The door lock clicked open immediately.

Upstairs, he let her into the tidy flat and went to reassure his partner that it was fine to stay in bed. It had been years since she'd allowed herself to come here. She felt like an invader, tainted with a darkness that would spoil everything good he'd built here.

Tal returned to the kitchen quietly and went about making tea. She knew he was giving her time to take it all in, to calm herself with figuring out her surroundings as he had taught her. She drank in the homey touches, counting the signs of a life made in everyday moments. Stacks of mail here. A hook hung with reusable grocery totes there. Photos and mementos tacked to the corkboard amid receipts and show tickets. She fingered an envelope.

"You got an invitation to Fashion Week," she said, smiling. "Finally."

"It's the second year, Evie girl," he said wistfully. "You should be there with me, you know."

She waited for the question. But he poured and sat down across from her.

"Mark is in trouble." The words rushed out of Evie. "It's my fault."

Tal exhaled.

"I have to help him." She wiped her tears and slid the last ledger across the table. "Remember the change of plans."

"The Amazon." He paled.

She told him about Valentin and the creatures, then Mark. She sucked in a hard breath to calm the tremble in her voice. "Valentin has to pay for what he's doing, one way or another. I'm planting my feet. That's what you told me to do."

"*Now* you take my advice?"

They both laughed. Evie was going to miss him. One way or another, she was sure she would never see him again.

"I knew it would come down to helping someone." He cupped her chin, staring as if trying to memorize her face. "I've never been able to cure you of your righteous streak."

"You didn't try very hard."

"Do you need anything, money—?"

"'We mortals must be content with lesser victories. Smaller but more profitable.'" She shook her head as she finished the quote she used at door. Even without the money she'd given Vi, she would be ok. She just had to get to her other stashes and vanish. After she'd gotten Mark out. "I'm set."

"Maybe you were paying attention after all." He sucked in a hard breath and circled his tea with both hands. "What's the plan?"

"I get Mark out and I run."

"Alone?"

She swallowed, fingers tapping the tabletop in a numerical pattern. "Not alone."

He watched her for a minute. "Multiples of two?"

"Squares of whole numbers," she said gently.

"That's a bad sign, Evie. You only tap squares when you're afraid."

She shrugged her shoulders, despair rising in her. She wasn't afraid. She was terrified. But not of her powers or Valentin. If anything happened to Mark, she didn't know how she'd live with it. "I love him, Tal."

"You said that." His gaze and his fingers settled on the notebook.

"I didn't." She looked up at him sharply.

"You didn't need to." He smiled. "You're not the only one who can read a person. If I have to march up to the gates myself, I will. When?"

"As soon as you can?" she said. "I don't know how long it's going to take for her to figure it out. But I need a window to get Mark out before she gets there. And it has to be her, Tal. I'm sorry to ask, but..."

"I know." He nodded grimly. "Don't worry about this part. I haven't been dressing Prague's elite all these years just for the money. You never know when you need a favor."

She kissed him on the cheek one last time, breathing him in. And then she wiped her tears and headed back out into the night.

Her second stop took her south of the city, along the river before crossing over. As she slipped off the tram, she looked across the bridge to where Vyšehrad rose like a phantom against the night.

She'd learned enough about the rival organizations over the years. The Vitezovi were new in the city—moved up from Moravia, their territory small but well protected, mostly clubs and a bar or two.

She couldn't just knock on the door though. So she went to the bar rumored to be the central point for the Croat gang and ordered a drink. She probably should have worn something a bit more appropriate for a night out, but perhaps it got her the right amount of attention. The bartender said something to the doorman she'd illusioned herself past, and he sidled over.

"Miss," he said. "This is—"

"I need to talk to your boss," she said, meeting his eyes. This time she looked at the face that appeared, a gray-haired old man with eyes closed. She kept looking, and it changed to a little round-faced boy and then an angular, pimple-faced teen.

Her focused stare must have unnerved him. He cleared his throat. "Who—?"

"Someone who knows where to find his family." It was a guess. A big one. But she'd read the articles. The Croats hadn't given up their performers without a fight. This wasn't just business, stolen resources. Families protected each other, fought for each other, died for each other.

The words rocketed through him. "Don't try to leave."

"I wouldn't dare."

He disappeared.

Evie sipped her glass of wine, ignoring the stares of the men who passed, sizing her up and likely moving on for something in a shorter skirt with less tension-wracked faces.

"Miss, if you will come with me." The doorman returned with three stocky men, less well presented for public work.

She stared back at their curious, vaguely threatening faces one at a time. She found the ones she could not see had other attributes. It was as if Teta's words had lifted the veil from her eyes. One that, she was sure, was supernatural of some kind.

"Miss." A command.

She nodded, slipped off the barstool. She hummed a little, feeling metal vibrating around her as the men closed ranks. Armed then. All of them.

They took her through the back halls and the kitchen to a tidy open-air courtyard.

The doorman stepped in. "Miss."

She understood, lifting her arms for a brief but thorough pat-down.

He came up with a key, studying it.

"That's mine," she said calmly.

His fingers started to close around it.

Evie hummed, lifting her hand as the key flew to her. She slipped it back into her pocket calmly as the men around her leaped back in alarm, going for their guns. She narrowed her eyes at them.

A man called out, and they backed down. He was tall with a head of sandy hair, and his long limbs moved with feline grace. She let her eyes lose focus. Instead of a death mask, she saw a mountain cat's sleek head and ears.

Switching to Czech, he took her in. "Welcome. You are Russian?"

She shook her head instinctively before correcting him. "I'm with them. I'm not— I work for…"

A young man leaned in, whispering.

The big man's smile grew. "You're Valentin's girl."

"No, I'm his bookkeeper," she said, prim as a schoolteacher. "I pretend to be his mistress so that no one will suspect what I really do for him."

The men looked around at each other, voices rising in a low buzz of wary curiosity. She could see the avarice in a few of them. She would make a valuable pawn. She ignored the bead of sweat trickling down her back.

But their leader merely smiled. "This takes balls. Coming here. Telling me who you are, what you are."

"I believe we have a mutual interest in stopping Valentin's new income stream."

His head jerked up, the sated cat replaced by a hardened soldier. "Income—"

"He's selling supernaturals," she said, voice even. "To the Red Death, I suspect. He has your circus, and I'll help you get to them."

He'd begun pacing as she spoke, a lion in a cage. "In exchange for...?"

"He has my man." The words came before she could consider them, how natural they felt. "I have to get him out of there."

"And you need us to do it."

"Valentin doesn't know, what he is," she said, weary of all the subterfuge. She grieved for a life where she could be herself, love the man she did in daylight, not just in the shadows. "He doesn't know what I am either."

"Which is?"

"A witch," she said, the words out loud for the first time in her adult life. That too felt like a liberation. "Daughter of witches and descended from sorcerers. Metal is my ally."

"She has a key," the doorman supplied, voice shaking. "She took it from me without touch."

"To be fair, it was my key." Her brow rose.

The big man's attention swung to the doorman. He flushed, lowering his gaze under his boss's stare.

When the big gold eyes switched back to her, Evie smiled with a faint shrug. Truth was truth.

He gestured to the chairs at the patio table. "Please sit. Tea?"

He even held her chair. He seemed to realize the mistake of putting her at a metal patio table belatedly, but he smiled. Up close, he looked weary, red-eyed, and unsteady. Her guess had been correct. The performers weren't just an act for entertainment. As a shifter, he could pass as human. Those he loved could not. He provided a life for them. And he'd failed to protect them.

"We need certain guarantees that this is not a trap," he said. "You will stay with my men until it is done."

She shook her head. "I can't do that. They're already suspicious of me. I had to sneak out of my apartment. I need to be back by dawn, or they'll know something is wrong. I can give you plans to the building, the timings of the guards, and my word—on my soul."

The men around her gasped. Witches and necromancers weren't the only ones whose blood allowed them to wield words as bindings. Even minor supernatural creatures knew the power of a spoken vow.

"And this." She slipped the key free and set it on the table as the tea appeared, served by a squat barback covered in dense, dark hair. Part ogre? Troll?

"He means that much to you?"

She ignored the question because if she answered, she might break down, and that could not happen. Not yet. Not until Mark was safe. "They're being kept in a recently built-out basement. An alley runs behind the club where this door is located. It's an old door on the other side of the loading docks. It's mostly forgotten. But I don't know if that's changed. I have to go back to work and pretend like I don't know anything about this."

"Sounds like a risky plan for you," he said. "Your man—"

"He's worth it." The words tangled in her throat. It was all she could do to keep her chest from hitching in a barely constrained sob.

He poured. "I understand."

He called in three big men—bear shifters—who all greeted her with polite curiosity, and then they sat down to business. She went through everything she knew about the club layout, the security, and the space.

"There's a spell," she said. "Some kind of compulsion. I don't know what exactly it does, but it could make it difficult for some of your... people."

"You did this?"

She shook her head. "One of the dancers. They forced her."

"Thank you for the warning," he said. "But this we can prepare for. You are not the only witch in town."

"They're going to move them soon, and once they do, we've lost them all."

"Understood."

With a few hours before dawn, he walked her to the back exit. "Do you need a lift?"

"My apartment is being watched," she said. "It would not be best."

The late trams ran slower, but Evie made it back in time to slip through her bedroom window. She took a long shower. She slipped her documents into her go bag. She dressed for work, choosing shorter heels than usual and something she could move quickly in.

Then she marshaled her courage and went to work. There was one more piece she needed to close the trap on Valentin.

# CHAPTER THIRTY

NIKOLAI SPENT most of the morning across from her desk.

Evie pressed her palm against the spot between her breasts, where the divinestone hung beneath the layers of a billowy silk blouse and the trim vest that hugged her waist. Was it her imagination, or was the stone warm?

Unsettled, she returned to her magazine, ignoring Nikolai's prolonged stare. As expected, Valentin arrived before noon and called him into the office. He paused at her desk, lowering his voice. "Alexi, make sure our Evie has everything she needs."

The youngest man beside the door slipped over obediently, his gaze catching on her for a moment too long before finding his boss.

"Yes, boss." Alexi was young, new, ambitious but stupid, and easily bowled over by an attractive woman. She blessed her luck. He took Nikolai's place.

When Nikolai was gone, she rose.

Alexi scrambled to his feet. "Where are you going—?"

"Valentin will want his lunch," she said lightly, checking the slim, elegant watch that had been an "anniversary gift" from Valentin. "In about fifteen minutes."

"But the boss said—"

"You want to tell him why his lunch does not arrive on time?" She smiled brightly. "Plus, if I go downstairs, they make me tea while I wait. Coming with?"

He shadowed her down to the kitchen. The cooks greeted her cheerfully, offered to let her try the sauce for lunch, sample the cheesecake for dessert. Alexi looked unsure at first but relaxed as she puttered around, tasting things and teasing the chef while keeping up a lively conversation with the busboy who made her tea. The kitchen staff had a football game on the small TV by the walk-in, and Alexi drifted into the crowd of servers, pausing to watch the latest charge to the goal.

Evie poured two cups and then brought one to Alexi.

He waved a hand, shrugging her off. Evie smiled.

She sipped her own tea, moving toward the back of the room. She met the cook's eye in silent question. He nodded.

She slipped out the back door with the tea service and a few more cups, moving quickly down the hall. In the security room, she tapped at the door. The banks of monitors lined the wall from cameras all over the club, tapes stored across the wall. She recognized Aldus and Sergei.

"I owe you a cup of tea, Sergei," she said cheerily at their puzzled expressions. "Here."

She tripped, spilling the whole mess across the counter, soaking their newspapers and the keyboards. Both men leaped up, yelling frantically. Aldus hurried to get the keyboards out of the way as Sergei lumbered off for something to mop up the mess.

Evie dropped to her knees to pick up the pieces of porcelain, scanning the bank of monitors as ceaseless apologies tumbled from her mouth. Each camera was labeled with the location of its placement: OF, MF, DR, KITCH. She paused. Dressing room? These scum. BB must be the basement. Strangely, there were monitors only for the waiting areas, though two of the recording decks were labeled ROOMS. She tracked to the wall of tapes. The newest tapes were at the bottom. Very few were labeled BB. She slid behind Aldus under the guise of chasing an errant piece of porcelain.

"Valentin is going to kill me," she moaned. "Please, a bag for all these pieces?"

He nodded.

When he was turned, she grabbed the last two basement tapes from the rooms, from the previous eight to twelve hours. She tucked them in the back of her waistband, under her vest, and kept cleaning. With the bulk of the service removed, she made her apologies and slid out of the room. She headed down the hall.

In the dry storage, she closed the door and hurried to the crates near the back. In the early days, when she had worked on the floor, the girls had taught her all sorts of secrets about the building. There was an old door here to the basement, and she thanked them, every single one, as she pushed enough crates aside to access it.

A set of creaky old stairs let out on the far side of the basement, where the old rehearsal stage had been. It was how the girls who were late managed to slip in without Madame Laureline noticing.

She hurried down, barely registering the prick of splinters in her palms as she gripped the old railing in an effort not to stumble in the dark. The air pressure changed as she descended. She yawned as though to pop her eardrums. The room had been altered. Something magical had been cast over the space. The divinestone heated on her chest. It was all she could do not to reach into her shirt and yank it away from her skin before it burned. When she checked it, she half expected blisters, or at least redness, when she peered at the spot it usually rested. Instead, there was nothing.

The growing sense of wrongness hit her stomach with every step, sending what little she'd eaten roiling in her belly and giving her a mild headache. It was like stepping into a viscous fog she could not see. The divinestone's protection usually felt nebulous, like a perfume that she occasionally caught the scent of. Now it hardened against her like a shell, and she could feel the edges pressing in against her skin as it resisted whatever had been done to the room.

She slipped into the space, carefully avoiding the camera eye. She changed her glamour again, filling her body out and darkening her hair. The cameras were grainy, so hopefully at a glance, she would not be recognizable.

When the basement door to the alley opened, she froze. Three unconscious bodies slid inside, followed by a tall, graceful man and three stockier ones, all unmasked and armed.

"It was guarded," the Vitezovi boss said. "Sorry we're late."

One of his men dragged Valentin's guards to the corner, tying and binding their mouths.

"Right on time." Evie shook her head, fighting the urge to hug him. "Do you feel the room?"

"It's like pressure on the skin." He shook, catlike. "You can open the doors?"

She stepped to the electronic panel of the outer doors. She put her hand over the surface and sang. Electronics shorted and sparked as wiring melted. But the metal tongue slid away. The door popped open. She moved inside, shadowed by the big man. Each door took time, but it was the only way she could avoid overdoing it. She peered inside as she passed, searching for one face impatiently.

She saw a shabby winged creature with a tail and the face of a lion and a tall, slender man who appeared to have fire instead of hands. An incredible, rafter-rattling thumping came from behind one of the still-closed doors, something powerful vying to be free.

The last two doors were opened. One cell was empty, the other crowded. Inside was a vaguely humanoid female creature with exceptionally long arms and a bulbous head and three child-sized beings who looked like something out of a terrible dream.

The round-headed woman crouched beside a familiar shape lying on the floor. Evie recognized his work boots first and then the single hand, long brown fingers, and the strong palm.

"Mark!" She ran, stumbling through the space toward him.

"The witch!" one of the hideous miniature nightmares cried as she approached. The second moaned. "She's cursed this place." The last bared jagged, sawlike teeth. "Trapped us."

She dropped to her knees, ignoring them. Up close, the woman had scaled skin that glittered faintly and long, knobby fingers tipped with suckers. Locks of her matted, dark hair smelled vaguely of river shallows and rotten cattails.

"Peace." The woman held up a hand to the smaller creatures, her attention on Evie. "He is yours?"

Evie nodded and pressed her fingers to his throat. His heartbeat was slow, his breathing thready and choked. His inhales wheezed, hitching in his chest.

"He tried to help us," the woman said, "but he's got the worst of it."

"I didn't do this." Evie met the woman's filmy eyes. "He's sensitive to craft. It makes him sick."

Evie slipped the divinestone from her neck and unhooked the chain to put it around his. Without the divinestone, the weight of the air settled around her like a heavy blanket.

There was no purpose in going anywhere, no way to escape this. She ought to just sit down, sit and stay here. What could she do?

"It's not real. Whatever you're feeling, it's not real," the woman whispered, eyes wide.

"Evergreen," Mark wheezed, rolling onto his elbows.

Now she understood the enchantment placed on the room. It worked the same way Violet's glamour did—the look came with a feeling. Making them *feel* powerless, hopeless. Evie took a deep breath and held it as long as she could.

She slung Mark's arm over her shoulder and levered herself to her knees. It was like trying to lift an anchor while a little voice whispered in her ear that it was time to give up. But for twenty-four hours, fourteen-year-old Evie had ignored people who told her she wasn't strong enough to clear the rubble from the building that was her family's tomb. She'd reached for rock and glass and shingles until she could no longer stand. This was just a sensation.

"All these muscles are heavy," she said through gritted teeth.

He chuckled. The beautiful sound cracked her heart into halves of joy and terror.

He tried, pushing onto his knees and one hand, then dragging a foot beneath him. It wasn't going to be enough.

Evie stroked his cheek, drawing his chin up so she could look him in the eye. "Come on, Hellhound. Help us out here?"

His eyes flashed yellow, just bright enough to let her know she'd been heard.

Mark staggered to his feet, and she pushed her shoulders underneath him, bearing as much of his weight as she could. She kicked off her shoes.

"*Vinko!*" The bulbous-headed woman ran to the Vitezovi boss.

He pulled her into his arms, kissed her before shouting a command that had to be *run* or *get out*.

The woman returned and tugged Mark's other arm over her shoulder. "They will cover us."

Together they lurched for the door. The three squat, nightmarish beings raced ahead, the shabby bat-winged creature being borne on the shoulders of one of the bearlike men.

Evie fought for every step, half carrying, half dragging the man beside her. She hadn't prayed to a god in years, had stopped believing in everything that night in the rubble. She did now, calling on every spirit of wind and desert her father had given her a name for and every household charm and guardian her mother left an offering for before bed at night—the name of gods old and many and singular.

*Just let me get him out of here. Take me if you need. But get him out of here.*

And then they were outside, shoving open the door with such force it bounced against the wall and rang with a clatter. A light summer rain had begun to fall, and the fresh, damp air flooded her lungs, taking the sensation of hopelessness with every exhale. Mark sagged to his knees.

A running van waited in the alley. The door slid open, and Evie watched the other supernaturals be carried and urged inside, saw the relieved faces of the ones who greeted them.

The driver looked around at her. The doorman from the club. "You weren't supposed to be here."

"Plans changed." She grunted.

The bulbous-headed woman climbed in first, helping to ease Mark inside. She held out a hand to Evie. "Come."

Evie slipped the tapes out of her waistband and placed them in the woman's hand. "The tapes from the room cameras, proof you were held. If you can get these to Elise Le Seppe, she'll know what to do with them."

"And your man?"

"Take him with you please." Evie choked. "There's an address inside, someone who can help him. Ask for Barbara or Beryl."

"Who's asking for me?"

Evie looked up at the low, husky voice from the front seat as the passenger looked back. The woman from the yoga studio. Mark's mother. "You... are their witch?"

Familiar, soft brown eyes bounced between them.

"Mom?"

"What the hell are you doing here?" Beryl gasped, scrambling to undo her seat belt and slip into the cargo space.

Evie shrank back, her chest aching with unshed tears. "I didn't mean for any of this to happen."

Mark grabbed her arm. "Don't go—"

"I have to."

"I love you."

Her fingers fanned over his face and swept the wetness away. "I love you too. Both of you."

Then his eyes rolled and he lost consciousness.

"He's just got too much of that shit in his lungs." Beryl checked his pulse, his eyes. "You need to come with us now."

"It'll only make things worse if I'm with you," Evie said. "They'll be looking for me."

"We'll protect you," Beryl said with absolute certainty.

"I see where he gets it from." Evie shook her head, smiling sadly. "But I—"

At the sound of gunfire from the basement, they all flinched. They'd run out of time. Valentin's men had caught on sooner than she'd expected.

The bulbous-headed woman extended her other hand. Beckoning. "Come."

Evie almost took it. *Plant your feet and refuse to be knocked aside.*

Even when she had told the Croatian boss her plan to slip back inside and return to her desk, unnoticed for her part, she knew it had been a long shot. There was no going back now. She was certain Valentin's men had seen her. But she could still do some good.

"They need help." She backed out of the van, reaching for the door handle.

"What will you do?" the bulbous-headed woman asked.

"Whatever I can." Evie smiled, grim and ready.

What had Mark said about the expense of the unnecessary steel? While it was true some supernaturals were impacted by old metals, iron mostly, they hadn't considered the ones for whom it might prove an advantage.

She stalked toward the door. She took a deep breath before she entered, holding the fresh, rain-damp air in her lungs so she wouldn't need to breathe the room's compulsion in again. Then she stepped inside. She kept herself close to the wall.

Nikolai and his crew had come in through the main door, cutting off the big man and the remaining creatures at the doors to the cells.

Evie flattened her palms against the wall. She reached out beyond her fingertips, feeling for the metal, the cells, and the chains. She called to it all at once, a command coated in a siren's song. Her glamour fell away as every bit of her notion turned on a single goal.

She called again, and metal answered.

The floor splintered. Fissures formed under her feet as even the rebar under the concrete responded. Walls buckled as nails and screws clattered to the floor.

She released the walls and the ceiling—no good bringing the whole building down on them. Drawing the fittings together, she flung them at Valentin's men.

From the cells, a wall exploded as the source of the thumping inside the cell burst free. A giant of a man charged through what was left of the cell wall and door, swinging massive bull horns. The fighting ceased as shocked men backed away, and then the giant charged.

Bullets thudded off his pelt. He descended on Nikolai and the Russians, roaring. The fire-handed person ran in his wake, throwing sputtering balls of flame that did not catch but induced enough panic to end the fighting.

Vinko's men herded the rest toward the door, covering their escape. Evie lagged as her notion dimmed and wavered. The bull-man came last, a meaty hand propelling her forward through the door before slamming it shut. He had been wounded, and blood poured down his face. Vinko waved him toward the waiting van as he threw his own body against the door.

Evie braced her heels back against the cold metal as the first impact came.

Vinko fumbled the key, fingers shaking. He was younger than despair had made him appear in the dark courtyard, no more than twenty. The key tumbled from his grip, clattering across the broken pavement.

Evie reached but too late. The silver key glinted, disappearing down the storm drain.

Vinko's face held an almost childlike expression of surprise when his eyes met Evie's. The door bucked against their weight. The two of them were barely holding it alone with their feet braced on the edge of the step. If Evie ran, he would go down. Realizing the trouble, two of the bear men had started back for them, but they weren't going to reach them in time.

His face hardened. "Go."

At a particularly strong blow from the other side, the door bucked into them, hitting Evie's head hard enough that she saw stars. Solid metal.

Evie spun to face the door, both hands spread over the old steel. There was no time for melody. She screamed. A call to battle. The metal wailed back, and the door sealed itself to the frame as if soldered. The knob and keyhole folded inward, forming a solid chunk of metal.

Vinko's eyes were wide, taking in her and the door.

She sagged against the thunder of fists on the other side of the door. Her notion was spent. She wouldn't have been able to lift a pin. "Now we go."

Evie pushed off the door. The van was running, people shouting at them. She turned away.

Vinko grabbed her arm. "Where will you go?"

She tried to smile, but the left side of her face wouldn't cooperate, numb. "I always have a plan. Take care of him. Please."

He put a fist over his heart. "On my soul."

Evie ran. She headed to a small café owned by a server who had once worked at Blossoms. The woman took one look at her and dragged her into the back room. She gave Evie the envelope she'd been entrusted with, a hot cup of coffee, and a small sandwich. When she returned from the storeroom, she handed Evie an old pair of tennis shoes.

Evie opened the envelope full of money and tried to give her a few hundred crowns, but the woman refused, saying, "I wouldn't have this place without you. We're even."

Evie kept moving. She bought clothes at a booth in the next metro station, changing in the bathroom and dumping everything she'd come in with. Perhaps it was good she couldn't glamour herself—with her scars visible, she looked nothing like what Valentin's men would have recognized.

She couldn't go back to her apartment. When they discovered she was gone, they would head there first. She'd given most of that money to Violet anyway. Instead, she cleaned out a minor cache she kept by the memorial hill in Žižkov's enormous park and got a cheap hotel near the conference center in the south of the city that was buzzing with low- and mid-level executives from other parts of the territory. She planned to sleep and buy enough time to wait to pick up her next cache when the national museum opened in the morning.

Restless, she paced the closet-sized room, thinking of Mark. He was fine. Beryl had him. He was safe as he could be.

Around midnight she found herself leaving the hotel. She didn't know where she was headed until she had gone through Vyšehrad Park and walked down the steep wooded slope, emerging on the street facing the mint-colored building.

There was a figure on the porch, a thin bead of cigarette smoke rising above them. Evie started to turn away, but the figure called out her name.

She fought off the instinct to run until it was Barbara's face she recognized in the low streetlight, a cigarette pinched between her index and middle finger.

"Do you mind?" Evie asked.

Barbara nodded, scooting over on the step. "You look like you could use a rest."

Evie sat, eying the cigarettes. "Can I?"

"Don't tell Tobias." Barbara held out the pack.

"If his nose is anything like Mark's, he probably knows," Evie said, plucking one out.

Barbara made a complicated rolling motion with the knuckles of her fingers, and a lick of flame appeared above her thumb. "You're right."

Evie took a long drag, filling her lungs and coughing lightly.

"Don't have to take it all in at once."

Evie laughed.

They sat, smoking.

Evie could hardly look at her. This witch had welcomed her into her home so completely, knowing she was a fraud and a liar. But she could no longer bite back the question. "Mark?"

"He's going to be fine," Barbara said softly.

Evie didn't realize how much worry she'd been holding until that word settled over her. She brushed away tears, unable to keep the hitch out of her breath.

Barbara dug around in the pocket of her jacket, handed her a tissue. Evie gasped thanks because once she started, she couldn't stop.

"Mom cleared him up." Barbara gave her time to collect herself. "He's wiped out though. I don't know how much more of that he would have survived. Your friend did a number on him."

Evie sat up a little straighter. "She didn't have a choice."

"There's always a choice."

It was no good arguing—a woman like this probably had no idea how bad life could get for people like Evie and Violet. How much of your humanity you'd be willing to give up to keep yourself—and the people you loved—safe when you had little to bargain with.

Barbara waved a hand at Evie's face and cheek. "I didn't notice that the other night."

Evie had forgotten what it was like to have her scars on display. She expected to feel the familiar twist of old grief. Instead, she heard the words leaving her mouth as if at a distance, spoken so calmly she could have been responding to a request about her day.

"It happened when I was a kid." She held up her hand, flipping it to reveal the broken nails.

"They hurt?"

"Not anymore." The truth felt new, unvarnished.

Evie contemplated her options: apologize, explain, convince. Barbara's unflinching gaze gave her no hint which might work best. Anyway, Evie was done lying, trying to sell a story. "Mark is the best man I've ever met. I never meant for him to get involved in this."

"Involved?" Barbara blinked hard. "That man will go down fighting for the people he loves. Do you want that for him?"

"I didn't want any of this to happen." Evie's chest grew impossibly tight. There wasn't enough air in the world for the thought the words left behind. "I didn't want him to love me. I didn't want to love him back. But I do."

Barbara sighed, and for the first time, Evie thought maybe there was pity in her eyes. "We'll take care of him. You should probably... skip town or something before they come looking for you."

"That's the plan." Evie swallowed the knot in her throat, feeling her nose get warm and her eyes sting again. She couldn't stand to cry again in front of this strong woman, a witch who owned her power. "Don't tell him I came. Please."

"Are you sure?"

Evie nodded, rising. She took a last drag, then put out the cigarette and pocketed the butt with the used tissue.

"Smart," Barbara said. "Never leave tears or saliva with a witch."

"I know a few things." Evie laughed softly. "Good night."

She was doing the right thing.

If only she believed it.

As soon as the national museum opened, she emptied out the storage locker she paid extra to keep there. She wouldn't have gone back to the apartment except she'd left her documents. She could have others made, but they were expensive. And she'd have to make the right connections first. It would be cheaper to travel with the ones Valentin had forged for her. At least for a while.

She cased the apartment for an hour. The Mercedes was gone. She assumed her apartment was abandoned.

She was wrong.

"Looking for something?" Valentin asked.

Evie reeled to a stop in her kitchen at the voice she never expected to come from the bedroom. Valentin emerged, her emptied go bag in one hand, the papers scattering all over the floor.

It was a nightmare she'd had for months now, only in the flesh. She reeled away, but strong arms grabbed her from behind as Alexi stepped out from behind the door.

He wrenched her elbow, twisting hard to bring her arm behind her back. She screamed as something in her shoulder tore. She reached for her notion, but there was nothing left after yesterday. Her knee buckled under the pain. The muzzle of a gun pressed against her rib cage.

"You cost me a lot of money, you know," Valentin grunted in her ear. "But there's a way we can fix this, you and I."

Evie stopped thinking. She went limp, forcing Alexi to catch her and pulling him off-balance. She expected the gun to go off, to feel the sharp shock of metal in her lungs, shredding the dense muscle of her heart. She didn't wait for it. She lunged, twisting, and jammed her elbow into his solar plexus.

He buckled and his grip loosened just enough. She grabbed his collar and planted her knee in his groin. Then she ran.

She made it to the front door as two suited men entered the garden, a sleek black Mercedes on the curb behind them.

She looked over her shoulder to where Alexi smirked. He rose, catching up to her.

Valentin's men closed in. Their death masks were a mess of bruises, a few gunshots, and some curiously blank expressions.

She held her hands, palm out, at waist level, surrendering. "Hello, boys. I missed your faces."

"Get her out of here," Valentin said from the doorway. "I will join you in a few hours. And then we will talk about how you can make this up to me, my dove."

He turned and closed the door of her apartment. She wanted to scream, to run, to fight, but there was nowhere to go. She was outnumbered and drained of her magic. Useless as the day her family had been buried under the rubble of bombs. This was how it ended. But she wasn't afraid.

Mark was safe. That's what mattered. And she wouldn't give up her dignity. She would hold it as long as she could.

She faced Alexi with a straight spine, keeping her gaze impassive.

"After you." Alexi grinned, all teeth, and gestured at the car. "My, you are truly ugly without that shit you do to your face."

She ignored the insult, limping toward the car. She recognized one of the faces around her. "Sergei, if you please."

The older man opened the rear door. Evie stepped toward it as they closed around her.

Alexi slipped inside, next to her. For the first time, it wasn't a calculation when she smiled at his death mask.

"What are you grinning at, you little skank?" he snarled.

"You're going to die." She waved a hand at her chin. "I can see it. In your face."

The slap made her see stars.

She wiped the blood from her lip and looked out the window. "Where are we going?"

"To dig your grave."

# CHAPTER THIRTY-ONE

EVEN WITHOUT OPENING HIS EYES, the wolf knew he was home by the scent of his pack, the distant rumble of a tram on the tracks, and cars clattering over cobblestones. Evie's scent came from the pillow next to him. *Evie*. That was good too. Safety.

The bulk of the healing was done. The wolf rested, settling into Mark's marrow, the depths of his muscles, the flow of his veins.

Mark had long suspected that Chris really could sleep anywhere. Case in point, when he opened his eyes well after dawn, his youngest brother was sacked out in the reading chair by the closet, head lolling against the wall and long legs stretched out in front of him.

He opened his eyes after Mark did and yawned.

"Skipping too many leg days, little brother." Mark kicked his legs over the side and sat up.

The remnants of the enchantment in the basement still ran in his blood. His body weighed too much. His vision spun. He rested his forehead in his hands.

"Ha fucking ha." Chris grew an extra three inches with a stretch before levering himself into a seated position. "This chair is extra uncomfortable, man."

"Really? I couldn't tell." Gods, he stank. No wonder he could barely smell her on the sheets. "Need a shower."

Chris's silence said everything.

Mark wanted Evie back in his bed. Not even for... anything in particular. Just to have her close. To breathe her in and listen to her sleep. But he wasn't going to her smelling like a dirty gym bag. Shower first. Gallon of water. Was there anything to eat in his fridge? Chris was still staring at him. "Not going to fall and crack my head open on the floor if that's what you're worried about."

"Nope." That lanky liar sighed. "But you do look kinda seasick. You should probably get back to bed and let Bebe give you the once-over first—"

"Where's Evie?" He hoped Barbara wasn't giving her a hard time. Or his mother. Jesus, he'd told Evie he loved her in front of his mother. He was never going to hear the end of it. He couldn't wait to tell her again.

Chris stared at him. "What about Evie?"

"She's upstairs or something, doing some witchy initiation thing with Mom and Barbara." He lurched toward the bathroom and turned on the tap. Hot water made him want to slide onto the floor and curl up for another nap. He switched it to cold and gasped when his heart lurched from shock. That did the trick.

Chris was still talking. Mark forced himself to focus.

"Mom and that cool-ass lion dude brought you home. Did you know there were lion shifters?" Chris called after him. "We got you inside, and Mom let Bebe practice the purification spell. You should have seen it. It was sick. Then Mom took off to go help the Croats. A couple of theirs are in bad shape too. She left Bebe in charge—who is a fucking tyrant, lemme tell you."

"Evie wasn't with them?" Mark didn't give a shit about lion shifters.

He turned off the water and reached for the towel that was usually outside the door. It was gone. "My car?"

"Get decent. Bebe is on her way down." Chris tossed a towel at him. "Nice necklace, by the way. Where'd you get divinestone?"

Mark touched his chest, unease doubling at the feel of the smooth stone and the delicate chain. He'd check her apartment first. Then the club. *"My car."*

"What about your fucking car?"

"Watch your godsdamn mouth."

"Fuck you!" Chris roared. "I can't believe you went back in there alone—what the hell is wrong with you? Why didn't you tell us what was going on? We could have helped. Mom said if they hadn't broken you out when they did…"

Mark had never seen his youngest brother so angry. Speechless, he glared.

"What is going on in here—who's shouting?" Barbara's voice came through the apartment. Man, he wasn't ready for Baby Witch right now. He could smell Tobias in her wake—as usual. Mark's apartment was his sanctuary. Now the place was a revolving door.

"I'll go put the brakes on the witch," Chris said, all his usual ease gone. "Get dressed."

It was handy to have him around.

Mark found clean jeans. The gray sweatpants he'd loaned Evie were thrown over the chair.

"—going to get him killed, or worse!" Barbara's voice reached him from down the hall, raised in a sudden shout.

Mark grabbed a T-shirt, yanking it over his head on his way to the door. He'd had quite enough of a pint-sized witch playing matriarch. "What's up, lovebirds?"

Barbara jumped, spinning on her heel. Tobias stood in her shadow, arms crossed over his chest, studying the floor at his feet. He was just dying to say something, Mark could tell by the constipated look on his face.

"You tell him." Chris spread his hands in a go-on gesture.

"She chose that life," Barbara said, turning to Mark. "She almost got you killed."

"You almost killed Toby," Mark countered. "Pinned him to the floor with the drawer handles before you torched the place."

"I was *possessed*."

"Please, you two." Chris sighed.

"It doesn't matter," Barbara said finally. "She's gone."

"Gone?" Mark's stomach dropped. Not without saying goodbye. He ransacked his memory. She loved him. She'd told him as much—*both of you*. And then things went a little fuzzy, probably because he'd passed out.

"That's because you told her to leave." Tobias looked up, arms crossed over his chest and a solid glare beneath his glasses.

Mark went cold, the rage boiling up under his breastbone with the wolf. "You told her to *what*?"

"Don't you yell at my wife." Tobias flushed, realizing his mistake. He stepped in front of Barbara to face Mark, shoulders up and his teeth beginning to edge toward lupine.

"Whatever happened at Little Blossoms has blown up." Barbara grabbed Tobias's biceps, propelling herself around him for a clear view of Mark. "It's all over the news. The cops are looking for anyone connected, and you know they'd turn her over to Azrael in a heartbeat. She came by last night to check on you. I told her you were okay but that she should go if that was her plan."

The wolf pressed out of his veins, spreading into his bones and scratching at his skin. The howl built in him, need tearing at the recognition that she was gone.

"Bebe—" Tobias yanked off his sweater and his glasses, his eyes on Mark. "Mark, don't."

Both ignored him.

"Stay out of it, Toby." Barbara's hands flexed at her sides, fingers moving in unconscious protection wards. "For her own good, Mark. And yours. The necromancer's people are looking for her."

"You had *no* business." Mark snarled.

"She almost got you *killed*." Sparks danced off Barbara's fingertips.

"Guys, really." Chris lifted his hands in a calm-down motion. "Come on. Let's just take a deep breath."

Barbara lifted a hand, flicking her fingers. Chris stumbled back with a canine yelp. He shook his head as if struck and tumbled into the wall.

Mark lunged. Toby met him halfway, mostly wolf and all teeth. Mark dodged and slammed a shoulder into Toby's solar plexus. Toby gulped as the air went out of his lungs. He tumbled over Mark's back. Furniture skittered across the floor as Toby scrambled to keep his footing.

Markus charged Barbara as the color stripped from his vision.

Her fingers knotted, she swung her hands in front of her chest. A quick shield, elastic enough to absorb his charge, bounced him across the room. He slammed into the dining room table, sending chairs clattering all over the floor.

She lifted her hands, no longer on the defensive. "Try that again, wolf."

# CHAPTER THIRTY-TWO

LUKAS ENTERED the building to the sounds of a dogfight upstairs. Not dogs—wolves. He took the stairs by threes, making soothing sounds to the lower-floor tenants who poked their heads out to see what all the commotion was about.

"Christof is dog-sitting for friends," he reassured them. "I'll sort things out."

He reached Markus's apartment. At the sound of his oldest son's voice, he slipped the car keys into his pocket. He'd gone to pick up the old Škoda after seeing it in the alley behind the club on the news reports. No point in leaving anything connected to Mark that close to the necromancer's investigation. But Markus was supposed to be in bed. Beryl had left them all with strict instructions.

When he rounded the corner, Markus was definitely not in bed. He and Barbara were squaring off, Christof was on the floor by the wall, and Tobias was trying to get to his feet.

The air was thick with the musky smell of adult wolves and the pepper-and-tangerine aroma of Barbara's magic.

"*Das ist genug*," Lukas bellowed. "Stop it. All of you."

"Dad," Tobias gasped from the floor. "Don't."

Lukas marched into the space between wolf and witch, glaring at both. "What would your mother say?"

The wolf retreated from Markus's face. He paced away, throwing off the shredded remains of a T-shirt and tugging his jeans back into place.

Barbara lowered her shield, ignoring Tobias as he patted her down for injuries.

"Toby, leave it." She shrugged him impatiently away. "Did you hear from Beryl?"

"What are you going to do, tattle?" Markus sneered.

"You self-absorbed asshole." Tobias took a threatening step at him.

Markus snarled, showing teeth.

Lukas met the wolf's yellow eyes, pointing a finger at his chest. *"Genug."*

The wolf retreated again abruptly, leaving Markus glaring in surprise.

"Beryl is safe. She says if it weren't for Evie, she never would have found them." Lukas reassured them all before turning to his eldest son. *"You* are supposed to be in bed."

Markus started to argue, but all the strength went out of him in one final shudder. If Christof hadn't caught him, he would have landed on his face. The youngest Vogel lifted Markus easily, slinging an arm over his shoulder.

"Come on, big guy," Christof said with a stern gentleness that reminded Lukas of their mother. "More sleep. Toby'll make you some pancakes when you wake up."

Markus's unguarded face was a study in misery. "She had to go."

Lukas hadn't seen his oldest son cry since he was small. It broke his heart. Barbara gaped, her face drained of color.

"Bed," Lukas ordered. He followed the boys down the hall.

Markus was almost unconscious again by the time they tucked him back in. "Dad. I need to check—make sure she got away okay."

"We'll take care of it," Lukas said. "I promise."

He followed Christof out of the room, closing the door behind him.

The youngest Vogel sighed. "I knew he was gone for this girl, but man. He's *gone."*

In the living room, Tobias had his arms around Barbara. She wiped her cheeks. "I thought I was doing the right thing. She said…"

"Her apartment. Does anyone know where it is?" Lukas sighed.

"Dad," Tobias said.

"I'm just going to drive by, make sure everything looks… all right." He had no idea how he would know if it wasn't, but he had made a promise.

"Wait a second." Barbara broke free of Tobias and ran out of the apartment.

She returned with a scrap of paper. "I did a location spell a couple of weeks ago for him. He wouldn't tell me who for, and I didn't need to know… He just had to see who he wanted to find for it to work."

Tobias stared at her. "You've been doing magic for him?"

"She bumped up his masking spell, didn't you notice?" Christof chimed in.

"I did not," Tobias said, his eyes on his guilty wife.

Unsurprising, considering Tobias had always been the least comfortable with the truth of the family's magical identities. He was still learning what he was capable of and how to live with his wolf in ways his brothers had long ago mastered.

"You have been enabling—"

"He asked nicely," she said. "For once."

Lukas sighed at all of them. Children. "Stay here, keep him down. I'll call as soon as I know anything."

◆

LUKAS DRUMMED his fingers on the steering wheel, considering what to do as he drove past the garden gate at the address for the third time. He parked and watched it. No one came or went.

At the gate, he let himself in. He knocked, peeking in the windows. The place was a mess.

"Scheiße." He liked nothing about this. His phone buzzed in his pocket. Beryl's face appeared on the screen. He swore again. "Scheiße."

He glanced at the building, then the phone. Stalking back to the car, he answered the call.

Beryl sounded tired but not in distress. Some of the weight sloughed off his chest. He listened patiently, hearing more than her words. She was exhausted. The Croats had managed to rescue their people, but they were in bad shape. Healing took more energy than anything else—she would be drained for days.

"Come home, let me make tea and read to you." Lukas pushed the worry from his voice.

"That sounds like heaven." Beryl sighed. But she would stay a bit longer to make sure they got safely out of the city.

A figure in a vintage double-breasted jacket with gold buttons and a navy bow tie passed by the gate, carrying a too-large garment bag. Lukas admired the man's shoes briefly—brogues in a rich shade of cognac. The man made a second pass, just casual enough to appear to be double-checking the address, but something about his pinched expression tugged Lukas's attention.

"Is everything okay there?" Beryl asked, yawning.

The man entered through the garden gate.

"Yes, fine. Everything is fine here. Markus is resting. Christof is keeping an eye on him. Tobias is making pancakes. Barbara has them all running like clockwork. Stay as long as you need."

"Are you sure?"

Lukas ignored the suspicious note in Beryl's voice. "Yes, of course. Everything is... Well, I have it in hand."

"*What* do you have in hand?" Her voice sharpened attentively.

"Nothing. A small matter really. You know, boys."

The suited man still hadn't emerged.

"*Our* boys?" He heard the phone shift from one ear to the other. "Lukas?"

Lukas cleared his throat. "Yes, my love?"

He stepped out of the car, bouncing the keys in one hand.

"Where are you? Are you driving?"

"A quick errand," he murmured. "Taking care of something for Markus."

"I can't wait to hear more," she said slowly.

"I can't wait to tell you all about it." He headed back to the abandoned apartment. The garden was empty, but the front door was open. "Must go."

He peered into the open front door. There was no sign of the man, but the garment bag was laid over the chair.

"Hallo?" Lukas tapped on the door.

He stepped carefully around broken glass and dishes, overturned potted plants.

The man emerged from the hall. Up close, he was just past middle-aged, short and stocky, with graying curls beginning to emerge from beneath a classic fedora. His eyes widened. "Who are you?"

"I could ask you the same thing." Lukas smiled, adjusting his glasses.

They stared at each other.

"You know Evie?" Lukas said finally.

"I am her tailor."

"Her tailor." Lukas's brows rose. "Delivering empty garment bags on a Saturday."

"Who did you say you were?"

"I didn't." Lukas drew up, one old man to another, and grinned. "Lukas Vogel."

"Vogel." The little man's eyes widened. "The foreman. Mark. Evie said... Well, she arrived in the middle of the night on a mission, and this morning I saw the news of the club and I suspected. Is he—?"

"She got him and the others out. But I understand she had her own plan."

The man sighed. "That's Evie."

"Was she able to complete it, you think?" Lukas looked around grimly at the wreckage of the apartment. Perhaps she had wrecked it to make it look like a burglary to cover her escape. He wanted to believe it.

The tailor shook his head. Before Lukas could ask how he knew, the shorter man lifted a notebook in a battered leather cover. "She would never leave her sketchbook behind. They caught her."

Alarm pricked over Lukas's spine. "They?"

"The Crimson Saints," the tailor said, voice low. "She worked for them—against her will, I'm certain. She gave me copies of her ledgers to deliver to Elise Le Seppe when she runs. It proves that her boss was selling supernatural creatures to Saint Petersburg."

"You still have them?"

"I came here first when I saw the news." The tailor had begun to shake, his voice a tremor. "Le Seppe thinks she's involved. And if they have her when the necromancer's people show up..." He shook his head, wiping at his face furiously. "Godsdamn, Evie. You have to try to save everyone. Foolish git."

Lukas looked around again. The place had been turned over, but there was no blood. If Valentin knew she had copies of the ledger, perhaps he'd try to get them back first. That meant they still had time.

"Let's go."

The tailor stared at him, blinking. "Go?"

"We're going to get your books to the necromancer's Amazon," Lukas said, determined. "And then we're going to find Evie before they do."

He turned, stalking out of the apartment. When he looked back, the smaller man stood in the doorway, gaping.

"You are... not afraid?"

Lukas bared his teeth. "You haven't met my boys."

◆

MARK ATE the pancakes in front of him obediently. They'd taken his phone. Barbara had threatened to bind him to his apartment until he agreed to stay put. He'd play along. When he needed to he'd slip out, and nothing the three of them could do would stop him.

"I whipped up that cream *by hand*." Chris leaned over the counter, setting down a plate of bacon. "Could you at least act like you even taste it? Here, protein."

"Dad call yet?" Mark asked around a mouthful.

Evie's disappearance sat uneasily in his gut, turning the pancakes into lead. He'd been preparing himself for her eventual departure. That was always the plan. But things had gone so wrong in the basement.

If only he had waited before trying to get them out. Instead, Evie had been forced to take on Valentin's operation alone. For him. All because he couldn't keep from rushing in, trying to be the hero.

"Cowboy," he muttered guiltily. His jaw slowed.

"This isn't your fault," Chris said softly. "You tried to help. You always do. We get it."

Mark focused on his plate. Evie got out fine. She got him out, didn't she? She had a plan. She could change her hair and her face, chameleon into anyone she wanted. She had money to last for years. She would disappear. Valentin would never find her.

He wished he believed it.

The front door opened, and he knocked his chair to the ground in his hurry to rise. Chris looked at him, wary, but stood in his wake.

Their father entered with a short, middle-aged man in a fine suit. The wolf recognized the scent, secondhand, something often tangled with Evie's. The smaller man carried an oilcloth wrapped bundle tucked under one arm.

His dad made a half turn, his expression lightening with a brief smile. "Tal, these are my boys. Chris, Mark, Tal's going to help us get Evie back."

Tal took a tentative step toward Mark, extending a hand. "You mean a lot to Evelia. She's never spoken of anyone like she does you."

The sting in his chest eased, but then his father's words caught up. "What do you mean, get her back?"

Dad held up his hands—a gesture that never in a million years worked to calm someone down and only sent Mark's blood racing. "She's been taken by men I imagine are in Valentin Dimitrov's employ—"

"Taken?" The word echoed through the sudden hollow in Mark's chest, a yawning pit that made the world slant on its axis and threatened to tip him into it.

It was all he could do to keep the wolf raging in his throat from lunging into the city, howling after her.

"Evie figured out Valentin was selling supernaturals to the Red Death," Tal said. "We think they might hold on to her to see if they can find out where she stashed the proof."

"The same creatures Mom was looking for," Chris said. Mark nodded impatiently, and Chris turned to him, pale face marked with two spots of high color on his cheeks. "You *knew*."

"Evie and I were going to get them out," Mark said. "Shut down the whole thing *without* Mom getting involved."

"You hypocritical fuck." Chris's nostrils flared, his eyes wide. Mark had seen his youngest brother annoyed and irritated. Mark was one of the few people in the family who could evoke either emotion in their easygoing sibling. But never this. The combination of disappointment and anger was palpable. He scented the younger man's wolf, no longer a pup.

Mark couldn't meet his eyes. Valentin had taken Evie. Which meant Nikolai had her. At the thought of that latent violence unleashed on Evie,

Mark's chest tightened and the wolf again pressed under his collarbone. He met Tal's eyes, presumably the only person in the room who knew who truly did the Saints' dirty work. The other man nodded.

"I know where they took her," Mark said.

"Jevany," Chris announced. "The villa."

Mark nodded sharply. He hadn't wanted them to know, to try to do something stupid like go with him or after him. "Give me my keys."

His dad faced him, hands in his pocket. "You are not an army of one, Markus. Your brothers and I—"

"Are staying the fuck out of it," Mark shouted. "All of you. Nobody else is getting hurt."

"Haven't you learned anything, jerk?" Barbara sighed. She and Tobias must have heard Dad come back. They stood together in the doorway, her back against his chest, his attentive glare focused on Mark and his ears a little furrier than human. "We are not going in without a plan. And a backup plan. But we are going. All of us."

Tal did a double take, his eyes widening in recognition of something, and then he scanned the group again. "What kind of people are you?"

"A family. A rather strange one sometimes," Barbara said with a little smile.

"Beryl's a day out of town with the circus," Lukas said. "Even if she could get here—"

"She's doing healing," Barbara finished. "That's going to take a lot out of her. We're on our own. But I think I know how to get the books to the Amazon."

Tobias looked at her sharply. "Zeman's already suspicious."

"Then he'll move fast." She shrugged. "He's really our best shot unless you plan on marching up to the castle and knocking on the front door. Maybe you impress the scary one in the suit with how polite you can be in German and ask him to hand them to her next time he sees her?"

"It's not funny." Tobias shook his head.

Barbara put a hand on his arm. "You want to help."

"I meant to go in with Mark and Chris and take care of business."

Mark wanted to laugh. A few years ago, Toby was afraid to let his wolf off the leash. Now he was "taking care of business." Barbara was good for him.

"I know you did." Barbara smiled. "And you will. Because if Evie gets picked up by Azrael's people with the rest, who knows what they'll make of her—and what they'll do. We need to grab her before they do and hide her until this blows over. She can stay at the cabin."

"Perhaps I can help you with your errand," Tal said, stepping forward.

"You are... like Evie. That makes this Zeman fellow wary? I am as mundane as they come, and I do work for Valentin's dancers, so it is plausible that I would have access to this information. I can be very convincing with these kinds of things."

It made sense. Some of the tension drained from Mark's chest. The wolf trembled with rage and eagerness to be off. But it waited, watching the pack and recognizing strength in numbers.

"I know a back way onto the property," Mark said.

"They may be ready for you," Chris warned.

"Count on them being ready for you," Barbara said. "If you were in those cells, they know what you are. We need a diversion. And another way in."

His dad showed teeth in a smile that lacked any warmth. "I may have both. An old friend in construction owes me a favor. Barbara, what do you say you and Tal and I take that fancy car of yours for a spin? A drive in the country would do us all some good."

"Wait a damn minute," Tobias groused.

"Tobias, pick up the van with your brothers," Barbara ordered.

Mark looked between them, knowing a plan was coming together but not entirely clear on all the pieces. He wished he had his shit together. After the surge of adrenaline cooled, he felt woozy again and unsteady. He stepped forward anyway.

"You're gonna sit your ass down." Chris planted a hand in his chest. "And finish your pancakes."

Mark started to protest. Did they think he was going to stay behind?

"Rest now. You'll need your strength when we get there," Barbara said before he could argue. "I can help a bit, but the best cure for what ails you is your wolf. Evie is counting on you. Now, where do we meet?"

He met her eyes as the last of the tension slipped from between them. Barbara gave him a hesitant smile. *You see, we're stronger together—all of us.*

She was part of the family now. Based on how well she marshaled the troops, they were much, much better for it. Godsdamn, he liked her more than he wanted to admit. Just as stubborn and headstrong as the rest of them, she fit right in.

She gave a little shrug. *I'm sorry, Jerk.*

Against his will, he smiled.

"Remind me not to piss you off again, Baby Witch." Mark grabbed a piece of paper and a pencil. "I know the spot to meet."

# CHAPTER THIRTY-THREE

EVIE HAD ALWAYS HAD a trouble staying awake on long car rides and, despite the circumstances, she surrendered to exhaustion in the car. The next thing she knew, she was being dragged into the warm night air. She hit the ground hard on her hip and leg, feeling places where paving stones scraped skin.

She fought, scrambling as Alexi dragged her down the long drive, trying to get her feet and bearings. She recognized the high walls surrounded by trees first. Fresh, woodland air flooded her nose. Jevany. She lurched to her feet.

Nikolai strode out of the main house.

Alexi opened his free arm victoriously. "Look what I found."

Nikolai's fist hit him square in the mouth. A follow-up body shot folded him in half.

Evie shrieked, and Alexi lost his grip.

"You were not to damage her." Nikolai caught Evie, an arm around her waist the only thing keeping her on her feet. He smelled like gun oil and *venik* and the sour tang of old sweat.

Alexi had the gall to look bored as he stood up, spitting a mouthful of blood at Nikolai's loafers. "Who gives a shit about this fucking whore?"

Evie's vision doubled as a ragged hole opened up where Alexi's left eye had been. Startled, she stared. This was not the death she had seen in the car. It changed. The color was vivid. Possibilities.

Nikolai drew on him, and the young man found himself staring down the barrel of his boss's pistol a second before it went off.

Evie's vision merged with reality as the body crumpled in the driveway.

Nikolai holstered his gun. He pinched her chin, yanking her face around to survey her split lip and the bruise forming on her scarred cheek. He turned to the remaining men, who mumbled apologies, a few leveling accusing glances at Alexi and the growing pool of blood on the driveway.

Nikolai shrugged, rolling his shoulders in his suit as he narrowed his gaze on Sergei. "Take her up to the study. Then clean this shit up."

Inside, Evie was escorted to the book lined room overlooking the driveway and the gates. Valentin stood by the window, arms clasped behind his back. When the door closed behind Evie, he turned.

"Nice to see you again, Evelia." He poured two glasses of scotch and brought her one.

Evie was proud that her hands didn't shake as she took it.

"We've come a long way together, you and I," he said as they watched the groundskeeper hose the blood off the pavement. The body had already been wrapped in burlap and lay on the manicured lawn, a dark stain spreading beneath it.

It was a messy, bloody business performed with startling efficiency.

Valentin frowned, displeased. She knew he preferred to keep that side of his work out of sight.

"A long way we have come," he repeated, musing. "And much of that is thanks to you. Your skill with the books has been a great service to me."

Evie sipped, feeling the heat and instant buzz in her head that said she'd burned through her last meal long ago. The alcohol gave her distance, a sense that she was floating just outside her body. Nothing could touch her here. It wouldn't last. But she would appreciate it while it did.

"But it seems we must go our separate ways now," he went on. "A disappointment. And one that I lay squarely on your shoulders, my dove."

Evie didn't bother speaking. She knew how this went.

"Now, you must return the favor before you are… released."

"Before I am bound in sacking and thrown into an unmarked grave in the woods like Alexi?" The sound of her own voice startled her with its strength, calm.

Valentin appraised her, eyes narrowed. "You do not plead for your life?"

"Would you grant it?"

He shrugged mildly, as if she'd asked to take the Bugatti parked in the driveway for a spin and he must regretfully decline.

"Then what would be the point?" A quiet had settled over her.

Death had come for her at last. There was no fear. No more fear. Only the certainty that she would take her secrets to the grave.

"I admire that," he said. "And this will go much easier."

"This?"

"We lost a great amount of money. In addition to the regard of our buyer."

She gave him the total, calculating the number of creatures in the basement based on the figures she'd been staring at for months—a stableful of Bugatti. The payment for the basement remodel twice over.

"Very good," he said. "You haven't lost your touch. It appears there is a way to salvage this... situation of ours."

She downed the scotch. At least it would take the edge off the pain that came next.

"The Necromancer Vanka's true interest is in ones that transform. Animal to man, man to animal. She has a special interest in such abilities."

Chill spread through Evie's bones that even scotch could not touch. How could he know? Mark had only been there a few hours, in the dark. They couldn't have possibly seen the tapes. The world around her went silent as she focused entirely on his next words.

"It has been made clear," he said, annoyed, "that were I to recover one or more of these creatures, I would be welcomed home and this unfortunate business put behind me."

He shrugged again, palms spread, and lifted the scotch bottle. Evie shook her head.

"Azrael will let you go?" She couldn't hide her surprise.

"The Angel of Death has been assured that this was a onetime event, an overreach on my part."

"How fortunate for you."

"I have been made aware that you know at least one of these creatures."

"So it's to be an easy death or a hard one."

He looked disappointed in her. "You think so little of me."

She frowned, unwilling to give herself a glimmer of hope.

"It appears Kolya wishes to remain in the service of the Petrov." He wrinkled his nose. "He has asked for you. You should know he is quite fond." He gestured out the window at the evidence.

"And some women get only roses," she said mildly.

"You have grown into quite a woman, Evelia." He laughed. "So different from the cowering little mouse reciting numbers while pinched in the trap."

*I have been loved by a wolf. No matter what happened to me, I have survived. And so will Mark and his family.*

"It is best that you prepare the sacking," she said quietly, setting down her glass.

Valentin's jaw flexed, the only sign of his displeasure. The study door opened, and Nikolai entered without looking at Evie.

"It has been a stressful day, and our Evie needs a clear mind to make a decision," Valentin said. "We will resume our conversation at dinner, kitten, yes?"

Nikolai's shoulders tightened a bit at the reminder that she still belonged to Valentin. But he held out an arm.

Evie ignored it. She stopped on her way to the door, turning toward them.

Valentin had already turned his back to her, but he angled his head slightly.

"You should know," she said, "whatever happens to me, the necromancer's people will receive ledgers for the past few months and the tapes of the basement. Le Seppe, was that her name? It seemed she would be interested in such a thing."

Valentin stilled. Nikolai looked at her sharply, as though seeing her for the first time.

Valentin barked a command, and the housekeeper skittered into the room. "Show our guest to her suite. Kolya, a moment."

The woman escorted Evie to a lavish guest room upstairs and locked her in. She returned with warm water, antiseptic cream, and bandages.

"There is no point," Evie said in Russian.

The woman ignored her, shaking her head and laying everything down on the dresser. She wouldn't meet Evie's eyes but gestured at the chair.

"I can do it." Evie tried again.

The woman didn't leave.

Evie bit her tongue against howling as the woman cleaned the gravel from assorted scrapes.

They both jumped at a quick rap on the door.

Nikolai opened the door, a box under his arm and a series of bags in hand. He leveled a stern glare at the housekeeper. "Go."

The housekeeper fled. Nikolai set down his packages, taking in the bloody towel and water in a quick glance.

Evie grabbed the antiseptic and held her palm over the bowl.

He took it from her and dropped to one knee.

"I don't need—"

"You don't know what you need," he chided as if addressing a small child. "Or what is good for you, it seems."

Evie set her jaw, refusing to wince as he finished cleaning her palm and her elbow. "Just let him kill me and get it over with."

"You think it will be as easy as with Alexi? A bullet and—" He snapped his fingers. "You cost him money. You broke his trust. You just revealed that you've betrayed him to Azrael."

Evie glared at the door, swallowing hard. "I haven't done anything. As long as I survive—"

"Survive." He laughed. "When what is left of you is dumped on the streets in Prague, you will wish you had not survived. And if that wasn't a bluff, he will have what remains of you hunted like an animal."

He wrapped her hand in silence, with a nurse's efficiency and a surgeon's precision. His touch was so gentle. "I promised you protection, and I mean to keep my word."

Her gaze snapped to his face. She couldn't help it. Fathomless dark eyes waited for her, flat and black as a shark's. But there was something else. "You still want me."

"Even though you behave like a spoiled child, yes. You are powerful. We will be powerful together."

"You're like me?"

He refused to look at her, instead taking up another roll of gauze. He cradled her arm around her scraped elbow. "I have an instinct for what people would hide from me. How do you think Valentin got this far? Until you came and made his money flow and I could better protect him. I appreciated you for that. It made it worth the risks I took to keep what you truly are hidden from him all these years."

"You knew what I was?"

"Who do you think told Valentin only that you'd stabbed that man in the booth that night?" he said. "Burned the body before anyone could find out that he bore no marks. Messy business that."

Evie was silent.

"And how you repay me," he said idly. "Sneaking out into the woods every day for weeks. It is truly amazing how much work you got done so quickly between cavorting with that animal. When our friend Markus arrived, he was another puzzle. Until the wolf started turning up in the city, near your apartment. Then the pieces came together in my mind."

He inspected the bandage, let his fingers linger on the inside of her forearm, and traced the veins beneath her skin. He met her eyes. "Does he fuck you as the wolf too or just as the man?"

Evie swung without thinking. He caught her wrist in an iron grip and yanked her into his chest. His next words were uncharacteristically rushed, urgent.

"Valentin is running out of time. He is willing to overlook many things. Give him his way out. He will take his wolf to Vanka in exchange for his forgiveness. You remain here, with me. I will provide for you, see that you have everything you need, certainly more than that hovel you lived in.

Whatever offspring you produce must be given to Lady Vanka—but that is a small price for your freedom. Yes?"

"My children?" Evie's voice shook.

He released her hand with a sneer. "Dress for dinner. And do... whatever it is you do to make your face passable. I don't want to see... this again. Understood?"

He stalked to the door. Evie picked up the dish of bloody water and hurtled it. It shattered against the wall, staining the pale cream wallpaper dusky rose. He spun on her, teeth bared as he reached under his jacket.

Good, let this be done now. They wouldn't use her for bait.

"Never," she said, knowing her eyes were wild and too bright. "I will never, ever choose you, Nikolai. I would rather die a thousand times."

He froze. She saw it in him—the drawing of the pistol, the flash of muzzle fire. Her body registered a phantom burst of pain and then the gasping leakage of her own life.

He drew himself up, tugging his jacket closed and buttoning the single button. She didn't know what to make of it. Then she saw the vivid echo of a face over his, still and gaping in death. No wound she could see, but there were a hundred ways to die that didn't involve a headshot.

He said nothing, only smiled at her and left the room.

The dress in the box fit like it was made for her, but the work had been rushed and the quality compromised. Evie eyed the uneven seams and loose threads and frowned before slipping it on. Not Tal's work then.

Reluctantly, she abandoned the running shoes in favor of needle-thin stilettos on thick platforms. They buckled at the ankle twice. Getting them off in a hurry was going to be tricky. She almost laughed at the folly of any escape that didn't end in an unmarked grave. And yet.

She did not waste her energy pacing. Instead, she ran numbers, calculating her chances with every potential escape plan she could imagine. The odds were abysmal, but she was done playing safe. If the opportunity to run presented itself, she would, even if it ended in a dark hole in the forest.

She was faintly aware of all the metal in the room in a way she hadn't noticed until it was absent. Her power was coming back. Evie sat on the bed, building the miniscule connections of sparks into solid threads. She experimented with her glamour. It took more effort than usual, but it came. An hour passed. Maybe more.

"It would be better without the bandages," Nikolai pronounced.

She stifled a gasp. She hadn't heard him come in.

He'd changed his suit, showered, and trimmed his beard and mustache neatly. She tried to see him as handsome, to allow her mind to travel along a future where she took his offer. But it was a closed door.

She rose.

"You still cut a stunning figure." He hooked her chin with his knuckles, turning her face. "Impeccable. If I didn't know better, I'd think you flawless."

"We shouldn't keep Valentin waiting." She strode to the door, leaving him in her wake.

The dining room had been set lavishly, and as she walked into the room, one of the two seated men rose. Valentin's skin was sallow, drawn, and some of the cool that he had so effortlessly exhibited earlier in the day was gone as he stalked toward her. Yan Petrov, the head of the Crimson Saints, remained seated, watchful.

"Mr. Petrov." She angled her head in deference.

Nikolai's solid bulk filled the space behind her.

Valentin waved him away, settling his sweaty hands on the back of her chair.

"You are a fancy piece of work," he murmured in her ear. "You and your threats. I am going to enjoy taking you apart."

Evie experimented with her returning power. His heartbeat sounded in her ear, the liquid pump of blood moving in his veins. She recalled the taste of blood in her mouth when she'd been struck, the metallic tang on her tongue. Blood held iron.

Once upon a time, the girl she was had drawn the iron in a man's blood from his body in self-defense—an automatic response even she hadn't understood. When Nikolai had broken down the door to the private booth, she had been screaming, covered in the man's blood, and shoving his lifeless corpse off her. She knew only that she was responsible but not how. She did now.

She met Valentin's eyes, smiled. "I'm sure you will try."

But there were too many people between her and the door, and it was too soon after the basement. *Conserve, Evie girl. Think, plan. Wait for an opportunity.*

She took her seat, drawing it in herself when Valentin left her to take his own at Petrov's right hand.

The meal passed in a blur. Like Persephone, she did not eat or drink. No one seemed to care or even take note. The one moment of excitement came at the crackle of a two-way radio from one of the door guards.

Nikolai rose, striding for the door. He returned, frowning, in time for dessert.

"Stupid fucking tourists," he muttered, sitting down. He looked up into Petrov's cold stare, Valentin's anxious one. "Lost and looking for directions. The old man saw the flag and thought he'd found a fucking embassy. Pretty little piece with him, young, bookish…"

Evie kept her eyes on her plate while her mind grasped the words in his explanation with something that felt dangerously like hope.

*Careful now, Evie girl. Stay focused.*

"I suppose you have had time to think about our generous offer," Valentin said after the table had been cleared.

"You didn't find my books," she said without question. "You tore up my apartment, floor to ceiling, but they were gone."

"The money—"

"My money?" she said gently. "Every blood-soaked crown I earned, scrimped and saved. Let me walk out of here, and I will tell you where to find the books. You can keep the money."

"Ungrateful, plotting bitch," Valentin snarled. "I'll kill you myself."

Evie never saw Valentin draw. Nikolai rose from his seat with a shout, moving between them.

When the gun went off, she flinched, expecting shock to give way to pain. But it was Nikolai who collapsed, knocking over chairs as he stumbled to his knees and fell. She flung herself away from the table, grabbing for the cloth napkin. He landed on his back, mouth gaping as the stain spread across the carpet beneath him.

She went to her knees at his side, pressing the napkin to his chest with one hand. She watched burgundy blossom on the white starched cloth, spreading. She looked up at Valentin. "How could you—?"

Nikolai's fingers crept around hers, squeezing. She reached out her awareness for the bullets, but they had exited cleanly, and there wasn't enough strength in her to pull a wound that large back together.

Horror ravaged her. Dark eyes met hers, blood already foaming at the corners of his mouth. Those red-rimmed lips moved one last time to form a single word, and then his eyes went flat, empty. The word echoed through her like a whisper with the disconcerting brush of an invisible hand. *Run.*

Evie rocked back on her hips, ankles tucked beneath her and fingers working frantically at her heels, using the steak knife she'd snatched from the table in the commotion to tear through the ankle straps on her cheap shoes.

"It seems you are not the only one capable of terrible acts, kitten," Valentin said, downing his scotch. "And unlike you, he had no further purpose. I don't need you to be willing to be bait."

Petrov smiled. Valentin holstered his pistol.

Evie flung herself off the floor, lunging barefoot for the door. She almost made it. The click of a hammer cocking stopped her in her tracks.

"That's enough histrionics," Petrov said flatly. "Drop the knife."

Evie froze, inches from the wood and freedom. Her throat burned. *Run.* She couldn't do it. They'd brought her to Jevany on purpose. She could still help Mark. She let the knife clatter to the floor.

"Bind her."

One of the door guards yanked her arms, pinioning her wrists at her back.

"And use zip ties," Valentin said. "No metal."

Thin plastic sliced into her wrists, and almost immediately her fingers went numb. She lunged away, but he held fast. The guard spun her to face Valentin.

"I saw the video." Valentin poured himself another scotch. "The black wolf prowled the walls, looking for you for weeks after you stopped sneaking out to see him. He'll come for you. Tell the men to keep their distance and the dogs hidden. I want him inside the walls before we spring the trap."

As Valentin dragged her down the driveway, she made out figures in the darkness. A dozen soldiers in armored tactical gear. Four held two big, savage-looking dogs apiece. What frightened her most was how silent they stood, no baying or even sniffing. They didn't even seem to be breathing.

"Fall back to the courtyard," he ordered, tossing a chain and padlock. "When he comes through, seal that gate. Nothing gets out."

Valentin dragged her through the garden and to the ivy-covered back gate. The ivy had been cleared away, leaving the old gate exposed, bare and skeletal in the dark.

"Open the gate," Valentin demanded. "I want your scent all over it."

"I don't have my power back yet."

"Then use your fucking hands." He tossed her at the bars.

She caught herself, barely. She pressed blood and sweat into the gate. The metal sang back, a low vibration in her chest, the rusted hinges protesting softly as old bars slid apart. As a last effort, she grafted her warning to the bars. *Not this way. Danger.*

The cottage was stuffy and dark. The ghostly shapes of furniture under the muslin drapes made it seem foreign. Valentin dumped her unceremoniously on the floor and gagged her with a handkerchief that smelled of tobacco and sweat. The bile rose in her throat. She fought it back.

Valentin crouched beside her.

He patted her cheek roughly enough to bring a sting to the skin around her scar. "Wiggle around a little bit if you would, scream or something. Make it convincing."

She glared at him, silent and still.

"Suit yourself."

He grabbed her pinkie and twisted. Even muffled by cloth, her shriek bounced off the cottage walls. Tears came and she fought them, allowing herself grunting whimpers as she wriggled away from him.

"Better," he said, rising from his crouch. "When this is done, we have some business to settle, you and I. I'll see you soon."

# CHAPTER THIRTY-FOUR

"RIGHT HERE—IT'S THIS ONE," Lukas said, lowering his voice to hide the nerves beginning to buzz in the pit of his stomach.

The black Citroën slowed as Barbara let off the gas. The circular lights at the gate of a walled villa illuminated the darkness ahead.

"Are you sure you want to do this?" Barbara pulled off the road while they were still in shadow.

Tal leaned forward from the back seat. "Are you sure you can get me in?"

Lukas tipped the seat forward for him to slip out. "You understand the charges and the timing?"

"Your good friend Anton was quite thorough." He wore a bulky work vest over his fine suit. "Let's do this."

Barbara eased onto the road and headed down the driveway toward the gate, as Tal slipped along the shadowed hedges lining the wall. The car's small, round headlamps cut golden swaths of light against the bars.

Lukas rubbed his knee where a soreness had taken up whenever the weather turned.

"Keep it simple," she murmured under her breath. "But keep them talking."

"Here goes," Lukas said, gesturing for Barbara to crank down the driver-side window.

Two men emerged from the guardhouse, both wearing a nondescript uniform. They waved, making clear hand signals that the car was to turn around. Lukas looked at his daughter-in-law, her face drawn tight and her gaze turned inward.

Lukas ignored their orders, flapping open a paper map over her hands and the steering wheel and pointing wildly while speaking in halting Russian. Eventually the gate rolled open and a dark-haired bruiser of a man emerged, glaring into the car's headlights as he approached.

"What is the matter here?" the man growled.

Lukas smiled genially as if relieved to finally have someone reasonable to talk with.

Out of the corner of his eye, the air seemed to ripple, bending in the light as it moved through the open gate. He resisted the urge to look at Tal and draw attention to the cloaking spell Barbara was working. He was running out of conversation when he felt Barbara tap his knee beneath the map. The signal. He folded up his map, begging apology.

Barbara threw the car in reverse, tires squealing.

"Easy now," Lukas said through clenched teeth as he kept this gaze locked on the armed men. "Slow and steady, no need for alarm."

"Speak for yourself," she muttered under her breath, but she managed to complete the maneuver and return to the road smoothly.

When they had left the house behind in the darkness and vanished into the twisty turns of the forested road, she released a long breath. She checked the mirror. They weren't followed.

"We're clear," he said. "And Tal?"

"In." She nodded, grimly pleased. "It's not true invisibility. When the gate opened, he slipped in."

Lukas gripped the door as Barbara bounced the little car off the road and onto the pitted driveway of an abandoned farm. She drove down the lane, switching off the headlights. This time of year, the orchard was redolent with the scent of ripe fruit going to rot, the trees like specters in the darkness. The waxing moon curved overhead, plenty of light for lupine eyes.

She parked beside a familiar Mercedes Sprinter van and shut off the engine.

Mark and Tobias were already outside, Chris sitting in the open side doorway, munching on a jerky stick. Tobias met her at the door.

"I'm fine." Her words were muffled against his chest. "Tal's in. We need to give him as much time as possible. He knows exactly where to go, thanks to Anton."

"No thanks to Anton," Lukas said.

It had given him a distinct pleasure to show up at Anton's unannounced with the crowbar he'd found in the back of Mark's car.

Anton assured Lukas that he'd had no idea Mark was in danger. And when he suspected something was off, he tried to call—after all, his own nephew was involved. He'd never let harm come to his family.

*Your* family? Lukas snapped. He'd never wished harder that he did more than carry his sons' gift in his veins than he did at that moment. He wanted to take Anton apart with his teeth. Instead, he jammed the crowbar against the man's throat, shoving him into the wall with a surge of strength that made the bigger man gasp in shock.

Barbara's small hand on his arm was the only thing that stopped him from crushing Anton's windpipe. With a tiny shake of her head, she faced Anton.

*You are going to get us the plans,* she ordered. *Come to think of it, aren't construction companies as large as yours authorized to keep a small quantity of explosives on hand? We require it as well.*

Lukas had stared at his petite, polite daughter-in-law in shock.

They left Anton to finish his hurried packing. Lukas had the feeling he would never see his old friend again and couldn't be the least bit sad about it.

"Fine, no thanks to Anton," Barbara agreed when they gathered in the abandoned orchard. "Are you boys ready?"

Mark stripped off his T-shirt and kicked out of his shoes. A pale wolf leaped out of the open van.

"Glasses." Barbara held out her hand to Tobias.

He dropped his glasses into her palm, placing his clothes in the van.

A moment later, a gray wolf pressed against her thighs, whining softly as she tucked the frames into her jacket pocket.

"You too, sweetheart," she said before opening her hand to Mark. "Keys."

He tossed them to her. "Remember, I don't know how far—"

"Depends on what condition she's in," Barbara said. "I know. What about that necklace?"

"Stays with me." Mark shook his head and dropped to four paws, his yellow eyes bright in the dark. The divinestone winked amid the dark fur on his chest.

Lukas so rarely saw his sons in their other skins, he could hardly tear his gaze away. They were unearthly and wild but as familiar as his own heartbeat. A pang of longing and pride in his chest surged at the sight of them.

Barbara called again, gently. "Dad—"

Lukas jingled the Citroën's keys. "I'll get it back safe and sound. Promise."

"I'm not worried about the car." She sighed. "Beryl is going to kill all of us."

"Don't worry, I'll be first in line," he said merrily before reciting his part of the plan. "I'll pick up Tal."

"We meet here," Barbara said, taking in three wolves and Lukas in her gaze, which was as much a command as her words. "No extra risks. If the necromancer's people show up, clear out, lie low, and let them sort it out."

Mark growled.

She jabbed a finger at him. "Evie is smart and tough. A survivor. She doesn't need you to fight her battles. If it comes to that and she's going to have to hold her own against a necromancer, my money is on her every time."

She met Lukas's eyes. He nodded, fighting the urge to snap a salute. She had the makings of a formidable witch.

When they were all gathered, she set a blessing over them, a ward wrapped in a bit of Libuše's favor, which had been bestowed on her. And he stood beside her as the wolves disappeared into the trees.

Mark looked back once, yellow eyes in a field of dark so uniform Lukas couldn't make out the shape of him.

"Go," Lukas whispered. "Bring her home."

A shadow within the darkness shifted—the flick of an ear registering a sound or the twitch of a tail betraying eagerness to be off.

And then there was nothing but night.

❦

EVIE WASTED no time working herself onto her side, then her knees in the bedroom. After no small amount of fumbling, she'd dragged away enough of the muslin from the mattress that she could stick her fingers between mattress and frame. Her fingertips ran over the knife she'd stashed there months ago.

By the time she got the knife, she was weeping outright, snot and tears staining her face, accompanied by low, sobbing grunts of effort.

Valentin would be so pleased.

Now to figure out how to use the knife on the plastic ties. Her fingers were nearly dead from lack of blood flow. Mercifully so perhaps—she could no longer feel her pinkie.

Noise from the front room startled her into silence.

A familiar head poked around the corner. Ignoring her muffled protests, Tal hurried to her side. She rolled to her shoulder and let him take the knife. He slit the zip ties first, dropping the knife to work at the knotted handkerchief at the back of her head.

Evie clutched her wrist and tried not to scream as the blood returned to her fingers. Her pinkie throbbed.

Tal cradled her hand. "It's dislocated, not broken. Are you ready?"

Evie clenched her jaw, but a shriek escaped her when Tal set it back in joint. The pain changed immediately, only a dull ache but not the sharp, mind-numbing agony.

"What are you doing here?"

"No gratitude?" Tal said brightly.

"The books?"

"On their way to your Amazon," he said cheerfully. "Thanks to one Havel Zeman. Odious man and definitely not quite right in that peculiar way." He rapped on the floorboard with a knuckle in their old signal. "But he got the gist quick enough. And if he's as eager for Azrael's favor as I suspect, the necromancer himself might be on his way right now."

"How did you get in?"

"The front door, of course," he said. "With a little help from your friend Barbara. I'm supposed to be setting up the diversion, but I saw you here and I thought maybe I could give the rescue crew a head start."

"This isn't part of *our* plan." Relief squeezed Evie's heart in her rib cage. "You weren't supposed to come—"

"You are a fool if you think I wouldn't," he said. "Though I admit I am the *least* formidable of your rescue operation."

"But you are brave," she said, clutching his cheeks in her palms. "And you are clever."

He pressed her forehead to hers. "Runs in the family."

"They know about the gate." Evie kept her voice low. "They know that's how I got out. They're going to be waiting for us. They have dogs. Strange ones."

Tal's face tightened, grim. "Good thing we're not planning on using the gate."

"What is your diversion?"

He opened the strangely bulky vest to a row of pockets. Most were empty. Three contained what looked like small bricks.

She gasped. "Are those explosives?"

"Turns out to be quite handy to have a friend in construction." Tal winked. "Just need to drop a few things off."

"I can help."

He shook his head. "That's not the plan, Evie. You're going to need to be ready to run."

"When?"

"Any minute now."

"Watch the guards. They're not right—and the dogs."

Tal nodded. "Zombies. Barbara's spell should keep me invisible to them. We hope."

When he was gone, Evie dragged open the drawers to the linens, tore sheets into strips, and wrapped them around her bare feet. That would offer some protection. She found a second knife stashed behind the toilet and wrapped her fist around it. Then she pressed her ear to the back window of the cottage where she had seen one armored man take up position. The faint sound of his radio crackled.

"Movement in the trees."

"—as fucking mastiffs." A voice on the comms said in Russian. "What the fuck kind of wolves—?"

"Keep this channel silent."

The radio went dead.

She put her back to the corner and waited.

THE WOLF WAITED in the deep shadows, eyes locked on the solid wall ahead of him. The gray wolf appeared from his trip past the north wall, where he'd allowed himself to be spotted prowling a few times. The pale wolf came from the other direction, chuffing a laugh as he bellied down in the cool dirt. He'd gone by the guardhouse and, based on his expression, enjoyed giving the guards at the gate a good look.

The black wolf snapped his jaws twice, and the mood shifted. Their eyes turned to the wall as one. At the slight click of a fuse, familiar to the man in the wolf's mind, the sharp ears tipped up.

A half second later, a series of explosive cracks echoed through the villa as one of the walls crumbled, shaking the ground beneath their paws. The black wolf barked.

The gray wolf and the pale one raced into the clouds of dust, followed by shouts of panic.

The black wolf dropped back into the shadows, circling around toward the gate.

It was unattended when he arrived. The sound of his brothers wreaking havoc as a second and a third charge turned the villa walls into swiss cheese must have been enough of a distraction. The radio exploded into chaotic chatter. The wolf lost a bit of the sharpness in his senses as he retreated, rising as a man to examine the gate.

Mark saw the loose hinges, the open bars. He read the warning Evie's blood had impressed on the metal. He didn't care. She was hurt. He was going to kill someone.

Inside the walls, he dropped to his paws again. The garden was empty, but he picked up the scent of dogs and the stench of undead—the zombie servant of a necromancer.

He padded through the garden to the front of the cottage. When she saw him, Evie dropped to her knees, arms around his neck. "You came."

Arms were better for this, hands, fingers. The wolf retreated.

Mark held her for a long moment until soreness made her whimper. "We have to go."

He wanted more than anything to spirit Evie out of here, to make this all go away. And then he saw her bruises.

"Kolya is dead," she said, meeting his eyes with startling clarity. "Let the necromancer take care of Valentin and Petrov."

"Petrov is here?" Mark hesitated. A hunger for vengeance burned. He needed to fix this, to right whatever had happened to her in whatever way he could.

"Please. Let's just live." Evie's hand settled on his cheek. "I'm ready."

Mark checked her feet, impressed with the improvised coverings. He unclasped the necklace and put it back around her throat. "You forgot something."

Her fingers settled over the chain and stone, warm from his body. Her eyes shone. He had what he'd come for. Let the rest sort itself out.

"We head back to the orchard. Run as hard as you can. I will be with you. But if we're followed, I may have to drop back to take care of it. Look for a pale wolf. That's Chris. Keep moving no matter what you see or hear. I've got a few surprises. The woods are ours tonight."

She laughed, voice watery. "This brings back good memories."

"The best." He kissed her soundly. "Let's go."

They were halfway through the garden when the sound of baying dogs stilled Mark. A second later, the agonized howl of a wolf cut through the night. Tobias.

The dog noise rose to a furious pitch, drowning out the snarling of wolves.

"They have dogs," she hissed. "Strange dogs. I've never seen—"

"Run." He pushed her through the gate and slammed it shut behind her.

She thrust her hands against the gate, trying to force it open. "No, Mark. No, please."

"Change of plan." He grabbed the abandoned padlock and chain, looping the chain through and slamming the padlock shut. He tossed the key into the yard and gave her a savage grin. "Get to the orchard. I'll meet you there. Go now."

He spun, and the wolf raced into the villa's interior.

In the courtyard, a dozen of Valentin's men had managed to corner the two wolves because the gray was wounded. His mangled foreleg hovered over the stone, streaks of carmine darkening his coat and puddling beneath him.

Their prey bloodied, the cries of the zombie dogs rose to a new, fevered pitch. Of the eight, three were down. The remaining lunged at their short leads, forelegs scrabbling at the air for purchase as spittle flew from their jaws.

One slipped its lead, overpowered its handler, and raced at the gray with single-minded focus.

The pale wolf collided with it midstride, its mouth full of dark fur. The dog hit the ground hard, tried to roll, but was outmatched. The wolf was all teeth and focus—throat, leg, belly. The youngest wolf fought well, Mark noted.

The dog lay still and the wolf surged, bloodied but undaunted. He paced a tight semicircle around the gray, and his inside ear kept flicking back to the wounded wolf. *Now what?*

"We need them *alive*," Valentin bellowed. "Lights!"

The subsonic whine of an enormous draw on the power came before light flooded the courtyard. The wolves recoiled from the bright glare of the artificial floodlights. In front, the pale wolf squinted, his darker gray companion a shadow.

"Tranquilizers don't slow them down," the guard shouted.

"Dart them again!"

"That could kill them."

"Fucking do it."

"Where's that black bastard?" Valentin called, squinting into the darkness.

*Right here, asshole.* The man's thoughts met the wolf's motion as the black wolf exploded into the cluster of armed men around Valentin, ripping through two of the zombie dogs before they could register his presence.

A bullet whizzed past his ear.

*Guess they gave up on tranquilizer darts.*

"Alive, godsdamn you," Valentin howled, but he didn't sound entirely convinced that was possible.

*Good.*

"The net!" someone snapped.

One of the guards stumbled away from the new threat, forgetting about the old one. The pale wolf saw an opening and pounced, dragging the screaming man to the stones. But it left the gray exposed. The soft, gusting noise of compressed air released, and the whizz of fiber sang through the air.

The gray wolf hit the ground with a thud.

The black took another zombie down, but he wasn't fast enough to catch a second lunging past him. It collided with the pale wolf, and the two went down snarling.

Mark despaired when the pale wolf yelped in pain. He wasn't going to be enough to save his pack.

"Enough," Valentin shouted.

The gray wolf thrashed in a net and then went still. The pale rose over the downed zombie dog, but his coat was darkened with blood.

Valentin had gotten a knee on his neck and the pistol pressed against the back of his skull. The gray wolf held perfectly still—his nostrils flaring but his eyes fixed on his brother.

"So you are not stupid animals," Valentin shouted at the black wolf. "There are men in there. Would you see his brains on my driveway, over a woman?"

The black wolf growled, low and threatening.

Valentin smiled, never releasing his aim. "That is you, Markus. I suspected as much. You see these dogs? They arrived special from Saint Petersburg. A gift. They are single-minded. They will not stop. No matter how far you run. Turn yourself over to me, I let the wounded one go, and I put the dogs down myself."

The gray wolf loosed a sharp whine and exposed two rows of teeth. His eyes did not waver. *No deal.*

But the black wolf backed up a pace, whined softly.

Evie was free. The pack would track her down, get her out of here. Protect her until she could run. If not for him, she would have disappeared already. She just needed a chance.

The pale wolf coughed in disbelief when Mark rose to his feet, his palms spread.

The men swore. A few crossed themselves at the sight. Before he could speak, all eyes went over his shoulder.

"New deal." Evie stepped through the mess of downed soldiers and dogs. "Let them all go, and I'll let you live."

The air around her vibrated with the crackle that came before lightning. She glowed as if the moon herself had come down from the sky, and the night darkened around them. The artificial lighting dimmed and flickered skittishly.

Her face was pale, but her eyes were bright. Liquid moonlight raced down her skin, puddling beneath her and leaving gold prints in her wake. She cocked her head thoughtfully. "If you start now, you might just escape Le Seppe. But I wouldn't be seen in the territory again if I were you."

Valentin swung his pistol in her direction.

Mark lunged, but it was the wolf's jaws that closed on the man's biceps as the gun went off.

Valentin went down hard, the back of his head striking the pavement with a wet thump.

Mark shook his head once, twice, whipped the screaming man like a rag doll at his paws. He would have shaken until flesh gave way and bones shattered if Mark didn't stop him with a single thought.

*The gun had gone off.*

The wolf dropped the man abruptly, gaze seeking her.

Evie stood, unmoved, except she held her fist out before her. She flipped it over and opened her fingers. The bullet rolled off her fingertips and clattered to the ground.

She raised a brow and took a step toward the gray wolf. The pistol in Valentin's hand crumpled, folding in on itself. Valentin scrambled backward as she kept coming.

The guards muttered and swore. The dogs quit snarling and were still.

Evie positioned herself between the men and the wolves. The black wolf pivoted to her side.

"Chris, the net," she muttered, tossing a knife toward the fallen wolf.

The pale wolf reared up, and Chris snatched the blade out of the air. He went to the ground at the gray's side, working on the netting.

A moment later, two familiar check-in barks sounded. The black wolf huffed a command: *Go.*

The two wolves scrambled through the nearest ragged tear in the villa's external wall.

Evie's fingers threaded through the stiff hairs at the base of his neck. The touch sent sparks through them both. But it also betrayed the tremble in her limbs. She was tapped out. The light show, the bullet, the gun was all she had. The rest was a bluff.

He pressed back against her thighs, crowding her toward the wall. *Run. Run now. Go.*

"Goodbye," she said with all the theatrical foreboding of a fairy-tale witch. "And good luck."

The black wolf huffed. *Move, woman.*

She turned finally and started for the wall. She was leaning on him now, but she made a good show of moving under her own power, a death witch and her hellhound.

They just had to make it through the gap. The black wolf kept his eyes on the men.

A sharp, pained gasp left her, and she stumbled, going down to one knee. Her light flickered out, and she sank to the stones.

A half dozen rifles rose with the renewed snarls of single-minded undead animals.

The black wolf crouched over her, facing them.

"I need him alive," Valentin shouted as one of the men tied an improvised cloth bandage around his forearm.

"The girl?"

"The dogs may tear her limb from limb for all I care. Let him watch." He turned and started for the house, calling over his shoulder. "And I want the two in the woods. The gray is wounded. He won't make it far."

The dogs closed in.

The wolf narrowed his eyes, snarling.

Everything froze at the quick twin taps of a car horn and the rare rumble of a gasoline-powered engine. A set of headlights came down the driveway —a sleek, black Audi leading a train of matching Sprinter vans. The headlights spilled over the cluster of men and dogs in a semicircle around the crouching wolf.

Valentin lifted a hand over his eyes. "Who the fuck?"

The passenger door opened.

"Nice to see you too, Valentin," a woman's voice said, cool and amused. "And so very soon."

The car doors slammed, followed by the sound of boots and the click of well-soled heels.

The wolf couldn't see in the light. Also, he couldn't carry a fallen witch.

Mark scooped Evie up, slipping back toward the wall.

One of the dogs caught his movement and lunged, its handler off guard. It slipped the startled man's hold, racing for its prey.

Mark turned away, shielding Evie's body with his own. If he could get her to the ground, the wolf would take care of the rest. He braced for the pair of teeth to sink into his shoulder.

It never came.

The dog's body slid to the ground at his feet. The head kept rolling before rocking to a stop across the driveway.

A tall, suited man with impossibly blue eyes stood in the space that had been empty a second ago. Gregor Schwarz, the necromancer Azrael's enforcer, winked at Mark, the blade in his hand so black the sight of it burned into Mark's retinas like an afterimage.

"You seem to be a man of action." Gregor cocked his head. "I imagine there will be many boring questions to sit through. Still, it would be best for you if you did not make me have to track you down for answers."

He crossed the courtyard so quickly the motion blurred. The blade turned to smoke when he moved before solidifying as he took the heads from the remaining zombies.

The blade disappeared, sheathed in some invisible space against his spine, and Mark wasn't sure it had ever been there in the first place. It certainly didn't have the realness of the nine millimeter he drew in its place. Gregor joined Valentin on the walk.

"Turning animals is underhanded work," he said idly. "A violation of code— Which is it, Lysippe? The master has so many, I cannot be expected to keep track of all the numbers."

"You've got the gist," the Amazon said wryly. "Shall we all step into the house? Lord Azrael will be here shortly."

Mark considered making a run for it, but when he looked up, those impossibly blue eyes pinned him in place.

Evie stirred in his arms, and even though the situation had gotten much, much worse, the relief that swamped him at the sight of her eyes blinking open almost took him to his knees. She glanced around, but he clamped her tight against his chest with a little shake of his head. The alarm grew as she recognized Valentin, then the Amazon, and Azrael's Black Blade before she found his eyes again.

"It's going to be all right, I promise," he whispered and hoped that he wasn't lying.

# CHAPTER THIRTY-FIVE

"A CURIOUS PACKAGE arrived at my office today." The woman whom Evie now doubted had ever been named Elise Le Seppe began, laying the ledgers on the sideboard.

The way the suited man, Gregor, had pronounced it had sounded different somehow—running it all together, dropping any implied hint of French and making it sound older.

Evie and Mark had been shuffled into the sitting room with the rest by strangely quiet soldiers who had emerged from the black vans—the necromancer's security forces. All undead, though they lacked the blankness of the dogs.

Valentin's men had been rounded up. She counted a dozen. Valentin stood apart, stripped of his gun and his bravado. He seemed deflated somehow, a ghost of himself.

Mark had taken the pale damask sofa on the edge of the room and ignored the mess they immediately made of it when he set her down. He dragged the nearby throw blanket over her tattered dress and bare arms. As though he wasn't naked and covered in blood and dirt with healing wounds from where the teeth of the zombie dogs had found their mark.

Evie stared into space, feeling as hollow as an empty carton until he pressed a cup of tea into her hands with a murmur. "Drink. It's safe."

Tears had smarted at the corners of her eyes, and she struggled to hold them back.

She'd dragged him into the dark cesspool of her life. Not just Mark—his loving, magical brothers and his prickly, loyal sister-in-law. The secret they'd hidden in this city all their lives had been revealed to people who would capture them, sell them. And now, the necromancer, who had forbidden all supernatural creatures from exposing themselves to humans. It was the first of the codes—number one.

Because of her.

She wanted to put down the tea and beg his forgiveness for dragging him into this.

She took a drink instead. It was a strong black tea—Valentin's best. The warmth, and likely the caffeine, rocketed through her. The strength was an illusion, but she would take it.

The ghost of a smile brightened his eyes, lifted the shadows from the stern lines of his mouth. That he could still smile at her tore her heart.

The doors opened. Beside him strode a man she'd only seen in feeds and on television.

He seemed less grand in real life but more deadly. Handsome in a way that reminded her of her own father in his youth, with dark curling hair and sharp features that evoked the warmth and dry air of the high plains.

Except for the eyes—there was nothing human left in the silver coins of his eyes. They were so bright, so metallic. She almost reached out to see if she could rattle them as she often did idly with the small change in her purse.

But calling more attention to herself than absolutely necessary was a mistake. No, the best chance she and Mark had was to remain silent and hope the big players in the room would forget they were there.

In a fit of inspiration, she began the spell to hide them. Her power stuttered, and she could feel the headache building behind her eyes that always came when she drew too much, too deeply, on it. She called it anyway.

Mark rubbed her biceps briskly. His voice rumbled through her. "Cold?"

She shook her head once, fighting the urge to tell him to be quiet. Azrael was going to look at them any moment, and there would be no more hoping that this would just go on around them.

"She did it!" Valentin shrieked suddenly, pointing a finger wildly at her. "She had me under her spell. She made me—"

Yan Petrov strode across the room, backhanding Valentin so hard he tumbled into the wall. "You lie to me and now you lie to him? What do you think happens to you next? Have the sense to shut your fucking mouth."

Azrael watched, revealing no interest in what went on around him. She could not read him, and a shiver raced over her.

He cocked his head, and then his gaze settled directly on her. The fragile net of the spell fell away, a cobweb dissolved in a gale. He smiled, a cold and terrible thing because it was empty. There was no pleasure, satisfaction, calculation, discovery. Whatever human had once been in the expression was gone.

The tea rose in Evie's throat, and she clamped her jaw hard to keep from vomiting.

Azrael looked toward the door expectantly. Gregor opened it, but Lysippe took point. Gone was the expertly structured couture designed to flow effortlessly with her movement. Tonight she wore black—tactical pants and boots and a chest plate—and a polished baton at either hip.

"It's clear." Lysippe answered an unspoken question. For their benefit, Evie assumed. "This is all of them."

Gregor fell into Lysippe's wake in a move as unhurried as it was familiar. At a glance, his suit, the tailoring, the shoes fit in with the rest of the company. But he moved like an apex predator, and Evie feared him with an instinct as primitive as the need to breathe. He checked a watch more expensive than the car parked in the driveway and surveyed the room. "There are a number of bodies in the yard. It appears to have been a busy night, even by Jevany standards."

Evie's vision doubled. Neither was completely unarmed. The smoky afterimage of a blade hilt rose between Gregor's shoulders. A bow crossed Lysippe's back, a quiver full of arrows on her hip that kept seeming to multiply, the number shifting so rapidly Evie's temples began to throb and she had to look away. She got the sense the quiver never emptied.

"We're combing the woods now." Lysippe jerked her chin at the assembled men. "But this matches my records."

Tension raced through Mark. His nose gave an inhuman twitch, and she pressed her hand against his thigh above the knee. The skin prickled with hair that was no longer crisp human strands.

She lowered her chin, knowing her eyes were wide and her expression at the edge of panic. *Not here. Please. We have to trust they made it. We can't help them if you lose control.*

"The clubs are shut down, and the Aegis is working the city," Lysippe went on. "A few of the vermin will slip through, but we'll have the operation locked down by dawn."

Valentin looked sick, and even Yan Petrov paled.

Azrael inclined his head. "You thought, perhaps, she does not know the name of every man, woman, and child on your roster? That after a thousand years of running such arrangements for me, she wouldn't have every detail accounted for?"

A thousand years. Evie looked between them and tried to imagine that much time. No wonder Azrael no longer resembled anything human.

"They always imagine themselves to be the first, master." Gregor actually laughed.

"Sir," Petrov began, and Evie thought a word had never sounded so foreign on a tongue. The next words were even less believable. "My lord. I assure you."

"I would be incredibly careful. About your next words. And to whom you address them." Azrael lifted his fingers from his thigh, twitching them in a silent movement.

Petrov's lips pressed shut, but his throat bobbed and his eyes widened, indicating how involuntary it had been.

That was when Lysippe tapped the notebooks sitting on the lacquered table beneath the framed portrait of the family: Valentin, his wife, the three daughters.

Looking at the notebooks, Evie felt curiously detached. They were such small, shabby things. Her years in Prague distilled to a dozen books. Her money was gone, her plans destroyed, her life forfeited.

What did she have to show for it?

Love. That was enough. Even if they died tonight—at the hands of a necromancer or the mob—she would never regret him. And there was still a chance. She had one chip remaining.

Mark squeezed her fingers, the message clear. *Let them sort it out.*

"I was willing to let your first story about the circus stand, contrived though we both knew it was," Lysippe said to Valentin, laying out the notebooks. "To maintain the accord."

"I would have been delighted to scrape you and your ilk from the face of my territory after what we found in the basement, the truce with Saint Petersburg be damned," Azrael said, as though indicating a wine preference.

"The problem with the mob is that they're cockroaches." Gregor chimed in with the patience of an old argument. "Stamp one out and the next appears. It's just easier to manage the situation."

"Better the devil you know," Lysippe said, concluding his point.

He narrowed his eyes at her, lips pressed flat. Lysippe shrugged, amused now as she ignored his ire and flipped open a page.

Gregor smirked. They looked like they were having fun.

"The problem is, she hates being underestimated." Gregor jerked a thumb in Lysippe's direction.

"Fool me once..." Lysippe's fingers tapped the notebooks restlessly. "When these turned up."

"Lies," Valentin whined. "She kept the books for years. She could have manufactured—"

"Anything is possible," Lysippe allowed airily. "Gregor."

He opened his coat and set down a familiar pair of tapes. The security footage from the club. "These arrived as we were leaving."

"What's on them?"

"Didn't have time to make popcorn, never mind watch." Gregor shrugged.

"I'll tell you." Evie stood, proud that she only wavered a little. Unable to look at Mark for fear his expression would break her, she clasped his hand in hers, brought them both to her belly, and held on for dear life. "You'll let this man go and any others like him you come on in the woods. I'll tell you whatever you want to know. I'll give you anything you ask. Names. Conversations. Dates."

"You bitch," Valentin shouted, lunging for Evie. "Everything I did for you. You murderous little whore!"

Lysippe's first blow shattered his jaw. The second buckled his knee and sent him to the floor. He howled. Evie hadn't seen her draw either baton. Like Gregor, she moved faster than it seemed possible.

The Amazon slipped the batons thoughtfully back into the holsters at her hips and pressed a finger to her lips with a stern expression. "Hush."

"Who is she again?" Gregor leaned in to murmur, eyeing Evie.

"Bookkeeper," Lysippe supplied. "Came up from the floor at the club. Forged papers."

"And a true metal witch." Azrael's silver eyes focused on her with that same dissembling intensity. "That was your work in the basement. The beams."

"Trafficking is against the codes." Evie nodded, her throat sticky and dry. "He captured them, intending to sell them."

"And you enforce my law?" On a being more human, she would have said his expression was amused. Instead, it looked like a mask. She shuddered.

"He caught someone dear to me." She shook her head. "I panicked."

"You revealed your powers to nearly sixty humans," Azrael said. "Patrons a floor above had their silverware drip right out of their fingers and run through the cracks in the floor. Gregor?"

Gregor went through a laundry list of damage. They would condemn the building to cover the story, but even that would do little to stop the spread of rumors that were already creeping like smoke through the city.

Evie's stomach turned over.

"You defended your own," Azrael said, his gaze skating over Mark. "And the others?"

"Freed," she said, finding the courage to look into the face of one of the eight most powerful beings in the world. "Gone. But it wasn't the first time. There were others I did not protect. And for as long as I live, it will haunt me."

She saw nothing but his features. No death but no past either. Why should she? He was death incarnate.

When Azrael's attention moved on, it was as if a weight had lifted from her chest. She sucked in a breath, and her vision wavered.

Mark pulled her down into his arms. His mouth pressed against the hair at her ear, and his whisper tickled her skin. "Of all the stupid, brave, beautiful things. For gods' sakes, from here on out, sit still and be quiet."

"I will not," she hissed into his shoulder. "Not if I can save you."

Azrael flipped through the pages of the notebook carefully. One at a time. At last, he looked up and nodded at the Amazon as if in response. "As you wish."

Her smile fixed, hardening.

"We will keep his men," she informed Petrov. "One hundred years of servitude."

The mob boss blanched. "Understood."

"As for this trash…" She angled her head in Valentin's direction and left an opening wide enough for Petrov to bumble through.

"I will take care of him," Petrov volunteered. "He will disappear."

"And Saint Petersburg?" Gregor added.

"I will make explanations," he said hurriedly. "I will smooth things over. I will do this for the accords. Allow me to make this right. For peace."

"Be sure whoever you put in his place minds their manners," Lysippe said.

Valentin's men were herded from the room. It took Azrael's men to drag Valentin along. Yan Petrov followed, looking alternately furious and relieved. The Amazon crossed the room to answer a call.

When the room was empty save for the three immortals and a handful of his undead guard, Azrael turned his terrible silver eyes on the sofa again.

"You may go, wolf," Azrael said. "Your life has been paid for. But remember how close you came to losing it and be more careful to whom you show your coat next time." Azrael flicked a hand, removing his attention from them. "Take the witch."

Witches, like many supernaturals, could not be made into the undead. Her death would be a final one.

Three of the necromancer's undead approached the sofa. Mark's arms closed around her.

Gregor watched impassively. The man's sharp blue eyes were not on her but on Mark's face. If Mark tried to fight, Gregor would be the one to meet it. The image of the zombie dogs in the courtyard twisted in her core. She rose. She would not meet her fate afraid.

"No." Mark stood beside her. "Lord Azrael. No."

"No?" For the first time, an emotion registered in that blank, leonine face. Surprise. He held up a hand, and the undead halted in place, uncertain.

"Please," Mark lifted his voice so that it rang like a command. "Rumors are... just rumors. The city is full of them. They'll be forgotten. For so long, she didn't have a choice. But when she did, she helped so many who were bound to be sold, even if it meant sacrificing herself—"

Evie clutched his hand.

Azrael studied them for what felt like hours.

"Master." Gregor broke the silence. He might have also been one of two people in the room who did not lower their gaze when Azrael's cold silver glare settled on him. He stared impassively back. "It might be advantageous to have a powerful metal witch in the city who owes you a favor."

The words came out flat, pure speculative consideration.

Azrael looked to Lysippe.

She had disconnected the call to follow the proceedings. "He has a point." She scooped up the notebooks. "Saved me a good deal of work getting to the bottom of Valentin's little venture."

Azrael waved his hand, and the undead retreated. "You will remember this when one day you, or one of your line, is called upon, witch."

"Lord Azrael." Evie bowed her head. She was tempted to curtsy, but she wasn't sure her knees would hold and not drop her to the floor in a quivering heap of relief.

Without another word, he left the room, the undead in his wake. Gregor stared at Mark and Evie, the calculation in his glacial blue eyes unknowable. He'd spoken for them for some purpose, and she didn't like that she couldn't think of a single reason why.

Then he followed in Azrael.

Lysippe remained, the notebooks in a satchel slung over her shoulder, her phone in one hand. She busily tapped out a message, frowned at the reply, and tapped again.

When she looked up, she seemed surprised to still see them there. "Do you need... a ride to somewhere?"

"Yes, please." Evie nodded as Mark said, "No."

Amused, Lysippe looked between them. "Are you sure?"

Evie stared at him, trying to convey her sheer exhaustion.

"The ride would be great," Mark said, nodding. "Thanks."

"Better find yourself some pants first." She sighed, heading out the door. "Gregor hates having bare ass on his leather seats. I'll meet you in the court-yard. You have five minutes."

When the house had emptied, Mark and Evie just held each other.

"We're still breathing," she said, amazed.

"Not how I thought the night would end," he said wryly.

"Pants."

They found a pair of shorts and a T-shirt in one of the guest bedroom drawers. She emerged from the closet in a sundress and tennis shoes. She held up a hand victoriously.

"Flip-flops?" Mark groaned.

In the courtyard, most of the mess had been cleared by the necromancer's undead, though she tried not to focus on what was under the large gray tarp on the lawn.

The necromancer stood beside it, hands spread, palms facing down. There was a curious sucking sensation as if the air pressure had changed sharply. She stretched her jaws. And then it was gone. The courtyard felt emptier, less foreboding. She thought of how many had died at the villa, unmarked graves in the nearby woods. He had released them all without the slightest effort.

She took Mark's hand, and they started for the black Audi. Movement caught her eye. At the far end of the driveway, near the back of the house, Yan Petrov faced Valentin. Something flashed in his hand, light glinting off metal.

"Perfect timing." The Amazon jogged down the steps from the house. She had a sandwich in one hand, a bite already half-chewed. "I wouldn't look if I were you."

Gregor stood in the Audi's open driver's side door, displeased. "Shouldn't you both be... running off into the woods or something?"

Evie reconsidered. They *could* walk. After all, the orchard wasn't far. If the wolves had gone, they could sleep in the old barn and walk into the village in the morning.

"We're giving them a ride," Lysippe said between bites.

Gregor looked them up and down. "To *where*?"

"Hotel Olga," Evie said as Mark said, "The village."

"Hotel is closer," Gregor snapped. "Get in."

"Evergreen, I don't have a wallet," Mark muttered in her ear.

She nodded, reconsidering. Maybe there was another stop they should make.

Lysippe held the front seat cocked so they could slide into the back of the two-door sedan. Evie paused at the sound of a single gunshot. But she did not seek its source. And when the car pulled out of the driveway, she did not look back.

Once again, she'd emerged from the rubble of a life she'd thought belonged to her. Now it was time to make her own.

When the Audi had left the house behind, Evie cleared her throat. "Actually, Madame Le Seppe—Lysippe... Mr.—"

"Schwarz," he said.

"Mr. Schwarz," she said. "Could you drop us off here?"

"This is the middle of nowhere." The Amazon frowned.

Evie nodded. "I know. We have something to pick up."

Even Mark was looking at her strangely. But Gregor seemed happy enough to oblige, pulling off the road.

"Do you have a flashlight," she said, "we could, um, borrow?"

Outside, they stood on the gravel beside the pavement as Gregor rummaged through the trunk and emerged with a military-grade flashlight that probably weighed enough to stop a charging bull if swung exactly right.

"Where should we, uh, return it?" Evie asked.

"Keep it," he snarled.

"Should we wait for you?" Lysippe asked, clearly curious.

"No, ma'am." Evie shook her head. "Thank you. We know the way from here."

Mark watched the taillights disappear into the darkness before he frowned at Evie. "We do?"

"Come on." She led him through the woods, the beam cast ahead of them. The pond emerged from the trees, with its wooden bench and the little grove of birch trees where one hot summer day she had been rooted to the spot by the sight of a gorgeous naked man emerging from the pond. She led him to a small pile of rocks overgrown with brambles.

"Can you dig here?" she said, stooping down. "Maybe ask the big guy? I had a garden spade last time."

The yellow eyed wolf dropped to four paws and started digging. He stopped when the earth gave way to something plastic and soft. Evie scraped carefully at the rest. She shook the dirt off the plastic, inspecting the package, pleased to find it had not leaked or torn.

Mark was pulling the shorts and the shirt back on when she rose and showed the contents to him. His eyes widened.

"The work I did while I was here, going through all the books," she said. "Bonus money. I stashed it out here. Just in case."

"You stashed..."

She nodded. "I gave most of what I had in my apartment to Violet, and Valentin got what I'd retrieved from the national museum. But that wasn't all of it anyway. This will at least get us a hotel for the night."

"For the week," he said. "But Toby."

"I'm worried about him too. Let's check the orchard and then go to the hotel. We can use their phone."

The van was gone, but parked beside the old livestock barn under a drop cloth was a black Citroën convertible. The keys were tucked under the driver's visor with a note.

"Meet you at home." Mark exhaled a long breath. "Bebe."

Car rides had been Evie's weakness since she was a child. She always fell asleep. But she usually woke when they ended.

This time it was nearly dawn before she opened her eyes, and she was lying in a familiar bed. The muted orange glow of streetlamps still framed the dark drapes over the window. The black wolf slept beside her, stretched out end to end on the mattress with paws dangling over the edge. She touched his shoulder.

Mark rolled over, facing her. "Morning."

He'd managed to get her into one of his shirts. It was a denim button-down washed to almost velveteen softness and smelled like him. She fought the urge to bury her nose in the collar. Just a little sniff. She tucked her chin and inhaled.

When she opened her eyes, his were locked on her.

"Now you know how I feel after you've been rolling around in my bed for a while," he said with a little self-satisfied smirk.

"How's your brother?"

"Fine," Mark said. "Getting henpecked by Baby Witch."

"Tal?"

"Dad put him up in Toby's old room. They were up till two talking about Yiddish jazz in London. I didn't know that was a thing."

"Tal plays the trumpet, very badly." She laughed, her heart sore with affection. "But he loves jazz."

"You pulled the metal out of the wall and the floors." He tunneled through the sheets to draw them skin to skin. "Stopped bullets and crushed guns."

"My metal affinity."

"Yeah, Mom wants to talk to you about that," he said, grinning. "When you're ready."

She sighed, rubbing her face in her hands. Now that they weren't on the run for their lives, now that she was safe and he was home, the reality came crashing in. She was right back where she started. It didn't matter how good she was with numbers, who would hire her with no certifications, references, or formal education? She didn't even have legitimate identification.

"Hey, hey." He grabbed her hands, drawing them away. "I can hear you worrying from over here. I thought we would talk last night on the drive, but you were out like a light. Which I get, all things being what they were."

"No promises." The words tasted like ash in her mouth.

"After I got you settled, I went up to check on everybody and got the lecture of my life about not being a team player. They're right," he admitted. "I've been assuming I have to fix things for everybody else for as long as I can remember. And instead of living my own life, I've been focused on theirs. My sister is so tired of hearing me judge her choices she barely speaks to me." He rubbed his face wearily. "I said that 'no promises' bullshit because I didn't think there was enough of me left over after all of that for anybody else. Especially somebody like you."

"Me?" She scoffed.

"Ambitious, beautiful, smart, outdoorsy, witchy in this really sexy, dangerous way." He grinned. "And for whatever reason, you're totally into me."

"Into you?" She laughed.

"Tell me you're not."

"I'm not."

He froze, uncertain. She gripped his hands with every ounce of strength she could muster. "I'm in love with you. All of you. You are so kind, and your heart is bigger than this building, and you really should be naked all the time."

Satisfaction made his smile sweeter than she had ever seen. And a little bit of mortification didn't hurt either.

"I know I said no promises. I know that was the deal. I understand if you're not ready for anything else. This place is probably full of bad memories. If you still want to go, I can figure out how to be okay with that." He paused, looking endearingly bewildered by his own logic but full of conviction. "But if you want to stay, stay. With me. And if being surrounded by nosy Vogels gets to be too much, we've got a cabin in the woods to disappear to whenever you like."

Snot clogged her nose, and her eyes were so wet she could hardly make out his face through them. "You think I'm beautiful?"

"That's the takeaway?" He laughed, tracing her scar with his fingertips. "You're fucking gorgeous. Did I mention how hot the metal thing is? I mean, I'm strong, but bending metal by singing to it—that is a turn-*on*."

Laughing through tears was a joyfully messy experience.

"I'm yours. We're yours," he said, looking equal parts hopeful and panicked. "Let's make promises. Maybe we raise some feral wolf-witch kids in the woods or just be a terrifically bad influence on Toby's little over-achievers."

"How many wolf-witch children would there be potentially?" She laughed.

"How many would you like?"

His eagerness terrified her. Excited her too.

"I will be overprotective," she said helplessly. "I will not let them climb trees that are too tall or swim in ponds that I don't know the depth. Or leave my sight until they have their coats or can pull the iron out of a man's blood."

"Then they'll be lucky to have you," he said. "And so will I."

So many things could go wrong. And one day Azrael would call in his mark.

"Worry about whatever it is when we get there," Mark said, rubbing her forehead where a line formed between her brows. "Anything can happen. And you might actually be able to see most of it coming, so we have that."

"You will be stuck with a fortune-teller who counts compulsively and owes a necromancer a favor."

"You're going to have to put up with a lot of family dinners," he said. "Family. Period. You met them. I'd say we're even."

"How does that make—?"

"That's the offer." He stuck out a hand between them. "Deal?"

This bewildering, amazing, ridiculous man. Her man. "You want to shake on it?"

"I want to fuck on it, but we gotta start somewhere," he said brightly before sobering. "And you're not beautiful. Not just beautiful. You're the moon in my night sky. Every time I lift my head to the stars until my last day on earth, I'll be calling to you. My badass metal witch."

Afterward, they slept again, his nose in the nape of her neck. The second time, she woke first.

His eyes opened before she could ease from the bed, fingers flexing on her hip. She read the unspoken wondering of his heart on his face. She brushed her fingertips along the twinkling constellation dotting his cheek and made her promise. "Deal."

# THANKS FOR READING

**Reviews help other readers find their next favorite book. Please consider recommending it to a friend or leaving a review wherever you purchased this book.**

Want more Vogel Brothers?

Be the first to find out about new releases at www.jasminesilvera.com where you can also find deleted scenes, extras, and other goodies!

# ACKNOWLEDGMENTS

Firstly, I do not suggest writing a book during a global pandemic. The benefit to *my* mental health was certainly questionable. If you must embark on a book in the middle of a terrifying and uncertain time (and aren't they all, in the moment), my best advice is to find your people and keep them close through multiple outlines, discarded drafts, hellish revisions, and that final, glorious light at the end of the tunnel (you will especially want them there for this part, it's more fun to celebrate together)

But, as in all things, YMMV.

I am enormously grateful for the earliest readers and location experts that helped give this book a sense of place: Lucie Greenidge, Beth Green, and Geoff Engle (who gave a thrilling tour of Jevany that I thoroughly cherry-picked to suit my own machinations)

Thanks to Eva Moore and Bethany Robison, who are always in on the beginnings, and Erin Evans, Rhiannon Held, Shanna Germain, Corry L. Lee, Kate Marshall and Susan J. Morris, who deftly advised on the final polish.

Anne and Linda of Victory Editing helmed a dramatic rescue operation all my poor abused commas *and* helped me to find the word I *meant* to use every time. Sylvia, and The Book Brander team, came through with another stellar cover. Elena Kononova and Jenny Kraft provided Russian translations and double my German, respectively. Any remaining errors are mine alone. A special thanks to Nathaniel Glanzman of Writing Diversely and Helm & Anchor Editing for generous and attentive sensitivity reading.

Writing may be a solitary act but being a writer doesn't have to be. And having other writers in my circle somehow makes the whole endeavor seem a *lot* less shriek-worthy most of the time. Heart-full thanks to The Ponies! Chris Henderson-Bauer, Elle Beauregard, Kelly Blake, Jen Comfort, Melora Francois, Alexis de Girolami, Lin Lustig, Kate Maybury, and Jo Segur—for shared meals, writing games, and the introduction to the hoodie snuggie (huggie?) which I am wearing as I write this and may never take off again.

To my soul's sisters Aarthi, Joanne, Kay, and Michelle: from the world's worst Lyft ride to a year's worth of Zoom happy hours, inspire, delight, and uplift, always. Thank you for coaxing me out of my head and back into my heart.

Wrapping up a long year of political fuckery and societal upheaval, 2020 concluded with the early passing of my father. In addition to being my gateway to science fiction and fantasy, he enjoyed the hell out of a good gangster movie—we traded lines from Miller's Crossing relentlessly over the years. Thanks for giving me lots of material to work with, Dad. This one's for you.

And last but never least: dearest readers, thank you for continuing to take this journey with me and for giving each story the chance to win your heart. Every time you buy, read, review, or otherwise share the love, you help make this possible. Thank you.

CPSIA information can be obtained
at www.ICGtesting.com
Printed in the USA
LVHW091558130123
737037LV00006B/542

9 780997 658293